Acknowledgement

Many thanks are due to those kindly individuals who have tirelessly encouraged me to persevere – in particular my Masters tutor Roger and my good friend Alison. Both gave me reason to cheerfully hope that one day my writing would be enjoyed by many.

The Tailor's Grace

About the Author

Susan Collis is a teacher, researcher and writer who has previously published several academic articles, a book and reviews. Her interests lie in family, history, art and the countryside.

She lives in Kent and continues to work full time with families.

Susan Collis

The Tailor's Grace

Olympia Publishers
London

www.olympiapublishers.com

OLYMPIA PAPERBACK EDITION

Copyright © Susan Collis 2016

A CIP catalogue record for this title is
available from the British Library.

ISBN: 978-1-84897-570-5

(Olympia Publishers is part of Ashwell Publishing Ltd)

This is a work of fiction.
Names, characters, places and incidents originate from the writer's
imagination. Any resemblance to actual persons, living or dead, is purely
coincidental.

Published in 2016

Olympia Publishers
60 Cannon Street
London
EC4N 6NP
Printed in Great Britain

Dedication

For my son Tim

One

'He from his lasse him lavender hath sent
Showing her love and doth requite all
crave ...'

Alone in her parents' room, Ellen gazed down out of the window, looking beyond the lilac tree which stretched upwards almost reaching where she stood, and thought how desolate everything seemed to be. She would have welcomed the beautiful sight of the blossoming plumes of frothy, delicate, and purple flowers from where she stood just then, but everything in the room and the yard was completely devoid of the sweetness and bounty which nature sometimes possesses; she longed for deliverance from the weeping world around her. She knew that the resurrection of this outer world would inevitably come in the spring but she needed saving now.

The tree was clothed in a sheen of moisture which darkened its twigs and branches, and as they tipped to the earth the wetness gathered into tiny rivulets which dripped gently from its boughs. She imagined that the tree was sorrowing with her and that the sap and the misty rain had combined, forming conduits of grief. She did not want to turn away from the emptiness of the yard even though she could find very little to interest her there, only the solitary lilac tree; she had to keep looking out, out through the dripping branches so as not to have to look at what lay within.

Behind her lay her mother's body, washed, wrapped and laid out in white linen sheets. These, only two days before, had been flung over and dried on the privet hedges below. She recollected how she had folded them and then placed bunches of dried lavender between each clean sheet.

There were no other flowers she could bring her mother now, to lay on the crisp whiteness of her shroud. She felt the stillness around her, and sensed the importance of this small, low beamed room, looking out over the Lime Walk in the distance, and the Old Rectory set east of the massive trees.

Thirteen and a half years before, she had been born here in this silent, seemingly unremarkable room. At that time the prevailing emotion must have been very different from the one today.

She imagined that on the day of her birth she had lain with her mother, curled beside her, surrounded by the beauty of the Summer meadows, for her brother Tom and sister Hannah would have walked over Botley Down with their grandmother, and gathered fistfuls of clover, hawkbit, meadowsweet and knapweed, and would have presented them cheerfully but reverently to their mother and their new tiny sister. Later, over the years, other babies, Agnes, Henry, Emily, George and Frederick had come, given birth in this extraordinary room.

"What is i' you're doin'?" The anxious voice of her brother Tom brought her precipitately into the present. She heard the door latch lift and his slow, careful tread as he entered.

He was certain to find her here, because for the past three weeks she had hardly been anywhere else. He had occasionally glimpsed her, passing unhurriedly by the workroom door below stairs, into the back kitchen, where she had prepared her mother's meals. And he had seen her take them and the various remedies, thyme tea, coltsfoot lozenges, the covered bowls of steaming herbal infusions, back slowly up the stairs.

His daily routine hadn't varied. Working alongside his father, he was learning to tailor as his father had done before him, from seven thirty 'til nine most days. He was seeking self-improvement, just like the other young men who were connected to the High Street businesses. A son of an artisan, he wanted to emulate his father who was his master, and had decided and was determined to acquire the knowledge and skills which he had observed and admired in his father, and use them well.

"It's alrigh' Tom," Ellen responded, not seeing his fearful look, "You can 'elp if you like. Take these sheets down, would you please?" The linen which had covered the breathing, living mother needed to be removed and washed clean.

"Is tha' all I can do?" Tom was relieved that he was required to do something, but felt he needed to do far more to support her because he had done so little. After all, he considered, she had been through the worst; he could see her desolation but he, himself, also felt deserted and could not bear the thought of mourning the loss of his mother alone. He laid his hands on her shoulders, but she did not turn to look at him. She felt afraid and abandoned and could not understand the aching bitterness she felt.

She had done everything their doctor, family, friends and neighbours had suggested. Old Mrs. Bloomfield and Grandma Lambourn had advised and directed her, and she had tried faithfully to watch over her mother without resting for a moment. Had she done everything that she was required to do, or had she forgotten something important? Had she really cared for her mother enough? Had she been right in her decisions? What was it that caused her mother's sudden deterioration? Dr Stocks had called a few times and once towards the end had assured her that she should continue with her remedies, but that was all that was said.

She felt Tom's hands and realised he was close behind her. Unable to look at him, but longing for relief from her miserable reflections, she turned and immediately laid her cheek against his breast, closing her eyes, and then, she wrapped her arms about him. She felt his brotherly warmth and his empathy as she felt him reciprocate, as he placed his hands on her back, and drew her close to him in his arms.

She felt his power too; he had become an almost fully developed man, his shoulders had widened and his chest had deepened. Ellen realised then that her brother had grown in stature and in strength beyond her recognition. She thought for a moment that he had become a stranger, that the sensations which she now experienced were due to changes which had completely transformed her brother, and felt dismay as she felt his intense embrace. His frame and flesh had matured in masculinity, and her heart responded to this new sensation of being closely held by someone who had greater physical power than her own. She felt it but was not afraid, wanting to yield unconditionally to this unfamiliar but potent strength.

Below stairs, their father Thomas, holding his youngest child George in his arms, knew it was time to face the moment for which he had been preparing himself. Whispering to the child, and leading the other children, he went before them.

"Come to see our beloved ma, now children, to say goodbye and kiss 'er cheek … come now, 'ere she is, ready to invite us in to see 'er". Thomas spoke no more. Entering the bedroom and pausing at the door beside the bed he stopped in astonishment at the sight of Ellen and Tom holding one another, closely intertwined within one another's arms. For the briefest of moments his mind was totally absorbed by their embrace, but in an instant he turned his swollen eyes to the bed and gazed, not at his wife's lifeless face, but at her smooth, white hands, which had become inert, flaccid and still. Ellen and Tom had sharply released one another on hearing the arrival of their father and their younger brothers and sisters, and were both irrationally confronted by feelings of embarrassment and confusion.

The children, Agnes, Henry, Emily and George had been brought from the home of their neighbours, the Rowe family, where they had been taken two days earlier when their mother's health had worsened. Now they had returned to see her.

Her heart had given out; Dr Stocks coldly described the cause of death. 'Hannah Lambourn's condition was a respiratory one, pneumonia, which is deadly'.

She had left them and would not come back.

As they stood around her bed, Ellen looked at her brothers' and sisters' faces. Emily and George were both whimpering and sniffing as they looked into the face of their father, feeling afraid and lost because to them everything had become unfamiliar. For some time all the family had missed their mother's music in their home, her voice, her laughter and her peaceful spirit and gazed without understanding at their mother's body. Their father had become different. Something had transformed him. He spoke strangely. He looked unlike himself. To Ellen, however, he only appeared fatigued and sombre and that was all. She wondered if there was any feeling in her own face. She did not know, but recognised a frightening change within her consciousness which she knew would alter the course of her life.

As she reflected on what had caused this burning pain within her mind, she heard the arrival of Hannah, her mother's namesake, her elder sister, lightly running up the stairs. On coming into the room, she hesitated for only a moment, but seeing her father, she cried out, "Pa! I came as quick as I coul'!"

"Stand 'ere beside me. We're together now." Thomas Lambourn's voice was abrupt and commanding, but he secretly felt some comfort at the arrival of this daughter, a fresh young woman, untouched by the misery of the past few weeks. The family circle was complete. He observed Ellen bow her head, and her hands reach out to Tom and young Henry on either side of her. He found Hannah's hand, relieved to feel its familiar roughness, and then, to his delight, there followed a responsive, consoling movement as his daughter gripped his fingers.

His vocal prayer lacked assurance but sounded grateful. His own heart felt absent. He could not summon any feeling and showed and felt no emotion. He thanked God for the life of his own dear helpmeet Hannah, for her gentleness and strength. He prayed for strength to provide and care for his family. He pleaded that he might be able to go on, that he would be able to bear his life as it now was. He promised God that he would try to lead his family in righteousness, as his father had done with his. He asked that his fear and anguish be removed. The children listened and did not fully understand their father's torment.

For those who were old enough to comprehend such things, there was, it seemed to them, no doubt that the Lord would support them, but unknown to them, Thomas' faith did not fully include the possibility of the Lord always being there for him. Now his heart had been forced to close to the possibility of help and protection. He had come to believe now that the Lord would only provide if He saw fit. He questioned the meaning of adversity. What if these terrible events were divine interventions designed as a test which could bring the family to its knees? How should he respond to such a test? Would his friends lose their respect for him? Would his business falter? Would he be able to maintain his position and standing in the village? His faith had diminished, and he was looking to trust in his own abilities, thinking that the Lord had abandoned him, because that is what he deserved. This was a punishment. He would need to be unbending, resolute, self-reliant and strong.

"It's time now. There's things we mus' do. Ellen, see to some tea for your sister. We'll go down, and ge' se' onto the arrangements. Tom, I 'ave to speak with you."

* * *

Once Hannah had returned to service at the Grange, life for Ellen at home had seemed almost normal. Tom had never really left his duties in the shop, whilst she and Agnes continued to share the family responsibilities as they had done before their mother's illness. Their father had returned home off and on, carrying on in a business-like manner, speaking rarely, except to give orders or inform the family of the funeral arrangements.

Their mother was buried in the village churchyard. Her parents had come from Lymington, their seaside home to attend. Nineteen years before, Tom had been born in their home, because their daughter had needed to be with her own mother at the birth of her first child, and had made the thirty mile journey. They had not visited the family since that time, but now they came to see their only daughter placed in the ground. They witnessed the burial, and then visited the grave of their youngest grandchild Frederick who had died just five months before his mother.

Her grandparents' stay with them had consoled and comforted Ellen. She had felt the death of the baby had instilled an intimidating darkness into their home, which had deepened mercilessly when her mother had died. Grandma and Grandpa Timms had obviously felt this when they came, and done what they could to dispel it, despite their own pain. Ellen knew that her grandma had lost several babies, and only two had survived; yet, now that there was but one, Grandma Timms still did what she could to lift everyone's spirits. Like her daughter Hannah, she loved to sing and wonderful times were spent every evening singing joyful songs and hymns together. Ellen watched her grandmother and saw a woman of great faith and assurance who clung to the hope that all would be well.

With the return of her everyday struggles once her grandparents had returned home, Ellen was forced to consider the future and realised it would inevitably lie in following in the footsteps of her sister into service. Time had passed, and the family had settled into some sort of routine without their mother. In the weeks since her mother's death, Ellen began to realise that she could not envisage a life in service as being the right course for her.

She and Agnes were working together in the back room. As she washed the glass chimneys of all the oil lamps, and her sister used soda and water to clean the various parts, a job they had been doing for some considerable time, she began to imagine what her life could become.

"I want more than cleanin' and servin', Agnes, I know tha' I could be more useful than tha'."

Agnes looked at her beautiful sister, and noticed how thin her face had become, and how large her hazel eyes were.

"Wha' you thinkin' of then?" She wouldn't admit that she instinctively knew her idiosyncratic sister would do more than just fetch and carry for the rich folks.

"Tom's goin' to teach me my letters, and then I'll know. I've go' to ge' on, Aggie, I can' stay 'ere. Tom says the shop's not doin' so well now tha' the departmen' stores are openin' in South'ampton. Factory clothes are cheaper, 'e says, and that's where the money is. 'e's told Pa 'e can't stay."

"What's Pa goin' to do if you go as well? 'e'll break 'is 'eart!" Agnes pleaded with Ellen, but she knew from her sister's cool expression that she would not be touched by such things. Ellen considered that her father's heart was not available to her or to anyone.

"Pa'll be alrigh', I think 'e's wantin' a new wife, and then…"

"Please don' say tha'! You don' know! Pa does n'a care for anyone else!" Agnes was crying; her tears fell unabated because she desperately wanted her mother, and this unrequited need was constantly present; very little encouragement was needed to activate within her a strong emotional reaction. Ellen wished immediately that she had kept quiet.

"Aggie, I'm sorry, I should no' have said i'. I don' know why I say such things. Please forgive me and stop your cryin'," and Ellen leant towards Agnes and hugged her, placing her chin on the top of Agnes' head.

Agnes never found it difficult to do as her sister told her, and within a moment, the tears were brushed away and all was forgiven. The oil lamps were carefully and cheerfully dried and reassembled. Agnes hurried off to carry them to the shop, seemingly as shining and bright as her load.

∗ ∗ ∗

Sunday came, and the family attended church. On her return, Ellen lay her best black straw bonnet on the kitchen table next to the family Bible. She was longing for the return of Tom from Church, hoping that he'd have remembered his promise, to begin today, to help her to learn her letters, so that she would be able to write as he was able to do. She had learnt to read from the Bible at Sunday School and had attended the Dames School when she was not needed at home; but now her mind was set on writing, on learning to form letters and words; she knew that her future dream would depend on her acquiring the ability to apply ink to paper, to record clearly, to make notes accurately and to document whatever was required. Tom had said that he couldn't see why she was so set on such a thing, and yet, secretly, he intuitively knew that she was right to want this thing so badly; he was confident that somehow she would achieve it with or without his help.

He could imagine how she was feeling, imploring him to come home quickly. Indeed, she *was* feeling flustered, caught in the unremitting grip of powerful emotions she always felt when she contemplated what learning might do for her. She thought he *must* be on his way home from Church by now.

As he walked home alone, he was quietly preparing himself for the 'lesson' ahead. He would give just a little instruction, and then occupy himself with his usual Sunday pleasures. The villagers saw him as he strode home unhurried, a tall and dark figure, like his father, quiet and reserved with little to say to anyone. He would be forthcoming with his sister though and he would not deny her; he would do what he could to meet her demands cheerfully and magnanimously.

However, Ellen's younger sister Agnes was not so willing to accept her ambitious sister's aspirations.

"We're 'appy as we are, are n'' we? Wha' do you wan' to se' your 'eart on such things?"

16

"Why Aggie, it'll 'elp me to find the spiri' to do all tha's righ', to make the best of the time I do 'ave."

"Fetchin' and carryin', and cleanin' and washin', tha's all we'll ever do. Pa'll need us now, and the little 'uns." Although only eleven years old, Agnes knew well the responsibilities of family, and her mind was very clear on the subject. She wanted Ellen to stay with her, be with her in *her* life. Now they had been thrown back together again, after their forced separation, her life had felt more comfortable, more organised than before. She felt troubled by Ellen's insistence on wanting things beyond their present experience. Why was n't she happy as she was herself?

"Aggie!" Ellen's tone was one of rebuke. "Don' try 'n stop me, I need to do this. I don' expec' you to go along with i', bu' don' make it difficul' for me!" Agnes was fearful as her sister's determined character emerged; so she decided to withdraw her objections for the present, and switched her thoughts to contriving a happy occupation for them both which would cement their sisterhood and delete their differences.

"When you're done, can we go to the river? We can see if the Mar'ins are back, and watch them collectin' mud, and see them catchin' flies." Agnes spoke excitedly, hoping to diffuse Ellen's anger with her excitement.

The Sabbath was the one day when they could enjoy being out of doors, and she was always wanting to watch the changing natural order of their life, and was filled sometimes with wonder with what she saw. She was not allowed to take up her needlework today, nor was she able to do any form of work. At least, if she knew she had a country walk to look forward to, the minutes spent waiting for Ellen to complete her writing tuition would not be so difficult to bear.

17

"Alrigh', but mind you keep quie' and don' star' getting' impatien' with me! The Mar'ins are n' goin' anywhere, you know." Agnes was satisfied with this reply, and smiled back at her sister, and immediately imagined ahead of their walk what would occur.

She would lead and then carry her little brother George to the Hamble River waters' edge, and tell him all about the plants and flowers on either side of the path, the bending willow herb and the elegant iris, and she would point to the beautiful Martins diving over the river and up into the early summer sky, and would delight him with stories bound up with one hundred year old oak trees and with simple songs and rhymes of country ways. She knew that Emily and Henry would come to listen too, and watch with her the fleeting movements and delightful antics of their newly arrived bird visitors. She noticed things and loved to share her excitement with those around her. She opened the Bible where it had been marked by her father, who had read from it the previous Sunday. She tried to find the place that she remembered.

"Con-sid-er the li-lies of the f-ield…'ow they grow, they toil not neither do they spin, and ye' I say un-to you Sol'mon in all 'is glory was na' ar-rayed like one of – these. Wha' does it mean Ellen?"

"Lillies are lovely and God takes care of them."

"Did n' pa say tha' they are the mos' beautiful of God's makin'?"

"Yes, and God takes care of us more than the lilies, because we are more beautiful to Him."

"God thinks we are beautiful?"

Ellen hesitated. She knew the ugliness of some people she had come across, and wondered for a moment what the Almighty made of them. Not that they were ugly in their person, but she

18

recognised something very hard and unfeeling about their behaviour.

She had once seen a small mongrel stray in Winchester Street cruelly laid into by a lad, because it had chanced to cross his path. She had run to its rescue, as its cries had touched some part deep within her and she could not bear to hear its suffering. Without fear, she had flung herself at the youth, challenging him in an anguished fury, until he had been sufficiently reprimanded, and had become silent. He had mouthed back at her, but he was no match for her fury.

"Wha' do ya think you're doin'? Leave the critter. Ge' off him, 'aven' you go' any 'eart? Look wha' you've don'. 'ow could ya? You're a 'orrible bully to cause such pain and sufferin'!" The accusations were followed by an equally emotional outpouring directed at the animal itself. She gently whispered to it, displaying a deep distress at its pitiful state. It lifted its shabby head, its ears hanging like rags in the dust of the street. It did not snap at her hand, but lay weak and trembling, as she gently put her hands under its bony body. Berty, for that is what he came to be called, was a very different dog now, well fed and enjoying the lap and affection of Ma Rowe, but the memory of her hands on that poor creature as he was, brought her back to the present and Agnes's question.

"He does! He does think us beautiful!" Ellen recalled a song. "I wish that his hands had been placed on my 'ead, that his arms had been thrown about me, that I migh' have seen his kind look when 'e said, 'Let the little ones come unto me'."

She sang with hope in her heart knowing how the Lord had touched her and shown her how much he cared. Her mother's love had shown her the Lord's hand, like He was always beckoning to her to do the best she could, and then blessing her with her mother's praise. She hoped the song would answer Aggie's question. She was always asking questions, and Ellen often resorted to explaining the answer not in an obvious way but in a story or a song she knew. Aggie always joined in with the songs, but this time, unusually she remained pensively quiet, listening silently and thoughtfully.

Tom was heard coming through the back door, wiping his Sunday boots clean of the street dust as he entered. Ellen's face was fixed in anticipation of his coming, whilst Agnes's mind was transfixed by a vision of beautiful Madonna lilies growing in the fields around her country home.

*   *   *

That evening, after the family's meal of vegetable hot pot and warm bread prepared by Ellen and Agnes, it was time for scripture reading, and so, as usual, they all gathered at the table to listen to their father.

"Matthew, chapter 7, Judge no' tha' ye be not judged. For with wha' judgemen' ye judge, ye shall be judged: and with........." Her father's voice gradually faded, as Ellen's mind turned to her triumph of the day. She could write her name! She glowed with self-satisfaction and triumph. She felt she was somebody! What a small and insignificant achievement it seemed to be, and yet, it had altered the image she had of herself in an extraordinary way; now, she totally believed that she could become equal to anyone. She could be Ellen Lambourn, and not feel ashamed of herself or beneath other people!

"How much more shall your father which is in heaven give good things to them tha' ask him … Ellen, wha' are you smilin' abou'?" Her father had noticed her inattention and was impatient and irritated at once. In truth, he was tired of his daughter's disrespectful attitude. She worked hard enough, but she had to be told so often, she had to be reminded to do things; she seemed almost unwilling; and now, as he had glanced around at his family, he had been shocked to clearly see that she was not listening to him at all.

"Pa, I was thinkin' on the times that God 'as given us things." Ellen had become adept at lending half an ear to the proceedings, having learnt her lesson a few weeks before, when her father had caught her dreaming, and become so angry with her that, without any warning he had lunged at her and struck her hard across the back of her head and neck. She had been flung forward and her face had caught the edge of the table. Her cheek hit hard against it and she slithered to the floor clutching her face. She curled into a foetal ball and waited terrified. The other children looked at their father and then at Ellen and did not move. They had no understanding of what their father had done, and waited watching.

Then he had been so incensed by her insolent, disinterested stare. Now, he had relived the same simmering revulsion for Ellen, who clearly was once again showing a thoroughly diminished sense of duty to her whole family and more specifically to him. It was intolerable to him. He could not allow it. This defiance, this unforgivable ingratitude had become very noticeable since Hannah's death. He could see that his natural anxiety for his family had become heightened since then, but he had become increasingly aware of his daughter's self-imposed distance from him, of her wish to be separate; her obvious contempt for him had become apparent; she was unwilling to accept or immerse herself in the life which he had provided for her as if it was not good enough for her.

"I did na think tha' you though' much of your 'ome … you show little interest in i'."

"Pa, we've 'ad such pretty things given us." Ellen recalled the generosity of her grandparents, who had passed on a tea set, decorated with daisies running through a blue and gold band. The handles were turned and delicate, and felt fragile between her fingers. Many smaller gifts had been received from her father's patrons, especially the Turners, whom he visited nearly every week.

"We'll go on with our readin' now," he spoke with some relief, thinking that maybe he had been in error and that nothing was out of place, whilst Ellen, gratified that she had avoided another beating from her father, felt completely in control. How clever she had become! Tom, however, felt uneasy. He had glimpsed something calculating in his sister's eyes, which he had never seen there before.

* * *

Walking from Botley High Street to the Grange was not a regular occurrence for the younger members of the Lambourn family. The distance was considerable, and there was not a reason usually to visit the grand house. An urgent summons from the Grange had been received to directly make contact without any delay, and the duty had befallen Ellen. Her father had not been present when the gardener's boy had come to the door, delivering the message to Tom which stated that something was amiss with Hannah. An uncustomary correspondence such as this had to be adhered to immediately, and so Tom had directed Ellen to go. He had thought little about it and had assumed that Hannah was in need of some trivial feminine assistance, and so it was that Ellen had

22

hurriedly pulled on her bonnet, thrown her shawl about her and left the house.

She had not seen her sister since the day of her mother's funeral five months earlier. Hannah had seemed well enough then, and Ellen had difficulty imagining the cause of her commission. She hesitated to hurry, afraid of the peculiar nature of her errand. She paused as she passed down Broad Oak Lane, and glanced at the activity to the north of the way, where the hay was being cut, and the delicious smell of coumarin drifted across towards her. How sweet this moment felt! It was so familiar, yet so potent! She suddenly felt more comfortable, recognising the inevitability of some aspects of her life over which she had no control, but which provided her with the pleasing sensation of belonging.

She hesitated, not wishing to acknowledge or smile at the young men in the field, who had paused, seeing a female figure pass along the edge of the field. They had instantly recognised the young woman, only a girl really, who always drew both admiring and curious glances in the village. They knew her to be the tailor's daughter, a cut above a farm labourer's daughter. She rarely went about, except to visit relations, or go to Church. She did not attend the village dances or any of the village celebrations, excepting those at Christmas and on May Day.

This past spring, some of the young men had noticed a change in her. May the first had been a warm and beautiful day. The parade of the garlands had passed through the village to the green, where a bower had been constructed and entirely covered with primroses and hawthorn. Here Ellen had sat, crowned the May Queen, and from there she had watched the young children skip and turn around the ribboned Maypole. The doors of the houses had been decorated with greenery, and she had led a procession around the village, knocking on the doors and singing, 'The first of May is Garland Day, so please remember the garland; we don't come but once a year, so please remember the garland.' Crowned with blossoming hawthorn, she had seemed as lovely as her crown as she sang, waved and smiled at everyone.

Ellen hurried on up the rise into Grange Road, turning the bend out of sight of the hay cutters. Her face had burnt with their stares, and she was sufficiently confused as to be completely unaware of horsemen coming down upon her at a fast trot from beyond the turn in the road. Suddenly, she became aware of the horses' hooves and their breath almost upon her. She instinctively drew back against the hedge, leaning backwards, almost collapsing, but still managing to hold her spine stiffly upright.

"Take care, take care," a shout rang out above her.

"It's alrigh', no 'arm done," she called. She'd expected the riders to continue, but the horses had been reined in, and were shifting about on a spot quite close beside her. She was not afraid, but felt unnervingly trapped.

"Please, sir, please to go on, sir."

"Very well, though I should warn you that to not look where you are going in the future may in all likelihood lead to an unfortunate mishap!" The young man was laughing at her, and she was forced to agree that he had a point.

"Indeed, sir, you are righ' bu' remember you yourself are no more able to see round a corner than I am!" She felt embarrassed now, not because of his words, but because she felt the awkwardness of her present situation, and she was struggling to retain her dignity. "Good afternoon! Sir!" and with these words she pulled herself out of the hedge, and in one movement, turned and pushed against the flank of the horse. She retreated hastily.

Not once had she looked at the riders, nor thought to observe the young men who had unwittingly dispatched her into the hedge. Her unseeing eyes were fixed on the way ahead. She had however realised that her assailants were the young sons of Sir Russell Turner, as she had seen them from a distance at various times as they had grown up. She had guessed that the young man who was addressing her was James Turner the older of the two.

"Good afternoon, to you, young woman! It's fortunate for you that I am able to control my horse!" His voice reflected his amusement at being the cause of the girl's chagrin. He had seen her disquiet, and recognised that her pride had suffered something of a blow, when she had found herself lodged in an uncomfortable hedge observed from above by two young men on horseback.

"I should 'ope so!" Her parting remark made the young men laugh, and they watched her as she continued on her way, sweeping up and round the corner.

"Who was that?" The younger was curious.

"She's the tailor Lambourn's daughter. Quite a lively girl, it seems!" James Turner had noted her bright eyes, rosy cheeks, and creamy complexion; her hair was a rich chestnut. He'd thought her an eye catching girl, and was curious about her.

His younger brother Alfred was ready to continue their ride. The girl had quickly left his thoughts, as would have occurred with most twelve year old boys. His brother, James, however, two years his senior, was still reflecting on their encounter when they returned to the Grange some two hours later.

If Ellen had heard herself described as merely 'the tailor's daughter' she would have been mortified. It sounded like nothing at all. However, if she had known that she had aroused the interest of the elder, it would, in some measure, have compensated a little for the unflattering title. She would have been satisfied that she had been noticed.

She was, however, at that time totally indifferent to the riders' reactions to her. Her mind had almost immediately returned to the object of her walk, her thoughts having reverted to her sister Hannah, and Sir Russell's message. The turning to the Grange was in sight.

The drive to the great house was curved, completing a semi-circle on its return to the road. The imposing house was set exactly at the half way point; hedged arbours, together with symmetrical lawns and straight gravel paths were laid out in the area at the front of the house. As she walked towards the Grange, she thought of her last visit, on Christmas Eve, when she, along with other villager wassailers had visited the Grange to collect alms in exchange for sharing a portion of the spirit of Christmas with them. They had stood outside the main door, the Turner family and servants within watching through the open door, as they had sung carols in the candle lit night. She recollected hearing Tom's voice beside her; it had been strong, confident and uncompromising, completely lacking in social deference. The wassail bowl had been passed around inside the house and then shared with the carollers. The distance that the bowl had covered from the inside of the house to where she stood had been small, only a few yards, but the space between them had seemed enormous to Ellen. She had not been able to make out the faces of those inside, but she had no desire to do so. She understood that her place was where she stood, with her family, and that the distance maintained by her 'betters' was an integral part of her life.

She now turned and approached the servants' entrance at the side of the main building. Their quarters were to be found in the east side of the house, tucked away from view.

"I've come about 'annah." Her voice whispered to the apron of the young woman who had come to the door.

"Where's your father? 'e should have come." The housemaid was, it appeared, aware of the circumstances surrounding the visit.

"Father is ou' making a call, he's not back until abou' four."

"Come in, come, wait a minute." Ellen was ushered into the dark corridor, feeling uncertain and bewildered, wishing she could find a way of taking command of the situation.

"I wan' to see 'annah!"

"Wait miss! We'll let master know you are 'ere, and then we'll see."

"What's the ma"er with 'er? She's alrigh' isn't she?"

"Wait dear, just a minute, come to the kitchen, you'll see 'annah presently." The maid was impersonally efficient in her treatment of Ellen, but there was also a faint note of kindness.

Ellen felt afraid, because she didn't know what to think. Uncertainty and anxiety had dogged her life just lately, but she had found the most powerful way of ridding herself of unwanted doubts was to do something, to act spontaneously.

"Le' me see Sir Russell!"

"My dear, *that's* not possible. Just come in here, and sit here while we arrange things." The housemaid, Charlotte, although only four years older than Ellen, was in possession of an undoubted authority which had come from three years of service. She knew how things had to be done, and so it was that she took Ellen into the kitchen, and left her there.

The young man sitting at the kitchen table looked up from his paper, and closely regarded the young stranger with interest and then with unqualified admiration. He stood immediately to acknowledge her presence, looked more closely at her and promptly found that he was being inspected too, noting the wide hazel eyes looking steadfastly at him. To her, his very fair skin and almost white hair had come as a shock. She had never seen a man with such a pale mystery about him; his steady misty grey eyes beneath a level, open brow created an intriguing and unforgettable impression which she found attracted her gaze and held her fascinated.

"I'm to wai' 'ere before seein' my sister." She felt the need to explain.

"Yes, I see ... do take a seat, while you wait. I'm Charles, Charles Coleman, just visiting like yourself." He came forward as he spoke, and although not particularly tall, seemed to hold himself well above Ellen, so that she suddenly felt shy.

"I'm Ellen Lambourn ... from the village." Her identity she simply stated, and she paused to clear her mind. Her shyness was a new sensation and it had overcome her usual ability to think with clarity.

He reached out to her with his hand. She was surprised by this but instinctively responded to his action placing her hand in his. She realised then as he had drawn closer to her that he was not much taller than her and imagined for a moment that perhaps he was not much older. She very soon discovered that in this she was mistaken.

When she gave her hand to him, she saw that her hand was completely enveloped in his. She could not help herself, and looked to examine his hand as he let go of hers.

It seemed so powerful to her, broad with expressive, capable fingers; it was strong and sinewy with the tendons and muscles clearly defined, and yet it had been soft and tender holding hers. His nails she noted were short and scrubbed clean and cut squarely across the tips of each finger. She decided that she loved the look of his hands and received the courage to lift her eyes to his face. He was smiling at her with such warmth and kindness that she felt impelled to smile bravely back.

"It's a pleasure to meet you, young Ellen. This part of the world is clearly a beautiful place to be." He appeared to be serious as he spoke, but there was humour in what he said which she noticed, and she felt warmed by what she had realised was his way of showing approval of her. She did not know what flattery was. Instead he was being friendly and attentive, as she imagined he was towards everyone, but Ellen, unused to society, and the social graces beyond her immediate family, concluded he was being particularly attentive to her, but did not understand why.

"It's the only par' of the world I know! You are not from around 'ere, I think."

"That's right. I come from Lyndhurst way. Visiting my sister you know. You say you have come to see *your* sister?"

"Yes ... I don" know what's the ma"er. Sir Russell 'ad sent for father ... bu' 'e 's away on business, so I"ve come."

"Oh, not a regular visit then?" He sounded concerned, and looked at her uneasily. Poor girl, he thought, she certainly looked in need of assistance, and decided to offer encouragement. "I'm sure that she's in good hands. Sir Russell is, by all accounts, a fair man. You needn't worry, you know!"

"No?" Ellen was unconvinced, but hoped that Mr Coleman had read the situation correctly. She wanted to believe him, to have faith in his ability to accurately interpret the situation. She could feel now that he was older and more confident than her. His manner towards her had taken on a more mature aspect, one of a kindly mentor. She concluded that, despite his stature, he was much older than her.

They both heard footsteps coming down the stairs, and turned to see the maid Charlotte, followed by Hannah enter the room. Ellen, overcome with relief at seeing her dear sister walking towards her and not lying on a sick bed, cried out in gratitude.

29

"Oh, thank God, 'annah, I'm so pleased to see you!" She rushed to hold her sister's hands, and looked up into her distraught face.

"Ellen, I've go' to be comin' 'ome. You must tell father, and 'e must come and fetch me. I can't stay 'ere now. I'm afraid tha' my time 'ere is over." Hannah hesitated to say any more. Ellen was such a child still. She could n't explain to her that her life had come to an end, that she *must* return to her family. She had to return to be hidden away, retreat to those who would be loyal to her, would protect her and keep her concealed.

Charles had drawn back as the sisters had met. He observed them closely. The older sister, tall, pretty and robust looking had appeared to him to be careworn and frightened, clearly worn down by life. With her plea to her sister his initial impression seemed to be confirmed. She expressed herself anxiously and impatiently; her words professed that a terrible misfortune had occurred and yet paradoxically her eyes shone with a glimmering fortitude and determination.

The other, Ellen, he saw as more vibrant and deliciously fresh than any girl he had ever seen, anxious like her sister but balanced by other emotions which kept control of her and which evidenced her strong spirit. She appeared to exude energy from every part of her body. He saw her as being very beautiful, like a glorious, newly opened perfect rose, created by the Almighty to His perfect design to enhance and demonstrate true sweetness in His world.

He observed that the sisters placed great value on each other. As they stood together looking at each other closely, he could see the trust between them, and although nothing more was said, he knew they had come to some kind of understanding.

* * *

30

Ellen had never seen her father so restless before. She guessed it was born of the shock of what had transpired in recent days, and had little to do with the normal day to day worries of his life. He had always possessed a quiet air of acceptance before the death of his wife, which others felt indicated that he was essentially a humble man, who cared little for the vain trappings of the world. He had always appeared content, and he had apparently loved his wife dearly. Their marriage had appeared to onlookers to be a love match, but he had since felt troubled that he had not been a more demonstratively affectionate husband, and that he should have given more of his time to her and protected her from the pain and troubles of their life together. At least she did not have to go through the latest ruination which had befallen the family, but he could try and rescue Hannah his daughter.

"Hannah, you have to tell me who is responsible." His fatherly instincts had been aroused and were the source of this demand, to seek retribution and not any paternal desire to protect his beloved daughter. She must have sensed this, because her reply was strangely cold and distant.

"Father, it does n't matter. Wha' difference would i' make? I'm no' goin' to tell, because i' can do no good. They've pu' me out, and 'ere I am, and 'ere I'll stay! I'll have nothin' to do with them. I wan' you to understand," Hannah summoned up some feeling and pleaded with him, "Please, pa, don' be ashamed of me! I know I've done wrong but ..."

"I'll no' agree with you, nor will I ever stop believin' tha' they're to blame, someone in tha' house is to blame! You've been molested in tha' 'ouse ... I'll get to the truth ... I'll be goin' round there to 'ave it ou' with 'em." Thomas looked at his daughter and could only see his wife. *She* would not have done anything morally

31

wrong. His wife had been pure and constant; she had been chaste, righteous and true all her life.

"Please pa, I could na bear it … it'll only make things worse than ever … you can see tha', please, I don'' want any 'elp from them … I know it looks bad bu' …''

"No, I'll finish with them! I'll no' be paid by tha' family any more. No, it would show them that I won't be made a fool of … for them to cast you aside without so much as a bye nor leave when all the time it was their duty to keep you safe.''

"Pa, I can' let you do tha' cos of me … Oh, pa, don't, don't!'' She slipped forward in her chair and flung her head onto her arms on the table. She felt utterly desperate. Thomas gazed at his forlorn daughter, torn apart and angry. He needed to have vengeance! He did not outwardly respond to her anguish. He made his decision which would provide him with a small degree of satisfaction.

"If you won't shame the man who defiled you, then I 'ave no choice in the ma''er … my work for tha' family is at an end … my conscience will not allow me to continue as if no injustice has occurred … that's my final word… But as far as the father of your child is to remain unknown … I 'ave to accept tha' for now bu' I 'ope that … one day, 'e'll pay for his sin.'' Hannah, desperate and fettered by the effects of horrible events was unaware at first of the consequences of her father's words, but sensed that he would obstinately remain firm in his actions, and would not relent.

Her unborn child would be hers and hers alone until such time as her baby's father would accept her as his wife. Until that occurred he would remain unknown and she would not, under any circumstances, be diverted from her decided course.

Then, her father's words began to penetrate her confused mind and she began to comprehend that her father was threatening to cut all ties to the Turner family and the Grange, and concluded that this could result in financial consequences which would be very damaging.

"'ow will we manage pa? I wish you wouldn't do it. I know tha' it is bound to be difficul' for you if you give Sir Russell up ...his family ... they're the best customers you've ever 'ad. Why can' you go on as before? Please pa, people will notice if you don' attend 'im and 'is family. I wan' to 'ave things to stay the same ... *please* pa." Desperate as she was, and wishing with all her heart that what had happened would go completely unnoticed, and that her family's life would be unaltered, she knew with a deep sorrow that this was not possible. Her father's need for some form of justice outweighed every other consideration.

"It is true that it will be 'arder for us, bu' it's no matter." Thomas spoke almost inaudibly, with a painful recognition that his decision would have some impact on the family, particularly as business had been becoming less productive. He knew that harder times were coming, and a remedy would be needed. "Tom has been wantin' to go and work in South'ampton, so 'e'll no' be 'ere for long. That'll makes things easier ... 'e'll contribute to the family, and 'elp where 'e can."

"Are you thinkin' of carryin' on the business alone pa"? Ellen had heard her father's announcement as she entered the kitchen, and could not contain her thirst for knowledge. She had to know what her father was planning, for she knew that whatever he decided, her life would be influenced more than any other. Tom would have his own new life. Hannah would have her baby and would help with the family. Agnes would help care for the children and go to school, and she had reached the age when she would be expected to work, to do whatever her father demanded.

Thomas, feeling anxious, troubled and frustrated with Hannah, became angry with Ellen at once, for asking a question which was not her place to ask, and which perfectly demonstrated her impudence and lack of respect. He angrily snapped at her, "Ellen, the children should be in their beds. Go an' 'elp Agnes! Your sister spends less time worrying abou' things tha' don'' concern 'er, and more time doin' the things that do, and you need to start doing the same!"

Ellen was bewildered and as had happened several times recently felt crushed by her father's treatment of her. Surely he could have shared with her his plan for the future, and she would then know what was expected of her. She could not understand why he would not wish to answer her or confide in her. Why wouldn't he share his plans, or was he just excluding her?

Ellen was as yet unaware that some men have implicit expectations of women, and are uneasy when the 'weaker' sex breaks the mould, and do not conform to the pattern expected of them. That her father had taken this view was also unknown to her. Unaware of this principle which defined many of the relationships within her world, she did not understand her father's dismissive response to her need, but due to a lifetime of conditioned homage to him, and a deep personal inclination to remain loyal to all those who were closest to her, she said nothing.

Her father watched her for a moment, and saw the pain in her eyes, but remained untouched. She could not look at him. She could not share what was in her heart, for she knew her path lay in obedience, and obey she must. Without a word she left and went to the stairs.

"Aggie!" Ellen called up to the bedrooms, to confirm that her sister was where her father expected her to be.

"I'm 'ere, Ellen, come and see wha' 'enry 'as done!" Aggie sounded excited, so Ellen went immediately, trying to control the tears she felt, which she knew she would need to express at some later time.

Henry at seven years old was a child who had found most of his life's experiences difficult and perplexing. He hadn't walked until he was five, had spoken only a few sparse almost indistinguishable words by the age of six, and had always remained withdrawn. Agnes had recently taken him to the Dames' School in the village, and it had been there that an important discovery had been made. Miss Sait, their teacher, had encouraged Henry to use chalks on a slate. For days he had just watched the other boys, showing no interest in mirroring their actions. Miss Sait, unused to such unresponsive behaviour, and unqualified as most would have been to know the best course of action, had determined to tell the family that there was little point in Henry attending school. The pennies would be better saved and spent on another of the children.

However, one cool day in June that year, a miracle had occurred in the form of a butterfly! It had flown into the classroom, unwelcome at first, through the open door, and settled its fragile fluttering blue form on a child's bench. Henry had been the first to discover it, close to where he sat. Making a cup with his small hands, he gently laid them over the butterfly, waited for a moment, and then, almost as if he was praying, brought his cupped hands gently together. He stood, and smiled, not knowing that he was being watched by everyone. Shuffling to an open window, the strangeness of his usual movements accentuated by the odd positioning of his hands, he reached it and held his hands out into the air outside. He raised and parted his hands in a salute to the sky, and the azure particle, a piece of a better, sunnier day, was released into its world.

Henry had stood there for some minutes, watching something beyond the butterfly. No one had ever known what it was, but some guessed it was that sunnier day, a brighter time ahead. He had eventually returned to his seat, taken up his chalk and slate, and with great deliberation, had gone to work. Miss Sait could not contain herself; she had to see what it was Henry was doing.

"Why children, everyone, Henry has drawn the loveliest flower and guess what? It has the most beautiful butterfly on it!" Although Henry's drawing was not like others produced by children of his age, Miss Sait's kind heart recognised the paramount importance of this occurrence in the development of Henry, and knew it was a moment for rejoicing.

Aggie had told Ellen, and communicated her own excitement and joy at what had happened. Ellen was ready to hear more.

"Why, what's 'e done now?"

"Aw, you won" believe i'! Look over 'ere!" Aggie could hardly contain her excitement, whilst Henry, passively lying on the bed by this time, appeared not to realise that he was the cause of the commotion. Aggie was staring at the chair beside the bed, and beckoned to Ellen. The simple beech chair had been decorated with a pheasant's speckled feather, a tiny banded snail shell, a knobbly white and black flint stone, a twist of wool left behind by a Southdown sheep, and a gleaming fragment of a blue-green, earth flecked blackbird's egg. Each object had been placed as part of a circle, the natural curves of each echoing the finished design.

"Is na i' wonderful? We should keep i', and no' change i'. I'm goin' to call i' 'enry's 'arvest! That's wha' i' is!" Both girls giggled, enjoying the simple knowledge that Henry was now expressing himself as he had never done before. For Ellen, especially, it was a joyful moment, having only just recently experienced a bitter anguish it was very good indeed now to encounter a sweet balm.

* * *

It was not long before the whole village knew of Hannah's condition and wretchedness. The valiant attempts of her father to protect his eldest daughter from the inevitable uncharitable expressions of non-approval and repudiation were seen by some as misconceived. Her present position was seen as the product of feminine weakness, which could have been avoided if she had been more virtuous. Her father's efforts in making it known that Hannah had been the victim of an evil seducer, were believed by only a few. Misguided some would say and disbelieved by most, his only desire was to alleviate her suffering and with it salve his pride.

Hannah, engrossed by her predicament, and feeling ruined by circumstance, remained silent. She would not tell, let people think what they liked. Whether innocent or guilty, it did not matter. She would *not* seal her fate by telling all, and would allow the jury to come to its own verdict. While she remained silent, there remained an uncertainty and as long as that remained, she could not be sentenced by anyone.

As her pregnancy progressed, Hannah became stronger. She threw herself into the daily chores, taking on the mother's role. She created a comfortable and gentle existence for the family, ensuring that each received answers to their physical needs. The unbaked loaves and cakes were prepared and carried to the bakery next door twice a week. The washing was mangled, the soap made, the dinners prepared, the range raked, stripped, blackened and lit. The passageways were scrubbed, the furniture waxed, the linen ironed. Working with Hannah, Ellen had time to reflect on how single minded Hannah had become, and how important it was to possess an order in one's life, because it allowed for the Creator to enter in and bring joy with Him. Order and industry allowed the appreciation of the most important things.

Without the kind of order which comes from hard work and self-discipline she decided, the chances that a passing blue butterfly, after venturing in, would be noticed, would be very remote indeed.

* * *

James Turner had been surprised at the quietness of the courtyard as he had entered it under the narrow archway. There was just room for horse and rider, between the uneven, russet coloured brick walls of the bakery on one side and the grocer and draper's shop on the other. Ahead of him stood a simple stable, wooden and tiled and room enough for two horses. He reined in and paused, hesitating in the stillness, unsure of his next move. His errand was awkward, and inwardly he had hoped for some kind of activity within, which might have made introductions easier, and would have resulted in a more comfortable entrance into the tailor's home. Here, behind the grocer's, tucked away from the busy street, there was no sign of life, no-one he could acknowledge, not anyone with whom he could exchange pleasantries. His entrance was not softened by a smile or a greeting on the way. He dismounted and led his horse to the rail beyond the tailor's shop window.

To anyone seeing this young man for the first time, he would represent the smartest element in the neighbourhood. The points of his high collar were crisply white, his boots were gleaming and spotless, his riding coat fitted impeccably across his shoulders moulding itself perfectly to his frame. His youthful face was handsome too, his brows and nose straight, and above the upper lip of his finely shaped mouth, there was just visible the beginnings of his first moustache. Only fourteen years old, but with the carriage of a mature man, James looked out from beneath the brim of his riding hat, seeming to gaze in a confident, self-satisfied sort of way. His look might have been interpreted as haughty and self-centred, a demeanour which would set him apart from others. He certainly was a serious young man, but to those who knew him well, he was a kinder person than he at first appeared, though he was naturally as selfish as a youth tends to be.

Ellen was not expecting to see anyone this autumnal Monday morning. She had only just returned from collecting water, and had set the copper on the fire, ready for the weekly wash. She was alone as Agnes had gone with the children to school, and Tom had left to work in Southampton, just a few weeks earlier. His father no longer needed him in the business as much as he had in the past. Work had lessened as he had predicted, and more was required in the way of simple repairs and alterations, rather than commissions for new clothes. His father could manage very well indeed without Tom, and so it was that he had gone to the new department store with considerable excitement born of anticipation, but also a little dread. But he had put aside his fear. Like his mother, he had a tendency to being positive about himself, others and life in general, and would tenaciously apply himself wholeheartedly to whatever it threw at him. Ellen missed him a great deal, probably because he reminded her of their mother, and she could never get rid of the emptiness she felt in her life, which had seeped its way into her heart at the time of her mother's death. At least when Tom was about his infectious optimism carried her along, and she felt easier within herself. Now, left to herself, the sombre emptiness had returned. Her mother had gone too early, and yet she knew that it had been too late as well. It had been late enough for the growth of a closeness of understanding between them; a precious friendship between mother and daughter had developed upon which Ellen had depended. Her mother had encouraged her, praised her and consistently tried to understand her. Her mother had never worried about her own life, but had serenely moved forward each moment of every day preoccupied with the care of her family. She had always recognised the good in others, too, and had encouraged each of her children to think the best of one another.

Her mother's influence was like a golden thread running through the fabric of the life of the Lambourn family, and it could not be unpicked or destroyed. It would always remain, Ellen believed, woven deep and intricately through their lives.

Ellen again reflected upon the last visit of Doctor Stocks. He'd said that their mother was dying. Ellen's heart had stopped, and she'd involuntarily cried out.

"No, my ma, mother! Say it's not true! Don't say i'. Say she'll ge' well, say i'."

She'd become familiar with death. She'd wanted to hold her baby brother's lifeless body, but Ma Lambourn had not let her near. Death was an unseen barricade, visible only through its effects on the living. It could not be overcome, it could not be vanquished nor surmounted. It was there, an insurmountable boundary, causing separation and tears. She was crying now, as she had often done when alone, longing not just for the comfortable and carefree life which had been hers beside her mother, but for the person who was her mother. The selfish desires of a child for an easier life had given way to the dawning of an appreciation and reverence for the giving and taking of love which she had learnt from her mother.

Her mother would carefully stroke her hair behind her ear when she was little and tired, sitting on her mother's lap. Her gentle touch conveyed an unspoken fondness which Ellen had felt. Her mother would also counsel with her and explain things that Ellen had not understood. She would laugh with her when Ellen made mistakes, and when she had grown tired and ill, she would smile at her, a smile that said, "Ellen, you are strong, you are not only my daughter but God's daughter too. Don't forget it!"

"I will remember, I will!" Ellen emphasised each word as she turned the laundry peg dolly down onto the washing. She watched the muscles in her forearms harden and shine in the steamy air. "I am strong, ma, I am!"

"The shop bell did ring, I am sorry if I've surprised you." James Turner had entered by the shop door, and hearing the sound of water coming from the back room, had passed directly through the shop as no-one had responded to his entrance. Ellen was startled, so deep had she been in her own feelings and thoughts.

Only just fourteen years old, she'd had little contact with her father's customers, and was very shocked to see a young man whom she vaguely recognised as the elder son of Sir Russell entering the back room. She could not think or say anything, and stood staring at him, her mind full of confusion and fear, her hands gripping the washing dolly for support.

James saw the young woman poised where she stood with anxious, doubtful, dark eyes fixed on him.

"It's nothing to worry you I assure you. I'm come to see Miss Hannah Lambourn if you please. I've come to the right place, I think?"

"Yes, she's my sister."

"Good, I would be grateful for a word with her. Please inform her that James Turner is here to speak with her."

"Of course, I … um … I don" know."

"Could I please speak to her now?" James' voice was even and calm and lacked emotion. He had removed his hat on entering the shop, expecting to see a member of the household employed in the shop premises. Instead he was faced with an attractive girl who conjured up a vague memory. He'd seen her before, somewhere he knew it, but as he tried to remember, she interrupted him.

"She's no' 'ere."

"When will she return please?"

"I don" know. It's no' arranged as ye'. She's gone away with my father, you see, to stay with family."

"So, you've no idea when she might return, is that right?"

"Yes, but Ma Lambourne, my gran'mama migh' 'ave some idea." Although this visitor had entered unannounced, she felt less fearful now, probably because she recognised qualities in this young man which made him address her with some politeness, which encouraged her to want to answer him and not be fearful of him. "Pa migh' 'ave told 'er when 'e and 'annah are comin' back." She hesitated to tell of more private matters. "I don" think 'annah will be back for a good while."

"Ah, I had no idea that she planned to leave." As he paused to consider this unexpected news, he recollected that he had arrived without warning. "I'm sorry to come in upon you like this. Would you be good enough to tell me who you are … I'm sorry to have startled you." He gently nodded his head at her.

"Ellen Lambourn, sir. You know 'annah well, sir?"

"Yes, a little. She was in service to my father and uncle."

A moment passed as they both searched to find words to express, and James noticed the brightness of Ellen's eyes, as she looked about her, trying to find an appropriate reply. It was then that he recollected the day of their previous encounter on the road to the Grange. His earlier attraction to her, her eyes, skin, and beautiful hair, was rekindled, and he began to feel uncomfortably warm in the steamy atmosphere of the wash house.

"Is there anything I can do, sir?" She'd heard her father say this many times to his customers. She had learnt to listen carefully to his conversations as she'd not been allowed to speak when her father had visitors. She had always remained in the adjoining room, performing some household task, and had strained to hear every word.

"Maybe there is. I wonder would you be so kind as to see that Hannah gets this on her return. Since your father has not been coming to the Grange, it has become more difficult for us to communicate with your family. We didn't really want to send it to Hannah, you see, and we felt that it would be the most sensible thing to bring it to her, but if you could see that she gets it on her return." His hand had reached into the side pocket of his coat, and drawn out a square envelope. His hand, still covered by a fine leather glove, lightly grasped the slightly crumpled paper. He held it out to her, hesitating as he spoke, hoping that the feelings of disquiet he was beginning to feel were not evident to this girl who possessed such enquiring eyes.

"Of course, I'll give i' to 'annah. I'm sure she'd be pleased to receive i'." Ellen was bemused by what was taking place. She

43

could think of only one reason why anyone from the Grange should want to write to Hannah, and that was because she was more than an ordinary friend. He was quite young, no older than herself she thought, but had such a confident air about him, she began to think the unthinkable! She blushed at the thought, and felt confused by the emotions that she was feeling. She hastily moved forward and took the letter, her head bowed and eyes averted. James was momentarily amused by the girl's shyness, and realised that the moment which now presented itself was a fitting one for his escape.

"I have trespassed long enough. Please convey my kind regards to your father and sister, and also those from the rest of my family. We are all indebted to your father. Good morning!"

* * *

When anything out of the ordinary happens in the life of an individual in an introspective and confined village, it is not surprising to discover that the unexpected event takes on a significance which dwarfs years of other experiences. Ellen could not stop thinking about the episode with James Turner, about what she had said, about what he'd said and about the mystery of the strange white envelope. She'd secreted it safely in the bottom drawer of her mother's bedroom chest, not wanting it to reside in a familiar place, but keeping it somewhere where it would hold a special and secret place.

Her mother's drawers had not been emptied completely. They still contained some of her mother's intimate possessions which her father had obviously made the decision to keep. Ellen looked down on her mother's starched blouses, some of her embroidered handkerchiefs, her best bonnet and a small bundle of letters, upon which she carefully placed Hannah's letter. Here was a fittingly sacred place of safety for this amazing acquisition. She pondered on the startling realisation that it represented something both perplexing and mysterious.

Before Hannah had left to stay with her grandparents, she had never mentioned the paternity of her child. Her decision not to divulge the circumstances of her pregnancy had remained firm and she resolutely committed herself to silence on the subject. Her intention was to bring up her child alone, within the supportive framework and love of her family. Ellen neither challenged nor questioned her sister on this matter. She'd accepted that Hannah had good cause for her taciturnity, and did not try to come to any conclusions on the matter. Hannah appeared well enough, and so Ellen had absolved herself of any interest, that is up until now. She had become intrigued, and grew impatient of the time when her sister would become acquainted with the contents of the letter, and hopefully share them with her.

She had returned to the labours of the day, when Ma Lambourn arrived, knowing that Ellen was alone and would need help with the household's washing, she had come back from her own home, which was situated just a little further down the main street after seeing to her own domestic arrangements. They were setting to together when Ellen remembered something she wanted to know.

"Gran'ma, when did pa say 'e would be back?" Ma Lambourn thought it strange that her son had not told his daughter when he would return.

"Why Ellen, 'e's back tomorrow, 'e asked me to stay close by until then." The older woman was relieved that her son would soon return. She had found keeping an eye on his family a thankless task, particularly when she could not understand the purpose of his absence. Everyone knew that Hannah was with child. There appeared to be no apparent reason for transporting her to Lymington. A long journey just before her confinement was foolhardy; she knew that better than anyone.

"Do you think tha' 'annah will be long in comin' back?"

"As for tha', I've no more idea than you, though I suppose i' migh' be a good while before she comes back. Your mother used to stay a month. Your Pa thought the sea air did her good, bu' I never saw an improvemen' in 'er."

Ellen felt the urge to tell someone about the letter, but for some strange reason did not feel that her grandmother should be the one. They were not close, and this was reflected in the lack of communication between them. As is generally the case, the tone of a relationship between an adult and a child is set by the former, and Ma Lambourn, a widow for twenty years, had remained single, supported by her two sons and, embittered by her own solitary state, had made little effort towards Ellen and her other grandchildren. In the first place she had disliked Hannah her daughter in law, and in result had felt little affection for her granddaughters. She had little patience with her elder son's behaviour in relation to his daughter Hannah, and could not understand the attention he was giving her. Other young women in her position went to the workhouse in Winchester to have their babies. They were looked after. That would have been her choice for Hannah.

Ellen had remained silent, knowing that her decision to not relate the unusual circumstances of the day to her grandmother was the right one. She would wait for Hannah's return, and see her reaction. In the meantime, the washing needed to be rinsed, mangled and pegged out to dry. The beautiful young man faded just a little in her mind, in the hot water, steam and sweat of that warm September wash day.

* * *

A period of frustration in various aspects of life can result in an increased sense of self, and an awareness of those sensibilities which lie deep within us. Ellen, longing for her sister's return, and with an equal desire to remain in her recently acquired happy state of independence and personal fulfilment, felt irritated by the conflict in her heart, and knew that this was something that she would have to learn to live with. At regular intervals she had found a degree of peace in immersing herself in writing, recording some of the homespun remedies and home comforts which had been handed down by her mother, who in turn had received them from older generations. Tom had given her a small plain booklet and a simple wooden handled pen for her birthday, and since that time, to ward off the contradictory emotions within her, she had collected together and written all that she had learnt.

Plants, their leaves, stems, roots and flowers acted merely as a distraction at first, but they gradually became her passion. Their properties, created, she believed, by the hand of God for the good of all, became for her a source of enquiry which turned her attention to the past and gave her a view of her own progenitors, and consequently a better understanding of the place in the world they had made for her.

She had begun to feel more kindly toward her family and she would try harder to please her father in particular. She had also begun to feel differently about her grandmother Ma Lambourn. She had approached her to ask her questions. Her grandmother, flattered by Ellen's interest in her own understanding of plant properties and their application, had conceded that Ellen had at last shown some sign of maturity.

"It's a blessin' to see the change in Ellen," she spoke with surprise to her elder son, during his customary visit one early winter Sunday evening.

"Wha"s th' mean Ma?" Her son had not shared his mother's vision of his second daughter. "I canno' know wha' you're meanin'." He had not considered how little he noticed Ellen. He had deliberately distanced himself. It appeared to everyone that this child was a disappointment to him, and this had led to his gradual emotional detachment which had resulted in his almost total impassivity. His wife had thought she had known part of the real cause. Ellen, unlike the other children, had posed a threat to his emotional stability. Ellen had enjoyed a deeply affectionate relationship with her mother which was undoubtedly the cause, amongst other things, of the father's unease and jealousy.

Ma Lambourn seemed oblivious to her son's disapproval and negative feelings towards Ellen.

"My son, Ellen is growin'. She's almost ready to make her livin'. You mus' talk with her, and tell her of your plans."

"Ma, now don" you start tellin' me wha' should be 'appenin' in my own house. You know my feelin's on the matter, and I won" be askin' Miss Mary to be wed until 'annah is back and settled in with the baby. There's plenty of time ahead to talk to Ellen."

"Don" think I'm no' knowin' tha' you've got everythin' in 'and. But Ellen 'as told me she's not sure wha' she's needed for, once 'annah returns. You should tell 'er." She had somewhat surprisingly sided with her granddaughter. She had grown to like her lately, seeing as she had been so interested in what she could tell her about the local plants and recipes that had been handed down to her by her own mother and other women in the village.

"'annah will return before Christmas, an' when the family is together, tha"ll be the time to make things plain to Ellen. They'll be a position for 'er. I've made a few enquiries. I' shouldn" be difficul' to get 'er settled." He spoke with confidence. His contacts had provided solutions to family difficulties before. Hannah had been offered the housemaid's post at the Grange because of the family's respect for him. It hadn't turned out well, but then that was no fault of Hannah's. He knew her to be like her mother, chaste and trustworthy. Nothing could persuade him otherwise. She would help his new wife in running their home. He felt very comfortable with his intentions. He stared at his mother.

She was aware of his courtship of Mary Crook. He'd visited her at her parents' home, and had been attracted to her from the time he had first noticed her as a young woman. She smiled warmly at him when he spoke, and seemed to him to be a very pleasant young woman. She was very attentive, and although only a farm labourer's daughter, had good manners, and was clean and homely. He'd noticed that she was happy to listen to sermons at church on a Sunday. He'd intently watched her and was relieved to see her apparent piety. Her solemn face and averted gaze perfectly matched what he hoped for. Here was a woman who would fit into his ways, and who would provide the warmth that was missing in his life. The thought of her in his bed filled him with an agreeable sensation, which he recognised as an overriding desire within him which needed to be satisfied. Long before he had intended to, he had asked her father for her hand, and being a highly respected tradesman in the village, he had not expected to be rebuffed. So it was that he had very quickly become engaged to Mary.

The age difference of twenty years meant nothing to him or to anyone else apparently. Mary had seemed excited, and had moved close to him when he'd told her of his love for her. Her face had been close beneath his own, and she had laughed up at him. Her eyes had flashed at him, and her beautiful young mouth seemed to be asking to be kissed. He hadn't dared. He had felt strangely shy in the presence of her confident approach. Memories of Hannah, the only other woman he had courted and kissed, haunted him, as he remembered her shy reserve which was such a contrast to Mary's bold manners.

He hadn't been able to resist the strong attraction however. He had wrapped her in his arms, and lovingly held her. Just for a moment the anxieties of the past months dissipated, and he was only conscious of her. Then, the door had abruptly opened.

"Ah Mary, it seems that there's a weddin' to plan." Mrs. Crook had been informed of Thomas Lambourn's request for Mary's hand in marriage, and was overjoyed at the prospect of seeing her only daughter securely established.

"Ma! Is n'a wonderfu'?" Mary had fallen back from Thomas's embrace, when he'd hurriedly released her. Her heart was pounding, and her face burnt with excitement. She had felt his longing for her, and was delighted by the power she knew she had over him. Her mother was thrilled to see Mary looking so radiant.

"Yes! Your father tells me tha' the weddin' is to be next month. It will give us enough time to make it special for you, though nothing fancy, mind. I said to pa tha' you'd 'ave to be satisfied with a simple service. Nothing fancy, Mary!" Thomas had been surprised but relieved that Mr. Crook had agreed to an early ceremony. He would need to break it to his family. He had made up his mind, and did not believe there was any benefit in any delay putting his decision into action. So it seemed that everyone was satisfied by events, and the happy couple would soon be united in the holy state of matrimony.

News had arrived from Lymington that Hannah had given birth to a very healthy baby boy, and would be returning to Botley accompanied by her grandmother as soon as the weather began to improve in the spring. Her father's reaction to the news was not favourable.

"'Somethin' must be done. I'm no' postponin' my weddin. Why can' she brough' back before Christmas, like it was decided upon?"

"Thomas, there must be good reason. 'annah will come back when she's ready. You know she is a sensible girl, and would na wan' to deliberately upse' you." Ma Lambourn had been shocked by his reaction.

He, however, had made up his mind to be married at the beginning of December, and now his beloved daughter was not coming home for months. How was he to wait so long for Mary?

"Ma, I can" believe tha' she would do this to me, when the weddin' day is all bu' set. I suppose I will 'ave to put it off."

"Listen, we don" know all the details, we don" know how the baby is doin'."

"Oh, I know, ma, bu' how am I goin' to wait so long. I..." Thomas suddenly realised that he could not confess to his mother the strength of Mary's hold over him. He knew that a wise man would carefully consider before making such an important decision. Maybe the time of waiting would be a time of reflection for him, which would provide him with an opportunity to better prepare the children at home for the arrival of his new wife and he should postpone.

"Consider the next few months as bein' a special time for you to 'elp Ellen and find 'er a good position."

"Mm, yes, Ma ... yes., yes." He sounded impatient now as yet again his mother was showing unwanted concern for Ellen. It irritated him that his mother did not appear to understand the way he was feeling, and was more interested in his awkward daughter. Apparently it did n't matter to her that his wishes and plans had been thwarted.

"I have na forgotten abou' Ellen, nor the others. Bu' I'm wonderin' tha' the weddin' can still go ahead as planned. Oh I know 'annah 'll be disappointed at missin;' it, bu' I know she'd understand and wish Mary and me joy."

"Oh, I'm sure, son." Ma Lambourn's sarcasm was born of the shock caused by her son's easy dismissal of his eldest daughter attending the wedding. She had n't really seen the hold Mary had over him but he was certainly in a rush to have her. "What's the hurry though? Why not wai' a while? You're not afraid you migh' lose 'er are you?"

"Ma! Mary'll always be faithful to me, of tha' I am sure."

"So, let it be a 'appy family time. Wait for 'annah's return, my son, and 'ave all your children around you." Ma Lambourn spoke gently, anxious to try and prevent her son from making hasty plans, which were less than satisfactory. Thomas turned to the mirror and gazed at his reflection. The long hours of painstaking work were reflected in his sunken eyes and dull skin. His cheekbones were too prominent now, whereas before, in his youth, they had provided a handsome, gentler curve to his profile. His looks were fading. He no longer looked or felt a man of youthful vigour. He glanced at his hair, and noted its thinning. With feelings of anxiety born of pride, he turned once more to his mother, his mind made up irrevocably.

* * *

The news of Thomas Lewis and Mary Crook's marriage had been viewed by various members of their families as unwelcome, and once the wedding had taken place as soon as the Banns had been pronounced, just four weeks from the time of its announcement, it was judged as overly precipitous. No one had openly remarked upon it in public, but much was shared in private.

"Wha' you goin' to say to pa when he comes in?" Agnes had witnessed Ellen's earlier outburst concerning their father's behaviour. Her inbred desire to please her father had dissipated as she had felt deeply wronged by the hurried wedding arrangements, because of her over-riding loyalty to her mother. She had noticed too his heightened irritability and impatience with her despite her efforts to conform to his will. Neither could she approve of her father's decision to act in a way which did not in every way consider the wishes of *all* of his family.

"I shall tell 'im I'm to go, as soon as I'm able, tha''s all," Ellen's voice was quiet but Agnes felt the determination expressed within it. She felt afraid and confused, hoping that a way might be found for her to go with Ellen. That seemed to be the obvious solution, and yet she knew there was no probability of that happening. Life without her sister, who reminded her so much of her mother, would be bleak indeed.

"Please stay, Ellen, I know it'll be difficul', but we'll manage with each other 'elpin', and we'll stay as a family, and wha' about 'enry? You know 'ow he loves you and follows around after you. You can't leave 'im, 'e'll miss you too much, and 'e'll cry…" Agnes ended in tears, her hands clutching her cheeks and her small body shaking, she'd not known such deep anguish since the

53

day of her mother's funeral, when she had hidden herself away and had been inconsolable. Her grief had been reawakened by the stirring of other deep emotions, bitterness and resentment, born of the seeming indifference of their father. They were expected to share their father's joy. So why did she feel so dejected, so devastated, so miserable?

"Agnes, Agnes! I'll no' do things hasty. I'll wait. Please remember, Pa's the head of this 'ouse. It's 'im that'll decide what's to 'appen. I'll wai' 'til I'm told, alright, alright, Agnes?"

Agnes felt a little comfort, but needed reassurance.

"I'll go with you, won" I? When you go, you'll wan' me to come too?"

"Pa won" wan' too many of us around, I'm sure." She looked across at the familiar but unusually empty kitchen, and realised how full it would become once her father and Mary, Hannah and baby Frederick, Emily, Henry and George, and finally Agnes and herself were all living there. No, her life and possibly Agnes's too would soon be centred upon another world beyond the tailor's small home in the High Street. Her spirits began to rise again and she smiled warmly at her vulnerable younger sister. She would try to take care of Agnes, as well as take care of herself.

'Into the nothingness of scorn and noise –
Into the sea of waking dreams.'

I'm not sure what got me going on this. Perhaps it was the fact that I've been trapped in this bed for the past month. That's enough to make anyone focus their attention onto better things, rather than stare at an uncompromising ceiling. Ceilings don't amount to much, excepting there is some life up there, if you give yourself enough time to explore it. I've discovered an animal kingdom up above, which incidentally, does not frighten me in the least.

What does frighten me is the future, but I'm not going to dwell on it. I am hoping for better times. But I feel so ill and afraid. I don't want anyone to notice me. Maybe it's because I don't want to draw attention to myself by screaming or sobbing or squirming in agony in this bed.

I know there was an occasion when I shared a bed – was it this bed? With my husband? With a sister? Surely my duty now is to try and maintain a degree of peaceful composure which should be present just in case. Anyone who has tried sharing a bed with someone screaming, sobbing or squirming knows that that wouldn't be a comfortable experience.

So here I lie, gritting my teeth in a stricken smile, gulping the gravy tasting soup and herbal teas when they arrive and being a model patient. Trying to make these other people's lives pleasant and trouble free- that's been the glue of my life which has stuck to **me**!

There have been men who have fluttered in and out of my life, they might testify to that, but only if they'd been sprinkled with 'tell the truth' fairy dust!

Time for cards on the table. This trait of devotion to others hasn't helped me achieve what my mother had in mind I feel sure. I thought she wanted me to be kind to everyone and everything, but something often got in the way, and the something was usually me. I did try to do it for her, as a memorial to her. I reckoned that being a model carer would solidify my relationship with her, and engrave my name with hers on a marble slab for all to see. She cared constantly. I think she saw the 'caring' principle as a reasonable way of achieving lifelong happiness, and isn't that what parents want for their off spring? My mother certainly did, or I supposed so at the fragile age of thirteen when her influence was at its height. I needed to live, but then, I wanted to be buried with her.

Being at home as a young woman was like a form of burial. Pa's grief was short lived, and so was his liaison with his new wife. Their marriage was hasty, and his regrets prolonged I think. She had what she wanted, apparently. She possessed a comfortable home, a husband who was incapable *of making real demands upon her, and the freedom to enjoy herself at her husband's expense. I don't think she deliberately hurt pa. It was like she'd caught this big fish, and then forgot to take the hook out. Pa was fastened to her line, and no amount of writhing and contorting on his part gave him any comfort or relief. He had been ensnared, lassoed, trapped…the greater his struggle, the harder he was held and finally, he weakly surrendered. I dreamt of his silent presence, he never spoke when she was present. When she was out, which was often, he constantly reminded us of our duties, was moody and bad tempered, and I think he may have hit all of us children as punishment for every crime, but I can't remember.*

I think now that he felt crushed by her indifference, and tried to rescue his pride by playing the overbearing master of the house. I was not around then I think. At some point I had tried to separate myself from his person, but I failed to break free from the cords he had tightened around me and I grew to fear him.

I never pitied him. Maybe I should have done.

My brothers and sisters may have felt the same way, but we didn't discuss pa. Us girls though, our hopes and dreams of finding a decent man to love and be loved by did fade for a time. Pa's violence and my dependence on him, made it impossible to confidently and accurately assess the goodness of any man. Consequently, I was always in the dark!

My dream was to escape and find freedom. I made plans. I schemed. I remained silent. I learnt patience and waited for the moment to arrive.

But now, I am still trapped in this bed; the stranger comes again and gives me spoonfuls of a bitter liquid; but then, suddenly, I am freed; I remember, I remember flying along being held up high and then, yes, another bed where I am constantly warmed and find gentle repose.

Agnes watched the little train leave the station. Her beloved sister Ellen had climbed aboard, and had sat surrounded by the summer's strawberry crop, piled high and ready to be transported to Winchester and Southampton. It had been a good year, and some of the better fruit, it was rumoured, was even destined for London. Ellen had travelled on the strawberry train, where only one carriage was provided for passengers, whilst the rest was filled with the region's most celebrated commodity. The air smelt sweet and luscious. Agnes had been the only member of the family saying goodbye that day. For her, the parting was a wrench, but she knew better than to believe that it was wrong. Things had happened during the six months since the arrival of Mary which had convinced her that she would follow the pattern set by her sister, and so she had watched and learned as her sister prepared and departed. Now she knew how she could follow.

Ellen had not taken much with her. She was to begin her new life beyond her early home, in a doctor's residence in Parchment Street, in almost the centre of Winchester, as an under house maid. She had not been undermined by the realisation that this was her destiny at this time, because she believed the Lord had a greater work for her to do. She put her trust in Him, prayed earnestly as her mother had taught her to do, and was able to acquiesce to humble beginnings.

At first Agnes had been shocked by Ellen's attitude, because she felt that by accepting something which she had sworn she never would, Ellen had not been true to herself nor to her, and had betrayed them both. Her path would have to be different, because she wanted more. Her lust for excitement and beauty had never dimmed. Her way would have to be a contrast to Ellen's. So she returned home, remembering Ellen's genuine smile and embrace as they said good bye.

"Will you write to me? Let me know wha' you 're doin'. Who you mee'. Don' forge' me, Ellen."

"Aggie!" Ellen had noticed Agnes' disappointment when she had told her of the plan. She had misunderstood, thinking that it was simply that Agnes wanted to come with her. "We can mee' in Winchester. There will be times when I can see you. I wan' to see you. I wan' to know how you are."

"Yes, yes, please, Ellen, and come home too, if you can."

"Alrigh', maybe.... perhaps I shall." Ellen had no intention of returning but could not reveal that to her much loved sister. "Please keep ou' of pa's way, Aggie. I know this must sound strange, bu' he's not the same as before ma died."

"No, I know that.... I know that pa is ..."

Ellen interrupted. "I shall miss you Aggie, stay close to the Lord, and He will direct your path."

"I will," and Agnes knew that Ellen's path had been forced upon her, in a way that the Lord would not approve of. She had heard pa shouting at Ellen several times. But the worst occasion was just recently. He had sounded like a man out of control. She had not heard Ellen's replies. She had heard a chair scraping along the floor, and an enormous crash as something or somebody had been thrown across the workroom below. She, listening intently to the terrible violence from her room, had heard someone crying and knew it was Ellen. Her father was cursing and screaming, the words were too horrible to think about. Ellen's voice sounded muffled and strange, as she struggled to speak. Ellen never spoke of what happened, but it became clear that the decision for her to leave home had been made at that time.

The following day, their father had made enquiries, and had found a position for Ellen, which in her eyes, would have to be an improvement on her present circumstances. She had n't said good bye to him. She had left wounded, and afraid. Her spirit, however, had been strengthened, but she feared for Hannah, Agnes and

Emily especially. Would their father try to control them in the same way as he'd tried to control her?

She was hopeful that she was embarking on a life without fear. Her father had terrified her, but she need not dwell on that. She had escaped, and put it down to prayers being answered by a loving God, who was mindful of her. Now she could wave good bye and take with her the knowledge, skills and talents she had acquired. However, most importantly, her faith and strength had remained firmly embedded in her soul. Not even her father could deprive her of that.

* * *

Agnes watched the train disappear out of view. She turned back, and wondered how long it would be before she too could depart the home she had once loved, but which now had become a frightening and lonely place.

She knew that Hannah held a special place in their father's affections, and seemed content in her roles of housekeeper and mother to Frederick.

She had returned to Botley earlier in the spring and had quietly resumed her position in the household, attending to everyone's needs, including Mary's. Baby Frederick was a quiet baby, and Hannah watched him constantly, presenting the appearance of a loving mother. She was fully occupied, and ran the home with an efficiency which Thomas approved of. His first grandchild he largely ignored and he said little to Hannah excepting an occasional comment about the meals she prepared. Agnes was kept busy too, occupying the smaller children and attending school with them. At home, she was not noticed amongst the others, but was content to watch and wait for her moment. The only thing which disturbed their peaceful existence was the effect that Mary had upon them all. Their father remained entirely silent when she was present, Hannah would occupy herself with the baby, Agnes watched from a distance and kept the little ones quiet, and Mary, happy to hold centre stage, acted out various parts which depended on her mood. Most often, the part was a deeply wronged young woman who had been deprived of everything which would have contributed to her happiness. This was usually acted out at a time when she was wanting something, some money perhaps for new clothes or a visit to Southampton, and quite swiftly resulted in Thomas putting his hand into his pocket, and parting with a few shillings. At other times, Mary would talk incessantly about her own family, her friends and other acquaintances, in a very animated way, making Agnes feel that they were all very insipid in comparison. Mary seemed to enjoy pointing out her good connections, and reminding everyone of their poor relations and circumstances. Poor Hannah was not overlooked. Thomas took to remaining in his work room after supper, avoiding the lengthy diatribe which always seemed to accompany that time. Mary gloried in other people's misfortunes and was not afraid to use them to amuse and entertain herself.

One evening, Agnes found herself alone with Mary.

"Did you hear, there is talk about Hannah. Some are saying that the child's father is old Sir Russell. What do you say to that? I must say that I had wondered. It seemed a bit likely, especially as we now know that Alfred is probably his base born son. Sir Russell has an eye for a young woman it seems. Alfred's mother only let on, I've heard, because she's in a bit of difficulty. You know her, she was at the Grange a few years back. She lives down in Bishop's Waltham now, poor woman. I wondered who would have her, but some poor man has taken up with her, and wed her.

60

He's none too well at present, so I've heard. Some kind of accident. She was seen up at the Grange; expect she was looking for some help from her son. He's got some means I hear. Alfred is such a handsome young man. Sir Russell has been very generous to him. Of course James will inherit the estate, but Alfred will always be taken care of. I am utterly disgusted with Mr Lambourn's avowed disconnection from the Turners. It sickens me. I see no point in harbouring grudges. We must do all we can to develop good connections." At last there was a pause, but because Agnes kept her mouth tightly shut throughout, she was not ready to stem Mary's flow.

"Yes, I want to associate with the family. I hear that there will be a party in January to celebrate Mr Turner's sixtieth birthday, and I shall be wanting to attend. No doubt my dear husband will refuse to go. I will have to turn to my loving father, who would be delighted to escort me. Yes, yes, what an evening it will be. I will need a new evening dress. The finest families will be there. Sir Russell's sister's family, the Lawrences will come from Romsey, the Russells from Botley Park, and goodness knows who else. It will be something not to be missed, I can tell you. I would be wretched if for any reason I was prevented from going." Mary seemed satisfied with her expression of profound disappointment if she was to be frustrated in her efforts to enter a higher society, and turned to a different subject.

"It's Hannah, though, who deserves our pity. It's a punishment to have to go on as she does without any kind of support for herself. It's true that her pa is good to put up with a situation which so badly damages the reputation of this family. I am not so unfeeling as to want to see her in the Workhouse, but I cannot see any advantage to going on as we are. I've told Mr. Lambourn that a marriage must be arranged for Hannah. Agnes, you know of someone who is interested in her, don't you?"

Agnes was caught out, for she had been trying to ignore Mary's censure of Hannah. She looked at Mary blankly, but Mary did not notice. She was following her own thoughts still.

"Yes, I know a man who might suit. Nothing much to recommend him excepting he is thirty and single. William Judd. Someone told me he was a gardener at the Grange. I'll invite him to come for lunch one Sunday when he is free to do so after Church." Agnes had no idea who this gardener was, but hoped it was all empty talk, and no harm would be done.

Mary's schemes and plotting were based on comprehensive information which she obtained from various sources. She had, as they say, her ear to the ground and listened for the slightest tremor and any hint of scandalous rumblings in the village. Agnes was well aware of Mary's liking for exchanging reports, tittle-tattle and rumour. She tried hard to divert Mary's thinking.

"It's always pleasan' to make new friends," Agnes ventured timidly, "an' I'm sure pa would no' object to inviting this young man to dinner on Sunday. Maybe we should talk to 'annah abou' it firs' though, see 'ow she feels abou' it."

"Nonsense! What's it got to do with you or your father for that matter and Hannah will agree to whatever *I* suggest. You're just a child, what do you know about anything? You must run over to the Grange tomorrow, and see Mr Judd and give him an invitation. Tell him he can come here any Sunday if he hasn't another engagemen' to meet us all." Agnes looked forlornly at her step mother. What was the use of attempting to divert Mary's mind when it was made up? She did not attempt to speak. "Good, that's decided" Mary concluded the conversation her way, and was satisfied that she had a good plan in place which would be appreciated by Hannah.

* * *

Agnes did visit the Grange and met the said gardener, one William Judd, in order to placate Mary, and put her scheme into action. Hannah had been informed of the plan, and felt shame at the prospect of seeing someone from the Grange, but did not think of opposing it. It was true that William had noticed and liked Hannah, but there were few opportunities for them to become properly acquainted. He lived for his plants and outdoor life so it would seem, and she was tied to her household duties. The time they shared was over the meals of breakfast and tea. He rarely came in to the house for lunch, as it was brought to him where ever he was working, a slice of pork pie or some bread and a chunk of cheese, washed down with a jug of cider or beer. So his contact with Hannah had been limited by those times when he was always a little absorbed by the proper meal that had been placed before him, and his full attention was never really given to her. Certain of his appetites were paramount; William lived for food and fresh air.

Even so he did miss her when she was no longer there. He had been surprised when she had been suddenly dismissed, for he'd seen nothing amiss. She'd always been busy, cheerful and naturally accommodating, and he'd been unaware of the underlying reason for her dismissal. There had been no opportunity to say goodbye, and his life had continued without a pause. He'd hardly thought of her. Just occasionally, something reminded him of her tentative smile, or he remembered her strong, busy hands when they sometimes became very quiet, clasped on her lap or folded on the table and it was then that he missed her. She had a pleasing countenance, and an agreeable manner about her. So he was gratified when he received an invitation to Sunday tea at the Lambourn home and wondered that perhaps Hannah had missed him too.

"You will come, Mr. Judd, I hope, we always have a good tea on Sunday, scones and jam and cake and biscuits, if you just say the word when you will be able to come." Agnes enthusiastically pleaded with him. She liked the look of this man. He was large and somehow very solid, but possessed an air of gentleness at the same time which she found very encouraging. William was trying to overcome his astonishment and hesitating he replied, "Why, yes, I 'ope to do so, though, I am surprised at the invitation. It is over a year since 'annah left the Grange, and I wonder why after such a time, she should suddenly want to see me again."

"'annah 'as been busy at home you see and …you must know that 'annah has a little boy, Mr. Judd. She 'as lived quietly at home. I think she would be very happy to see you now, and 'opes you feel the same. You will come this Sunday won't you?" Agnes was beginning to feel a bit desperate, and had no idea what to say to this puzzled man. To explain Mary's scheme was impossible.

"Of course, of course," William nodded and tried to smile, "Mmm, yes, I see … yes, of course."

Agnes quickly left, hoping that William would conquer his natural incredulity and come to see Hannah again. William was indeed bewildered, and overcome by the knowledge that Hannah had had a child. The family had kept that very quiet, and he had heard nothing about it. He lived away from the village with his mother at Curdbridge. He was not sure how the news affected his feelings for Hannah. He hesitated and decided that he would definitely not go to the Lambourns. It all felt too uncomfortable, too embarrassing for him. He could not help feeling uneasy. He hardly knew her after all.

* * *

Hannah was not so much puzzled as angered by Mary's interference in her life. But she knew better than to allow her feelings to become evident. Mary's position at home was above her own. And she depended on Mary's good will in order to live a relatively comfortable existence. She knew that she could do nothing to change Mary's plan, and so she silently prepared the tea for her guest. She had liked William. He had always spoken to her in a way which made her feel he had singled her out. She noticed how he would look at her and observe her as she moved about doing her duties. He was interested in her, and she reciprocated by blushing occasionally when he held the door for her, or she would smile at him when he gave her the smallest wink across the breakfast table. She did not mind seeing him again, but not like this.

Hannah waited in the parlour for William. He did not come. Mary was elevated by Hannah's disappointment. Despite the failure of her plan, Mary somehow rejoiced in Hannah's humiliation, and triumphed in her step daughter's rejection. William had stayed away because it was an easier option. Although his life was devoid of female companionship and involvement, he had become accustomed to his easy way of life, and was content with it and the bachelordom which accompanied it. It was true that the complications which had occurred in Hannah's life had removed any longing on his part to renew their acquaintance. Nothing changed in William's life, but Hannah's was never to be the same again.

Hannah was not alone in finding her life had changed so disquietingly; so much so that she would look at her clothes some mornings, and was unable to see herself dressed in them. She had forsaken herself as a result of her disappointment, and this she had done to manage her feelings of degradation and abandonment. She was struggling, but managed to cling on, as many women have before her, because she had a child, and Frederick needed his mother. Her parenting of him allowed her to stand tall, and she could still hold her head high, knowing that this was something that could not be removed, that she would always be a mother.

But Agnes was plagued by her youth, and missed her older sister Ellen with a longing which remained with her almost constantly.

"Wha' would Ellen do?" was Agnes's response when she was confronted by a new challenge. Her dependence on Ellen's guidance became very apparent. Agnes had recently been summoned to the vicarage, and she had wondered what was expected of her. Hannah and Frederick had gone with her, as she had pleaded with her older sister to accompany her and Hannah had agreed as she went out very little, and balked at going out on her own, as she felt the critical stares of neighbours knowing them to be unfriendly and she could not face them alone. She happily accompanied Agnes, especially as the Reverend was one of the few who acknowledged her without any degree of self-consciousness, which always helped her to feel less censored.

They arrived at the appointed hour and were ushered in by the Housekeeper Mrs. Freeman who paused for a moment as she took in the presence of Hannah and Frederick. Frederick was generally a quiet baby who seemed to have become tranquil in the knowledge that his mother was not far away, which was always true. Despite Frederick remaining inconspicuous, Mrs. Freeman was unable to share her master's view of baseborn children and their mothers and remained silent and unwelcoming, seeing the child as an ill omen and wishing it and its mother elsewhere.

Parson Russell appeared, unconscious of his guests' initial chilly reception, and he smiled warmly at them, and shook Agnes and Hannah's hands. Mr Russell was considered a lively and popular sort of clergyman. He laughed a lot, and enjoyed playing little games with the children. He also enjoyed a glass of claret, and would look forward to a quiet evening at home when he could sip his favourite drink and mull over the events of the day. His ruddy nose and twinkling eyes combined with his full head of curly thick dark hair made him appear very impish and rather mischievous, and endeared him to many, particularly children. He had an interesting commission to fulfil, and wondered what the outcome would be, and was grateful that Hannah had come as the circumstances could well involve her also.

"Agnes, my dear, and Hannah, how good to see you both ... so pleased that you were able to come ... now, don't look so worried – I know it is rare that I get the chance to speak to you ... Sundays are always so crowded, and it feels like I never get a chance to talk to you young people. How are you both? ... You both look very, very well. And here is little Freddie." The parson placed a finger on Frederick's nose and watched for the baby's reaction. Freddie closed one of his eyes momentarily, and everyone laughed. He continued, "I see that your father is happy once more, what a blessing it must be to him and to you to have Mary's support." Agnes was about to make some sort of comment, but she noticed Hannah's quick reaction which was to look keenly across at her, and so she allowed the pause to remain unfilled and allowed Mr. Russell to continue.

"So, my dears, I have an idea for Christmas this year which I hoped would involve you both and your family. You see, I want to involve the children of the village in our Christmas services more than before. I have been impressed by Christmas Plays that have been put on by children in the past, but want something a bit special this year." He paused for a moment, and realised that the young women had not responded in any way to him. He wondered about this, and suspected that it was because they were in his home and were perhaps a bit overcome.

"Please take a seat both of you ... how is the little man, Hannah? He's well? ... yes, of course" Hannah awkwardly sat on the edge of a very firm armchair, while Agnes looked around for something near her sister, and finding nothing, crossed the room to sit on a cushioned divan. She felt strange and oddly privileged to be where she was.

"So you see about this play... a Nativity Play which the school will put together and do in the Church, but I want to include more music this time. As you will see, I hope to include the choir in all of this, and will need children and young people to sing." Mr. Russell steadily looked across at Agnes, and continued, " In fact, it has been noticed how much you enjoy singing Agnes, and that you have a very sweet voice, and so it was my feeling that you should play the part of Mary in our play and sing some of the beautiful Christmas carols." As Mr. Russell surveyed Agnes, she still did not respond. She was bemused as she had thought that he was going to offer her a position in service at the Vicarage. Now that she was twelve years old and no longer needed so much at home to look after the little ones since Mary had come into their home, she had been prepared to leave home and go into service.

"I … I do love to sing, it's true," and that was all she could think of in reply.

Smiling Mr. Russell nodded, and approved of her reply, suspecting that Agnes would, given a bit more encouragement, agree to be the central part.

"Yes, Miss Sait has informed me that you are happy to lead the younger children in their rhyming songs, and you do it beautifully."

He then witnessed how assured she became as he described her ability; she had visibly straightened in her seat, and smiled confidently across at him.

"That's settled then, but you will need to practice with Mr. Smith … he will let you know when you have to make time to meet with him." Agnes thought of kindly Mr Smith. He was so much kinder than the previous choir master who had been clearly disappointed with the efforts of the choir in the Church of All Saints. Her brother Tom had often remarked on it. No, Mr Herbert Smith was kind and gave sweets to the choir boys. She was not in the least apprehensive, and she hoped that she would learn something which would be useful to her. She had remembered the example set by Ellen and her lust for learning, and was excited at the prospect of being in the presence of someone who knew about music and wanted to teach her.

Mr. Russell turned to Hannah, and delicately spoke to her.

"You know my dear … we will be needing a babe to represent the Christ child … um … and I was thinking that if you did not object, your little Frederick might be quite happy lying in a manger … what do you think my dear?"

Hannah had been deep in her own thoughts. Why was it that everyone in her family seemed to have all the opportunities except her? Ellen was working for a doctor and his family, Mary was now responsible for their home and Tom had achieved a good position in Southampton. Now, Agnes had her opportunity to shine. And then she heard what the Reverend was saying and suddenly felt a fragment of joy, just a glimmer of gladness which was born out of her love for her child. Her child was a child of God just like any other, was he not? And Mr. Russell had confirmed that truth.

" Oh yes, tha' would be such a lovely thing … li"le Freddy all curled up and everyone looking a' 'im!" Frederick did not stir in his mother's arms, but her heart was leaping and pounding. Maybe now she and her child had a small chance of being accepted, as the village would see how Mr Russell had no qualms in putting Hannah's Frederick in the centre of an important event. Since William's rejection she had become unwilling to think for a moment that she would one day be accepted by anyone. Now she felt that if Freddie could be treated kindly, this would prove to be a form of acceptance which would be healing to her soul. Mr. Russell had indeed provided Hannah with the balm of Gilead, and she would remember his kindness and willingness to ignore the prevailing attitude to her and to Freddie.

Agnes had felt a moment of relief that she had something to look forward to and provide her with an opportunity to do something special and exciting. She had felt unhappy since Ellen's leaving, and had been low in spirit. The lightness of her heart which characterised her relationship with Ellen had been removed with her departure. As young as she was, she began to feel burdened by a sad depression bearing down on her heart. Motherless and without Ellen she had found it hard to enjoy her life, especially since Mary had become mistress of their home. She had noticed her father become more quiet, brooding and distant.

Once she had felt that her father had generally approved of her, but this feeling had evaporated as she had unconsciously supported Ellen, and her father had sensed this and resented it, seeing it as a form of betrayal. Thomas spoke little to any of his children, but Agnes had felt his coldness which she did not fully understand. She had begun to learn to fend for herself.

Agnes was preoccupied with her thoughts. "If it wasn' for Henry and the li"le ones, I don' know 'ow I would feel … they keep the sun shining." She smiled to herself as she considered Henry's unusual ways.

Parson Russell was entirely oblivious of the comparative miseries of the two Lambourn young women especially as both appeared to be most happy at the present time. Both were handsome in their way, as were all the Lambourn children excepting poor Henry of course; in his view Agnes and Hannah exuded a freshness, vitality and natural bloom which they had undoubtedly inherited from their mother. Their mother was admired by many. Mr Russell knew also of her faithfulness and virtue, and was aware that many villagers had mourned at her passing. She had, however, left a legacy in her children. It was a pity about Ellen, he thought, as he had come to hear that she had argued with her father, and that was why she had been sent away. Ellen of all the children had been quite remarkable, and particularly close to her mother, he had noticed, and he had wondered why Thomas was unable to manage a good relationship with her. Not being a father himself, he felt at a disadvantage. However, he wanted to care for all the children of the parish, and hoped that the Nativity Play this year would provide the children and young people with a wonderful occasion which they would remember for a long time.

As there was little more to be said, he gently invited Hannah and Agnes to follow him out into the hall. The vicarage had a lofty hallway, with large dark pictures and a sturdy oak staircase. Agnes and Hannah paused there to thank Mr Russell and shake his hand. It felt strange to them, as they had only ever shaken his hand after church services. His eyes glinted as he looked at each of them. They responded with a cheerful farewell.

"Thank you so much … for the invitations … um … we will look forward to playing our part …" Hannah blushed holding Frederick's sleepy face up to Mr Russell.

"Very good, very good my dears, I can see that some excellent decisions have been made today!" He laughed and tickled Frederick gently, so that everyone was merrily laughing as they took their leave.

Two

'Where the bee sucks there suck I,
In a cowslip bell I lie.'

Ellen had arrived in Parchment Street a little after four, and had anxiously waited at the lower door for a response to her knock. Dr Gibson's house was part of a terrace of town houses, decorated in stucco, grand in its proportions and, in the case of Dr Gibson's home, meticulous as to its care. Ellen noticed the brass door step and fixtures gleamed with a brightness which would have taken a considerable amount of time and effort to accomplish.

The street linked the thoroughfare of North Walls to a lesser way St George's Street, which ran parallel to the main High Street of the City. The part of Winchester where Ellen now stood was affluent and peopled by doctors, solicitors and successful middle class business owners. Parchment Street displayed all the attributes of wealth which had been acquired by this growing section of society. North Walls close by was busy with trades people's wagons and carts, with carriages and pedestrians. Ellen had had some difficulty making her way through the traffic and marvelled at the bustle and the speed of some of the vehicles. The way was dusty and the air felt unclean and cloying. She had been relieved to enter the quietness of the residential Parchment Street, there quickly finding her destination.

The arrangement made between her father, Dr Gibson and Dr Stocks was unknown to her, although the consequences of it were now happening. Here she stood, alone, in an unknown place, with only a small portmanteau as evidence of her previous life. She still felt bruised by her father's anger and physical blows, and she was very conscious of her injured face which still showed signs of disfigurement from his latest assault marking her from her left eyebrow to her jaw.

Her father had swung his fist with full force knocking her to the ground and she had only just missed the edge of the window sill as she fell. She supposed that once she was down, her father felt he had conquered and overpowered her and his anger became completely unrestrained. He removed his belt and beat it viciously across her back striking her violently; then he had left the room, shouting that she *would* learn to show him more respect; he would make sure that she did.

Her face had been hit with so much of his strength that she was still horribly marked and her face still very tender to the touch. Her back and neck ached painfully and felt badly bruised and aching; that morning she had had difficulty getting dressed. She had dared not look at herself and her injuries.

Her heart and spirit, strengthened by years of nurturing by her mother, had resisted but she had been torn apart by the cruelty of her father and felt broken like an injured rabbit gripped in a cruel snare.

The sound of someone unlatching the door brought Ellen back to her present situation, and she looked up hoping that her face was not so conspicuously damaged that it would be immediately noticed. She brought her hair forward over her cheek to try and conceal it. A quiet voice spoke to her.

"You must be Ellen Lambourn ... yes, oh ... you must have had a tiring journey ... come in, come in won' you? Is it you 'ave just one bag? Let me 'elp." Ellen looked into the eyes of the young woman not much older than herself who was reaching towards her trembling hand. Her eyes seemed both kind and apprehensive; Ellen supposed that she must have caught sight of her damaged face.

"Yes, thank you, the walk from the station was down 'ill fortunately, so I managed." Ellen hesitated as she stepped in to the house. She entered a dark, narrow corridor, with very little room to move. She noticed that the girl was wearing a stained pinafore over a dark blue cotton dress which she supposed was her maid's uniform. It was crumpled and very loose over the girl's slight body.

She had a long narrow face which accentuated the hollows in her cheeks and to Ellen her skin seemed to be unhealthily sallow like old parchment. Her eyes, though, were dark and bright and looked gently upon her.

"I am Ada Strong, I've been told to show you to your room ... we share a room ... please ... come this way Ellen, it's this way." Ada again smiled kindly at her, and Ellen, feeling slightly better, was convinced that the girl was someone who was good and considerate in her ways. As the days followed, she discovered that she had not been incorrect in her first assessment of Ada.

She led the way through the unlit corridor to the back of the house, along the narrow sunless hall; they passed a slightly open door on the left which Ellen supposed might be the kitchen, as she could hear the clatter of cutlery and could smell the delicious smell of baking. Ada hurried past until they reached a staircase.

It was narrow like the corridor, and dark enough to ensure that the climb had to be done with extra care. After two flights Ada slowed her pace, and Ellen began to be concerned as she could hear that Ada was struggling for her breath. She was relieved to discover that only a small flight remained leading to what she realised must be the attic of the house. There appeared to be several doors, but Ada stopped at the first and opened it, and then beckoned to her to follow her in to the room.

Despite it being summer and only early evening, the bedroom was dark, dank and cold. Ellen observed the lack of windows and the musty smell of damp walls and unaired beds with a sinking heart.

"This is your bed, I managed to ge' some clean sheets from the 'ousekeeper for you. I hope you donna mind 'avin' to share with me … I 'ope you can put up with me … Jess, the under maid before you was na 'appy … mind, I should tell you that she was less than careful abou' keeping 'erself clean. I think that she was dismissled because of i' … Dr Gibson says 'is staff must be presen'able and clean you see … 'e 'as 'igh expectings though." At this point Ada looked disapprovingly down the front of her soiled pinafore and continued, "Don' look at me. I've been cleaning the scull'hery, and it needed a good scrubbin' and now I do too … please don't be displeased." Ada smiled cheerily and removed the offending article placing it at the foot of her bed. She looked sheepishly at Ellen.

Ada was always afraid of being found to be wanting in some way. She tried with all her heart to fulfil her master's and the housekeeper's demands and felt shame when she perceived that she had in some way fallen short. She pleaded for Ellen's forbearance as surprisingly, she had already decided that she was in some way superior to her. She looked for reassurance that she had been excused her dirty appearance, and Ellen was slow to reply. She had not in her limited acquaintance come across anyone

76

as self-effacing as Ada but she recognised that she needed to say something which would hearten her.

"Oh don' be worryin' abou' me … I've been brough' up in a family which is large and good at creating messes … it's not possible to work 'ard around the house without gettin' a bit … soiled by it all!" Ellen tried to laugh, bu' Ada's doubts were infectious, and she could only smile wanly.

She had heard about Ada's recent efforts in the scullery with a heart that had sunk even further. Everything about this situation resonated with her as being unpleasant, but she would not allow herself to judge everything as hopeless so soon after her arrival. However, she could not help it, she *was* feeling fearful.

She had noticed Ada's tired, drawn expression, the pallor of her complexion, her poor marked and roughened red hands and the general lack of personal care which characterised her appearance; she had concluded that this was clear evidence of a life of drudgery. She had seen some poor folk in the village and recognised the signs. Ada's overall appearance was distressingly pitiful. Her lank hair was coiled around her head in a kind of plait and seemed held on by a layer of grease. Her nails were blackened and chipped as if she had placed them in coal and soot and had laid the household fires using only her fingers. Her feet were shod in canvas slippers made from what appeared to be some form of Hessian; there were several large holes in the fabric revealing her toes which evidenced their constant wear; beneath her skirt her stockings were wrinkled about her ankles and were an indescribable greyish colour. Her mouth seemed frozen in a pinched position, her narrow shoulders were drawn into a posture where they seemed to disappear, her back was swollen into a hump, and her long, fleshless arms dangled limply at her sides.

Ellen felt such pity for her, and wondered how long she had been in this wretched state.

Her sister Hannah had warned her that some lives in service were blighted, and Ellen could not help wondering if this was what she had been referring to; she had not been prepared to witness the effects of hard labour on a servant but considered that now she had come across it. She was roused to wanting to help Ada in some way, but knew from Hannah that a servant's situation so much depended on the attitude of the master and mistress of the house, and on the other staff that held positions of authority. Hannah had heard appalling stories of hardship and misery from some who had come to the Grange.

As Ellen became more accustomed to the dimness of the room, she noticed even more Ada's shadowed eyes and sickly pallor.

"Are you feeling well … you look … sick … why don' you si' for a minu'? … shall I ge' you somethin' … a glass of water?" Ellen showed Ada her concern immediately. She had gained a heightened awareness of sickness and its effects, as the nursing of her mother had brought these things very much into her consciousness. It is true that she had possessed a compassionate spirit before, but recently it had become the core of her existence.

"Just a touch of womittin' and faintin' … it will pass soon enough … I can't eat much a' presen' bu' I'll be righ' soon enough." Ada's eyes closed for a moment and she sank on to her bed, but remembering herself and wanting to conceal all sign of her sickness she tried to quickly stand but only succeeded in falling against Ellen and grabbing hold of her.

"Oh, I'm a bi' woopy I'm afraid, I'll be righ' by and by." Ellen wondered what was meant but Ada continued.

"My pa always used to say that it is be"er to 'old on to someone or somethin' than to be found callopsing … cos we should all 'elp another by 'olding 'em and stoppin' 'em from fallin'. Pa was always thankful to them that 'elped 'im in the street when he was a bit unsteady like … thank you for 'oldin' me." She straightened herself as best she could. Ellen wanted to ask her about her illness, but at that moment without warning the door swung open, and a young man stood on the threshold, eying them both, but giving particular attention to Ellen.

"Hello, hello … Ada, Ada, and who migh' this be?"

"You know 'oo was coming today John. Ellen, this is John Simpkins, Dr Gibson's man servant." Ellen looked up at John and was immediately overcome by his height and haughty air. She had never met anyone who dwarfed everyone around him as John did. He held himself very erect, the top of his head almost touching the attic ceiling and he looked down on her imperiously with narrowed eyes; she couldn't help but feel intimidated and was unable to say a word. Ada amazed her by being surprisingly assertive.

"Is there a reason for your burstin' in 'ere like this? You're wantin' somethin' I suppose?"

"As a matter of fact I do … Mrs. Golding wants you down stairs now, both of you, and quick about it!" Simpkins raised his voice as he gave the message, and Ada responded by scuttling out the room, towing Ellen behind her. Hurtling down the stairs at a break neck speed was not Ellen's choice, but they managed to arrive unharmed at the foot of the stairs and Ada flung open the nearest door and almost ran into the room.

As Ellen had at first supposed, the room was the kitchen, comfortably warm with a black range situated on the opposite wall and with banks of shelves holding numerous copper pans, dishes, crockery, tins and moulds on either side. A broad, rough-hewn oak table stood in the centre holding what appeared to be the beginnings of the preparations for dinner. There were piles of potatoes, carrots and cabbage, surrounding what appeared to be a large joint of salt beef, sitting in a large dish. Ellen had never seen such a generous portion of beef before on anyone's table, and her initial impression of the house as being affluent and well-kept seemed to be confirmed. At the far end of the table there appeared to be some kind of cake or pudding making going on in a large ceramic bowl; it was filled with a smooth pale yellow batter like mixture. Flour and broken eggs were scattered on the table and the floor. In fact, the quarry tiled floor was as messy as any floor could be. Ellen spotted a variety of ingredients, utensils and other items deposited at various locations, and she guessed rightly that they had been summoned to clear up and clean everything away.

Mrs Golding was the Housekeeper and Cook, and mistress of below stairs; she was used to getting this kind of assistance which Ellen saw as both unnecessary and demeaning. In her experience at home her mother and Hannah would always clean up after themselves when they cooked, and, she reflected, they were nowhere near as slovenly as Mrs Golding appeared to be. She was spooning the last of the loose mixture into a metal pan, and looked sideways at Ellen.

"I hope you're a sight be"er than the last under maid, because if you aint you'll not last … get to work with Ada, this kitchen has to be as clean as a new pin … Sweep up and mop …Ada will show you how the vegetables have to be done, but first you will serve afternoon tea in the drawing room; Ada will show you what needs doing." It was clear that she expected Ada to train, supervise and organise Ellen, and at the same time perform all her own duties.

The housekeeper was as proportionately stout and robust as Ada was withered and frail. She wore wire framed spectacles at the end of her thick nose which gave her a rather surprised and slightly quizzical look. Her face was large and seemed to descend in folds of flesh falling under her chin and around her jaw, depriving her of a neck and reminding Ellen of a bulldog. Ellen hoped that she would prove to be more amiable than her looks. Her critical eye had fallen on Ellen, and while she continued to slop the contents of the bowl into the pan she demanded, "Ada, the tea must be poured, it's 'alf past four, be sharp, Mrs Gibson will be calling for it ... tidy yourself girl, or you'll be looking for a new position ... 'elp me put the cake in the oven ... 'ere, there's some biscuits to go with the tea, set the tray, warm the pot, fetch the sugar bowl, there's the milk jug ... get a plate, the strainer."

Ada followed the orders given as best she could; she needed help as she shuffled and bustled to each command, putting on a fresh apron, washing her hands, placing the cake tins in the oven, rushing to the larder to fetch the milk, immediately grabbing a white laced cloth from a clothes horse and putting it on the tray with a cup and saucer on the table. All the time she repeatedly looked across at the cook, watching to see if there was any further instructions or words to her which she would need to act upon straight away. Ellen, wanting to assist, looked for the teapot but failed to discover its whereabouts. Ada rushed past her and disappeared through a door in the corner of the room. She reappeared with a blue teapot in her hand.

All this was done so quickly that Ellen was filled with admiration. Ada's movements were so precise and practised that she was able to accomplish the orders in less than no time. Ada made the tea without a pause, placed the pot, milk, sugar, plate of biscuits and strainer on the white cloth, and lifted the tray.

Ellen watched her as she proceeded to the door, but she turned and beckoned for her to follow. She found herself swiftly ascending another flight of stairs, much broader than those at the rear of the house, and discovered they led to a wide hallway, and there they continued on, stopping at a large chestnut door at the back which Ada gently knocked.

A reply from within could be heard, and Ellen opened the door for Ada noticing the fine, embossed brass door knob and brass door plate. As Ada entered bearing the tray, Ellen hesitantly followed, and looked about her. The room was decorated in a rich green, with patterns everywhere. The drapes, wallpaper and rugs were all elaborate, as was the furniture. The ceiling was ornately moulded with plaster at the centre and around the edges. An impressive gasolier immediately caught her attention although it was not yet lit. Ellen noticed several small portraits above and around the fireplace. There were two large comfortable divans in the room with wide arm rests and deep cushions as well as a velvet chaise longue.

A dark middle aged woman in a fashionable well-fitting afternoon dress with a full bussell and made from a beautiful, fine wool, sat back amongst the cushions before a blazing fire alone in the room. She wore a lace cap and her hair was arranged simply with just a few curls showing. A book lay unopened on her lap.

The air in the room felt over warm and stuffy; waiting and feeling the heat, Ellen slipped behind Ada, and wondered why she was there.

"Ma'am, if you please, this is Lambourn, the new under maid …

ma'am." She placed the tea tray on a small side table, and moved back.

"Lambourn, I would speak with you for just a moment. Strong, you may go." Mrs Gibson did not look at either of them except at Ellen for the briefest of moments. Once Ada was gone, Mrs Gibson began.

"You will assist Strong and you will apply yourself to helping Mrs Golding as she demands. Your pay is a shilling a week, and your hours are the same as Ada's ... she has one Sunday afternoon off a month but you must see to it that you are not off on the same Sunday. You have been sent to us by Dr Stocks, who has told us that you are to be here for a trial period ... you will need to prove yourself to be willing and hard working." Mrs Gibson, aware of Ellen's eyes upon her, glanced at her once again. Her look spoke of her disinterest in the new under maid. "That is all."

Ada stood in the corner of the kitchen, firmly grasping a broom and began to vigorously sweep away the remains of the cooking debris. Ellen was to learn that cleaning up after Mrs. Golding was an essential and necessary part of life. There was much more to learn, but miserably she realised that she was not in all probability incorrect about the kind of life that Ada had lived and that she herself would be now enduring.

* * *

Her life *did* become a grind of long relentless days with only Ada providing her with a measure of consolation; the living conditions and food proved to be so poor and meagre that she wondered how she might be able to remain healthy, and how she could continue to live without ill effects to her body. It was clear that

Ada was not able to, and just two years in service at Dr Gibson's had proved to be very damaging to *her*.

The work was relentless, from five in the morning until nine at night. The day began with cleaning and setting all the fires in the house and serving early morning tea and breakfasts in the bedrooms, heating water and then taking it from the kitchen for washing, emptying chamber pots, preparing baths and airing and making beds; this was followed by various chores including washing, ironing, preparing and serving food, cleaning and waxing furniture and floors, cleaning silverware, stairs, shoes and anything else in the house, washing windows, floors, curtains, walls, beating carpets, polishing glassware, pictures and ornaments and more. These occupations took place in all respectable households, but Ellen was not used to the constant daily drudgery with no evidence of appreciation or much needed times of rest. Her work and Ada's was constant and unremitting, and went unnoticed and unrewarded.

Mrs Golding appeared from the first to be lazy and slovenly in Ellen's eyes, and so there was, in Ellen's attitude, a lack of respect for her authority which the Housekeeper noticed and gave her ample cause to dislike her. This resulted in Ellen losing any benevolent actions which might have come her way. Mrs Golding was not naturally generous in her approval of others in any case, and showed no kindness to Ada whatever, despite Ada doing everything to gain it. She saw to it that she herself was well cared for, as self-centred people will always do, and with the minimum of effort.

* * *

The Sunday morning service at the local church was the only regular occurrence in their lives which allowed them to venture out and have some respite. Ada had apparently nowhere to go when she had leave, as she had only ever spoken of her father in the past tense and had never mentioned any other family members or friends that she could visit. She knew nobody and, in Ellen's view, had been exploited by the Gibson family who should have shown her nothing but kindness. Ada had been alone in a very hostile, uncaring world, unnoticed by anyone; that is until Ellen arrived.

It wasn't long before she understood why the situation was so bleak. Dr Gibson was not interested in his staff, and was rarely at home. His wife showed a constant preoccupation with money and expenditure, and was miserably stringent about the running of the house; but was generous with her own needs when it came to her meals and her clothes.

Above stairs, the family ate well, and so did Mrs. Golding and John below stairs. Ellen and Ada were provided with porridge or bread and dripping and a cup of tea in the morning and in the evening left overs and a cup of tea. The left overs might have been sufficient except that most of what remained was consumed by John and Mrs Golding. Ellen and Ada were given so little.

Ellen was seriously concerned about Ada and realised that her own health would deteriorate if nothing changed. Her hunger tormented her and her energy and her ability to think straight began to decrease. She decided to conceal items of food on her person such as would not be noticed, and these she shared with Ada in their room. She knew that in all probability her thieving would be detected at some point, for *thieving* would be what it would be called she was certain. Yes, she would be branded a thief, and dismissed; but she was not afraid and continued to smuggle out a piece of fruit or a slice of bread or a wedge of cheese and did it in a way that she hoped would not be detected.

By candle light one night, after enduring this life for a little less than a month, Ellen decided to write to Tom in Southampton. She could not return home, but perhaps he could provide a means of escape for herself and Ada. Ada's health seemed to be rapidly deteriorating, as she was often sick, and had become weaker as a result. Ellen was grateful for the writing set which Tom had given to her before he left. She was not sure what to tell him, but decided that the truth of her situation would suffice, and so she described the misery of her employment and Ada's ill health. She hoped that he would think of a solution, and would come to her aid. She believed that Tom would not rest until she was safely out of Dr Gibson's employ.

Her resolve to get away was interrupted when a strange summons came for her to go the drawing room after dinner one September evening. She had noticed Mrs. Golding's knowing look as John had informed her of Dr. Gibson's instruction. Ellen thought that they knew the cause; Ada tried to reassure her, and gave her a brief hug, holding her around her shoulders. Ada had shown Ellen such kindness during their time together. She was always watchful over Ellen, and helped her when she could despite being so unwell. She had even asked her about her bruising, but Ellen had not divulged the true cause.

She resolved to speak to Dr Gibson about Ada, even if it meant more trouble for her. She could not stand by any longer and watch Ada's health worsen any further. Dr Gibson's back was to her as she entered the drawing room. Ellen had had little opportunity to get to know him and his ways. When she had served him he had never acknowledged her, and had appeared to be totally unaware of her existence. Ellen examined him for a moment; he was barrel chested and stocky and possessed a head of thick wavy grey hair and eye catching bushy eyebrows. He looked at her from beneath them and advanced slowly towards her.

"Lambourn, yes, there are some things I need to discuss with you … I spoke to Dr Stocks yesterday and he assures me that you have to stay away from your home. He and your father arranged with me for you to come here … and there was no provision for you to ever return home." Dr Gibson paused and glancing very briefly at Ellen, he continued gruffly, "Mrs Gibson informs me that the economies of our home will not provide the means to keep two housemaids, and Strong's work has always been satisfactory. It is no longer convenient for you to stay here … we cannot offer you any further employment and so you will need to go elsewhere. You will have to go immediately, particularly as it has been made clear to me that you have on occasion been thoroughly unpleasant to others and there is, I am reliably informed an untrustworthy side to your character. Mrs. Golding has advised me that you have been consistently unreliable, and your work is generally less than satisfactory." The doctor watched as the unwanted under maid's face reddened, and he thought 'Well might she blush.'

"There is only one thing left for me to say … you must go now and put your things together Lambourn, and prepare to leave my house in the morning. My opinion and that of Dr Stocks is that you will have to go to the Winchester Workhouse in St Paul's Hill, as your family cannot provide for you. I have already informed the Warden of your imminent arrival … they are expecting you tomorrow as a new inmate." Dr Gibson looked at Ellen coldly, and shook his head uncompromisingly. "There is no

87

other alternative as I cannot recommend you for any service position."

Ellen, shaken by Dr Gibson's accusations and horrified by the prospects of not being ever allowed home and the Workhouse, still managed to gather some thoughts together, despite her being shocked and totally unprepared for what was happening.

"Sir, I am unable to reply to your false accusations. I would not wish to stay, and I am grateful for my release from your employ." Ellen glared at the doctor and continued without pausing, taking a deep breath. "Ada is very sick, and if you don't see to 'er, she will be unable to work, and then you will be judged for your neglect and lack of concern. Maybe you 'ave no care for some of the persons living under your roof, but I say to you, that you need to be concerned. Since I 'ave been here, Ada and I 'ave not been shown an ounce of respect or kindness. I *am* trustworthy and I've only lacked a desire to be pleasan' because I 'ave been treated with such disrespect." Ellen's eyes were filling with tears, and she brushed her sleeve across them. Her voice began to break as she continued, "So you see Dr Gibson, I am grateful to be rid of this house." Ellen's parting shot as she turned hurriedly rang out so that the whole house could hear, "And mind you take a look at Ada, that is if you have any decency in you!"

Dr Gibson's face had turned a glassy white, and he now knew that his worst suspicions were confirmed about Lambourn. He would be well rid of the disgraceful wretch. But before he could make a reply and place her in the ignoble and lowly position which was where she ought to be, she had gone.

*   *   *

Ellen surprised herself in her ability to speak in the way that she had to Dr Gibson. She knew that the injustice of what he had said had been the cause of her indignation. She had been shocked by his attitude to her. He did not know her at all, and yet he had felt that he could malign her and dismiss her. What gave him the right to behave in such a way? Where was his evidence? He had been unfeeling and callous. She felt a new emotion which had grown in her breast, a deep resentment bordering on hatred for her employer. She decided that she could not wait for the morning but would leave immediately, but there was one person she needed to see.

She sought out Ada before leaving, and managed to snatch a moment with her. She was adamant when she spoke to her.

"Don' you think for a minu'e tha' I am going and am forge"ing you ... somehow we'll be together, and you can depend on me ... Ada, Ada do you believe me?" Ellen had glimpsed a look of hopelessness in Ada's eyes, a forlornness which filled her with a similar feeling. She would not allow it to overcome her however. "Remember Ada, I won' forge' you, I will be free and so shall you."

"You going to the Workhouse? 'ow can you find freedom when you are in tha' place? You will be caged. There will be no way ou'." Ada expressed her sure knowledge that there was no possibility of escape from a place such as the Workhouse, but Ellen saw her situation differently and had other plans.

"I 'ave a kind brother who will 'elp me, and I will no' be goin' to the Work'ouse ... I will come for you as soon as I can ... 'old on Ada, until I can come for you."

After the girls had held each other for a long moment, both confused and trembling with feelings of foreboding, they parted, Ellen grasping her few possessions to her, as much needed replacements for Ada's embrace, and left without a backward look.

She knew that she had been 'caged' in the house just as she would have been in the Workhouse. Her spirit had rebelled, and would not be smothered in this way. She did not know what the future would be like, but she knew that Ada would need help; she was not in a position to help at this time, but, it might be possible soon. She had liked Ada for her goodness and humility. She had not complained. She was loyal to Ellen, and she had been a true friend. Her mother would have been kind to Ada, and would have tried to protect her, and so she was impelled to do the same.

Ellen walked to the Water Mill at the foot of the town and walked along the river, breathing in the air which was both warm and fresh. The river coursed swiftly under the bridge from the Mill, and snaked its way south to the sea. It had a way to flow, something like twelve miles, and this was the course Ellen had decided upon. She would walk to Southampton, and seek out her brother Tom who lived where the river and the sea met. Despite not having received a reply from him to her letter, she hoped that he would empathise with her and know what to do. The water would be her guide, and her solace.

Beside the river she knew there would be fertile ground, soil which brought forth rushes, watercress, willows and soft luscious grass. There would be life on the river, the coots and swans, the water rats and ducks and much more to enjoy as she left the dark world of the Gibsons and entered one full of colourful reflections and bountifully filled with light. The river was so beautiful to her; its world was full of vibrant colour which her eyes had once not fully seen nor appreciated but now she could feel her heart and mind rejoice at the sight of it. She marvelled at how completely happy she felt, despite being without parents, homeless, penniless and unemployed.

Being truly free, she decided, was not so much about a person's circumstances but it was more about possessing the capacity to be self-reliant and create opportunities to carve out one's own life.

With every step along the river she felt she was expressing her will and the feelings that come of empowerment which had gradually evaporated when her mother had died, but which now began to return. At her young age she gradually recognised the part the natural world, the existence of God given life played in lifting and ennobling a person. As she thoughtfully drifted along past the old St Cross Church and beyond towards the Downs, she looked about her at the darkening trees and misty waters of the river, and dusk began to draw in.

She continued on passing cattle quietly feeding in the water meadows. She watched the sun set. She walked with a purpose and was living in the moment. Her journey would remain significant in its own right. No matter what the outcome, she held fast to the feeling that if she followed the will of the Lord, she would ultimately find joy. The Lord would keep her and watch over her. Her mother had always instilled in Ellen a dependence on the Lord, and a desire to keep His commandments. And so it was with a feeling of confidence that Ellen embarked on her journey to find the one person who might be able to help her, and provide a continuation of this sense of freedom which filled her heart.

As the day further darkened, she looked for somewhere to sleep, first washing her face and hands in the river, and then drinking the cool water. It tasted so good and felt so wonderful on her tired skin that she splashed her face several times and then dried it with her petticoat. As she settled down sheltered by a willow tree she thanked God for the strength He had given her and the friendship of dear Ada. She prayed that Ada would be treated for her illness, and that her own family would be blessed, that her own father in particular, would be reconciled to her, and that he would be protected from harm. She prayed for her brother that he would know what to do once she had been guided to him. She asked to be blessed by the Lord, pleading that she might be given what she needed in her time of trial. Still with the prayer on her lips and lying exhausted, Ellen fell asleep.

* * *

Early the following morning, Tom, leaving for work, stood at the front door of his lodgings and looked incredulously at his sister who was standing on the steps, and who looked very different from the last time he had seen her. She was now decidedly gaunt, unkempt and frail looking. He felt confused by her sudden appearance and by the change in her.

"Ellen! What's happened to you ... Ellen?"

"It was tha' place Tom, I can" tell you 'ow bad it was ... did you ge' my le"er? I'm sorry to be a burden, bu' I was sent packing, and I could no' go to the Work'ouse." Ellen had waited for over an hour at the door to Tom's lodgings from the time she had found it, afraid to knock, but at the sight of Tom her words tumbled from her lips. Tom hesitated when he replied.

"No, no ... but I did get your letter." Tom had moved close to her and whispered beside her ear, not wanting any passing stranger to hear, "I thought that you'd be alright once you had settled there ... but I would not see you in a Workhouse ... but what can I do? ... Oh, I'm sorry Ellen, come in, come in won't you? How did you find me? … I am sorry it's such a shock seeing you … I can't believe it's you. Tell me everything, come in, we'll talk."

He tiptoed up a flight of stairs. Ellen quietly followed. Tom carefully opened the first door and revealed to Ellen a small room, clean and tidy with a bed in the corner, a single chair, a small round table and a small grate. Tom had a kettle situated in the hearth, and everything, thought Ellen looked most comfortable. Once Ellen had sunk into the chair, Tom managed to collect his thoughts.

"I don't have long … you see I was going to work … maybe we'll have to talk when I return this evening? Would you like some tea, something to eat? Yes?" Ellen had weakly nodded. She could not remember the last time she had eaten anything, and felt overcome with a kind of weariness which was new to her and she did not recognise. Tom quickly laid a fire and placed the kettle on its hook to heat.

"You can stay here … yes, I will speak to Mrs. Prescott, and find a way for you to stay with me for a while … father will not have you back, I realise that … I am going to work now. You rest, there's some cake if you want it. I'll be back at six thirty, and then once you have rested we'll talk." Tom spoke breathlessly and hurriedly. He did not give Ellen a chance to reply.

Ellen was surprised by how Tom's way of speaking had changed. She was not dismayed at what he had said, because she always knew him to be kind and loving towards her, but it was his way of speaking which had changed. He sounded like the better off folks, and she wondered how this change had come about. She made no comment however and quietly watched as Tom turned to go, hesitating for a moment at the door and looking with deep concern at her as he finally closed the door behind him.

He knew that Mrs. Prescott would object to his sister staying with him. It was not in the terms of his agreement that he could have people to stay. However, under the circumstances, what could he do? He would speak to her at the end of his working day.

Tom returned home just after six, having had a difficult day, his restless mind turning to thoughts of Ellen when he should have been concentrating on his work and serving his customers. Life at the Plummers Department Store had proved to be a fulfilment of one of Tom's dreams. He found that smart clothes could be affordable to him and to others like him because of the mass manufacturing of garments which enabled the price to be within many ordinary people's reach. He had assisted in the gentlemen's outfitters department at first and had used his knowledge of cut and fit to assist customers in finding the style and size best suited to them. He had been successful in serving many gentlemen and the Plummers family, and more particularly the eldest son Paul, had noticed him, and had given him encouragement and happily commission.

Tom had achieved a broad clientele, and as he had learnt some social niceties, and improved on his manner of speaking, he was able to attract the wealthier customers who appreciated being able to have a knowledgeable and presentable young man to serve them. His tailoring skills enabled him to see when and how garments needing adjusting a fraction for an excellent fit. However, today, Tom had been distracted, and his manager Mr. Phipps had noticed it.

After lunch, Tom had been told that he would need to ensure his work was 'to his usual standard' for the rest of the day. Tom realised that for the time being he would need to put Ellen's troubles into the back of his mind, and worked through the afternoon trying to dismiss his worries.

As the store closed, he completed the final checks of the day, ensuring that the clothes were all immaculately displayed, and that each rail could not be faulted for its neatness. It was not his responsibility to check the takings for the day. Mr. Phipps did this with painstaking accuracy. Once Tom was satisfied that his department was organised and orderly, he checked on his own appearance in a full length mirror.

He saw himself with fresh eyes. His reflection depicted a tall young man with dark sculpted hair and trimmed moustache, staring fixedly back at him. His eyes were clearly troubled, and he felt ill at ease with himself. Despite having a very well fitted suit, fashionable waistcoat and overcoat, and being shod with gleaming laced shoes and a high collared white shirt and wearing the latest fashion a neatly tied wide tie, he realised how quickly appearances can change, and how fortunes can suddenly swerve to an unfriendly course. His sister had been so vibrant when he had seen her last, with her beautiful skin, glowing hazel eyes and thick copper hair. Her figure had always been slim, well-proportioned and upright, and she possessed an air of quality. What had become of that person?

As he left the building through the wide oak doors leading out to the main city road, he noticed Paul Plummer getting into his carriage.

"Mr Lambourn, I would like a word." Paul viewed the troubled expression of his favoured employee which he had never seen before. Paul was an attentive employer who noticed a great deal about what was going on in the store. Tom had been made aware of this early on in his employ when Paul had mentioned something to Tom about a particular customer, and had noted

Tom's ability to put the customer at his ease. Tom had quietly and calmly shown a variety of garments to this rather nervous gentleman, and had quickly been able to make him feel comfortable, and persuade him that a particular suit fitted him as if it had been made for him. Paul had observed this process and had been impressed. He had shared his satisfaction with Tom and praised him.

Tom was honest in his work, and Paul had noticed Tom's love of clothes and also of the work. Paul realised he had a good employee, and wanted to make the best use of him. On this occasion he had taken Tom to one side and congratulated him on his perseverance in dealing sensitively with a customer who could have been very difficult.

However, today, he had observed a shadow over Tom's features and, deliberately waiting for Tom to leave, had intercepted him and requested a conversation with him. Tom was not used to a request such as this.

"Why yes, of course sir, I hope there is nothing amiss?"

"No, not really although I've noticed that, well, you have not been yourself today, and wondered if there was anything that I might do to help."

Tom was unaware that his concerns were so transparently obvious, and replied diffidently as he approached the carriage, "Why, sir, I suppose I am troubled about something at present, but I feel sure that there is a solution which has not come to me as yet."

"Come with me, if you like Lambourn and I will take you where you need to go, and on the way maybe you can tell me about this 'trouble' if that's what it is. It's possible that I might be able to help." Tom wondered why Mr Plummer was willing to do this for him, but decided, after looking at him and believing him sincere, that he would accept the ride, and take the opportunity to associate with his wealthy employer. It couldn't do him any harm, could it? The driver was given the address, and both men settled back into the comfortable seats of the carriage.

The thought of possible harm from disclosing his troubles to his employer, together with his lowly position prevented him from sharing all with his employer, but he gave the bare facts as he had come to know them, that Ellen his younger sister had been badly treated in service, and had come to Southampton to get help from him. He was unsure how he could help, but left it at that. Paul said nothing, but when it was time for Tom to leave the carriage, he thanked him and recognised that Mr Plummer was reflecting on what he had said, and for the moment did not have an answer. They bid each other goodbye, and Tom decided that Mrs. Prescott had to be his first priority. The carriage moved away, leaving Tom unsure as to how Mr Plummer had taken his news. He dreaded that Ellen's misfortune would turn in to his own.

* * *

Bugle Street led down to the harbour, and was a pleasant enough street. The buildings varied in size, age and maturity. Tom's home for the past year had been in a small Victorian house towards the sea end of the street. The lodging house was lived in by several single gentlemen and was owned by Mrs. Prescott, a careful, anxious widow who also lived at the property on the ground floor. She had several rooms including a parlour and dining room with a small kitchen and scullery. She was dependant on the rent from her tenants, and was uneasy about this. She had no means of her own, and had only the home bought by Mr Prescott during better times. Since his death, she had learnt to be thrifty and watched her tenants vigilantly. She had not known of Ellen's arrival because of the early hour, and was unaware of her existence.

When Tom Lambourn nervously told her of his sister's plight, she immediately replied as Tom had expected. There was no possibility of Ellen staying, and she would need to go straight away. Tom felt downcast, and showed it. If only there was something that he could do to ensure Ellen's safety. She needed a roof over her head and food on her table. How was this to be accomplished? But his landlady was adamant.

Ellen had fallen into a deep sleep after she'd had some of Tom's tea and cake. She woke and could not remember where she was for a moment, but then, fully realising her situation, hurriedly got up and began to tidy herself. She found a jug of water on the table and at the side of the bed a basin and soap and began to wash herself. She spent time brushing her hair and tying it back onto the nape of her neck. She tried to coax it into soft curls falling onto her shoulders. She looked at her clothes and realised they were shabby and unkempt and felt ashamed. What must Tom have thought of her? She wondered what else she could do before Tom's return and decided to go out and explore the neighbourhood.

She had appreciated so much the open air on her walk to Southampton, and this was still at the forefront of her mind. She replaced her straw bonnet and grey wool cape, and ventured out into the street. It was about two o' clock, and the street was empty except for a young couple walking arm in arm and a young woman pushing a baby carriage. They did not appear to notice Ellen as she turned down the street towards the sea.

The road dipped gradually and then swung to the left, and as Ellen approached the bend she felt a change in the air, and felt the brush of a breeze which was cool and fresh, shifting her skirts about her and tangling her hair. She had never experienced anything like it before, and wondered what was causing the changeableness of the air around her. She grasped her bonnet as she felt it lift from her, and smiled as she struggled to keep her cape about her. Her skirts were lifting too, and she knew her discoloured petticoat was on view. And on view it certainly was as she had discovered there were other people walking where she was walking, and that her route had suddenly become busy with persons of many descriptions. Street sellers occupied every few yards along the way, selling small useful items and treats and as she progressed along the sea front she glanced at their trays for a moment, but was quickly persuaded to look away as her gaze was inextricably drawn to the sight of the sea.

Its colours were constantly changing and shifting to multitudinous shades of grey, turquoise, green and blue. It tumbled, tossed, rolled, foamed and splashed, and its movements were rhythmic but constantly changing. Ellen could not take her eyes off the undulating patchwork of movement and reflected light. She crossed the road as soon as she was able, and stopped to gaze out at the expanse of water, looking at the tiny boats and vessels in the distance riding the restless, flexing frame of water and salty foam. She had tasted the salt in the air, and felt her hair loosened by the vigour of the wind. She loved the feeling this experience was giving her, and wanted this moment to remain so that she would have time to really relish it.

Then the thought came to her that she had recently taken her life into her own hands after having to occupy her time since her mother's death in complying with other's demands and following what others were telling her to do. She stood facing the wind, the restless expanse of breathing water, rising up and descending like the exhalations of a gigantic creature and felt she was being released. She smelt the strange smells of sea, fish and weed, and other unrecognisable smells which were carried on the breath of the wind. Her mind seemed to be invigorated by the water and air, and the many questions which had remained in her subconscious began to surface.

'Why had she been left alone to care for her mother? Why had her father stayed away? Why had he changed so dramatically towards her at the death of her mother? Why had his attitude to her become so hostile? He had never hit her mother, so why did he turn on her and strike her? What had happened for her to be sent to a place where the people were unwilling to show her or Ada any kindness? Why did Dr. Gibson say those terrible things about her? They weren't true were they?' Ellen had so many unanswered questions, so much that she felt unsure of; she needed the answers. How was she to accomplish this, particularly as most of them revolved around her father? He had apparently disowned her. Had this been because of his marriage to Mary? No, she had marked a change in him prior to that. How was she to discover the answers? She desperately needed to know why these things had happened to her. Why did she now find herself alone in a strange place, totally unfitted to make her own way in life, and yet having to do so? As she pondered, her mother came to her in her mind and in her heart, and she could not restrain her tears.

She wept for her mother, for herself, for the misery and anger of her father, for Ada and for Agnes. She cried for her home, for her mother's arms, and for her own desperate state. Her face was marked with sorrow and desperation. She turned once more to gaze outwards to the sea, and then, gradually, she felt the lines being smoothed and washed away by the buffeting wall of air and mist which pounded her cheeks and her forehead. Her eyes were swollen but they were brightened by the vision of what lay before her. She would continue to have her mother's strength which would be hers if she prayed for it. God would provide her with the answers, and so she brushed away her tears and walked on.

Tom arrived back at his room with a troubled heart. He had nothing of a positive nature to share with Ellen. He found her reading, but she quickly dropped the book as he entered the room.

"So how have you been today? I have to tell you that I've been worried all day. It was difficult for me to think about work. What have you been doing?"

"Oh, Tom," Ellen hugged her brother and was slow to move away from him, "I've been ou' and seen the sea. I' was wonderful and so many people abou', I loved i'!" Tom grinned at her as she was so clearly overjoyed with this new experience of the sea.

"So you've decided that the sea is a pleasant enough place and that Southampton suits you! Well, I hoped that it would be possible for you to stay, but at present ... it seems unlikely." Tom bravely told Ellen his bad news. "Mrs Prescott will not allow you to stay here, and at present I do not know of anywhere that you might be able to stay. As you have no work it makes things difficult, you see ... and father will find out soon enough that you have not gone to the Workhouse, and I suspect he may think you have come here and I don't know what he will do." Tom paused when he saw his sister's bleak expression. She was beginning to see that her situation was desperate, and that there did not appear to be a way out. She knew that she needed to work, but was confused as to the kind of work she should be engaged in. Surely it needed to be something in which she had an interest and some skill already.

She was fifteen and had gathered some skills. There wasn't much she didn't know about keeping a home. She knew how to make a poultice and how to make infusions with herbs. She knew how to use a wide variety of fresh and dried leaves, roots, stems, flowers, bark, nuts and fruits to create recipes that were wholesome and remedies for all kinds of sicknesses and complaints. If she had access to some of these ingredients, she might make a living supplying remedies, providing people with treatments and preparations which had been handed down, tried and tested and used for centuries. She knew her grandmother had acquired many of the recipes from her mother ... who knew how long these recipes went back? She remembered she had written many of them down, and was grateful that for some reason she had always kept these writings with her. She felt she should share her thoughts with Tom.

"You're right ... I don't think father will want to see me a' the presen'. I've not been in 'is favour for some time you know. I don' know why 'e should 'ave turned against me, but I do know that 'e is unlikely to wan' to help me ... so, I 'ave to find a way of making a living, some'ow, and the only thing I can think of is to use my understanding of 'erbs and such to provide people with potions and remedies ... I mean people will always wan' something for their ailments, and they can't always afford a doctor, so I though' ..."

"And how do you suppose you can set yourself up to do such a thing?" Tom became impatient with Ellen because what she was saying did not seem feasible to him and in his view could not be done. His critical view of her hopes was elaborated. "You would need the ingredients and all the equipment to make the remedies, a licence to sell, premises possibly, goodness knows what else. And how would you get your customers? You couldn't just go out into the street and go up to people."

"But maybe I could … I've seen the street sellers ou' on the sea parade, they seem to do well as there are lots of people walking up and down, and 'avin' a look at their wares. Why not me? I could sell some simple recipes to begin with – I would just need some twists of paper to wrap them in – maybe camomile tea leaves for calmness or cough drops for sore throats - maybe just a few things to start with until I find out what people wan' and need." Ellen was flushed with her ideas and her wish to convince Tom of their veracity; she felt really excited at the prospect of using her knowledge to help others.

"What about the ingredients Ellen? You'll have to buy things and if it has n't escaped your notice, you have no money." Ellen looked blankly at Tom and realised that he was not seeing what she was seeing, but she realised that he had a point. How would she get started?

"Ellen, we'll have some supper and maybe talk again later. Of course we have to find you somewhere to live, that's our first job, but let's eat first!" Tom had brought a package in with him under his arm, which unwrapped revealed a newly baked loaf of bread, slices of ham and some cheese. There was a jar of ginger beer which they shared, and then they settled down to discuss their future. Ellen lay on the bed overcome with tiredness, and drifted off to sleep wondering if she could manage to make and sell her remedies and then had a happy dream of sailing on the sea selling her remedies to satisfied and happy fishermen.

* * *

The practices for the Christmas Nativity had been full of music and, for Agnes especially, opportunities for learning. Agnes had relished the challenge which had given her a chance to try new things, to venture into an unfamiliar world. Some of the music had been unknown. A lovely new carol called 'O Little Town of Bethlehem' was introduced to her, but she had learnt it without difficulty. Mr. Smith had made comment several times on her inborn musicality and her ability to very quickly memorise melodies, phrasing and rhythms.

Agnes had certainly felt nervous at first. She lacked confidence in her ability, not having had any kind of opportunity to build any kind of assurance in her musical talent. Nevertheless, she was reassured by her teacher's constant expressions of faith in her, and slowly grew to believe in herself and her natural aptitude. As the time drew nearer for the performance on Christmas Eve, Agnes threw herself in to completely remembering every move, every word spoken and every musical note. It dawned on her that she felt ready and became excited at the prospect of the play, and any anxiety she may have felt was not apparent. Not so Hannah, who did not have a direct part in the performance, but was very apprehensive about Freddie's central role.

"I'm thinking that I will need to make sure Freddie has his feed just before the performance, or 'e might decide 'e's 'ungry in the middle ... what do you think Agnes? Do you think I should give 'im something extra to really settle 'im? It would be a terrible thing if 'e suddenly burst ou' crying in the middle of i' ... and wha' could I do? I couldn't very well take him ou' of the manger to calm him while everyone is looking on ... could I?"

"You know Freddie is a happy baby, and does n't fre' when you're around ... he'll be 'appy to lie there and listen to the lovely music and watch the flickerin' of the candlelight I'm sure ...

'annah, 'e's sure to be as good as gold." Agnes could see that her usually calm sister was deeply worried about this occasion in relation to her son's involvement. She thought that it was probably more about the whole situation than about the possibility of Freddie crying. Hannah's wish to be accepted by the community and for Frederick to grow up amongst people who did not care about his beginnings was all she really wanted and Agnes knew this. She thought she knew her sister as well as anyone. She had noticed how Hannah loved her child, and spent as much time as she could holding him and talking to him and seeing to his needs. Freddie responded to Hannah and was indeed a very contented baby.

He bore no physical resemblance to the rest of his family except for Ellen. His hair was tinged with coppery tints and his skin was fair. He was always dressed in clean linen and hand knitted garments, and his face was scrupulously clean and devoid of those traces of food and dribble which babies often possess. Agnes saw clean and immaculate Freddie as the personification of everything that was good about her older sister.

The final practice had begun, with Hannah and Freddie in attendance. Agnes had felt a little hesitant before her entrance but once she had begun to sing, she blossomed and felt very much in command and happy to be performing publicly, particularly singing. Everyone hearing her was struck by her lovely clear voice which had a hint of an occasional tremor which some more perceptive members of the audience glimpsed and interpreted as evidence of not only her lack of experience but also her fragility and vulnerability.

Agnes was not aware of this aspect of her character, as her youth had not allowed her mind the time to be too occupied by those things which had upset her life and led to her suffering. She had not yet experienced the turning of her heart and mind fully to the effects of grief, of losing those who were closest to her.

She had heard only one bit of news in relation to Ellen from Tom, who had told her that she had travelled to Southampton and visited him and had been trying to think of various ways to support herself. The last he had known of her was that she was on her way to grandpa and grandma Timms.

Tom had come back to Botley alone when the leaves had just started to fall, and Agnes had been happy to hear of Ellen. At this time that she was thinking of her, she expressed to Tom the question that was bothering her; why hadn't Ellen come at the same time as Tom. She had hoped that Ellen would return any day, so that they could be close again, but Tom's words took away that hope.

"You know Aggie, pa would not have Ellen back … he would not want to see her … something has happened between them, and I don't think Ellen would want to return. I'm sorry … I can see this is hard for you but it won't be for ever. When you're older you will be able to see Ellen if you wish. It's time, that's all. Maybe father will relent; perhaps the rift that exists between them will be mended … maybe you'll see Ellen sooner than you think."

Despite Tom's attempt at consoling Agnes and providing a glimmer of hope, she could not help but feel down cast. She desperately missed Ellen, and thought of her every day. At times of uncertainty she would continue to ask herself 'What would Ellen do?' and this would in some measure console her as she reflected on how Ellen had acted in similar situations.

Agnes had been shaken by her mother's death so much, but she had allowed herself only a brief moment to feel her loss, and then had continued with her daily care of the younger children. That is until Mary had married her father. She had carried on doing what she could for the younger ones, particularly Henry, but had chosen to occupy herself more with studying and in, recent weeks, with her music.

Mr. Smith had proved to be as kindly as he was thought to be. Unknown to her, his time and effort with Agnes were enjoyable to him. He thought he could see the beginnings of a significant talent, and enjoyed playing his part in its nurturing. Agnes enjoyed the work with him. He was not a singing teacher as such, more a music teacher, and assisted Agnes in understanding the structure of music and appreciating its intrinsic power. Agnes learnt about tempo and phrasing. She learnt how to enunciate the words. She learnt how to soar over and above the high notes so that they sounded effortless. She learnt a little about expression and about how music could uplift and pacify, could excite and energise, could do so many things.

The final practice came to an end, and Agnes returned home with Hannah, Frederick, Emily and Henry. She felt buoyant and happy, and was eagerly looking forward to Christmas Eve.

Everyone in the village came to the Church on that night and the Church was full and filled with excitement. The places where the congregation stood or sat were predetermined by status and family. The Turner family were positioned at the front on the right, while other families with property were seated at the front on the left. James and Alfred sat on either side of their father with their uncle Colonel Matthew Turner beside Alfred; Sir Russell's sister Elizabeth Lawrence always visited the Grange at Christmas and was sat close to James. Everyone noticed how very severe Lady Elizabeth was in her appearance as she had followed the lead of Queen Victoria and had remained in austere widow's black since the passing of her husband four years before. She was like her brothers very upright, with a superior air which reflected her wish to be separate from the society of ordinary people. The Colonel visited at various times of the year and not having a family of his own, often visited at Christmas.

The two brothers James and Alfred were contrasting in their appearance. James was careful with his appearance while Alfred did not really attend to his. His hair was dishevelled, his coat loosely fitting and his overall demeanour was overly relaxed. He appeared bored by the proceedings and showed little interest in his surroundings and in the play. However, this completely changed when Agnes made her entrance and sang the first verse of the first carol, 'The First Noel', with the choir and company all joining in on all the other verses. Alfred's attention was fully upon her, the sweetness of her voice and her loveliness; the young girl who stood before him dressed in a simple blue robe, glowed in the candlelight.

Agnes's blond hair was left loose beneath her head covering, and Alfred could just glimpse a few fair waves catching the light as they fell down on either side of her face to below her shoulders; her blue eyes caught the glow of the candlelight and shone brilliantly; she was quietly serene; as she sang her lips opened wide and joyously, and she appeared to be smiling.

Her performance was full of contrasts which Alfred noticed; he listened to her high and then deeper notes, her gentler tones, her more strident, joyous choruses.

Despite being only a little older than her, Alfred had begun to take notice of young women. Agnes was just becoming aware of changes taking place in her own body, of the beginnings of female menstruation, of her physical shape changing in recent months, but she was still very innocent in her outlook and interests. She had no idea that her loveliness as a woman was emerging, and that it would not be long before she would have more than one suitor.

Alfred watched Agnes and was drawn to her innocence which he was not able to understand as yet, but which he recognised; he felt its effects on his own feelings. He suddenly felt entirely happy to be where he was. He could have listened to Agnes all night, and watched her intently. As far as he was concerned she was an angel, and recently he had acquired a particular need for an angel in his life.

His father was always unhappy with him these days. It seemed that he could not please him. He always showed his preference for James, and rewarded him. He had begun feeling that his illegitimacy would always in some way negatively influence how his father treated him, and would ultimately prevent him from being fully accepted by him. Alfred's growing surliness was due to his view that he could n't ever attain his father's complete approbation, and he felt bitter about it.

His understanding of his father's attitude to him was based on his attempts at rectifying Alfred's propensity to indulge in reckless and inappropriate behaviour which, Alfred was loathe to accept, a loving father would be expected to have. But Sir Russell Turner's criticisms of him, he believed, were based on the unfair comparisons he made between him and James.

James had a level head, but Alfred was accused of being inconsistent. Alfred would be slow to do what was asked of him, but James completed tasks without delay. James was studious while Alfred never wanted to spend time reading or studying but liked nothing better than to ride about the countryside, particularly on his favourite horse, Stardust, a beautiful grey who responded to every nuance of his riding. Alfred showed little interest in any occupation while James had several aspirations which he had discussed with his father. His younger son was, it appeared, a grave disappointment to him. This was Alfred's view.

However, Sir Russell did appear to see his sons differently but not in a judgemental way; he just felt the need to guide Alfred more than James, but it was out of concern only and not because of any less charitable motive. The resentment which Alfred felt was self-induced, and based on his own feelings of inadequacy around his older brother.

James sat on the other side of his father and appeared to be a young gentleman of true distinction. He was immaculately dressed and had taken painstaking care with the tying of his cravat and the fit of his caped great coat. His hair was carefully brushed forward close to his head, and trimmed meticulously. His neatly trimmed moustache, side whiskers and cheek bones were shaved carefully and evenly. He was tall despite being only fifteen, and although still very loose limbed, was clearly going to possess a strong frame and musculature when he matured. Compared to his father he was much more prepossessing, being taller than Sir Russell already, and broader in the shoulders.

Their uncle, sat with them, was little known and nothing of great weight was spoken about him; Matthew Turner had remained in the Army since enlisting as a young man; his commission had been bought, and he had, it was rumoured, fought in various conflicts. Some said that he had travelled to South Africa and others to Turkey. Through his endeavours, everyone supposed, he had been rewarded by reaching the rank of Colonel. Observers noted that he was a quiet man who said very little, except to make some reply to the comments of others. He remained an enigma, as he had never associated with members of the local community when he stayed at the Grange. He appeared to those who scrutinised him as being a typical gentleman, who had distinguished himself in the army, and who valued his brother and his family. While at the Grange he was happy, it seemed, to remain in the shadows, beholden to his wealthy older brother, and content to ride about the countryside and stay at home in the evenings, not venturing out to the village at any time.

Further back in the church the Lambourn family had congregated. Thomas sat with Hannah on one side of him holding Frederick, and Mary on the other, and Tom beside her; George sat on his father's lap. Henry and Emily were involved in the Nativity, so they were with Agnes getting ready.

The church looked beautiful in the candlelight, with winter greenery and scarlet ribbons decorating the choir stalls and the sides of the congregational pews. Everywhere there was the sweet smell of pine and of oranges, a special Christmas treat given by the Church to every child in the parish. Hannah rocked Frederick in her arms. He was wrapped tightly in a new white shawl, had been well fed and was content, and Hannah began to enjoy the wonderful feeling present in the church as everyone from the village gathered on that chill December night to celebrate the birth of Jesus.

She watched the play without moving, totally caught up in the music and the story told by the children. Henry was a shepherd boy and held a lantern high as he sang with the shepherds. He appeared to be unaware of the audience and was entirely absorbed by the music. Emily was dressed in a white dress which was adapted from a choir garment. She looked like a diminutive angel, and drew smiles out of many of the congregation.

During a congregational carol towards the end of the play, Hannah slipped quietly forward, and gently placed the baby Freddie in the wooden manger which was lined with straw and hay. He slept throughout and was much admired. Later, as members of the congregation commented on what they had witnessed, it was generally agreed that Freddie was a beautiful child.

It is not an exaggeration to say that for Agnes the evening was the highlight of her life up until that point, and she had one regret only which was that Ellen had not come. She was not clear as to why, but hoped that it wasn't because of her father, and that the reason was due to a circumstance like a previous engagement which could not be changed. It wasn't long, however, before her disappointment had evaporated, and she had immersed herself in her portrayal of Mary, the mother of Christ.

The end for her came too quickly. She felt that she had found out something special about herself that night, which she would never forget. No matter what others had thought of her performance, she was blissfully happy, and retained a desire to repeat the experience whenever she could and as soon as she could. Her mind was set on it and her heart too.

She would find ways to express herself through participating in plays or musical events, but had no idea at this time how this might be accomplished. She felt unclear about the future but hoped that somehow the opportunities would come and that she would be able to experience these wonderful moments again.

"Well, Agnes, it seems that you 'ave surprised us all."

"Father, did you enjoy the play? Wasn't the music wonderful? Frederick never made a sound did he? Did Mary 'ave a good evening? What' did she say abou' it? Wha' did you think?"

"It was a wonderful evening my dear Agnes, you showed us the sweetness of Mary tonight." Agnes felt so happy that her father had approved of her, and she exclaimed, "Music *is* wonderful ... I never knew that music could be so beau'iful father!" Agnes wanted to thank Mr Smith for his kind and careful tutoring but could not see him. He had opened her eyes to the potential of music to lift, to inspire, to calm, to create mood and drama, and generate powerful emotions. It seemed to her that music was the best thing that had ever come into her life. She had sung songs with Ellen and her grandmother, and had enjoyed joining her voice to theirs. But singing alone was a different experience for her, and she had begun to appreciate what her own voice could do.

Mr Smith was nowhere to be seen, and so she contented herself with the adulation of her family except for Hannah who had retrieved Freddie from the manger and had hurriedly made her excuses wanting to take him home out of the cold.

Agnes meanwhile was revelling in the kind words and praise which were coming her way. She was, however, completely unaware of the adoration of a certain member of the congregation who would remember her performance for the rest of his life. It had been his introduction to her, and Alfred Turner would firmly base his future relationship with her on the opinion he had constructed of her on this Christmas Eve.

*   *   *

Christmas morning arrived for the Lambourn family with the giving and receiving of gifts. All the children received an item of clothing from their father. Agnes had a new soft blue wool skirt, and her brothers each had new shirts. Emily had a pretty winter dress with a touch of lace at the collar and cuffs. Everyone recognised the lace as the handiwork of grandmother Timms, who had also made a new knitted outfit for baby Frederick. Thomas received a pair of socks made by Agnes and from his mother some handkerchiefs with embroidered initials. Hannah had also made him a thick muffler which would ensure his warmth on colder days. Tom had provided some items of clothing from the store, and was the recipient of a new tailored jacket and waistcoat made by his father out of a fine, green, woollen material. Ma Lambourn had also provided the family with a fruit cake and a plum pudding, which the family would be having later in the day. Henry and George had also received wooden toys, Henry a large brightly striped spinning top with stick and string, and George a beautifully carved and painted wooden horse. Hannah was grateful for a new cape made from local wool and dyed a rich dark blue. Her father had bought the material and fashioned it with a warm lining and Hannah, delighted with the gift, clung to her father for a long moment, and kissed his cheek. Thomas seemed to soften a little after this, and even smiled at Mary when she opened her gift.

"I can see tha' you 'ave spent more time and money on this dress, my dear Thomas ... were you thinkin' tha' I needed a new dress for Sir Russell's birthday party? ... Does this mean we shall be going? Oh I do so love to dance ... the material is very fine my dear ... I've never 'ad such a dress before." Everyone looked on as Mary held the dress against her. It was a deep russet and had volumes of material at the back. The skirt was so full that Mary appeared very small indeed behind it. Mary's very dark hair shone, reflecting the amber highlights of the satin. The neckline scooped across from one shoulder to the other, and would reveal a considerable amount of Mary's throat and bosom. Clearly Mary recognised this and ventured to say that it was 'very much the fashion'. Thomas replied with a warm smile, and the family felt happier now that they could see their father was content with Mary's response.

After a moment he turned to the family and reminded them, "Come it's time to ge' ready for church. Be quick, as we need to leave very soon. 'enry, pu' your coat on now!" He left the room to fetch his best coat and hat, and stood at the door inspecting each of his children as they emerged ready to leave. Shirts were tucked in and hair brushed back, collars tightened, caps and bonnets straightened and buttons neatly fastened. Henry was suitably dressed, and Thomas thought that his second son was at last beginning to behave like a typical eight year old; but the coat had been thrown on by one of his daughters, because they knew that Henry was not yet able to accomplish it alone.

Agnes had quickly dressed in her new skirt, and put red ribbons in her hair. Her bonnet also was dressed with red bows. She felt happier this morning than she had felt for a very long time, and was looking forward to returning to the place where she had performed with such acclamation. She had enjoyed all the admiration, and had felt for the first time in her life that she was of some consequence. Everyone of note had complimented her, and she especially had appreciated the comment of Sir Russell. She had memorised his words and reflected on them once again as it had occurred the previous evening.

"Agnes, is it? Why I must congratulate you on a wonderful evening. I know that everyone could not have failed to notice how beautifully you sang ... clear as a Christmas bell ... in fact you were the belle of the evening ... ha, ha! Yes indeed."

Agnes had smiled up at him, and had been unsure as to why he was laughing, but he had clearly enjoyed her singing, and that was a great compliment. Alfred stood beside Sir Russell and watched Agnes. Thomas intervened at this point and made an excuse to leave. Agnes was taken by the arm and shepherded out. She saw Mr. Smith at the door as she left, but was only able to give him a cheery wave which he reciprocated. He had smiled broadly at her, and felt as good as a celebrated maestro might have done having performed at the highest level. Herbert was a humble man but had felt great delight in assisting with what many would have described as an insignificant and provincial enterprise. But he did not see it in that way. Every endeavour, he believed, required his best efforts, and the night had certainly been very enjoyable and had delighted the audience. He had recognised the positive influence he had on Agnes's achievement, and revelled in her accomplishment. She had sung with confidence and with feeling. For one so young she had successfully portrayed Mary as a pure and lovely young woman blessed by God, and it seemed that nearly everyone had been captivated by her performance.

As Agnes returned to the Church on Christmas morning, her mind was full of herself and she only gave a cursory thought to Ellen. Everyone in the family was there except Ellen; she was conspicuously absent, and not mentioned by anyone. Agnes was not so troubled by this as she would have been if she had remained the ordinary Agnes Lambourn with nothing remarkable about her. Nevertheless, she did still miss Ellen, and wished more than anything that she could have been present at her triumph. But it was not to be, and she was feeling too happy to allow her attachment to Ellen to deprive her of a moment's pleasure.

She led Emily and George into the Church and looked eagerly around her to see if she was being noticed. She was pleased to see that there were a few smiles and acknowledgements directed at her as she passed down the aisle to the family's pew. The village had once again congregated together, warmly dressed, and ready to celebrate Christmas. It was a simple celebration with Christmas carols and readings, a sermon and the whole was concluded with a prayer. The church was filled with every family, and if they were so fortunate as to have servants, they also attended standing at the back of the naïve.

The sermon which the Reverend Russell gave was an encouragement to the parishioners to make a renewed effort to read or listen to the words of the Bible, and to try to think about how they might apply them to their own lives, especially as the New Year was only a week away. Agnes sat during this part of the service, deep in thought, thinking of the New Year, and wondering when her next opportunity to perform might come. Her whole mind was focussed on this, and she did not want to think about anything else. She became irritated by her younger siblings when they became restless or wanted her attention. She wanted no distractions from her own musings, and when she did listen to the sermon, was much like everyone else in the Church, wondering what the Reverend meant and what the connection was between the Bible and her life.

It was then that she suddenly remembered Ellen, and thought of their conversations about their relationship with God. She knew that her sister had understood something which she had tried to share with her, but she only had a vague idea of what was meant. She missed Ellen immediately, and her eyes began to sting with her pain, and she folded her arms tightly around her, and slumped forward in her seat. Thomas, watching his children with eagle's eyes, reached across to Agnes, and roughly squeezed her arm. Agnes felt her father's firm hand and was brought back to the present; she straightened her back, and looked briefly at her father, who dispassionately observed her tears.

The walk home was a time to wish other walkers a merry Christmas. The day was bright and crisp, and the villagers shouted and called to one another across the street and down the lanes as they walked home from church.

"Merry Christmas Thomas, Mary ... compliments of the season ... merry Christmas." The village returned to their homes wishing one another the best of days, and the Lambourn family shared their good wishes with all who crossed their path. The tailor's shop was less than a five minute walk from the Church, but this Christmas morning the walk took considerably longer as everyone stopped and acknowledged one another along the way, pausing to wish each other well and shake hands. The young people watched as the older members of the community addressed one another, recognising that this event was special to Christmas Day, and a village tradition.

The Christmas dinner was prepared by Hannah. Mary was not inclined to cook the meal for a large family, as she'd had no experience of it and in any case she did enough cooking the rest of the time. She was going to relax on Christmas Day she decided. Hannah had helped her mother in Christmases past, and was able to roast the goose and prepare the vegetables. The meal was ready at two o clock, and the family eagerly came to the table. Each member of the family sat in their usual place, excepting Ma Lambourn who presided at one end of the table and her other son, Stephen who was placed at her side. The meal was set in the centre, and Thomas prepared to carve. The smell of roasted bird, potatoes, root vegetables, rich gravy and stuffing filled the eager noses of the children. Their eyes widened as they watched their father raise the carving knife and fork, but then, disappointingly replace them on the table.

"We will thank God for the blessings we 'ave". He clasped his hands, and bowed his head. All the children put their hands together, and closed their eyes.

"Almighty God, our Father, we thank thee for this Christmas day and for this meal which 'as been prepared for us. We are thankful for this family, and ask that each of us might remember the blessings we 'ave, and that we might be able to do those things which thou wouldst 'ave us do, and become the family thou wouldst 'ave us be. 'elp us to do what is right, and please provide us with all that we need. 'elp us to know who we are, and to do the best we can. Please bless all our family wherever they are, and please prevent those things that will cause us suffering. Please teach us gra'itude for the blessings in our lives, and 'elp us to love one another." Thomas paused momentarily and the children opened their eyes wondering, but he continued in a very quiet voice, "Please forgive us our trespasses as we forgive those who trespass against us … in Jesus' name, Amen." Everyone chorused Amen, and the carving began in earnest.

Three

'The holly bears a blossom
As white as any flower'

The children eagerly watched the slicing of the flesh and the spooning of the stuffing. Their plates were soon full of a delicious combination of tastes, meat and vegetables moistened with a flavoursome, dark gravy. Hannah possessed a culinary gift which had been encouraged by her mother.

To anyone watching this family from the outside, it would have seemed that here was a group of people without a care in the world. They would witness a strong father and head of the house, a contented, submissive wife, and obedient, happy children who lacked nothing. There was not much conversation it is true, but that would probably be seen as the fault of a scrumptious meal and a generally held view that conversation at the table is not required. Christmas festivities can conceal the challenges and deficiencies in a family.

The Lambourn family were subject to many challenges, and all except George and Emily were in some measure weighed down by difficulties and concerns, but none of these would have been evident to a casual onlooker. As Christmas Day drew to a close, the children played with their toys, the grownups washed up, tidied and cleared away, and then it was time to sit around the hearth and roast some chestnuts. The little ones being full of rich food soon became sleepy and Agnes lifted them one by one and took them to their bed. It had been a day free of work in the usual sense, a day for the family. Agnes wondered about her family, and realised that the oneness which she had felt when her mother was alive was now absent. Things were not the same naturally, but there were extra burdens to carry. For each the burden was different, but instead of sharing with one another as they had used to do, the family members struggled in isolation, and did not seek the needed support from each other. Agnes did not share her burden with anyone once Tom had returned to Southampton. Thomas kept his troubled thoughts to himself. Mary was unable to talk about her bitterness in relation to her disappointing marriage, and Hannah could not disclose her child's paternity and her fears for her child. Henry was locked into his own world. Ma Lambourn remained intransigent in relation to her son's foolish behaviour, and made no comment. The Lambourn home had shifted into an uneasy quietness.

> 'But of this medicine, love,
> which cures all sorrow ...'

I did not recognise the young woman as the one who was to become my sweetheart the first time I saw her. You see it was at a time when she was still very young, no more than a girl really, although I did notice her a bit, and knew her when I saw her again months later – so there must have been something special going on. I tried to stay close to her as she grew, because I loved her, not as a husband loves the partner of his soul, but as the dearest of brothers loves the sweetest of his sisters.

She did grow into a beautiful young woman, one to whom I could hardly speak at times because it felt like she had me held in a kind of spell, and my mind would not reason or focus, but my heart yearned for her, and for her approbation.

Sometimes she would be distant with me; well that's how it felt to me, and I was left wondering what I'd done for her to remove herself from an emotional closeness which I felt existed some of the time. I tried to work out what was happening. Why did she found it difficult to maintain an attachment to me? And what was it that made her change? I thought when I was away from her that I would ask her to marry me, that we would be betrothed, but this did not happen. Not in the way it should have done anyway.

I had met with my love as I regularly did for Sunday lunch with her family. I was a familiar visitor, and these occasions became the best and happiest times of my life. Her family proved to provide her with the means of being natural with me, and she never showed any signs of aloofness towards me when we were with her family. I became particularly confident one Sunday, and suggested that we go for a country walk as I was determined and felt absolutely confident in knowing what lay ahead for us both and, being alone with her and feeling so content, I resolved that I could not fail to appeal to her to be my wife, and that she would accept me.

As we walked through the town to the river estuary which was a favourite place of ours I ventured to touch and hold her hand; she did not flinch but her hand was unresponsive and lay limp in mine. I was not deterred, and quietly as we at last were in sight of the sea, I told her how much I loved her, that I would and could not be whole until she agreed to be my wife.

We had stopped in the path and I had taken both her hands in mine, hardly knowing what I was doing, but only knowing that what I was doing was right. My sweetest rose looked steadily at me, her eyes so wide and wet that I could hardly keep my gaze upon her. She did not speak but with tears alone she gave me her answer. We walked in silence until we parted.

I did not see her again after that day for nearly two years. It gave me the time to consider the reasons why she had not been able to accept my proposal of marriage. I reasoned that she was too young to make such a commitment, that maybe she did not reciprocate my love, that there was some unknown obstacle to our liaison which was unknown to me, that perhaps my love was not sufficient for her. I know the reason now but it is of no matter.

I met my wife two months after that day. She encouraged me in loving her, and so I did, and we were married within two months of our meeting. She became pregnant very early in our marriage, and she, being one of a large family, seemed to look forward to the time when we would increase our family, and become truly one as a woman and a man in the birth of our first child.

I was happy to plan my life with her; but I had made a covenant with God and her that I would be true, and I was racked with a torment that I was not as faithful to her as I should because my mind and heart would sometimes turn to my first love, and I would wonder and reflect on the love I had had for her. I had not been released from that love, and was consumed by thoughts and feelings which would not be extinguished. I still longed for her, and knew my love for her would never perish, but that my love for my wife would grow if I was steadfast to her, and if I clung to her and to no one else.

The baby came early, but her mother would not bear another child in this life. Very soon after the birth, the midwife returned and called the doctor, but within two hours of little Amelia's birth, her mother died. We had not spoken one word in that time. I had remained at her side, but she had only looked at me with a deep impenetrable desire in her eyes which I did not understand.

My wife's mother and father came as soon as they had received the news of the death of their daughter. They came and saw that I was broken, death had entered my life again, and I could not bear it. My only thought was that my life was utterly condemned to misery and emptiness. I had sunk into a lonely place where no one could find me.

Her parents recognised that the baby could not stay with me, and so it was that my first child was taken from me, with the consent of which I was capable of giving at the time, and has been nurtured by them.

Somehow I will need to recover; my mind is unclear as to how this will happen, but I know now that the healing which needs to take place can only begin after a time of prolonged isolation and grief. Somewhere deep within me I know that I will rise, the wounds will not pain me and I shall become whole again; I will be able to reconnect with my heart, but the means of doing it never has become entirely clear as yet; the hoped for desire of my heart though is to be reconciled to my dearest sweetheart.

* * *

Tom had not made Ellen leave that first night, as he knew that she would have nowhere to go, and he needed time to think and make some kind of plan. He was anxious that his work at Plummers would take priority, and he could not allow the problems with Ellen to interfere with his employment. He was clear about that. His feelings when he had been with Paul Plummer had drawn him to the conclusion that his sister's plight, desperate though it was, was nothing compared to the possibility that he could lose his job, and then he would not be in any kind of position to assist her. He thought that he had glimpsed Mr. Plummer's disapproval of what he probably saw as the impediment of poor relations, and had not offered advice or displayed any form of sympathy. No, considering this, he would have to remain constant in his work, allowing no change in his efforts and character which might jeopardise his position, and somehow engineer a way of supporting Ellen, with the least amount of disturbance to himself.

He and Ellen slept at either end of his small bed, and he did not sleep well. He kept waking and felt troubled by the plight of his dearest sister. He arose early, and quietly completed his preparations for the day. Ellen lay unmoving, apparently deeply asleep, and he realised he would need to rouse her before leaving for work.

"Ellen, it's time, I have to leave, but we have not thought about what you must do, as you cannot stay here." Tom looked anxiously at the dark head almost covered by the sheet, and touched her shoulder, and despite there being no sign of life felt impelled to continue. "There isn't anyone that I can ask for help here. I have thought the only place for you now is Grandpa and Grandma Timms. You would be able to stay with them I think. What do you say?" Thomas waited for Ellen to show some sign that she had heard. He had thought how she might accomplish this and suggested, "You could travel on the Stage, I have a little money saved." He had no idea how much she would need and what she would do when she got there, but he knew of the kindness of their grandparents, and resolved to encourage Ellen to throw herself upon their mercy.

Ellen's voice came from the pillow, quiet and controlled. She felt empty of all feeling, and stared ahead at the wall, fighting the need to turn and look at her brother. But she could not look at him.

"Yes, Tom, thank you … though I don" wan' to take your money." Ellen, strengthened by the gratitude she had expressed, turned her head without raising it to smile faintly at Tom, and he felt reassured that despite him having to tell her to go, she had not apparently seen this as a total rejection or that he was abandoning her. He believed she was able to understand most things, but he did have a concern that festered in the back of his mind, that in her present condition she would find it hard to travel or to work. And she would need to do both.

Ellen's face showed that she was, by this time, struggling with her emotions. She was feeling afraid of what was expected of her. Her treatment by her father and those in the Gibson household had had a debilitating and devastating effect on her confidence and her self-esteem. She thought that she had little to recommend her, and she began to see the desperate situation that she was in. She hurriedly sat up in bed, and the blackness faded a little. She still had her strength, and she'd had her mother's love. She would do whatever needed to be done. Tom dared not look at her, as he was struggling with the desire to be loyal and to ensure that she was alright, but he had reasoned that he had to keep aloof from her. He had to continue with his life as before, when things were going well, and his employer and manager were satisfied with him. He could not allow anything or anyone to distract him from that path.

Ellen had eaten breakfast, a warm roll with butter and honey, with a cup of warm milk. She felt for the first time for weeks that her stomach was full, and she was ready to begin her day. Tom had suddenly gone, and she needed to quietly leave before the Landlady was about. She straightened her hair, unseeingly checked her appearance in the mirror, and left, leaving Tom's money where he had left it and closing the door behind her without a sound.

Ellen had to see the sea before her departure, and turned down the street, holding tightly onto her bag which held her few possessions, her recipes, her pencils and paper, and a few items of clothing. She once again looked out to sea, and was once again transported by the energy and movement of the writhing Solent. The morning had become even more blustery, and she could see some fishing vessels being violently tossed on the waves in the distance. She watched the antics of the boats and realised despite the apparent dangers that they were in, that they kept bobbing up and back to their rightful position. She was heartened by their ability to stay upright despite the turbulence around them, and knew that she would need the same kind of resilience at this time to withstand the tempests and upheavals of her life.

A sense of optimism had once again entered her mind, as the salty gusts of wind smoothed her face, tangled her hair and pushed her off balance; she was ready to do whatever was needed to stay afloat.

Her course had been set. She had been directed by Tom to attempt the journey to Lymington, imagining that she would find a haven there with her grandparents. She was ready to begin this journey, but did not know the direction, and stood wondering which way to turn. She looked to the west, and felt unsure. She knew that Lymington was located beyond the New Forest, as she had heard her father mention it and his sightings of the deer and ponies as he had travelled through. But as she tried to recognise the forest in both directions she could not see anything that resembled it, only sea and boats and harbour and sky.

Her mother had taught her to pray at those times when she felt uncertain or anxious about what she should do. She walked a little way and discovered a seat housed within an open fronted structure. It opened out to the sea as if to encourage those who felt like lingering to spend time sitting and contemplating the beauty of the sea and the life to be found on it. Ellen sank to the open boarded seat and bowed her head. She turned to God in her moment of indecision, and felt prompted to ask Him if the way she should go was to the west. After a moment listening to her feelings, and quietly considering the Lord's reply, she turned her face to the east and began walking.

Almost immediately she was on the point of passing a woman carrying a large basket which appeared to contain fish as Ellen spotted a silvery thin tail protruding from the piece of linen thrown over as a lid. She looked into the woman's face and saw a pair of mouse-like eyes peering at her out of folds of skin, the colour of wet shingle on the foreshore. Her cheeks resembled a newly ploughed field, furrowed and dark and Ellen had never seen her like before; however she did not hesitate, as the woman had paused and was looking curiously at her. She asked, "I am travelling to the other side of the New Fores', and I wonder, could you tell me if the coach passes this way, and where i' may be picking up passengers?"

"Why you need to go to the Dolphin 'otel, my dear," and the woman indicated with a turn of her head where that was situated. "You might jus' make it if you walk smartish, bu' i' follows the Shirley Road, so you won't see i' if you miss it." Again the woman indicated where this might be, and pointed to the west. Ellen was satisfied that she had been given the answer she needed. Thanking the woman with a smile and warmly clasping her hand, she turned to follow the woman's first instruction.

The woman with the fish watched her leave her feeling concerned, as she had never received a handshake from a stranger before, and had seen that the girl was very thin and to her surprise, dressed even more shabbily than she was herself. The stranger's cloak was edged with mud and frayed threads, her dress where it could be seen was marked with smears and stains, but the girl's face filled the woman with the greatest pity as she had observed a child's eyes drenched in privation and loneliness, a skin pinched tightly over protruding cheekbones and a neck bowed by cares and hardship.

Unknown to Ellen, she was being watched until she was out of sight, and then her observer thoughtfully went on her way thinking that the child was clearly in need of help, but she could not see how she might provide the help needed. She did not know that she had already done so.

Ellen wondered why the Lord had sent her in the wrong direction initially, but then realised that He had directed her to someone who would be able to clearly tell her the direction she needed to go. And so it was that she set off confidently, thanking God for the fish woman and for the answer to her prayer.

The wind had lifted and with it the rains had come. Ellen was poorly clad and had insufficient covering for a journey in the rain. Fortunately her cloak had a hood and she was able to swathe her head in the warm material, and with her head bowed, as soon as she had reached the Dolphin, she turned to the west and began her steps to reach people she was confident would take her in and offer her shelter. She knew she would receive a welcome from her grandparents, and so it was with resolution born of hope that she set off. Indeed Ellen was consoled with the picture that she would soon be in the arms of her mother's mother.

The weather grew worse, cold and very wet with a fierce wind. The rain beat across her face and body, buffeting her incessantly. Ellen needed to find shelter, and within a half hour she came to a towering viaduct which she quickly discovered provided a dry and comfortable sanctuary; she tucked herself beneath one of its supports where she was to some extent protected from the relentless lashing rain.

She lingered there for an hour waiting for the storm to decrease, feeling wet and cold to the marrow of her bones. She felt she should move on despite the conditions, and determined to keep going for as long as she could. She left the relative comfort of her sheltering place and once again began her solitary journey.

As she passed along the flooded tracks an occasional carriage or cart would pass her and she longed to sit in the comfort of one of the covered wagons and be effortlessly carried, snug and dry. She did not know how she would respond if she was indeed offered a ride, if perhaps a tradesman would see her and take pity on her in her drenched and forlorn state. She knew how she must look, but cared little. She used to have some pride but this had evaporated into the chill and saturated air. As it was no one paused to consider taking her aboard. She continued on her way, past the estuary and upward through small hamlets and isolated farm houses. She noticed how the covering began to gradually increase, and by the time she had been walking for about five hours, she felt sure that she had reached the Forest as the road passed along a way which was closely shrouded in trees on either side and vehicles became less frequent.

She had passed one or two walkers like herself who were heading in the opposite direction and they were heavily burdened with large baskets and bags. They carried wood, vegetable produce and other items for sale. One lanky traveller topped by a tall and misshapen hat had numerous pans, cups, kettles and ladles attached to various parts of his body. She had seen tinkers before, and recognised the clanging and tinkling accompaniment of these traders. She admired his long swinging strides and returned his polite salute.

The weather remained unpleasant, but despite the conditions, she was able to keep her spirits up by being interested in who and what she saw on her journey. Ellen, imprisoned and maltreated for the past three months, and before that abused by her father after her mother's death, relished the feelings she had which were born of escape and freedom, and her spirit felt buoyant.

As dusk came, she realised that she could not go on walking through the night. She did not know how much further she needed to travel, had passed Lyndhurst but was now conscious of the ever increasing darkness. It would not be long before she would not be able to find her way, and she hastily looked all around her for a shelter of some kind. She found the trunk of a smooth beech tree close to the road, and sat against it, and slept.

Morning broke and Ellen did not awake.

* * *

Ellen had not found an adequate shelter except for the tree, and had remained at the roots of the beech tree not far from the forest track. She was seen in the early hours by another traveller, who had happened to catch sight of her, sensed that all was not well and had approached her; and when she had not responded to his call, he had dismounted from his horse and ventured to touch her and had found that her face was drenched and flushed and her hands icy cold. She did not move at his touch and he then realised that the girl's situation was serious. He had looked up and down the forest track looking for a sign of assistance which he knew Ellen needed. He would need to transport her to the nearest home, and get medical help.

This passing stranger, fortunately for Ellen, personified the compassion exhibited by those people who had seen works of charity and also have been the recipients of compassion themselves when it has been needed. He was Jack Woodley, a local young man, on his way to visit friends in Lyndhurst. His nature was naturally kind, but due to the example of his own father whom Jack had seen taking in and sheltering unfortunate individuals from time to time, Jack had learned the rightness of his father's actions and had chosen to think and feel the same way. He did not hesitate to put his own plans to one side when he found a poor creature collapsed at the side of the road. As he considered his next course of action, he remembered that set back in the wood there were a few foresters' cottages. He lifted Ellen easily from her resting place and headed for the cottages.

Ellen did not know how she had come to be laid out on a straw mattress with a warm grey blanket thrown over her. As her eyes opened for the briefest of moments, she saw the covering below her chin, and she thought she saw someone looking at her earnestly standing near her feet. But her eyes were dragged shut and she did not open them again for several hours.

When she felt the blanket again against her neck and chin she opened her eyes more easily, and was able to take in a little more of her surroundings. At the side of where she lay, a small table held a china bowl and spoon, and a small oil lamp which glowed dimly. There were soft shadows in every corner of the room, and in one she thought she noticed a seated figure of a woman with her head bowed. She looked steadily at the person, and then realising that she was being observed, she saw the person rise up onto her feet, and rush to the bed side.

"Lor' the girl is awake ... ma, quick, she's awake, come quickly." The person's high pitched shouts were definitely heard by another as rapid footsteps came into the room, and another person, a smaller woman also came to Ellen's side and touched her face.

"It's my yarrow tea tha's done it, I'd swear by i', though I did 'ave me doubts abou' the lass, but I can see the 'erb 'as worked its magic, ther's no doub'."

"Ma, she *is* be"er isn't she? 'er face 'as colour in 'er cheeks. Oh, ma, I am so 'appy to see her be"er."

"Maggie, she 'as a lot of improving to do. You will need to keep making 'er them 'erbal teas and gruels, and givin' it to 'er regular, or she won' get no be"er."

"I'll do it ma." The girl who had been watching over Ellen since she had been carried here, and had poured tiny quantities of liquid into her parched mouth every twenty minutes or so over the past two days, did not hesitate. Maggie had followed her mother's example in understanding the importance of caring and ministering to sick animals and people. She had had ample opportunity to minister to the former, as the family were involved with many creatures which needed attention from time to time. She had applied a potion made from small amounts of tobacco to cuts and grazes on their goat, their dog, and a forest pony. She had also applied all kinds of treatments to neighbours, following her mother's directions. She had given peppermint tea to provide relief from colic and other dietary difficulties. This had proved to be very effective if used promptly. She had gathered and dried thyme, lavender, rosemary, mint, dill and other herbs. She had experimented with the use of roots, stems and flowers. As for many woodland labouring folk, the only form of medicine was of their own making.

Ellen had been the recipient of yarrow tea, and soothing compresses and bandages soaked in warm cider vinegar applied to her wrists, throat and forehead. The fever had gradually abated, and Ellen weakly turned to her nurses and whispered, gasping for breath, "I don' know who you are, but I am so thankful to you … I know I must have been a nuisance to you … and I know the trouble I must have caused … I'm sorry … sorry." For a moment Maggie smiled but her smile turned to an anxious look at her mother when Ellen once again became silent and her eyes closed.

"It's alrigh' my dear, it's just tiredness, she'll need a lo' of sleep." Maggie's mother held Ellen's wrist for a moment and was gratified to feel a steady pulse and a warm hand that remained still. She turned to Maggie and praised her, "You've done well, Maggie, an' you can come away for a bi' now, as the girl is past the crisis, and will sleep gen'le like for a while. Come away now and have your tea." Maggie and her mother hugged in a close and warm embrace, Maggie laying her cheek on her mother's shoulder. She loved it when her mother praised her, and would do anything to receive her approval.

* * *

Jack Woodley had not hesitated in enlisting the help in the first instance of the Grist family at the first cottage he had come to. The girl showed no sign of life, and his face was anxious as he approached the door, hoping to discover a willingness to assist him which he realised might not be the case. The Grists clearly were poor, but as he had approached the door of the dwelling, a woman had observed him coming with Ellen and had rushed to open the door, and with anxious looks had quickly understood the situation, and had not hesitated but had invited him in immediately.

The cottage was divided in two, the one room being a living area, and the other a sleeping. There was little in the home which indicated that the family had anything in the way of possessions. However, Jack saw the concern in the woman's eyes, and her immediate wish to see what could be done to help the girl. The woman had taken charge. After feeling Ellen's forehead and wrist, she had charged him to lay Ellen on a bed which she had summarily stripped of its blanket and sheet. The woman quickly began to try and remove the saturated clothing on Ellen's shaking body, and seeing this, Jack left and waited for instructions in the adjoining room.

Help was needed, and so Alf Grist was sent to the Robinsons' home across the forest way where help and advice of a medicinal kind might be obtained. Jane Robinson and her daughter Maggie were soon fetched, following Alf to where Ellen lay. With more hands the task of undressing Ellen had been accomplished.

"That's it Maggie, 'elp lift the girl, gen'ly, we 'ave to take off all these we' clothes … tha's it, I'll lif' as well and you take her pe"icoa' down, that's it … Mister!" The woman called to Jack, "Pour some wa'er into a bowl … it 'as to be warm mind, so use some wa'er from the ke"le will yer, and bring it in."

Mrs. Robinson had seen a fever like this many times before, and knew that the young woman would need to have her wet clothing removed, her body chaffed to disperse the chill, and then warm compresses would need to be applied to those parts of her body which displayed the most concerning heat, to try and depress the fever. Only so called qualified men could apply the leaches, and they required paying. And so it was that Ellen was

135

spared bloodletting, but had access to all that the local folk lore could provide. Ellen would have approved of her treatment if she had been aware. The painstakingly careful application of remedies that had prevailed for centuries amongst country people was generously given to her.

Ellen was to discover that her own knowledge in such matters was scant, for later she gained some insight into her own limited understanding during her recovery. She had the opportunity to talk with Maggie, as she shared her views and knowledge of plants and the wondrous properties they possess; Maggie had been given a much fuller and more extensive introduction to the world of botany and biology than herself.

Maggie's knowledge had come from generations of her family being called upon to practice and apply natural medicines and treatments. Their position, as healers in their community fluctuated; at times, her family had been rejected and vilified by their neighbours, but then, in contrast, they were sometimes respected and honoured. Their standing in the forest community was high in circumstances where their treatments resulted in recovery, but there was always an element of unease born of ignorance and uncertainty. Death was often at the door and when poverty was often the underlying cause of misfortune, those who professed to cure and heal would often provide those who grieved with ready scapegoats; superstitions would come to the fore, and prejudices would rise to the surface. This made the Robinson family's position in their community very uncertain and fragile.

Ellen had not understood the circumstances of her rescue nor did she fully understand to whom it was that she owed her gratitude for giving her shelter. Her rescuers had been many. Jack had arrived at the home of Alf and Judith Grist, an older couple who had managed to hold on to their home despite Mr. Grist's advancing years. He had worked all his life as a forester, employed by a forest verderer, Jonathan Matthews, a gentleman of property and influence living in Lyndhurst. His was the responsibility to ensure the numbers of commoners' livestock grazing the forest did not exceed what was acceptable, and he appointed labourers to clear and plant the land and maintain the area under his control. This arrangement ensured the proper care of the land and the necessary animal husbandry was seen to; Alf Grist had worked tirelessly for the Matthew's family over the years.

Judith Grist was the first to see Jack striding towards her front door carrying Ellen in his arms. She had very quickly realised that Ellen was in need of medical treatment and had acted immediately. And so it was that the Robinsons were summoned, and that Maggie was assigned to care for Ellen.

Maggie felt an overwhelming surge of contentment as she ate her tea the day of Ellen's return to complete consciousness. She had had little sleep for two days, but felt the satisfaction of someone who had relieved the suffering of another.

"It will be something I will always remember ... this feeling ... I've done it! Ma was so pleased with me ... I've done something good which no one can remove ... I'm so 'appy ... so 'appy." Maggie had been thinking and feeling the effects of the past two days and could not in the end remain awake. With her bread and jam virtually untouched on the plate, and only a sip of tea consumed, Maggie sank into an exhausted sleep.

* * *

Jack returned to the Grist's house on the journey back to his home three days later, and anxiously enquired as to the health of the patient. It was clear to him that the girl was exhausted and exposed to the unkind elements for far too long. She was a slip of a girl whose situation and background interested him. She had murmured something about her mother and someone called Ada as she was placed on the bed, and he sensed that the girl must have been overwrought with a terrible anxiety for both. He wondered how she could have ended up in such a state, and felt a sense of responsibility towards her.

"So good day, Mrs. Grist, how are you and how's the patient?" Mrs. Grist eyed him seriously, and shook her head. For a moment Jack's heart stopped, "No! ... Not good then?"

"She's no' 'ere Mr. Woodley, she's over at the Robinsons' place. We could na keep 'er 'ere you understand, so when she were strong enough, she walked over to their co"age, an' she's been gone since yesterday."

"Oh, I'm indebted to you Mrs. Grist, I want to thank you for taking her in ... please accept this for your trouble." Jack had lifted a half crown from his inside pocket, and, smiling with relief he quietly placed it in her hand; Judith Grist stood speechless. She stared at the silver coin in her hand and wondered how fortune could have come at such an opportune time. The rent needed paying and here it was with some to spare.

"I accept your kindness sir, and thank yer for i'. Tha' poor child needed some kindness, and it was fortuna'e tha' it was *you* tha' found 'er."

"It is good of you to say so, bu' I must away to visit the girl, as I will need to see her stronger if I am to feel easy about her ... if you understand?"

"Ay, I can see what you are saying sir, bu' do you know which way to go?" She pointed to a group of dwellings further back deeper in the forest beyond some yew trees. Once again Jack smiled at her, offered his hand, and turned away intent on seeing for himself that Ellen's condition had improved.

Jack had considered the plight of the girl he had found and needed an explanation from her which would gratify his natural curiosity; he liked to know the circumstances of people around him. His trade brought him into contact with many different kinds of people. His shoe makers' premises in Brockenhurst were well placed to attract customers, and he had taken total responsibility for the business at the death of his father a year before. Despite being only twenty two, his head was a business one and his father had taught him all the skills he needed, and so Jack had established himself as a fitting successor to his father. His younger brother John had followed in their father's footsteps too, and 'Woodleys' showed no sign of losing its name.

The brothers rubbed up against one another, it is true, Jack being solid and reliable while John was apt to forget his responsibilities, but Jack put this down to his brother's youth. In fact Jack was of the opinion that all men and women had the innate capacity to develop those qualities which would enable them to obtain the greatest rewards in life. He saw these as treasures of a heavenly as well as an earthly kind. Jack's view was that as the Lord recognises every sparrow that falls, so mankind has the potential to do likewise and recognise the worth of all things.

As he led his horse through the trees to the group of cottages he considered his overall impression of the girl he had found, and could not help dwelling on the thought that she may have come from a family of some distinction, as he had noticed that her boots were well made and thickly soled, despite being very worn and filthy. Her clothes too seemed to be better than those worn by those who laboured on the land, and he was led to the idea that she was a girl of good family who had, for some reason unknown to him, run away from home, and was at present striving to subsist on her own with no visible means of support. He felt an overwhelming sadness as he pondered the plight of homeless children, who usually, of necessity, were accommodated within the walls of the nearest Workhouse, places which offered poor living conditions and work that was the most menial. He knew what these establishments inculcated within their victims; he knew something of the hopelessness of those who had resided within them from some who had by some means escaped their walls and then described in awful detail their effects. It dawned on him that this girl was probably destined to be taken into just such a place if her family could not or would not provide for her.

He saw through the branches crossing the path that there were people sitting outside the door of the nearest cottage. The door was open and he could see into the darkness within. Outside the September sun had penetrated the wood, and the people were sat in its gentle warmth, and he saw that the group were deep in discussion and did not hear his coming. As he drew within ten yards of them, they suddenly looked straight at him, and jumped to their feet, that is two of them, while one remained sitting.

He recognised the seated person as the once unconscious girl, who was now wrapped in a woollen shawl and was sat leaning propped against the house wall. She too had looked across at him but had for some reason immediately looked away. He saw that it was Mrs. Robinson and her daughter Maggie who had risen in order to meet him, and they were advancing excitedly towards him. He tied his horse to a sturdy branch and, seeing them race towards him, braced himself for their welcome.

Mrs. Robinson spoke immediately. "Mr. Woodley, 'ow good i' is to see you ... 'ave you 'ad a long ride? Why, it mus' be a three days since you were 'ere … look, see for yourself, she is up and looking brigh'er, is she no'? Would you no' agree, Mr. Woodley?" Before he had time to open his mouth in reply, Maggie addressed him, in the same excited way, rushing up to him and almost running into him.

"Oh, Mr. Woodley, you will never guess, bu' she is now ea'ing stews and all sorts … you can see for yourself, isn't she looking be"er? It's wonderful, isn't it ma? I would never 'ave though' that she could have go' be"er so quickly."

"How do you do Mrs. Robinson … Maggie … yes, yes I can see what you're saying is true. It is remarkable to see the young lady so much recovered, and clearly you have to be thanked for it," and here he gave a special wink at Maggie, who blushed rosily and looked at her mother.

"I believe that Ellen, for Ellen be 'er name, 'as a strong body, sir, for there is no reason why it would have been expected for 'er to 'ave recovered as she 'as … bu' come over and see for yourself." Maggie and her mother jumped on the spot and turned like two children playing hopscotch only just avoiding each other. They moved hastily back to Ellen who looked at them smiling broadly.

She had grown accustomed to the Robinsons' excitable way of expressing themselves. They were enthusiastic about Ellen's journey back to health, about her appetite, about the glow of her cheeks, about the return of the shine to her hair, about her expressions of gratitude and almost anything that Ellen said and did. She assumed that this was there general way of dealing with people, and was amused by their cheerful and over congratulatory ways. She had begun to feel comfortable for the past day living with mother and daughter, for that was their entire family as far as she could make out. Their happy dispositions warmed her, and despite feeling that she must have been a burden to them, they never once did anything to make her feel that they saw her as such.

Maggie was naturally excited by the arrival of the rescuer. Jack did indeed present a romantic figure to an unworldly Maggie. He was tall, had dark hair which fell over his forehead and curled around his ears and a strikingly warm expression which he directed unwaveringly at those who conversed with him. His eyes were wide and green under dark arched brows, but Maggie had noticed at their first meeting that his gaze was full of concern for everyone, and she had felt at that time that he cared equally for her, her mother and Ellen.

Jack had not been able to return since the day that he had carried Ellen to the Grist's home. He had been fully engaged in business, and had had no time to ride back from Lyndhurst; but at the earliest opportunity he had come, and was very happy to see the improvement in the patient. Jack wanted to engage in conversation with Ellen, as there were so many questions unanswered as to her identity and the reasons for her misfortune.

As he sat on the recently vacated bench, he leant towards Ellen and took her hand. Ellen was surprised at this but did not take her hand away. She felt instinctively that Mr. Woodley was a kind man but was a bit overcome with shyness as to what to say to him. She hesitatingly began.

"Mr. Woodley, I know I 'ave you to thank for everything that 'as 'appened over the past few days. I was in a very bad way, and you did something which I will always be grateful for … you brought me to these kind people who 'ave taken me in, and treated me so well." Ellen looked at Mrs. Robinson who was smiling and nudging Maggie.

"I understand your name is Ellen, and I want to tell you that I am also grateful that I was able to assist you." Jack continued holding Ellen's hand, and looked at her in a questioning way. Ellen immediately understood this and replied, "You are wondering 'ow I came to be in the middle of the forest all alone, and I feel tha' I should explain … it is a long story, but for the moment maybe I should say that I was on my way to my grandparents in Lymington, but because of a lack of nourishment and 'aving walked a considerable distance, I was overcome with the cold and we', … and found that I could not go another step." Ellen had looked at Jack intently, and could see that he was giving her his full attention. She sadly realised that this man was more willing to help her than her own brother had been, and she felt confused.

She understood that family relationships could be fragile as hers had been with her father, but her longing for her mother and Agnes and sometimes Hannah had proved to her that these relationships could well prove to be the strongest and the most likely to endure.

Jack listened to Ellen and knew there was a lot that she was not telling him, but he judged that this was because she was very much a child and surrounded by adults, and would find it difficult to tell her whole story without considerable prompting. Jack felt kindly towards her. She had spoken quietly and with a gentle intonation. He thought that probably she felt shy of him because he had been the one to rescue her.

"Ellen, I feel that your journey to your grandparents is something that I might be able to assist you in, once you are well enough of course." Jack hesitated and looked closely at Ellen's eyes, as he could see that her expression had changed and she was feeling a strong emotion; he could only imagine the cause of it.

Ellen had once again averted her gaze; she had suddenly felt her eyes fill with tears, and then a strong feeling in her breast which she knew was due to this man's thoughtfulness and willingness to ensure that she was safely placed with her family, but she still felt so weak and afraid.

"Ellen, I will return in a few days, and we'll talk some more."

"Mr. Woodley, sir, I find it 'ard to understand why you are so willing to 'elp me. Forgive me, but your kindness is more than I 'ave ever known … but please know that I thank you with all my 'eart … and …Mr Woodley …,'" Ellen's hold on Jack's hand had tightened, but now she covered her mouth with her other hand and tried to dispel an overpowering feeling of relief and of gratitude which were compelling her to break down and weep uncontrollably. She could not prevent a sharp inhalation of breath followed by a series of deep sobs which wrenched Jack's heart.

It was Mrs. Robinson who then came and who embraced Ellen in a firm hold, and reassured her that, "It's alrigh' lass, yes, yes, you'll be feelin' be"er for a cry." Ellen instantly became aware of her foolish behaviour in front of comparative strangers and sniffing and wiping her eyes with her sleeve felt ashamed, and extricated herself from the woman's embrace. She sat very straight with her head bowed and became silent. Jack had watched the drama and realised that Ellen needed more time to get well, and was ready to acknowledge this.

"Ellen, I will leave you now, and will return when next I'm passing … then perhaps we can talk about your journey to Lymington and make a plan."

"Oh yes, Mr. Woodley, I will be well soon I am sure, and will be ready to make the journey … thank you, thank you, sir," and Ellen bravely summoned up a wan smile. She looked at her other benefactors and felt safe and content, and was reassured that she would be with her grandparents very soon.

As Jack stood to leave, he looked at each of the women in turn, and then he took each of their hands one after the other, and bowed his head slightly. The forest women were overcome and smiled and giggled. Ellen felt warmed by Mr. Woodley's deference and show of respect. She had seen her father behave in like manner when he was bidding farewell to the genteel women from whom he had received commissions. The memory upset her for a moment, and she realised once again that people were unpredictable and could not be trusted. Outwardly they might be kind and respectful, but inwardly their feelings and thoughts might well be unkind, judgemental or even vicious. Her lack of trust would act as her protection she decided, and so Ellen withdrew her warm smile and with a solemn face waved goodbye to Mr. Woodley.

The family had been generously paid for their trouble. It was clear to Jack that Mr. Robinson was no longer present in the household; that mother and daughter were surviving alone. He was therefore more generous than he would otherwise have been, and went away hoping that Ellen would be much improved by his next visit.

The days passed and Ellen's condition remained much the same. Occasionally she had experienced painful bouts of indigestion after meals, but had put this down to being undernourished for months. Maggie and her mother thought that this was probably true, and had given her lighter meals of mostly vegetables and soups. Ellen then experienced headaches, usually in the mornings, and felt wretched. It was after a meal in the middle of the day that she struggled with the most dreadful pain behind her eyes, and immediately felt very sick; she brought the whole

145

meal back up, and was quickly returned to bed. As she lay with the blanket over her to shut out the light, she felt even more weak and afraid than when she had been in the dreadful Gibson household. She knew that, for some inextricable reason, she was getting sicker and now had become, she believed, entirely at the mercy of her carers.

Four

'Dearest, bury me
Under that holy oke, or Gospel tree
Where, though see'st not, though may'st
think upon
Me ...'

The Lambourn household continued in just the same way after Christmas as it had before. The family was wrapped in a restrictive cocoon-like structure woven by Mary and her husband, who neither showed any inclination to involve themselves in the domestic arrangements of the household, but who expected the younger members to do all that was required. Agnes recognised that this represented a change in her father as when her mother was alive she had seen him spending time with her as she went about her domestic activities. She remembered him helping her string up bunches of lavender in the pantry. She also recollected her father regularly removing the beef from the oven and basting it at the kitchen table. Oh yes, there were so many times when he had quietly stood at her mother's elbow and offered his assistance. Agnes now saw what her parents had possessed in their relationship which was absent in her father's relationship with Mary.

Mary's main concern at this time was the birthday party to be held at the Grange at the end of January. Domestic tasks were not her interest. There was no need, as she had a readymade family who provided the work force. Hannah never tired of applying herself to these tasks. Agnes was a capable assistant and would mind the smaller children whenever it was required.

Agnes' education had virtually ended. She could not go to school when the younger ones, particularly George, needed attention. So she stayed at home and cared for him, sadly wondering what she could do to resume her musical education. She cared little for the requirements of school of reading, arithmetic, sewing and knitting. She wanted to sing, to sing so that the whole world would hear her! She had hoped that somehow and in some way opportunities would come her way to perform, but two weeks had passed since Christmas, and no one, not even Mr Smith had mentioned anything remotely connected with music.

She knew that occasionally the village hall played host to entertainers and that there were sometimes evening concerts put together by local people. She wondered how she could get involved but being young and inexperienced as to the ways of the world had no idea. Her mind was drawn to this predicament quite regularly and she became increasingly bored and frustrated with her life. Hannah had noticed Agnes's preoccupation, and hoped she wasn't still worrying about Ellen.

"Aggie, 'elp me get the washin' in off the line, would you?" Their conversation was normally restricted to their work, but Hannah went on, "I've been wonderin' if there is anything botherin' you, Aggie, you seem to be rather sad … is it you're missin' Ellen?"

"Oh 'annah," Agnes paused and looked at her capable and rather emotionally distant sister, "I don't really know what's botherin' me 'cept I need to learn some more singin' … I 'oped that Mr Smith would go on teachin' me, bu' that 'asn't 'appened, and I feel sort of lost …"

"Why don't you ask Mr Smith for more lessons? It could be that 'e would be pleased to continue with you, and maybe 'e would find you a performance now and again …" Hannah could see Agnes brighten as she spoke, but a cloud crossed her features as she replied, "I don' think I can speak to Mr Smith … he was so kind before, but surely 'e would have said somethin' if 'e 'ad the time or inclination."

"No, Aggie, sometimes we 'ave to make our desires known. There's no point in staying silent, you 'ave to speak to 'im if it matters so much to you."   Agnes felt that Hannah, her sensible sister, was telling her what she needed to do, and she vowed that she would see Mr Smith at the first opportunity. Agnes felt grateful to her sister and took her hands and promptly kissed one. Hannah was surprised at Agnes's action, and smiled at her demonstrative and exaggerated ways. Maybe Agnes was destined to move in creative circles where hand kissing and other conspicuous shows of affection would be commonplace.

Agnes was very different from herself she well knew. The only person she felt comfortable touching was Frederick, who at this moment was displaying the usual antics of a one year old, crawling around her feet. She bent to pick him up, cuddled him close, and walked with him and Agnes into the garden.

The sisters, absorbed by the simple task of unpegging and folding the stiff and dry clothing and linen paid no more attention to one another except to assist one another in the tidying of the bed linen. Frederick had been placed on the grass, and Hannah watched her child as she completed the task. As she considered Agnes's plight, she realised that she herself wasn't unhappy. Each day, thankfully, did not bring any terrors or horrors. She felt content, and despite being only nineteen, had no ambitions to urge her in to a different way of life. She recognised that Agnes was different, and would not be content until she had escaped into a world, which she surmised, was in Agnes's dreams far more colourful, vibrant and fulfilling than her present one.

Agnes was absorbed by her task superficially as many are who perform physical labours, but she did assume a mental state in which she imagined herself dressed in a pastel silk dress acknowledging the applause of a crowd of adoring people. She felt lighter and stronger as she removed the last of the clothes from the line, and lifting the linen basket high above her head, she sang an improvised tune to Frederick, "Come with me my Freddie my dear, follow me, follow me and do not fear." She laughed as she saw the child turn on his knees and watch her skipping away. He chuckled and was drawn to follow her. Agnes led the way in a dance, Frederick's small body slithered like a snail over the grass behind her, and quietly watchful and smiling, Hannah returned to the house last of all.

The preparations for the party were in full flow. Every day since Christmas Mary had raised the subject, and everyone except Thomas had been happy to share her enthusiasm for the forthcoming event. The apparel for the occasion was what preoccupied Mary. She had decided not to consider the possibility that Thomas would refuse to go. She made preparations, looking at every ribbon and trimming in the High Street, talking with the Burnett sisters who were the village experts in female fashion and owners of the only shop in Botley specialising in female dress and haberdashery, and meticulously planned her own, Hannah's and Agnes's dresses and hair designs.

She had not completely approved of the dress which Thomas had given her for Christmas. She had not warmed to the colour, and was determined to have a second dress, one which was entirely to her own specifications. Hannah, with her encouragement, had tried on the russet dress and it had, Mary assured her, entirely flattered her and would do very well at the party.

The dark evenings were not conducive to comparing shades and fabrics nor to the careful, minute stitching required. Mary's dress was taking shape during the day. Mary had encouraged Hannah to take this on, with the advice and help of her husband. The pattern had been provided by the Burnetts, but the fabric, a turquoise shade of organza had been bought by Thomas when he had visited a Southampton warehouse. He had loved the material because he knew that his late wife would have admired it. He had cut out the dress, and guided Hannah step by step in its sewing. The lining he had also chosen, a soft, fine, white silk material which would set the organza off beautifully, allowing it to fall and flow naturally. He realised that he was doing this for his late wife, because he had never made her an evening gown, and wished that he had.

Mary would go to the party in Hannah's dress. Agnes was not provided with a new dress, as the family's resources did not stretch that far. Instead, her best dress, made of pale blue cotton, was given fresh trimmings of lace and ribbon, and she tried to be satisfied with what she had. Agnes found this difficult as she jealously viewed Mary's dress as it came into fruition.

She was present when Mary had her final fitting. Thomas was satisfied. Mary shone as she turned, postured and posed. The gown reflected light, and shimmered in a soft haze of blues and greens. Mary, although not tall, seemed to possess an elegance wearing the dress which had not been present before. Her skin appeared whiter, more luminous and softer against the beauty of the fabric. Her blue eyes seemed more deep and translucent and had a sparkle which Thomas noticed.

"What do you think Thomas? Will you be ashamed of me do you think? Will you be proud to stand up with me in a dance? Thomas, tell me ..." Mary, turning excitedly around, and revealing the full train of the dress, had suddenly realised that she had once again caught her husband's attention, just as she had before their marriage. Thomas had remembered why he had married Mary as he examined her in the dress. She did look entirely feminine and alluring. He did not see her in this way for long however, as his mind quickly reverted to Hannah, and how she would have been utterly beautiful in the dress. He reflected regretfully that her amenability, her purity of character and inner beauty would always have outshone Mary.

He realised awkwardly that Mary was expecting his reply, and looking at her with as much affection as he could manage he assured her that the dress suited her perfectly and that she looked lovely. Although Agnes had desired a dress just like Mary's, she together with Hannah looked at Mary with the uncritical gaze of children. Despite Mary's preoccupation with herself, and her unwillingness to play any part in the maintenance of the home, which might have caused them to feel a certain amount of resentment, they viewed Mary at this time as a woman who had at last achieved something of value, and they wanted to applaud her. She appeared triumphantly better than her surroundings. Hannah who had sewn the dress tirelessly over the past three weeks had not expected any recognition. She was satisfied within herself that the dress was well made and a significant achievement. Thomas was also pleased that his eldest daughter had followed his instructions, had been obedient to his every word and had done well.

"Hannah, you show a talent for dress making. Your mother could make somethin' out of nothin' you know. Your work shows you 'ave a good eye and 'and." Thomas moved across to Hannah and touched her under the chin, a slow smile lifting his usually long, expressionless and dour face. Thomas's action diverted attention from Mary, as everyone in the room was watching him and Hannah; their gaze was totally fixed on one another. Mary's expression fell. Immediately her temper rose, and she did not hesitate to express the ever present under current of resentment and envy which she possessed in relation to her step daughter Hannah.

"Oh, I see 'ow it is, 'ow you dote on your daughter ... and don' spare a though' for me your wife, *your wife* ... everyone comes before me in this 'ouse, I could be wrapped in ... gold leaf and you would take no notice ... you don' care a button abou' me ...." Mary stood grimly gripping the back of a chair, shaking so much that the dress seemed alive. Her round face was distorted as her mouth twisted; her words ripped across the still space in the room. No one moved. Mary swept angrily out of the room, her movements emphasised by the fabric of her dress no longer reflecting grace and ease but irregular and ungainly spasms. Mary could be heard stamping up the stairs and into the bedroom above.

Hannah and Agnes waited to see how their father would react. Mary had had outbursts before. Sometimes the family had not known why Mary had shouted at their father, and were unaware of anything that might have caused her displeasure. Usually Thomas tried to ignore Mary's outbursts, and did not respond. He never looked at her during her furious accusations. He seemed to be simply waiting for the storm to pass, and this he did now.

153

Hannah had thought for some time that her father was unhappy. Agnes childishly looked on and wondered about the struggle between Mary and her father. Their relationship appeared to be far from mutually satisfying, and she desperately wanted to show loyalty to her father but wasn't sure how. She decided to follow Hannah's lead; she looked at her father and smiled, seeing his sadness and confusion as he wiped his brow and pushed back his hair with both his hands. He shook his head, and said nothing.

He was always angered by Mary's fault finding. He chose to keep this anger inside, but he knew there were times in the past when he couldn't, and he was then overcome and appalled by the force of his feelings. It was at these times, before Mary came on the scene, that Ellen had been the victim of his fury. Since her departure, he had had to use other ways of diminishing his anger, and his guilt. He would leave the house and walk for an hour or so, or he would visit the inn and have a jar or two of beer.

He saw his marriage as something which needed to be under his control, but Mary had always been able to command and disparage him and this he could not accept. He wondered why this should have occurred, but reflected that he had been weak in the early days of their marriage. He had wanted her so intensely, and she had recognised this and used it to her advantage. He had been rejected regularly. He could not forgive her for that, and he would punish her. He would find ways to get back at her, and he would rule her, he would control her. His plan was simple, and he would have Mary pleading with him for forgiveness.

He shrugged, picked up some clothing which was folded on the table and hurriedly left the room heading for his appointment at the parsonage. The Reverend had commissioned a black velvet evening coat and breeches, for the Grange party and the final fitting had been arranged for today. Mary had left his thoughts by the time he stepped out of the house.

Thomas did take his wife and two older daughters to the Grange for Sir Russell Turner's party, but did it with a degree of churlishness which was not missed by them. He had made some effort with his own appearance however, and had demonstrated some pride in his position in the community. He wore evening dress, a white silk cravat, a black waistcoat sporting silver trimmed buttons and his silver chained pocket watch, an elegantly fitted longer black dress coat and trousers made of the finest worsted cloth. His tall and broad shouldered figure was noticed by all those who came to the Grange. His appearance could not be faulted, and several remarks were made about Thomas Lambourn the tailor, who, they said, was thinking 'well above his situation'. Thomas was aware of the attention and did not mind; he was gratified. Perhaps the party was not going to be so unrewarding after all.

The family were greeted by Sir Russell himself, and Hannah was not surprised to see an awkwardness and curtness between him and her father which she had been prepared for. She had known that her father's distrust of Sir Russell Turner had not wavered, and had believed that it was born of her demise while in service at the Grange. Her father had not tailored for the family since, and had apparently removed himself from any contact with them up until now.

The house was alight with music. Agnes was immediately spellbound. She viewed the company, and envied the dancers who drifted by, the couples swirling in one another's arms and moving as one. She examined the room where she stood for the first time. It was high-ceilinged and of square proportions, providing ample room for dancing as the furniture had been moved to the perimeter. There were some large paintings of fashionable gentlemen and ladies presumably portraits of the family but Agnes recognised none of them. They were a series of vaguely smiling faces which peered down from the walls, but Emily thought they were colourless and lifeless. The colours of the women's dresses were far more worthy of her attention. She loved the soft spring colours of primrose and lilac. But her attention was drawn to an elegant woman, dark and tall, wearing a dress of the deepest green. She supposed it to be a taffeta material, as it was full skirted and fell firmly to the woman's ankles, but as the woman turned the skirt lifted into a bell like shape, and even the train almost left the floor; at the front the woman's ankles and calves were on full view. Agnes watched mesmerised and wondered if the woman knew that her legs were exposed.

She envied the woman, as she could see that the company were watching her, and the woman was clearly enjoying the attention. As she swirled with her partner she smiled and laughed, and clearly showed everyone her enjoyment. Agnes realised that the woman was dancing with Mr. Turner's older son, James, whose youthful energy was well matched to the woman's unconventional conduct and dress. He was laughing too.

The dance ended, and the couples moved to the edge of the dance floor while others drifted towards the salon doors, beyond which refreshments were to be found. Agnes knew that she would not be dancing, because of her age. Indeed, she had not expected to attend the party but had discovered that the invitation to Ellen had been diverted to herself, and she was pleased. The fact she would not be allowed to dance she viewed as a blessing, as she had never danced except at an occasional country dance at the village hall or on the village Green at the time of a festival. These occasions were very different from this situation. The three piece orchestra struck up again, and she felt a touch on her elbow. She looked and realised a young man had come up to her from behind holding a glass, which was offered to her.

"Alfred Turner, I think you are Agnes, Agnes Lambourn, am I right?"

"Yes, sir."

"Alfred please."

"Thank you … for the drink … 'ow do you come to know my name?" Agnes was unsettled by Alfred's approach. She looked at him, and noticed he was impeccably dressed very much as a true gentleman would be. She knew he was of a considerably higher standing than her and wondered why he had approached her. She imagined he was quite a few years older than her and was surprised that he should even notice her.

Thomas, who had been in conversation with Sir Russell's sister, Lady Elizabeth, noticed Agnes talking with Alfred and quickly excused himself. His paternal instincts were alerted, and he threaded his way to where she stood. He did not know where Mary had gone or Hannah, but Agnes was his first concern.

The room had become very crowded. The village tradesmen and craftsmen, their wives and older children were all in attendance by now, as well as the local gentry who counted themselves above the village storekeepers and stood apart from them. The music grew louder, and Thomas struggled to see Agnes. He looked to where he had first seen her, but she was no longer there.

Agnes had been encouraged to accompany Alfred to visit the music room. Alfred had disclosed how he had come to know of her, that he had enjoyed her performance at Christmas, and had wondered when he would have the pleasure of hearing her again. Agnes had innocently gone with him having enjoyed his compliments but had no idea of the impropriety of her actions. The music room contained a very large piano, standing dark and imposing at the far end of the room. Alfred sat at the instrument and invited her to sit beside him. He had some knowledge of playing, and began to pick out a piece by Mendelssohn, one of his Songs without Words. Emily watched his fingers nimbly lift and fall on the keyboard. She looked at his face, and realised that he was looking at her, and blushed as a consequence. She moved away from him, as she suddenly felt a little uncomfortable in such close proximity to someone she hardly knew, and a young man too. She was unsure as to what to do, but decided to return to the party, with a quick word of thanks to Alfred.

"Thank you, it is a fine pianoforte, I should be returning to my father and Mary." All was said without pause with her words tumbling over each other. She did not wait for a reply, but rose and swiftly headed for the door. Alfred reached out and caught her skirt and gripped it as she rose. She found that she could not move, and her unease intensified.

"What is it? Let go of my skirt ..." What was he doing grabbing her in such a way? She looked at his face a second time, and saw that he was enjoying himself. He was grinning and tugging at her dress, and clearly had no intention of letting go. Agnes pulled away from him as hard as she could with the result that the ribbon sewn to the waistband began to tear, and she was afraid that the seam underneath would split.

"Let go, let go, let ... *please.*" Agnes pleaded but she would never have known if Alfred would have let her go or not, because as she spoke, the door swung open and her father stood looking at her. She did not feel Alfred let go of her, but he did so, as his enjoyable game was clearly over at the arrival of the father. So she ran to Thomas and took his hand, looking up into his face with a heart full of gratitude.

Agnes was such a child, Thomas thought. She had changed very little during the past five years. She had been protected and kept close at home. He knew that she would be lovely like her mother. Her hair was the colour of ripening wheat. Her smile was cautious but endearing. Her expression always seemed to emanate an even temper and warmth. All these things were plainly visible but Thomas was afraid for this child who could, he believed, attract all kinds of attention. He already knew this to be true as it was happening now; and apparently Agnes was devoid of the intelligence, sense and skill to manage this kind of unwanted attention and manipulative advance.

Thomas chose not to speak to Alfred, but gave him a curt dismissive nod of the head, and holding Agnes close to him turned abruptly and delivered her in to the next room. Agnes looked into his face as they left, and found it to be unsmiling. He revealed nothing in his expression. She felt that he might be angry with her, for leaving the party with a member of the Turner family.

"My dear Agnes, you should be aware that there are folk here who would wish to damage our family's reputation. We need to be on our guard, you see, and do nothing which might incur negative comment … you goin' in there with Master Alfred", Thomas turned to look back to the music room door, "might be seen by some as inappropriate, and you would be condemned along with the rest of your family. I am only poin'ing this out as you are clearly unaware of the dangers of society. I should have realised that you would be ignorant of such things". Thomas paused for a moment and glanced momentarily at Agnes, who stood with her head turned away from him, so that he could not view her expression. "Look at me, Agnes ... You will remain with Hannah for the rest of the evening, is that understood?"

"Yes, pa, yes."

Entering the crowded room with her father was noticed by several onlookers. The women in particular had become astute in their perceptions having many years of practice. A small market town has little in the way of daily excitements excepting those small occurrences which are noticed and exaggerated by local descriptions and conversations. These are brought about by keen observation, in circumstances where there is time to linger and move to observe in close proximity. A single villager may be in a position to record the finest details of incidents which would in larger societies not merit a cursory glance. It was for this reason that Agnes's flushed cheeks were noticed, her tear stained lashes, her drooping chin and her twisted dress. Similarly, Thomas' demeanour was noted as austere and cold, with a definite grasp of his young daughter which was neither amiable nor gentle. Something very interesting was occurring, and the ladies of the company were, without hesitation, speculating as to what this might be.

Alfred was left to stew in his own juices, feeling as usual the injustice of what had happened, and he quickly began to plot how to right the wrong done to him.

Mary enjoyed the feeling of being noticed at the party. She had had conversations with people of rank, and had enjoyed the experience. A farm labourer's daughter had arrived and had accredited herself well. She felt triumphant, knowing that her dress was equal to those of the most fashionable women present. She had smiled excessively, and had danced with her husband and others displaying a natural lightness of foot and had enjoyed the experience thoroughly.

"Mrs. Lambourn, you have danced us off our feet! Where did you acquire such energy and effortlessness?" Colonel Matthew Turner stooped over Mary's hand at the conclusion of an energetic reel. Mary had been gratified by his attentions, as he was a striking figure in his extravagantly embellished red regimental dress, and naturally held a position of importance in society.

"Colonel, I think my feet have been unused to dancing for some considerable time, but they are making up for it, it seems." Mary was breathless, and glowed with the compliment. She felt that all eyes were on her. She was right in one respect. Her husband had not removed his gaze from her throughout her dance with the Colonel, and slowly made his way to her side at the conclusion of the dance.

At Thomas's approach, the Colonel's demeanour changed. He did not look Thomas in the eye, abruptly bowed and turned, leaving Mary gasping at his sudden departure. What was happening? Her husband was intent on spoiling her enjoyment it would seem.

"Thomas, I am in much need of refreshment, would you be kind enough to escort me in to the salon"? Thomas wanted to laugh out loud. His wife was talking to him as if she had suddenly become a lady. What a fool she was to imagine a dance with a few of the gentry would make her so. His belief that he had married a fool had been confirmed on numerous occasions. She provoked him and irritated him and filled him with a strong desire to silence her. This feeling had also existed with Ellen, and he knew that she could not stay close to him and would have to go away; but he could not solve this problem with his wife in the same way. Some other plan was needed.

Agnes weakly stood beside Hannah watching the dancers and taking very little in. She felt very small indeed, and wished for the time when she could go home.

"What are we doing 'ere 'annah? The purpose of our being 'ere is to be very much unnoticed don' you think? No one to talk to and no one to show any interest in us ... just to watch and wait for the end ... why do I feel so disappointed 'annah?"

"Wha' did you think would 'appen Aggie, knowing that I was once a servan' in this 'ouse, and you the daughter of a tailor who refuses to accept Sir Russell's patronage? I wonder why we were even invi'ed, as there doesn't appear to be any reason for it ... unless Sir Russell is trying to mend the breach, bu' why would 'e wish to do tha'? I've learn' from what's 'appened with Frederick tha' there are things which are far from clear, even though we may think that we understand wha' is 'appening around us ... and we allow our feelings to mould our thoughts. I don' know the answers to your questions Aggie; the only thing I know is we need to find 'appiness where we can. Remember what mother wan'ed for us. She would say 'walk your chosen path, and make sure there is some dappled sunshine. Then the rays of the sun will sometimes light your way, but not always because life has many shadows'. Maybe this is a time of shadows for you Aggie, but look for a sunny spot ..."

Agnes listened to Hannah wondering about the sunny spots of her life, and realised that there had been considerable joy in her life recently because of her love of music.

"Mother wanted us to be 'appy didn't she? I would feel differently if she was 'ere. I would be content just to be with 'er".

"Maybe that's what's wrong with your chosen path, something tha' you will just need time to put right. You were 'appy to walk alongside ma, her path was yours, and now you find that there is no path because ma is gone and her path with 'er. Do you see what I mean? It was easier for me, I 'ad left and made my own way. But I made a mistake, I thought that another person wanted me on his path, and I though' that in time our footsteps would be in harmony. We would plough the same field, and sow the same seeds together. And our 'arvest would be shared and enjoyed. A shadow has passed over me too tonight. Maybe that's why we are 'ere, to see a new path, to recognise that the path we are on is leading nowhere ..."

Hannah placed her hand softly on Agnes's shoulder. Agnes felt Hannah's warmth and leant against her. As she had sought to obscure the terrible loss of her mother by pretending that her ma was still beside her, she discovered that she had a true and kind sister who was here, now, and who could offer a gentle example.

The sisters had drawn closer in an unguarded moment, and Agnes feeling so changed looked again at the assembled company and saw things very differently. The music was merry, the room decorative and bright. As she gazed around from Hannah's side, she found a gaze fixed upon her, a look which enveloped her. Alfred watched her unwavering from a distance and was fixed in his desire to have Agnes near him.

* * *

In many people's eyes, the New Forest was now at its most beautiful, possessing burnished and tinged carpets and canopies, the latter becoming the former as winter drew closer and the life giving sap began to withdraw from the furthermost branches and twigs of oak and beech. As Jack rode towards the Robinson cottage at the beginning of November, he was only faintly aware of the gorgeous patchwork of terracotta and gold which surrounded him. His thoughts were focussed entirely on his fears which were centred on Ellen. She had been at the cottage for nearly six weeks, and despite showing an improvement the first time he had visited, her health had since then deteriorated, then improved illogically and then once again worsened.

If she was no better this time, he had made the decision to consult with the apothecary; his feelings of personal responsibility towards Ellen had not abated and he would not disown what had begun on that cold and wet September morning. He had recognised his duty then, and had been spurred on since by his father's unshakable example. His father would not have abandoned any soul in need of his charity.

The cottage showed no sign of life as he approached. It was early morning and a Sunday, and so he hesitated to wake a sleeping household, but he was so anxious to see Ellen that he dismounted and with a strong sense of urgency immediately approached the door. The picture he held in his mind from his last visit had remained fixed and concerning as he recollected the sight of Ellen, curled up in bed, but showing no inclination to talk or even open her eyes. She had dark shadows beneath her eyes, and her face showed no sign of healthy colour, being tinged with grey. The veins around her eyes and forehead stood out in an ugly way, and when he touched her cheek it was wet and cold. He was utterly dismayed to see her health deteriorate in such a way, and had talked anxiously to Mrs. Robinson, who assured him that although the fever had returned, Ellen's body was fighting it and would require further administrations which she and Maggie could provide.

The women were adamant that Ellen would greatly improve by the time he saw her next, and he felt some reassurance, but on his departure, after giving them a further six shillings, he had remembered that they had said the same thing once before when Ellen's health had deteriorated, and sure enough she had improved; but the same circumstance had come about once again, and Jack felt uneasy.

As usual when he visited Ellen he was on his way to Lyndhurst to visit his friend, and he thought that he would share his concerns with him. He had never mentioned Ellen to Charles before because he had imagined that his contact with her would be short lived and that his involvement would be brief. Now he needed to share his concerns with his closest friend. Charles was a shoe maker and repairer like himself. Their fathers had worked in partnership in Lyndhurst and had successfully developed and expanded their business, establishing another premises in Brockenhurst which had been run by the Woodleys.

Charles had remained with his father in Lyndhurst. His father continued to assist but had encouraged Charles to take on a fuller responsibility for the business, and this he had done. Both young men had learnt their trade from their fathers, and were engrossed with their labours. Both possessed the hands and eyes to design, cut, shape, sew and assemble leather foot wear in all its varieties. Their craft required a full knowledge of the materials, an expert understanding of the machines and tools required and a perceptive understanding of what each of their customers required.

Jack knew that Charles loved to speculate on the characteristics of humans whose shoes came into his possession for repair. He would remark on the evidences presented, on the chosen style, the apparent wear and the way the shoes had moulded themselves to the individual's foot. It was a game he played with his father, and they would amuse themselves in this way, as they worked.

"This is a dainty shoe, judging by the fineness of the uppers, expensive too … a lady of respectability no doubt who has a problem with a bunion on her left foot caused by ill-fitting shoes when she was a child. Clearly this shoe belongs to a lady who has not always enjoyed the privileges of wealth … her father struggled as she grew up, and could not afford to see that his children were correctly shod … am I right father? I think perhaps these shoes belong to an older woman who is now well married as there is very little wear on the soles and yet they are to be repaired with new leather soles." Charles would pause and catch his father's eye, who would bless him with a twinkle and a smile, and Charles would know that his observations were being correctly interpreted.

"Really, son you should be one of those detectives … 'ow you can fathom out so much from a shoe is beyond me!"

Jack had arrived in Lyndhurst by nine thirty, and witnessed the arrival of worshippers at the magnificent parish church at the summit of the High Street. He hoped he could get to the shop Coleman and Woodley's before the family departed for church. He knew the family well enough to know that that would be their destination. The business was at the other end of the High Street, and as he rode down it, he looked intently to either side to ensure that he would see the family if they were on their way. He did observe Charles with his parents and younger sister Sophie walking briskly in the distance past the shop fronts on the right, and called and waved to them as he approached. Charles and his father both waved back at him, and he quickly dismounted and turned to walk with them.

"Good morning Mr Coleman, Mrs Coleman, Sophie!" Jack reached forward and shook their hands warmly raising his hat, "I

166

hope you are well," Charles took his hand and put his other arm across his shoulders.

"We are, as you can see, dear boy", Benjamin Coleman was effusive in his compliments to his wife, "Mrs Coleman is looking particularly lovely as you can see, and is positively blooming you know." He was a smart and stout gentleman who possessed very short legs and a full head of silver hair who enjoyed complimenting his wife because he knew well that she took great trouble and some expense in looking her best. Mrs. Maria Coleman's plump cheeks lifted in a broad smile. She had always been content, very happy in her marriage, and so to be at the side of her husband who had been a wonderful provider to her and her three children.

Widowed at an early age, Benjamin had courted her as if she was the only woman in the world for him, and had accepted her family as his own. She was indebted to him but recognised that he had to be in some way indebted to her. She hadn't fully worked out what he gained from their relationship, except that she was reasonably attractive, a good cook, enjoyed gardening and making the home a pleasant place to be, and she tried to be an attentive and caring wife and mother. Yes, that was it.

She had made the decision early on that once she was married to Mr Coleman she would place him above her children, that if there was anything to discuss in relation to them, and if she found herself at odds with him, she would not oppose him but ask him to think about her opinion. She had found that as time passed, he would compromise and sometimes change his view to be more in line with her, and this had led to happy outcomes. She felt she was truly blessed and looked to the Lord as the 'fount of every blessing'.

She was pleased to see Jack as she had secretly hoped that he would marry one of her daughters. Sophie was the more obvious choice as she was prettier, but rather younger than Jack, and it seemed to her that he only viewed her as a younger sister. Charlotte, being that much older, might be a better partner for Jack, but she was miles away in service, doing very well, and was happily settled. In her last letter she had mentioned a young man on the gardening staff who had accompanied her on a walk after church. It sounded as if Charlotte had liked him and enjoyed his company. She had had little opportunity to find a husband up until now. Maybe this young man would be the special man in Charlotte's life.

Jack walked with Charles, and as Charles' arm had been flung around his shoulders, their heads almost touched, and Jack was able to speak in a confidential tone to him.

"Charles, I do have something I wish to discuss with you and that's why I have come ... it is something which has been plaguing my mind and I have not had an opportunity to discuss it with anyone. This is not the time or the place, but," Jack brought his lips close to Charles' ear, and whispered, "It is of paramount importance that you speak of it to no one, I hope you understand me." Jack did not fully understand himself why he had asked for secrecy and complete confidence. Perhaps it was a wish he had to protect Ellen from further misadventure. He did not know for sure, but only that he wished that his closest friend would be the sole recipient of his news, and that only he would be party to what to do next. At the back of his mind he felt something ominous, something deeply unpleasant, but knew that he was too close to what was happening to see things clearly.

Charles drew away slightly so that he could look into Jack's face.

"Of course, Jack, I hope that this is not as serious as you are making it sound ... is it something to do with me ... or the business?"

"No not at all, a personal matter you understand, which is tormenting me ... after church perhaps, we could go somewhere quiet, and not cause anyone to suspect that there is anything amiss." Charles knew Jack as well as a close brother, and realised that he was feeling very anxious about something, something personal, and responded cheerfully, "Yes, that sounds reasonable, we can say we are visiting Grandma Whitcher, and you can tell me all about it on the way ... how does that sound?"

Jack felt relieved that Charles had responded so positively. He had realised how little he had shared with Charles and had wondered if he would take him seriously. In fact Charles's nature was drawn to the very fact that Jack had not wanted to discuss his life with him in recent years. Their relationship had been firmly based on family and business, and so, when Jack divulged something of a serious nature to him, he was quick to see that Jack needed his opinion, and was happy to listen and give it.

Church was interminably long for Jack. He could not rest until he had divulged the cause of his uneasiness to Charles. Jack tried not to leave the church over hurriedly, and lingered with the family acknowledging one or two mutual friends. They informed Mr and Mrs Coleman that they were to pay their respects to Mrs Coleman's elderly mother, Mrs Whitcher, and knew this would be approved of. Jack gathered his horse and walking beside Charles tried to broach his uneasiness in regard to Ellen.

As they walked, Charles listened gravely. Every now and again he stopped to ask a question or to repeat back what he had heard. When Jack had finished, Charles felt that he would need to visit the Robinsons and see for himself what sounded to him to be a very serious situation.

He had pieced together, based on the information already given to him, two or possibly three theories of what was happening. He would need to question the women caring for Ellen to get to the truth, and this he offered to do at the earliest opportunity. He felt that there was something in what Jack was telling him which had truly unsettled him, just as it had disturbed Jack.

* * *

Grandma Whitcher was a lonely soul who was very gratified when visitors came to call. She had a particular fondness for her grandson Charles, whose visits were less regular than they had been when he was a boy. She lived on the outskirts of the town on the road to Ashurst, and had remained in her brick built cottage for the past thirty or so years. Her husband had been part of the business community in Lyndhurst, and had prospered. His interest lay in farming and in locally produced food, which had begun when he had worked for the town grocer as a boy, delivering orders and serving in the shop. He had gained a thorough knowledge of what lay in the surrounding countryside and had learnt to discern quality in milk products, fruit, vegetables and grain. His application to understanding and evaluating the produce brought its own reward as he was able to suggest and even recommend what was needed for the shop.

The shop expanded, and after twenty years, he joined the owner in partnership. His only daughter Maria had benefited greatly from her father's industry, and had married an up and coming tradesman, attached to her father's firm as an apprentice.

Three babies had followed but tragedy had struck with the early death of her young husband; she had returned to the red brick cottage where she had been raised, and became a Whitcher once more; but not for long, as she abandoned her parents once again to marry Mr. Coleman within six months of her widowhood. Her mother had been so happy for her daughter. It was the greatest of blessings that she had been given a second chance of happiness.

Grandma Whitcher, a widow of several years, enjoyed a comfortable existence because her husband had taken care of financial matters, and like everything related to business, he was capable and careful. A tidy sum was left to her, and she lived in relative comfort. She visited the church yard every Saturday, and laid flowers on her husband's grave. She waited for visits from her daughter and son in law and her grandchildren. They came when business and time allowed. She was not friendless and had an uncanny way of knowing what was being talked about in the vicinity long before her daughter.

She sat in a wide armed chair placed sideways to the window, surrounded by an accumulation of ceramic objects, pictures and oak furniture; she was placed so that she could see to sew or read and also, perhaps more importantly, to observe the lane outside and the activity upon it. She saw her grandson approaching and immediately felt grateful that he was visiting. She would still berate him for not coming sooner, but that was part of their relationship.

"Good morning, grandmamma, I can see you are in good form." The maid Betty had ushered the gentlemen callers in to the morning room, and Charles was quick to take his grandmother's hand and squeeze it gently.

"I may well be but it has nothing to do with the care you have been giving me I assure you."

"Oh grandmamma you know how constantly you are in my prayers and in my thoughts. How could you think otherwise? You know that as your only grandson I dote on you." Charles paused, gave Jack a wink and then, continuing to envelope his grandmother's hand in his, he gave her such a beautiful smile that she became flustered and muttered, "Get away … you could always charm your way back in to my good books." She tried to wrest her hand out of his, but only succeeded in drawing him closer and he swiftly kissed her lightly on the cheek.

"And so what is it that has kept you away this time? Forgive me Jack, it's been such a time since this dear boy has come by … you can imagine how I look forward to his visits, but of course it is lovely to see you too. Would you like some tea or something to eat? Dinner will not be for another hour you know … would you like to stop for that?" Jack hoped that Charles would accept something in the way of food. He had been on the road since seven, and was feeling in need of some refreshment. Fortunately for him, Charles accepted the offer of tea and biscuits, but declined dinner as they would be sharing a meal with his parents which had already been offered and accepted.

They settled down to talk about her health, her visits to various friends, and their visits to her. They examined her latest embroidery, and after the tea and biscuits had been brought, Jack ventured to ask her if she knew of a family called Robinson who lived to the west of Lyndhurst. At first she replied that she had no recollection of them, but after being told that they were healers, she recollected something which she thought might be connected to the family.

There had been an unfortunate death in the Forest. About a year ago a baby had been found by a family, and she was reasonably sure that the family's name was Robinson. It had been mentioned at the enquiry that the woman who had found the baby, a Mrs Robinson, if that was indeed who it was, had been a practicing herbalist. She had maintained that she had found the child dead, and had immediately contacted the doctor. No one knew of the child, the child was never identified, and was soon after buried by the parish at the back of the church yard. No one had ever come forward to ask about the child, and so the child's true identity had remained a mystery.

Charles instinctively felt uncomfortable when he considered this story. Jack also felt uneasy. He could see that there was so much that was unexplained. If it was indeed the Robinsons who had reported the death of the child, how did the child die and what part did the family play in its death? The thought of a dead child, and Ellen not much more than a child herself, being held by this family filled him with disquiet, and yet, there might be nothing to concern him. His imagination could be guilty of conjuring up a completely false set of circumstances. He hoped so, and looked to Charles to act with reason as his guide. They returned to Charles's home pensive and anxious to get to Ellen.

Jack ate his dinner without enjoyment. The Sunday roast at the Colemans was a meal worth savouring; mouth-watering beef with crisp and flaky potatoes cooked in the dripping and juices, with carrots, swede and buttery cabbage from the garden and moist slices of batter pudding with horseradish sauce. An apple pie followed, moist and sweet and spiced with a hint of cloves and topped with thick cream. The meal was enjoyed by everyone else, and Mr Coleman, after ceremoniously carving, left everything to Mrs Coleman who cheerfully ran from kitchen to dining room, carrying her creations.

She prided herself on her good cooking, and no one could have faulted her gravy which possessed just the correct amount of seasoning with a richness and flavour which was due to her vegetable and bone stock and her knowledge of the importance of concentrating the flavours by reducing the liquid to about half of its original quantity by simmering it gently and watchfully. Her pastry too was exemplary, crisp and light with a hint of butter and a light dusting of sugar. Yes, she thought that she had provided a meal that some would have talked about for a week, but she couldn't help feeling that perhaps she had overestimated her culinary expertise when Jack left most of his gravy, only picked at the delicious greens, and left half his pie.

After Jack and Charles had left, Mr Coleman reassured her that she wasn't mistaken in her judgement.

"Dinner was, as always, a triumph Maria my dear. Everything was just as it should be. Your creative skills in the kitchen are legendary. Nothing could persuade me from saying or thinking otherwise. No, my dear, dinner was perfect." Mr Coleman smiled knowingly across at the woman who had successfully fed him for the past fifteen years. Naturally, he knew what he was talking about, and felt that Jack's inability to appreciate the meal was not anything to do with his wife's cooking. Mrs Coleman was satisfied with her husband's explanation and they settled down to a happy Sunday afternoon, in front of the fire, reading and talking, and later preparing to attend Evensong.

Jack and Charles had immediately set off for the Robinson's cottage. Charles had not shared his theories with Jack, knowing that Jack might react in an unfortunate way, despite there being little in the way of certainty. His ideas were theories and nothing more. He intrinsically enjoyed creating hypotheses and possible explanations, but he would wait to see if on meeting the family, he learnt of anything which supported any one of his theories.

He did not feel that the girl was in safe hands. Why this should be he could not entirely understand. However, either the family were innocent of any crime and just incompetent at curing people, or there was something much more sinister going on. If this was the case their motive might be a continued supply of cash. However, there was always another possibility and that was that the girl was genuinely very ill, and beyond the capacity of her carers to cure, and would need to be seen by a professional medical practitioner as soon as possible.

What Charles saw on entering the cottage left him in no doubt as to the correct course of action. The two women had a strange relationship which he noticed almost immediately. The girl had concealed herself behind her mother when she saw Charles. She had not spoken, but had watched her mother and Jack, ignoring Charles completely. Mrs. Robinson behaved as she always had when in Jack's presence, smiling at him, and talking excitedly about Ellen and how there had been some improvement since the morning.

Charles asked her about the treatments and asked to see the remedies she had been using. There was no sign of the collected herbs in the room, and Mrs Robinson did not answer him. As he did not wish to delay, and as he rightly assumed the cottage was comprised of just two rooms, he immediately asked to see the patient and moved towards the only internal door in the room.

"Mr Woodley, do show your friend the way." Mrs Robinson appeared to be wholly compliant with Charles wishes, and smiled at them pointing towards the door.

* * *

Charles, later, moved by what he had then seen and believing that it might be possible to find out the true identity of Jack's unfortunate young woman, during the long night that followed the unfortunate circumstances of the day, he wrote to someone he hoped would have some sort of answer.

14, High Street,

Lyndhurst.

16th November

My dear Charlotte

It is unusual for me to write to you but something rather strange has happened, and I am hoping that you may be able to shed some light on the mystery.

I remember coming to the Grange last year to see you and I met two sisters one of whom was a maid working alongside you I suppose. I noticed how upset they both were, but did not know the circumstances. I think I have come across the younger of the two sisters in a very poor state of health, destitute and homeless. She is at present living here because we are at a loss to know where she comes from. I wonder if you could enlighten me as to anything you know about her family. I have been reliably informed that her name is Ellen but she has not been able to speak so that is all I know.

Please let me know if you know anything about the family, and if there is anything more that you are aware of that might assist us in helping us find the true identity of this unfortunate girl.

Your loving brother Charles

A reply was received two days later.

The Grange Botley

Dear Charles

There is not much to say but I do believe you are writing of the Lamborn girls Anna Lamborn worked as a kitchen maid but left quick the year before last and word has it that she has had a child not marred that is all but I know nothing of the sister Hope you can come and visit

Your loving sister Charlotte

Charles felt a degree of consolation that his memory had been proved correct, and that the young woman found by Jack and now in Charles's family's care was indeed that child who had clung to her older sister in the kitchen of the Botleigh Grange. He had thought that both sisters were attractive well above the ordinary, and the image of the two seeking comfort from each other had lingered in his mind.

The frail creature now lying in the room above the shop bore very little resemblance to the girl he had met that day, but something about her had helped him to recall her, and he knew that it had been her distinctive long, rich, waving, chestnut hair. He remembered it as unusually wild and free from pins and a bonnet. He had thought her very natural, younger in manner than her years possibly, and despite her hair now being matted with lack of care and fever, the auburn tones could still be discerned, and the volume and length could still be recognised.

The horror he had felt when he had first walked in to the room where she had been kept had not left him. The odours and atmosphere of the dark, stuffy room were horribly unpleasant to his senses; he had instantly recognised them as smells of sickness and human excrement. His hand had involuntarily lifted to cover his mouth and nose, as he had struggled to breathe. He found the truss-ell bed pushed into the corner away from the window, and could only just make out the form of a person lying on it. He was compelled to take the blanket in his hand and throw it back so that he could see what lay underneath. The time it took for him to sharply intake one breath was sufficient time for him to know what to do.

"Jack, Jack ... go to my horse, fetch the rug and coat tied to my saddle, do it quickly Jack, go now!" Jack hesitated and turned to look about the room; Charles must have decided that there was nothing there of any use.

"Will you go *now* ... *Jack*, hurry!" Charles's voice became more urgent. The women stood silently by the door for a moment but Mrs Robinson soon exclaimed,

"Yer not thinkin' of movin' 'er sir, that would be a mistake."

"The mistake would be to leave her here ... get out of my way!"

Charles had realised that Ellen's nightclothes were soaked with sweat and urine, but as soon as Jack returned, he did not pause but took his coat and wrapped it around her writhing body. He lifted her from the bed and taking the rug, swirled it around himself and Ellen.

"Jack open the door, there's no time."

There then followed a ride to Lyndhurst which was as fast as Charles could manage it. Jack had taken Ellen while Charles had mounted, and then carefully she had been lifted and held across the front of the saddle, and cushioning her head close to his chest, he had rode with her knowing that her life depended on swift action.

*   *   *

Charles had remained at Ellen's bedside the whole of the first night. He had watched her until the night had almost passed. He had written his letter. Before she could be allowed to sleep, he and Jack had supported her as she was forced to walk and keep conscious. The physician had told them that Ellen showed all the symptoms of poisoning and that she would need to be purged of the poison. He poured a vinegar solution between her lips and urged both men that they lift her and do all they could to keep her walking and awake. The doctor believed that the bumpy ride might have been responsible for Ellen still being alive, as she had been jolted into some form of consciousness. Ellen had vomited very soon after receiving the solution and whatever had lain in her stomach was expelled; and then she had been wrapped in warm blankets.

The doctor did not know how long Ellen's body had been subjected to poison but gravely gave his opinion that he believed that she had probably been poisoned by degrees but that this last dose might well have been lethal.

Charles had seen a change for the better in Ellen in the early hours, and had hoped more than he had hoped for anything before that she would recover.

While Charles had taken upon himself to watch over Ellen, Jack had ridden home wondering if there was anything he should do about Mrs Robinson and Maggie. If the doctor was proved correct, that Ellen was suffering from poisoning, then it was clear that mother and daughter had been engaged in the most terrible crime, and would need to be brought to justice. But, there might be another explanation, which Charles had been quick to point out when they had discussed the doctor's diagnosis the evening of the rescue.

"You must see Jack that the Robinson's may well be guilty of malpractice, but it will be our responsibility to prove that they had deliberately harmed Ellen. We do not know of an obvious motive, only that you were paying them handsomely for their care of her, and they might have possibly wished to continue this fruitful state of affairs by prolonging Ellen's illness. That is all. We must bide our time ... bide our time Jack, and wait to discover further evidence, before we accuse. You do see that as our necessary course? Jack what do you say?"

"I cannot bear to think that I had left that poor child in the care of monsters that would not stop at injuring another person almost to death for just a few shillings ... but you are right, there is nothing as yet that we can base our suspicions on and so we must wait ... but it is most irksome, and I think if I was to see those women I would not be able to prevent myself from saying or doing something."

"That is why you are to stay away from them ... do not go anywhere near them until I give you the word ... I need your word that you will stay away Jack." Charles spoke earnestly and expected Jack to assure him that he would not do anything foolish. "After all, if we were to act at this time, it would put them on their guard, and all they would need to do is deny that they had done anything illegal. We could lose every chance of justice, so we need to establish their motives and we also need to establish evidence which *proves* it was them who had administered the poison."

"Alright, alright, Charles, you are the thinker of the two of us, and clearly you have given this some thought already. I will do as you ask."

Charles felt heartened by Jack's response, and gave his hand to his friend. He knew that Jack had been very upset by Ellen's condition, and had deeply regretted not acting earlier. For some reason he had been blind to the seriousness of her condition, but Charles had reassured him that in cases such as this, people are known to deteriorate very quickly, and this was probably the case in relation to Ellen. He should not beat himself up about it. It was more important now to ensure that Ellen received the best possible medical care, and the two men had agreed that they would share the doctor's bills.

Jack rode home and passed the Robinson's cottage with hardly a hesitation. He had accepted Charles's argument, and would not act, but he did glance across the woodland to the cottage, and did see a light burning, but that was all. He would do as Charles said and bide his time.

*   *   *

Ellen got well slowly; she had to keep to her bed for two weeks, and it gradually became apparent to her that her kind benefactors gave her the best that they had. Mrs Coleman took great delight in providing her with the lightest of nutritious meals which would, she believed, gradually restore Ellen's strength. Ellen supped on the tastiest of broths made from all manner of winter vegetables and stocks.

Charles and his father cultivated a quantity of home grown vegetables and fruit using a large garden plot at the rear of the shop to good effect. It provided a wide variety of foods for the table, and Ellen, the invalid, was the fortunate recipient. She very soon began to look forward to Mrs Coleman's entrance with a steaming bowl of food and a benevolent smile, and although feeling somewhat guilty and beholden to the family for their unsurpassed kindness to her, she could not help but appreciate her treatment, and would never leave a mouthful of food on the plate. This of course pleased the enthusiastic cook most assuredly.

Charles felt a mixture of relief and sadness as he observed Ellen's marvellous recovery. He was naturally relieved and very much heartened by her restoration to good health, but he viewed it with a tinge of sadness as she, as soon as she was able, would be taken to her grandparents by Jack. Charles had grown to treasure the time spent with her, for the conversations they had had in recent days had been full of interest to him. He recognised in her a rare intelligence and a strong spirit to which he was irresistibly drawn.

"My mother's attention to you has I can see, caused a remarkable change in you."

"I am feeling so much better, and feel I am ready to get out of bed. I think if I stay here much longer, my legs will cease to function completely. Charles, would you help me?"

"I don't see why not. But first you just need to sit up straight and put your feet on the floor and stay there for a moment. Remember you have not been upright for weeks, and only two weeks ago we were afraid that you would not recover … it is too soon to be leaping about."

"I did not think that I would be leaping exactly!" Ellen smiled wistfully at Charles, thinking if only she could. "But, I may not be able to leap but I might be able to … lumber or limp a bit … if you could hold me?" She indicated with her hands and arms using large ponderous and laboured movements which described her idea of lumbering, and grinned at Charles.

"Lumber ay? I don't think your little legs could do anything like lumbering … maybe try standing and then shuffle your twigs an inch or two … hum … better hold on to me … that's it. That's right. Stop now Ellen, that's far enough for one day. You've shuffled far enough."

"Maybe you're right although I do object to your comparing my poor legs to twigs." Ellen was laughing because she enjoyed this kind of conversation with Charles. He liked to say things to her which he knew would get a reaction from her, and she enjoyed responding.

"They may not be very sturdy, that's true, and they are skinny as anything, but not that skinny … Oh!" She had suddenly felt that she was losing her balance, but felt Charles's arm close around her, and he held her close to his side. She leant all her weight against his chest, and she felt his body tense, but he did not move. His holding her in such a way felt strange to her, but it also felt in some way strangely familiar and yet she had never been supported like it before; she wondered why it should feel so recognisable and that she should feel such relief and comfort.

"Thank you Charles, I can see that I will need a bit of practice at this. I've lost the ability to stay upright for more than a few seconds!" Ellen giggled at her ineptitude. Charles had lost himself in the moment, and failed to reply. Ellen was surprised at his lack of response, and looked up into his eyes. He looked at her, so close to her and then leant to kiss her upturned face. His lips gently touched her ear, and Ellen, surprised at the gentleness of his mouth in contrast to his bodily strength, turned quickly away from him, and leaned towards the bed.

"Charles I would like to try and wash and dress. Do you think your sister or your mother would help me now?" Ellen's mind was working better, and she longed to be independent of everyone, and to regain some sense of her autonomy. Charles action had frightened her somehow, and being so young, she could only think that he had probably felt really sorry for her, but she definitely did not want his pity.

She was beginning to feel like herself again, but she was unclear at that moment as to who she really was; nonetheless, she was sure that she did not want to be a helpless creature. No, she wished to be anyone other than the pitiful human being she felt she had become recently.

She gathered all her strength, and pushed herself away from him. She could only fall against the bed, and Charles assuming that she was feeling uncomfortable and wished to be away from him, let her go, and she fell unceremoniously onto the mattress, and only just managed to stay there. She had arrived back on the bed in an untidy heap, and was amused. She did not feel the least bit embarrassed, as she would have done a few short months before; she straightened herself as best she could, and smiled bravely at Charles.

Charles responded, "I'll go and see if they can come and give you a hand now, if you wait a moment." Charles wanted to ask her if he had offended her when he had kissed her, but could not summon up the nerve to do so. Despite her probably being ten years his junior, he felt in some inexplicable way that she was somehow wiser than he. This had prevented him from speaking his mind and asking the question to which he would have so dearly liked to have had an answer. He didn't know why he had kissed her, but he only knew it was something to do with him wanting to show her that he cared and that he would be willing always to support her in every circumstance. She seemed to need someone, and he offered himself as a surrogate older brother which he assumed she did not have.

Very little was known about her family, excepting that she had grandparents living in Lymington, which she had mentioned to Jack, but so quickly did she become ill again afterwards, she never did tell him their names and exactly where they lived. Now that Ellen was out of danger and improving daily, Jack had submitted that it was necessary to contact her family as soon as possible to notify them of Ellen's whereabouts and to arrange her journey to

184

them. It was his assignment to talk to her and ascertain the identity and whereabouts of her relatives. He had said he was going to visit today for this sole purpose.

Mrs Coleman had left her sewing to go to Ellen and responded to her request to help her in getting washed and dressed. It was late afternoon, and getting dark, and so Maria did not delay in going to her. She brought a jug of hot water and soap and a large deep bowl with a clean, warmed towel. She had done what she could with Ellen's clothes but had ultimately despaired and offered Ellen some of Sophie's clothes, a warm wool dress and shawl and some cotton undergarments. Sophie did not mind at all as she was promised new replacements.

Ellen decided that she would try to complete her toilette herself, and thanking Mrs Coleman undressed slowly, laid the towel out over the edge of the bed, and sat with the bowl at her feet. She found it relatively easy to stoop over and wash herself from the top down and this she did, shivering a little as she did so. Anyone seeing her would have noticed her fragility. She still had only a little flesh on her bones and her eyes had blue shadows drawn around them; she washed herself as quickly as she could, wrapped the towel around her shoulders and dried herself. Seeing the clothes left for her at the end of the bed, she dressed feeling tired and ready to lie down again but she fought this feeling and did not allow herself to do so. She called for Charles, hoping that he would assist her in going down stairs. However, he looked at her closely when he arrived and suggested that she remain where she was.

"Oh please Charles, I am so tired of this room. Please allow me to spend the evening with you all. I know I can manage the stairs with your help."

"Then I will as long as you promise not to tire yourself by staying up late ... Jack is coming to see you, and will want to talk with you about arranging your transport to your grandparents ... I know he wishes for you to be reunited with them soon ... as we all do ... please remember though that we are at your disposal and want to see you happily back with them, but only when you feel you are ready."

"I feel so bad about the way I have trespassed on you and your family, and realise that if you had not come when you did, I do not know what would have become of me ... I just know that I am indebted to you and your parents more that I have ever been indebted to anyone." Ellen paused for a moment. She had not looked at Charles. She had planned this little speech for as long as she had realised that she had owed the Coleman family more than she could ever repay, and that to Charles she was in particular debt. He it was who had rescued her. She had wondered about the Robinson family, but as no one had ever mentioned them, she had decided to try and forget her experiences at their hands, and her memories of her time with them were fading. She continued, "What could I ever do to show how thankful I am to you and to your kind family, and to Jack of course. I seem to be beholden to so many people, and I feel so awkward about it, for there is nothing I can do at this time to show my gratitude."

"Ellen, really there is no need, it is reward enough for us that you are better, and will, I am sure, be enjoying the companionship of your family very soon. Please do not forget us though, as we do have an interest in you and in your wellbeing now ... which I hope you will remember without any degree of guilt or regret. I hope you will look back at your time here as being with friends, and not think that you are in any way beholden to us. My mother,

I know, has grown very fond of you, and would be unhappy if you chose not to remember her and your time here."

"How could I ever forget your wonderful family ... but I can't help but feel beholden ... maybe there will be something one day that I will be able to do to show my gratitude?" Charles remained silent, confused by his feelings and wondering why he hoped so much that Ellen would be happy to continue her association with him and his family.

Charles did assist her down the stairs, by going before her, and she placed her hands on his shoulders and followed him step by step. She arrived relieved at the foot of the stairs and looked about her. The shop was comprised of a spacious room which lay to her right. She could smell the new leather, the linseed oil and the oily warmth emanating from hot machinery. She could see that there were several boots and shoes being constructed lying on a central table. Various machines with wheels and belts were set against the furthermost wall. On the opposite wall were numerous cupboards and open boxes containing lasts, completed boots and shoes, nails, thread, glue and items which Ellen did not recognise. Leather aprons were hanging on pegs by the door, and another wall area close by had a variety of hand tools displayed neatly hanging on brackets. The room seemed to Ellen to be ordered and very business-like. There was evidence of a lot of work going on, and a stack of shoes and boots which had been completed. Ellen, with Charles' arm about her turned and walked towards the voices that she could hear coming from the back of the house.

Charles guided her into a warm and snug room which was the family's parlour.

Not many working men possessed a parlour, but this house in Lyndhurst had been extended by Benjamin Coleman, and the kitchen was now right at the back, and he had designed this comfortable parlour for the family, so that his wife could sit by the window overlooking the garden and do her reading or sewing.

Maria was happiest sitting in her parlour. It helped her to feel that she was truly 'comfortable' She sat in her chair with her husband a few feet away, and her daughter and son would also sit by on the divan or another easy chair and they would talk and discuss the events of their day, and the news they had of the world beyond their own. Maria had enjoyed having Ellen with them once the initial crisis was over. She had not seen it as a burden, and had noticed Charles's interest in the girl.

"Ah, Ellen, come and sit here close to the fire ... are you sure that you feel well enough to join us? Shall I get some tea, and perhaps a piece of cake ?... you know there is some jam sponge left from earlier ... here, here, are you warm enough my dear?" Maria gave Ellen a small hug as she sank to her seat, and smiled warmly at her. This kind woman had, without reservation, embraced Ellen into her home. Benjamin had not moved from his chair, and watched attentively as his family were engrossed in the care of this friendless creature. She was an enigma. There were many questions which were unanswered. At that moment, he heard the front door knocker sounding, and so he quietly rose, smiling at his wife.

"That's probably Jack, to see our lovely patient." He winked at Ellen, and she blushed at him. He was gratified. He still had the ability to make a woman blush. He had often thought that Maria had married him because he was well known in the town for his good looks. He wasn't particularly tall it is true, but he had thick blond hair, very blue eyes, and his physique had always been well proportioned and muscular. He had enjoyed many outdoor pursuits as a young man, and several young women had watched him and hoped that his eyes would turn in their direction. When he had chosen a young widow with three children, many were dismayed, including the widow in question. He had married her for love. He had seen how she had coped with her family, and despite the loss of her husband so young had faithfully nurtured her children. He loved her cheerful disposition, and her love of her family. He had had to be patient and persuasive. It had taken him three months of very persistent courting. He *would* have her and no one else. Everyone who knew him said that he was utterly determined to have her as his wife, and Benjamin persisted and was rewarded.

Jack stood at the door, and Benjamin shook his hand gratified to see the young man who had maintained a good business which had been set up by him and Jack's father; and who would surely take the young woman off their hands. Benjamin wanted his life to go back to how it was. Maria had hardly stopped for two weeks, and he noticed that it was taking its toll on her. He did not resent the sick girl exactly, but he looked forward to her departure, and then Maria could return to her usual routine which was primarily devoted to caring for him, Sophie and Charles. He liked things that way.

The Coleman's parlour was filled with chairs, and so it was without difficulty that the whole company were able to sit down together, and talk about the protracted plan to ensure Ellen's safe passage to her family. Jack sat with her, with Charles a little set back in a corner. His sister was on the other side of the room with his parents either side of the fire in their usual places. Maria was the last to seat herself having hurried off to fetch a knee blanket for Ellen, and once she had made sure that she was comfortable and warm enough, she finally took her seat.

The company was assembled, and Ellen, who had been shyly gazing at the attractive furnishings and impressive fire grate with a marble fender and patterned tiles which she had never seen in any homes of her close acquaintance, looked enquiringly at Jack and waited.

"Charles has told me, and we can all see, that you are becoming well Ellen, and we are all overjoyed … it has been a worrying time for us all, and we know that you have been seriously ill, and despite not knowing you before, we have grown to look upon you as our sister, and we have wanted you to look upon us as your family … unfortunate circumstances have brought us together, but now we need to see that your wants and needs as far as your true family is concerned are met. Yes, we are here to see that you are reunited with them."

"I do feel as if you have become my family. Such kindness you have shown me at a time when I seriously was in need of someone's charity, I cannot express how I feel … I can't repay you except in words of gratitude. I was convinced that had I been forgotten by all the kind souls in the world … but, yes it is time for me to leave you, I can see that, I would not want to be a burden upon you for any longer than is necessary … I am truly sorry for the burden I know I have been."

Everyone in the room was looking intently at Ellen, not knowing how to respond to the quietness and meekness of her speech. Charles was once again touched by powerful emotions, and felt again the unexpected humility of this slip of a girl who boldly sat before them. He recognised and appreciated Ellen's intelligence and her clear understanding of her situation.

"My dear, it must not be that you consider yourself a burden," Benjamin responded at last, "I would want to express on behalf of us all the relief we all feel that you are able to sit before us and prepare for your journey as soon as it can be arranged."

"Of course," Maria interjected, "It must be so, but I for one would want you to think that you would always be welcome here. We have watched you as you have returned from the edge of the grave, and we have marvelled at your courage ... Charles has often spoken of your indomitable spirit ... we have become attached to you Ellen, and hope that you will not entirely forget us." Maria ended with a broad smile at Ellen, who rose from her seat and went to her kind benefactor and knelt at her feet.

"I will never forget."

"My dear, you know we won't forget you." Charles had risen and had moved to his mother, and stooping, he took Ellen's arm and gently raised her to her feet. She knew without any doubt how much of her good fortune had been because of Charles' initiative, and was overcome with thankfulness towards his family and particularly towards him. She went with him, leaning on his arm, and held his hand for a moment. She felt the warm pressure of his hand, and the warmth of his arm. He had become a brother to her, and she knew that where ever she was that Charles would come to lift her up if that was what she needed. Jack noticed the exchange between Charles and Ellen, and recognised that their relationship had developed beyond what he would have expected in so short a time.

"Ellen, I would suggest that you travel to your grandparents by stage, as this is probably the most convenient for you, as you are still recovering; it will not require you to change as the journey is direct from Lyndhurst to Lymington. I will notify your relations of the time of your arrival ... are they in a position to arrange someone to meet you at the coaching house?"

"Yes, Jack, I would think so, but I am not entirely sure. Grandpa Timms owns a grocery store you see, and it might be difficult for him to leave the business ... but I don't know ... You

191

see I have not ever stayed with them before, but I do feel sure that they will welcome me." Ellen brightened as she considered the kindness of her grandparents; but she quickly realised the consequences of what Jack had said, "But who is to pay for my travel? I could not expect you to do that … is there a way that my grandparents might be asked to come and collect me? They have a small carriage I think."

"If you would prefer us to approach them, then of course we will do so. How are we to contact them?"

"I will write now that I am feeling better, and let them know of my whereabouts, so that they can make arrangements that suit them. That should solve the present situation don't you think?"

"It should … that is settled," Benjamin concluded the discussion. "And now my dear Maria, some cake and tea for our visitors if you please."

Five

'These sacred plants, if here below,
Only among the plants will grow.'

Samuel and Eliza Timms received Ellen's letter within a week, and were astonished that they knew nothing of what had happened in the Lambourn household. Their son in law had not contacted them at any time. It was therefore with a degree of consternation that they read the letter several times over.

Their relationship with Ellen had, in some measure, been influenced by what they had learnt from their daughter as the years had passed. They had noted that their daughter had demonstrated a particularly devoted fondness for Ellen. They had surmised that this was due to an unfortunate occurrence at Ellen's birth, when Hannah had suffered severely during the labour, and had had to be sedated with morphine; her mother unconscious, the child had been delivered by Caesarean section by Dr Stocks. Understandably Hannah had probably looked upon this child as something more of a miracle than her other children, and although she had never sought to treat Ellen as her favourite, she had once divulged to her mother that when she had eventually been well enough to hold her baby, she felt something different and this had never left her.

Well now it seemed that this child, who would constantly remind them of their daughter's devotion, needed to come and live with them. They could see that this would disrupt their comfortable existence. The shop was doing well. Their son Jacob and his wife Susannah did most of the managing. In fact, Samuel had left it mostly in their hands since the coming of his sixtieth birthday; he had resigned from hard and long hours, and was content to do so. The business had supported them and his son and his wife admirably. However, Ellen would need work, and Samuel wondered how she would earn her living while she was with them.

Eliza was thinking very different thoughts, and wondering about house hold arrangements and how Ellen could be accommodated. A life time of labour and tight belts had left its mark on both of them, but she felt confident that they would be able to manage. Eliza quickly decided that they should go and collect Ellen as soon as they could, because she realised that the letter, which was not revealing how she had come to be living in a strange place with people who were unknown to the family, *had* to be acted upon immediately.

So it was that the deliveries were cancelled for the next day, and that the business carriage was used to transport Samuel and Eliza to Lyndhurst to collect their granddaughter.

Charles and his father were busy in the workshop when the anxious couple opened the door of the shop. They paused momentarily, waiting for some recognition of their presence, and they did not have to wait long, as their entrance had been heard and Benjamin had left his tools ready to go to the shop door and meet a potential customer.

The couple who stood before him were both a lot taller than himself. This was not an unusual occurrence for someone who barely reached five foot six, but to be so dwarfed by a woman was a new experience. He must have shown a little apprehension as he approached Eliza, and she, sensing and recognising a reaction to her height with which she had become familiar, quickly held out her hand.

"Mr Coleman? Eliza Timms, Ellen's grandmother. I'm so pleased to meet you." Benjamin was a little overwhelmed by such a forthright woman, and looked hesitantly at Mr Timms, who quietly reached for his hand.

"Samuel Timms ... as you can see we have come to thank you for your kindness to Ellen, and to take her home with us ... we came as soon as we could ... we are in your debt ... if we had known of Ellen's plight we would have come before ... we had no idea ... I hope you will accept our heartfelt thanks and accept this small token of our appreciation." As he spoke he had turned and his son, who had driven the carriage for them appeared in the doorway with a hamper of groceries which Benjamin and Maria could only look at with unconcealed astonishment. The basket was filled to overflowing with bottled fruit, cheese, packets of flour, semolina and dried fruit, butter, nuts and jars of honey and jam. It was undoubtedly a very generous gift.

"Why that is very good of you, Mr and Mrs Timms, come in, come in, ... yes this way if you please," and Benjamin, smiling broadly beckoned to their visitors to follow him, and of course led them to the parlour. "Your driver, would he like to come in?"

"Oh Jacob ... yes, he's my son ... he will take care of the carriage ... I think we will not keep him long ... and this is?" Samuel saw Charles come in; he had followed everyone into the parlour, and stood looking at their visitors with undisguised interest.

"I beg your pardon sir, I am Charles Coleman ... I played a small part in bringing Ellen here ... it was my decision ... she was very ill and appeared to be friendless and destitute … I *know* I did right sir."

Mr Timms looked closely at the young man before him. He noticed the small stature, but his attention was caught by Charles's keen grey eyes and his intelligent expression; his gaze did not waver from Samuel, whose first impression was that Charles was telling the truth. Despite having only just left his workshop Charles had quickly realised the importance of this meeting in his own mind, and had switched from thinking about his work into an entirely different way of thinking. He had seen that the couple were nervous, and despite their generous gift, seemed unsure of the reception they would receive and the circumstances of their granddaughter's presence with these strangers; they were clearly a little apprehensive. He put this down to them not knowing the full facts of the matter, and wanted to put their minds at rest.

"I'll call my mother and we can have some refreshment. We must have something sent out to your son. Tea? My mother makes delicious shortbread … perhaps some of that while we talk things over … Yes? … I'll see to some refreshment but first you will want to see Ellen, so that your minds will be easy about her … I'll call her … please make yourself comfortable. Father, I'll close the shop while Mr and Mrs Timms are here."

Charles left with the full intention of doing exactly as he said. For some reason he felt he needed to impress this couple.

He passed along the hall to the kitchen, and finding his mother there completed the task of requesting food and drink for their visitors. His mother as expected was very happy to comply. He then hurriedly left to visit Ellen in her room.

He found her sat up, dressed in her nightdress in bed reading, and so retreated to a modest distance, and through a crack in the door informed her that her grandparents had arrived, and that if she felt well enough, she should get dressed and come down.

"I heard voices but I could not believe that it was grandma and grandpa so soon ... yes, I will do my best ... tell them I shall be down in a little ... have they come to take me home?"

"Yes, they have brought a large carriage ... your uncle Jacob has brought them."

"Oh, I'll be down ... as soon as I am ready ... I will have to pack a few things."

"That can wait. Ma is making tea ... later she will help you get your things together I am sure ... I'll leave you now." Ellen watched as the door closed. She took a deep breath, and despite feeling weak and fatigued, she slid out of her bed, out of her nightgown, and began to prepare herself to see her grandparents. There was a small mirror on a stand in the room, and she looked into it for the first time since being in the house, and for a moment felt bewildered by her reflection. Her face had changed in some way; her eyes expressed her feelings so transparently; she recognised the emotion clearly which she observed now, and she knew it was a fear and distrust which she could not eradicate. Her life, her future and her associations with other people all felt unsure and frightened her. She could not at this moment attempt to change her view. Shaking and feeling emotionally unsteady, she prepared to go down and face her future.

* * *

'After we saw you dead
You came back in a dream
I'm alright now you said.'

There is so much of my life that I cannot recall, and I suspect that it is in some way connected with significant people in my life. Why they should have eradicated memories, I am uncertain; maybe it's all about my unconscious wish to smother certain parts of my life, which are unbearably dark, and which would not have occurred if I hadn't associated with certain people. And so I justifiably choose to thrust the blame upon them.

Here I am near the end of my life I am sure, and I am trying to sift through the black sediment of my mortality, and find the golden grains of sand which are there, Oh yes they are there, they must be …

I think of the choices I have been forced to make because I could not stand to think of the life I had not changing; and so I made it change, and left as much of it behind me as I could. I gave up on it. Surely that was the right thing to do. I left my child. A husband.

Yes I know what you are thinking … I should have said <u>my</u> husband. He was as much my husband as was my child, it's true. The truth is that something triggered my disassociation from the love of my life. Why should it be that I automatically distanced myself from him? Who is he that he was forced to become just 'a husband'? What did he do to me to shift my affection to a place far removed from his love?

*He may have been the love of my life, but he was still **just** a husband. He was a father too, and our child only knew him as her devoted father and for a short time her mother too. I think I know what you have already asked. "How could a mother leave her child"? Well I did, and it was surprisingly easy to stay away. Of course I saw my daughter. I visited with her and her father. I treated him like my brother; he had become my brother. My daughter though could never be my niece. That was not possible; she would always be my daughter.*

My husband became my brother. My daughter remained my daughter, but she did not know it. I don't know to this day what her father told her, how he

198

explained where I was, and why I had gone. I asked if I could visit at Christmas every year. I could on her birthday. I went for a few years on my birthday. Those days came and went as the years.

Now my situation is fixed, settled into another sphere, and visiting is rarely possible, but I hope I will see them once more. They are not far away.

My family bought her a home and she has started a family of her own. I have three grandchildren, Lawrence, Frederick and Amelia, all born within four years. She seems happy and so like her father ... content.

Her husband's a soldier, and has leant to play a clarinet. I am very glad of that, because that's a golden grain of sand. I knew I'd find one at last; to think that music should be such an important part of my daughter's life; he is able to perform professionally if he desires, and has done so. I can't help feeling proud of my son in law's accomplishments even though I have had nothing to do with his achieving them. I have had nothing to do with him or my daughter. Her father has been the mainspring of her life, and has always been present, except for just after I left – am I envious of that now? Do I regret my complete severance from my husband and my daughter?

I can't weep now because I am on the point of entering another world, a place where I can rest; or have I been there for some time but my brain won't allow me to comprehend where I am and what has happened to me, and that's why although I want to weep, I can't? But I would if I could. But I am alright now.

The letters which Hannah received regularly from the Grange had ceased to arrive by the time Freddie had reached the age of two and a half. They had never been frequent, but had been delivered in various ways every three months or so. Thomas had of course been aware of the correspondence but had not questioned Hannah on their authorship, presuming that she would not wish to be examined on the matter. He continued to treat her with an excess of tolerance, and appeared not to appreciate the effect this would have on his wife; but the white envelopes no longer arrived, and Hannah grew anxious about the reason for this. Only known to her, the envelopes had contained no letter, and only a bank note; she appreciated the help she was receiving, and felt it was a clear indication of her lover's regard for her.

She was careful with her finances, and others in the household would hardly have known that she had personal means, excepting that she occasionally bought some wool, or some milk or fruit for Freddie, and sometimes she made a small contribution to the groceries. Hannah still had most of the money saved, and was grateful that she had been careful. It was possible that she would not receive anything in the way of help for Freddie anymore.

Hannah never made any comment to anyone about her letters.

She quietly accepted that she no longer would receive support, and resigned herself unwillingly to the complete demise of the relationship which had, in an irrational way, sustained her since the birth of her child. For a time she faltered. She was afraid and desolate. The only thing which had given her hope had been taken away. She found it hard to apply herself to the household tasks as she would normally do. Her heart was troubled, and her feelings were tender and filled with remorse. She wept in her bed silently until she slept. Her countenance was bleak and distant. Only Agnes noticed the change, probably because of her growing fondness for her and she was often close at Hannah's side employed in doing the daily chores. She had glimpsed an unfathomable distress which surfaced when their eyes connected.

"'annah, you're not the same as you always are … wha' is it? I know you are un'appy, please tell me wha' is troublin' you."

"I cannot deny tha' I am feelin' unwell, Aggie, but there is na anything anyone can do … bu' I would like it if you said nothin'

… Come 'ere and give me your 'ands, it'll pass, and I'll be well enough."

Agnes responded and held out her hands to her sister who grasped them and then put her arms around her and held her close. Agnes could hear her sister's short breaths, as she tried to control her emotions, and her lips moved close to Agnes's ear.

"Please … do … not say … any … thing … please." Agnes wondered why her sister was so adamant for her to keep her observation to herself, but she nodded assent and Hannah quickly drew away. She would talk about her shattered hopes one day perhaps, and be able to talk to someone about how she had once felt that she had been truly loved, and how she had come to know recently that she had been wrong.

He had been utterly convincing. He had persuaded her that he admired and respected her. He had willingly received her love for him without hesitation. Now she realised that it seemed as if their relationship had never happened. It now needed to be erased from her heart.

Freddie was a constant reminder of the rejection she had suffered, but it did not injure her view of him. He was a child, and there was enough of compassion in her for her to realise that children are not to blame for the sins of their parents.

Hannah then began to view her father's relationship with Ellen in a different light, and could not believe that any parent could utterly dismiss his or her child from their affections. She began to be suspicious and contemptuous of her father, and gradually her relationship with him suffered an erosive harm. She could not forgive him. Surely she had just cause to reject her child because of the complete rejection of his father, but no, she could not do it. She tried harder than ever to nurture Freddie, to demonstrate her love for him, and began to be noticed as becoming more anxious towards his care.

"I don' know what's go' into you 'annah, you're for ever fussing over tha' child." Mary put into words what everyone was thinking. They had observed Hannah changing Freddie's clothes twice before going out, as he, each time, had slightly dirtied them as he played. Hannah had not scolded him, but had insisted on his being spotless before they ventured out. He was now three years old, and was typical in his toddler pursuits. Mary had always looked to fault Hannah before in order to placate her own feelings of resentment and envy; now however, Mary's negative attentions increased, and Hannah was often the object of Mary's scorn.

"I'm doin' what any decent parent should do ... but then you wouldn't know about that."

"At least if I were to 'ave a child it would n't be a bastard."

"You're chances of having a child are very remote surely?"

"What do you mean? You ... ignorant ... *whore*!"

"I'm not a whore and never will be, but you, on the other hand ..."

Hannah's throat was gripped hard and strangled, but then suddenly, Mary fell back onto the floor, doubled up with her knees pressed to her chest. She had cried out as she was propelled by the force of both Hannah's knee and fists and lay writhing helpless at her feet.

"I'll tell you why you will never have a child ... because you don't deserve one, and father would never impregnate you ... if you ever touch me again, the outcome will be worse that it is today ... never speak to me in that manner again!" Hannah's face revealed her revulsion and frustration, her pent up anger directed at a woman she saw as a pathetic excuse for one.

She had failed to achieve any kind of liking for her step mother despite attempting to understand and sympathise with her. She had viewed her father's antagonism to his wife, and had always unwillingly empathised with him. Now, however, she had acquired an aversion to her father, her attitude to his choice of wife had been affected, and she viewed her with an increased distaste.

The altercation was witnessed by Agnes, Henry and Emily who were all thrown into a state of disbelief and shock. They had never seen Hannah react in this way before. Agnes had concluded that this extraordinary change in her sister had been brought about recent unknown events which had deeply affected her. It was almost as if the chemistry in the house had utterly changed. Hannah had become mistress somehow, and as a result Mary had suffered a complete humiliation at her hands.

Henry rushed to Agnes's arms, and buried his face in her skirts. Emily screamed as Mary's hands went around Hannah's throat, and ran to the door, shouting for her father. Agnes stood frozen watching as if the whole scene was not really happening. She never moved and stood transfixed, and did not even respond as her father entered the room. He saw Mary ashen faced on the floor, and rushed to her bending low at her side, kneeling beside her.

"What is it? What 'as 'appened? Mary, speak to me."

"It's your darling daughter …attacked me … she's 'as assaul'ed me … I wan' 'er out of 'ere … I will not stay in the same 'ouse as 'er … she 'as 'urt me bad, you … call … call the doctor … oh." Mary dramatically ended her speech with a prolonged cry, and hid her face in Thomas's waistcoat.

"Stand, can you? Agnes, come and 'elp me support Mary … that's it 'old 'er … 'old my arm across 'er back … gently now." Mary was half carried half pushed to the door, up the stairs and in to her bed. She groaned and complained the whole way, but once on her bed, lay still, and looked expectantly at her husband. Thomas did not speak.

He was thinking that here perhaps lay an opportunity to put his relationship with his wife on the right footing. He had been looking and waiting for a chance. He needed time to consider. He looked into his wife's eyes and saw nothing and felt nothing. He decided to try and use the circumstances of Hannah's attack for his own benefit. He reasoned that Mary's misfortune could lead to an improvement in his position, if handled in the right way.

Agnes had quickly left the bedroom, and hurried back to her brother and sister. It was fortunate that George had not been present. He had been taken out by Grandma Lambourn, which had become a regular occurrence once his grandmother had discovered that of all her grandchildren, he was the most amenable and easy to manage. Agnes felt relief as she knew that George would have been the most upset of all the children.

She talked happily to the other children, diverting them, she hoped, away from the scene which had so frightened them both. She made some tea, and poured out milk into two cups. She found some small buns which Hannah had baked and placed them in the centre of the table. She wanted to return to normality, and did what she could to conjure up this illusion.

The younger ones sipped their milk and nibbled their buns, and Agnes remained happily trying to talk about what the children had learnt at school, asking questions and getting no answers. The tea was just brewed when her grandmother returned with George, and the family sat around the table having their tea, with those who had witnessed Mary's assault thinking for the most part about her, who, unknown to her mother in law, had been taken to her bed and would choose to remain there for some time.

* * *

Ellen loved being with her grandparents, and, as time passed found an increasing amount of things to occupy her. They had made up a bed for her in their down stairs room which had been their sitting room. They showed no resentment at the loss of their private space, and behaved as if the bed did not exist. The evenings were still spent around the fire, talking, sewing and reading. Sometimes their son and his family would stay after work, and then the family would remain around the large kitchen table and Ellen felt more at home.

At first she tired easily, but within a matter of a few weeks, she felt she was getting her strength back, and tried to make herself useful. Her grandmother had written to Thomas on Ellen's arrival, informing him of Ellen's residence with them, but they had never received a reply. Ellen was made aware of this, but decidedly turned her heart and her thoughts to making a contribution to the business. She still harboured a desire to make something of her knowledge of herbal remedies and beauty treatments and one evening broached the subject with her grandfather.

"I've been wanting to talk to you and grandma about something … it's been on my mind that I want to help … I want to work and I know that I would be in service … but I want to ask you something."

"What is it my dear? You know we want the best for you now … and we can see that you need some occupation … I have spoken to Mr James the Apothecary about possible employment, because I know of your particular interest in medicine and remedies … did I do right my dear?"

"Oh grandpa, you are clever to know me so well, and I would like to learn more … do you think Mr James would have me? Would there be enough work for me? What did he say"?

"Yes, yes Ellen, he said that he could offer you some hours … only two each morning when he makes up his orders, and he would be happy to teach you … it is fortunate that he is such a good friend. I don't think he would have offered anything excepting that he wanted to gratify me."

"You mean that I can begin work with Mr James? Oh, that would gratify me! Thank you grandpa, I won't let you down." Ellen knew that the offer of so few hours was not the answer she had hoped for, and yet it was a start, and she could see that the rest of her time might be spent in working to help her grandmother, and maybe making some of her own remedies which she might be able to sell in the shop. She kept these ideas to herself as she realised that there were many obstacles to her making her own independent living. She had been thrown into the care of her grandparents without any warning. She was very grateful to them. She had to align herself to their wishes and feelings.

* * *

Christmas was almost upon the family, and Ellen reflected on past Christmases in Botley. She had only ever known Christmas with her brothers and sisters. This Christmas was going to be very different she was certain. She was free from the possibility of violence. She was free from the slavery of service. She was in the midst of a caring family and friends. Nevertheless, she slept only fitfully on Christmas Eve, thinking all the time of her father, Agnes, of Hannah, of Emily and Henry, and George. She wondered what they would receive for their gifts, and who would cook the dinner, and whether any of them would miss her.

On Christmas Day she attended church with her new family, and tried to forget those who felt like they had become strangers. She felt happy despite her longings and prayed and hoped that perhaps one day, her father would forgive her.

Six

'Thyme, for the time it lasteth, yieldeth
most and best honie ...'

To her surprise and delight Ellen very soon discovered that Christmas Day was a jolly occasion in her grandparents' home. After a day which included eating the most wonderful meal of boiled bacon with roasted vegetables and assorted Christmas treats including mince pies, and delicious nuts of every description which were dabbed in a dish of salt and eaten with relish, there were further delights in spicy pickles, creamy cheeses, freshly baked sour bread, fruity raisin cake and much more; then the family sang favourite Christmas songs and carols together sitting around a log fire; Ellen particularly liked 'The First Noel' because it told the complete Christmas story.

She recalled how her grandmother had lifted her spirits when she had visited them for her mother's funeral by leading the singing in the evenings. She had a clear, beautifully bright voice which rose and fell effortlessly. Then later, they played games. There were cards, and a strange board game with counters which was new to her. Everyone except Samuel joined in this amusement; he was content to watch their enjoyment from his place by the fire. He had had a few tankards of beer, and dreamily smiled happily at his family.

Jacob and Susannah had come for the meal and had stayed for a while, but as Susannah was heavily pregnant with their first child, they had decided that they would leave soon after the games, and were about to go, happy to have spent this special day with loving parents and a niece who had tried so hard to please her grandparents, when the family received a surprise visit from Jack and Charles. They knocked loudly on the door, and then regaled them with 'The holly and the ivy'. Everyone rushed to the door and enthusiastically joined in the chorus.

The family and the young men had such good strong voices, that the whole street must have heard the rousing carol. Everyone hugged one another, and wished one another a very happy Christmas.

Ellen felt as if her Christmas could not have been better; she was so happy; she realised that she was surrounded by people whom she loved and who, she felt reasonably confident in thinking, loved her. How could she feel so happy with people unless they cared for her? As the young men, Samuel, Eliza and Ellen sat gazing into the fire and into one another's rosy faces, the youngest member present realised with a dawning certainty that she felt more content now than she had since before her mother had died. She looked at the handsome face of Jack, who smiled broadly at her and mouthed 'Happy Christmas'. Ellen reciprocated and smiled so happily at him that everyone in the room noticed how lovely and attractive Ellen had grown at that moment, and deduced that Jack was the reason for this. Charles noticed this with an ache in his heart and with envy, but was quickly reconciled to the idea that as long as Ellen was happy he could be too. He observed Ellen unnoticed by her, and remembered the beautiful young woman he had met the first time at Botleigh Grange and considered that it felt a very long time ago.

Mary kept to her bed for two weeks after Hannah's attack. Dr Stocks was called, and he gave it as his opinion that Mary's nerves had been violently disturbed and that she was in need of complete rest. Mary was given permission to make the most of her demise. She insisted and demanded that Hannah should be driven from the house. She berated Thomas when he had claimed that Hannah would need time to prepare to leave. Thomas never once said that Hannah would not be leaving despite the fact that he, unknown to everyone including Hannah herself, had no intention of sending her away. She would stay, and somehow he would ensure that Mary would not be able to insist.

He would block her design with a myriad of excuses and placate her with pretended affection. His plan was to apparently be her slave, but beneath he would be waiting for the moment when he would enslave her.

The time that Mary malingered upstairs was given to bursts of his attentive care when he would ask her constantly if there was anything he could do for her. He would then respond directly, spending his time answering her needs in such a way that there was no doubt in anyone's minds, including Mary's, that here was the most heedful and diligent of husbands. He would then, after an hour of two of this treatment, suddenly take himself away and not be seen for several hours.

Mary would begin to fret, and having had the pleasure of his undivided attention devoid of any of his demands, and being the recipient of his most caring, devoted service, began to believe that he had taken himself off for good. She fancied that she was abhorrent to him; that her present state disgusted him. She had always been the one to refuse him because she knew that her youthful body was her main attraction. Now, though, she felt so despondent, and wept a considerable amount of her time and knew that this left her in a far from pleasing physical state. She knew she must look most unappealing.

But, she was in some measure comforted because she was enjoying these new attentions from her husband. Despite having been, for the most part, disappointed almost from the beginning of her marriage, because of his unfair demands on her and his lack of interest in her, she very quickly came to enjoy her husband's undemanding devotion, and longed for his return from his absences.

She recognised a caring attribute in Thomas that she had glimpsed during their courtship, and which she had imagined had gradually dissolved for some unaccountable reason as soon as they had been wed, but which she could not fathom.

She could not understand what was happening now, but knew well that she was on the whole the happiest that she had ever been when Thomas gave his attention to her. Her jealousy, yes, for she recognised now that that was what it was, directed at Hannah, and then, by association to his late wife had infected her relationship with her husband. Now, with the realisation of this fault, she had the desire to change.

Thomas played his game with Mary and played it well. He cheerfully lied to her, pretended to adore her, and then, when he had become sickened by his own deceit and revolted by her demands, he would leave and try to divert his mind away from her. He did not waver from his purpose, despite his occasional feelings of guilt which he knew were created primarily by his despicable behaviour in the past. He ignored the remorse and vowed he would conquer her, determinedly doing what he could to achieve that goal.

He spoke to no one. He confided in none. He remained silent around his children including Hannah. His relationship with her had to change, and he regretted that, but if he was to be the master, and ruler of his wife, then that was a sacrifice which he was willing to make.

He had calculated that Hannah would put up with anything, because she was not in a position to challenge his treatment of her. Although he was secretly indebted to Hannah for providing an opportunity to subjugate Mary, he could not allow her or anyone else to know of this.

Thomas was a man who had been trapped in a terrifying quicksand, and Hannah, in an instant had provided the means of his escape.

"Mary will be coming down this evening … Hannah, you will have to make yourself invisible. You can take Freddie to his grandmother's for the evening."

"Yes pa."

"Get along then, Mary will be down soon. I don't want any scenes in this house."

"Yes pa." Hannah answered without looking at her father. She made preparations to leave. "What time can I come home?"

"Try and stay with your grandma until morning if you can … it would be better if you did. Be back to make breakfast in the morning mind."

"Yes pa."

Agnes watched the departure of Hannah with a heavy heart. She had grown closer to her older sister since Ellen had left, and now it seemed that Hannah was now going to be taken from her. Although Hannah would only be a few houses away it felt like she had been removed a great distance. Hannah had been in control while Mary was in bed. Now with Mary's return into the midst of everyday life, another change was taking place which left Agnes feeling lonely and desperately wanting someone who would not leave her.

"I've got no one to talk to 'cept you Lord. Ellen said that I could always talk to you ... please send someone kind to be my friend ... Mother's gone, Ellen's gone ... now it looks like Hannah's goin' ... let me sing Lord, and let me 'ave my friends abou' me ... I've been wondering Lord ... I 'ave to stay 'ere to look after Emily and George, but could you please make it possible for me to see Ellen ... I miss 'er you see Lord, and 'ope she's safe, but le' me see 'er ... please Lord. I'll do what pa wants, and I'll be a good daughter, In Jesus' name, Amen." Agnes felt less forlorn when she had finished, and climbing in to bed, she silently wished that Hannah would return before she awoke, and then things would feel just like they always did.

* * *

Charlotte Coleman's relationship with William Judd had progressed in the natural way of things. They were, she had decided, alike in background, interests and opinions. She felt that she viewed things in a similar way as he, and felt at ease and comfortable in his company.

"Would you be having any more cake William?" The cook at the Grange knew very well William's appetite for her cooking. Most of the servants were present, and were used to this conversation.

"Why yes Mrs. Webb that would be very kind," and William held out his empty plate. Charlotte watched him as he began another portion of the raspberry sponge with enthusiasm. She looked steadfastly at him, and hoped he would notice her. She looked forward to their meals together, and hoped that at some point he would take the opportunity to speak to her.

"I suppose it won't be long before it will be wedding cake that you will be enjoying Mr Judd!" This remark was made by Mr Spreadbury the Head Gardener who had seen William and Charlotte out walking in the grounds on numerous occasions and enjoyed sparking off conversation with a controversial subject which might cause some embarrassment or comment. William looked blankly across at him, but the rest of the company were fully aware of Mr Spreadbury's meaning.

"Why Mr Judd, we all know that you have been walking out with a certain young lady … it's no secret." Mrs. Webb raised her eyebrows and smiled at Charlotte, and noticed that William was still looking bewildered.

"Yes, it would be lovely to have a summer wedding … we haven't had a betrothal or wedding here amongst us for several years … the last occasion if I remember correctly was the marriage of Sarah and Isaac … but that was all of, three years ago?" Mr Spreadbury looked across at Isaac Grace, the master's valet, who quietly nodded and smiled. The servants had entered into the feasting and celebrations of his wedding to Sarah Prewett, a chamber maid at the Grange, the eldest daughter of the local carpenter Samuel Prewett. They now had a home on the estate, and were already raising two children with the third on the way.

"That was such a wonderful day, and I believe my cake was equal to anything the master would expect." Mrs Webb beamed at the thought of the food she had prepared for the wedding tea. Everyone had been given the day off by Sir Russell and it being a warm July day, there was nothing to dampen the happy occasion.

The party had been given in the gardens of the Grange, and trestle tables decked in white cloths and decorated with glass bowls of roses had been laid out so that the staff, family and friends could all be seated and enjoy the spread and everyone's company. Mrs Webb was reminiscing and recalled the laughter and hearty appetites of that special day.

"Mrs Webb, I believe that your wedding cake was the toast of 'ampshire." Isaac had been very thankful for the wonderful tea provided mainly by her, and it was evident that everyone now present around the kitchen table that had had the good fortune to have been there at the Graces' wedding celebration agreed with him as now there was a considerable amount of murmured confirmation that what he said was true. Everyone in turn then voiced their agreement, and Mrs Webb, duly filled with pleasure born of the inborn delight in providing good food which would satisfy and give pleasure to its recipients, (which is probably true of all those who choose to engage in cooking) was motivated to ask "So, William, what have you to say for yourself? Will *you* be wanting my services shortly?"

William, noticeably reddening during the wedding tea discussion, appeared to be dumbfounded and failed to make any reply; so Charlotte, sensing that someone had to say something, and she was the most obvious one to do so replied, "Mrs Webb, I suppose you are referring to the regular sight of William and me walking out together ... well, William and me ... we 'ave not any plans ... it's as simple as that ... that's it William isn't it?"

William's cake had lain untouched on his plate from the time Mr Spreadbury had asked the unexpected question; he stared across at Charlotte, unable to think of anything to say. All eyes were upon him, and feeling that his silence would be interpreted as his agreement, and being unable to respond to a conversation which had astonished him, he resumed the eating of the cake.

Charlotte was rather unsettled by William's apparent lack of opinion of their relationship, and at the earliest opportunity decided to confront him on the matter. She would leave her questions to a time when there would be adequate opportunity to fully discuss what had transpired at the kitchen table. The times of their contact until then would be awkward, but she knew that in order for the matter to be resolved there would need to be no onlookers. And so it was that the customary walk on Sunday evening was used to clarify the situation. As soon as they had walked away from the High Street into a more private road Charlotte began.

"William what did you make of everyone thinking that you and I were to be wed?"

"I did not think on it a great deal … at first I was … as you may 'ave seen … rather surprised … I don't mean to say that it was unpleasan' to know that that was 'ow people was seeing us … but I 'ad not thought of it myself and that's why I was rather … astonished." William looked warily at Charlotte to see her reaction, and then his mind seemed to become entirely empty. She could see he looked troubled, his head was bowed, and his large forehead lowered. His eyes which were small and deep set had bulged as he looked at her and then furtively glanced about him. The lane was quiet he was relieved to see; not many came this way on a Sunday.

"Oh I see. I didn't realise that you were silent because of amazement. I rather thought that you said nothing because it was not an idea that you could entertain. Do you mean that it is not an unpleasant thought for you to consider that we might be wed?"

"Not at all."

"Ah, you are saying that it *is* an unpleasant thought?" Charlotte glowered as the answer came. William understanding her meaning replied hastily, "No, no, not at all, you misunderstand me."

"So you are of the opinion that it might be something we might consider in due course?"

"Why yes … that is if you … are taken with the idea."

"Did you perhaps … think that I wasn't?"

"Not exactly, but I thought that your feelings for me … that they 'ad not 'ad time enough to … grow … that you were unclear as to 'ow you felt about me … you have shown no sign tha' you care for me, you know."

"Oh I see … you were thinking that I needed more time … to know my own feelings." William was unsure as to whether Charlotte was irritated by his suggestions or that she was happy with them. He had no idea what she might be thinking.

"No … Oh not exactly … I've 'ad no experience … in these matters."

"Neither have I … what should we do then?"

"I'm not sure that we should do anything at present."

"I don't think I can go on as before William, now that this has happened … everyone around us is watching us … they has become aware of what is happening between us … it has changed things don't you see … I need to know … how you feel about me … and what you see as our future … do you *want* to marry me?"

* * *

The woman who had preceded Charlotte in William's affections, such as they were, was also considering her future. Hannah was standing in Grandma Lambourn's kitchen, getting Freddie dressed

217

ready to return early to her home having spent a very uncomfortable and miserable night trying to sleep on the floor. There was no room in this house for visitors, particularly as no one was inclined to give up their bed for her. Mrs. Lambourn and her second son Stephen, who had remained unmarried, had lived reasonably comfortably in the home provided by the late Mr Lambourn. He had been the tailor in the village and had been successful in striking up a creditable business in the area including the patronage of most of the local gentry.

His son Thomas had walked in his footsteps, while Stephen had always preferred more physical pursuits, and had joined the Botley Mill as a young man and had remained there. He had gained all the experience necessary to be a first class miller, and had risen to the position of assistant to the manager. The mill was functioning well and had expanded. It was the largest mill in the area. The labour force was generally content. Mrs. Lambourn had benefited from this circumstance, as Stephen's wage had continued to rise. She had, however, chosen to remain where she was. She had friends in the village, and the home suited Stephen also as it was only a short walk from the mill.

Two people who had achieved a comfortable existence, Mrs Lambourn and Stephen, were concerned at the latest developments. Thomas was behaving very strangely and unpredictably, telling Hannah she had to stay out of her home; Hannah had not disclosed the full matter, but enough for the grandparent to realise that Mary had to be the cause of this present upheaval.

Hannah had clearly seen the unwelcome looks of her grandmother and uncle. She recognised the coldness of their reaction to her request to stay overnight. She could not contemplate the possibility of her father's total dismissal of her.

Somehow she hoped that he would find a way to console and placate Mary and retain herself as the housekeeper. That is all that she expected. She had to do what her father demanded, and remained anxious in not knowing her father's intentions concerning her. If her dismissal last night was to be an indication of his treatment of her in the future, she was full of foreboding. This was because she was concerned about the effects of whatever was to come on Freddie. He had slept poorly, and had cried several times in the night. She had tried to make him as comfortable as she could but it was probable that small though he was he had sensed his great grandmother's antagonism, his mother's fears and had been upset by the strange and inhospitable situation and this had unsettled him.

As Hannah prepared to leave, he clung to her skirts, and whined unhappily in a way that she had not heard before. She lifted him, looked at him as brightly as she could muster, quietly kissed him and left, heading for home. She hoped that her home would remain with her father, but realised that there were changes taking place over which she had no control.

Despite it being only just after six, her father was waiting for her in the kitchen. He failed to notice the tired drag of her feet, and her listless expression. He had been thinking of his next move during his own sleepless night and despite feeling physically exhausted, resolved to make his next move.

"I trust your grandmother is well?"

"Yes father, she is well enough."

"What arrangements did she make for Freddie?"

"We slept on the kitchen floor. We had a warm blanket and were not cold."

"Um, I will need to talk to her … if this is to be a regular occurrence it will be necessary to arrange something a little more permanent."

"It's to be happening regular then? I wondered if another arrangement might be made. If you want me out of the house when Mary is about, that will require me to be away from home every day. Perhaps father it might be better for me … to go away altogether?"

"No, Hannah, I don't feel that will be necessary. It is just for a week or two while Mary gets her strength back … once she is well, I feel sure that we will manage at home and you will be able to do as you once did."

"Oh father! Do you really think so? I was afraid that you were angry with me, and that the wrong I have done you would hold against me … I know I did wrong, but I could not help it."

"You will have to learn to help it … you have done a great wrong. It is fortunate that you have Frederick, as I would not have hesitated in telling you to go, but for him. *He* cannot be cast out … Hannah you must promise me that there will never be a repeat of your behaviour."

Hannah broke in as soon as she was able. "Oh no father, I could not do such a thing again. I *have* learnt from my mistake." Thomas looked closely at Hannah for the first time since her return home and saw his beloved daughter with tears of relief flowing down her face. He did not know that it was relief which had resulted in her weeping. He assumed it was regret, but Hannah did not regret hurting Mary. Neither did Thomas. They both believed that she had received what had been coming to her. Neither would own up to their uncharitable thinking. Mary was seen by both as deserving of the punishment she had received, and Thomas was utterly determined to overpower her and ensure that she submitted first to him and then to Hannah.

Once he felt that Hannah had been dealt with as he saw fit he returned to Mary leaving Hannah to prepare breakfast.

"Are you awake my dear? Are you ready for breakfast? What would you like my sweetheart?"

Mary hearing that Thomas had returned to her bedside was comforted. She had felt him leave their bed very early, and she had wondered why. Last night he had returned to their bed for the first time in weeks, and for the first time in their marriage she had felt that he truly loved her. When last evening she had dressed before going downstairs, she had found that Hannah was absent, and that Thomas had cooked the evening meal. They had spent a very pleasant evening together. He had not gone out. She had been very content and had been warmed to be in his presence and to have his attention.

"Why yes I would like some breakfast. Maybe I'll try getting up this morning, and try to come downstairs."

"Whatever you wish, my dear, but you must be careful. Remember what Dr Stocks advised ... but whatever you wish my sweet." He held her hands and looked into her eyes, smiling in a way that made Mary believe that he thought only of her welfare.

"Perhaps I will stay where I am for a bit if you think it would be better ... though I do miss my friends and my mother. Has she contacted you at all? Does she know about my unfortunate experience?"

"Why no, my dear ... I thought it best not to inform her and your father. They would only be distressed for you, and it could do no good. Now that a bit of time has passed, if you wish to let them know what has befallen you, then by all means ... as long as you think your mother's nerves will be equal to it ... what do you think my dear?"

"I think ... yes ... I should consider my mother's state of health ... I feel it would be better ... for her ... not to know what has happened, now that I come to think about it ... I feel so much better now and I know that I am not in danger of another ... assault."

"You are absolutely right ... I know that Hannah has repented of what she has done ... however, she knows my feelings on the matter, and I would have you believe, my dear, that she is fully aware that the consequences would be very grave if she were ever to upset anyone in this household, and most particularly you, my love, ever again. Are you content? Does that satisfy you?"

"Oh yes husband, it would be contrary of me to be otherwise."

"That is a great relief to me."

"I will rest this morning ... I feel as if my strength has not fully returned ... my legs are still rather unsure ... do you think ... could you see to it that I have some sort of tonic to build up my strength?"

"I will see to it immediately ... is there anything that you had in mind? Are you thinking of some special food or herbal remedy? Anything in particular?"

"I will leave it to you ... I know I can rely on you to find something which will be just right for me." Mary looked lovingly at Thomas, who bent over her hand and gently brushed it with his lips. He returned her smile, and pulling the covers up over her, he bent to whisper something in her ear. She blushed coyly at him instantly, and covered her eyes with the counterpane. He took the moment to leave the room, just pausing long enough at the door to see if she was looking at him as he left, and discovered that she had emerged from under the bedclothes, and was looking at him longingly. He favoured her with another smile, and left.

Thomas was relieved to get out of the stultifying atmosphere of the bedroom. He longed to inhale the fresh air deeply, and made up his mind that he would leave the house immediately after taking his wife her breakfast, and go in search of a tonic for her which would have the kind of effect that he wanted.

Reaching the kitchen he found Hannah busily preparing a cooked breakfast. Agnes had brought down Henry, Emily and George by this time, and they were dressed and ready to have their meal. Hannah did not speak to her father, and so Agnes followed her example. Henry, unaware of his father's arrival having made a difference to the atmosphere in the kitchen, continued talking to Agnes about a picture he had drawn at school the previous day.

"Aggie, I was pleased with it and Miss said it was the best drawing she 'ad *ever* seen of a sparra'." Henry's voice rose with the excitement that he had felt when his teacher had heaped praise upon him.

"Yes, I know 'enry, you told me about i' yesterday … now eat your breakfast or you'll be late for school … time is running short."

"Oh Aggie, it was so …"

"*DID YOU NOT HEAR HENRY! … EAT!*" Thomas had lunged close to Henry and had shouted so loud that the child had jumped and then froze and his face had crumpled into tears. "Never mind that, stop crying at once, and *do as you are told.*"

Henry looked around him into all the faces which peered at him anxiously, and then knowing that he could not eat and that he could not stay, in one swift movement leapt from his chair, and ran for the door. Thomas could not prevent him from escaping, but followed him thinking he was going upstairs. He was surprised to see his young son go out the back door, leaving it wide open as he ran into the High Street and away.

Thomas did not remain angry with Henry for long. He had far more urgent demands being made on his feelings, and his heart and mind quickly turned to the task which he had set himself which was to mollify Mary into a state which would place her in his hands. The plan seemed to be working. Mary was showing signs of dependency on him which had resulted from her weakened state; he had not relished the part he was playing, but knew that it was right, and that Mary would soon be quite different from the argumentative and defiant wife she had once been.

He realised that he had never loved her, but that her youth had drawn him to her, and that she had been flattered by his interest, which in turn had gratified his pride. Now he could use her susceptibility to flattery to his advantage. The pretence which was a necessary part of his actions did not bother him, as he believed that the final result would be worth it. He had not ever considered that the deception would have to continue without end, and that there would never be any escape for him.

So it was that he continued on his course, collected his coat, and hastened out to find the 'tonic' which his poor wife had requested. He had no intention of buying anything but set off first for his mother's home.

* * *

The Timms' shop had a small new counter tucked into the corner which had been stocked by Ellen. She had chosen simple packaging, twists of brown paper held by twine. The contents of the packets were weighed and measured out of wooden tubs which had tight lids surmounted by attractive wooden handles, which made the removal of the lids easy. These wooden tubs labelled individually had been constructed as tea containers, and seeing as Samuel had several which had not been used for the purpose, Ellen had been the grateful recipient. She had chosen and blended a few simple mixes which could be used as infusions, tinctures or made into ointments and creams.

Spring had come and with it there had been an opportunity for her to collect a harvest of elderflowers, comfrey stems and roots, rosemary and other local wild growing specimens; and as summer followed, Ellen laboured and searched to bring home various herbs and plants. She had discovered wormwood, wild thyme, St John's Wort, plantain and a patch of common chamomile, all within easy walking distance of Lymington's High Street. Her supply of lavender had been kindly offered to her by the Coleman's who cultivated it in their patch of garden.

Drying the herbs had been problematic as there was little space in the grocers and in the living accommodation, but she had commandeered one side of the large larder which had the benefit of natural light from a window. She had had to resort to trying to dry some of the herbs in the small garden at the rear of the property. She had erected a rope line from which she strung her carefully bunched herbs on sunny days. She knew that the drying process was crucial to the collection of the medicinal properties of the plants, and that if this was not done in a satisfactory way, the final result would be less efficacious.

Ellen was absorbed by her efforts, and her work at the apothecaries was useful in reinforcing and developing her knowledge. She enjoyed working with Mr James although he was not always kindly towards her. He had established a good working relationship with Samuel Timms over the years, and they had come to a mutually agreeable understanding that the grocer would not in any way compete with him. He had established a good reputation in the town, and his business had more than supported him and his family. He was happy to offer Ellen a small amount of employment because of his friendship with her grandpa, but at first he did not view *her* in a particularly favourable light. After all she was only a slip of a girl, and would know very little. What could she know of all the complexities of remedies? It had taken him years of apprenticeship and study to get where he was.

Ellen learnt as quickly as Mr James taught her. He was incredulously impressed with her abilities, and could see that she applied them fully to her situation. He had never had a female to assist him before, but decided that if Ellen was characteristic of her sex, then he might not have any objection to having females work for him in the future.

Ellen was aware that she had impressed Mr James, if only to complete tasks before he had expected and to work sometimes unsupervised, knowing how to get on and do those necessary things without being told to do them. The strength she had gained over the past year in surviving abuse was now applied in thinking for herself and applying her mind to fresh situations. She felt happy, and hoped that Mr James was satisfied with her work, especially since her grandfather had stressed that her position was entirely due to the friendship between himself and Mr James. She had, at all costs, to make sure that she did not let her grandfather down.

"Ellen, I can see that you have cleaned all the bottles perfectly, you have kept your bench clean and clear of things that might get in your way. You are very good at remembering to put things away, which is extremely important. Everything has its place, you see, and you have ensured that my life is easier than it was ... I wish to tell you that your work has been good ... I have come to rely on you. This morning I am sending you home ... no, there is nothing amiss ... you have a visitor it seems, and Samuel has sent a message to ask if you might be spared, as the visitor has only a short time in Lymington ... I think as everything is in order you should go now."

"Yes, Mr James, but are you sure there is nothing left to be done? The orders are ready for you ... the lozenges you asked me to prepare have not been done as yet ... would it be acceptable if I made them tomorrow?"

"There is no particular rush for them ... but you must hurry home ... I gather your visitor is eager to see you."

"You mean the visitor has come specially to see me ... me?" Ellen's mind was excited but perplexed at this unexpected turn of events. Who could it be? She knew who she wanted to see more than anyone. Could Agnes have somehow managed to get to her? "I will go then Mr James if you are sure?"

"On your way young lady." Mr James watched Ellen as she grabbed her shawl and bonnet, and smiling in such a way that made him think that she was anticipating something special, she left the shop without pausing to thank him. She had to get home.

* * *

Charlotte Coleman and William Judd's banns were read during the month of August, with the wedding set for the first week in September. Preparations had begun in the Coleman household. The wedding breakfast would be provided by Mrs Webb, as she had wanted, but Mrs Coleman, being anxious and willing to demonstrate *her* cooking, was allocated those extra niceties which

227

turn an ordinary wedding into a very special affair. There would be a rare assortment of sweets and treats, cakes and biscuits as well as a sparkling elderflower wine which Mr Coleman judged as being as good as any he had ever tasted.

Charlotte, once convinced of William's love, was perfectly content and with a great deal of anticipation ordered her dress and veil and a travelling costume for the evening when she learnt with excitement that someone, probably Sir Russell, had arranged that she and William would travel to Bournemouth, and stay in a seaside lodging house for two nights before returning as man and wife to the necessary routine and requirements of normal life.

William's mother, unprepared for the suddenness of William's decision to marry, and knowing her son as she did, was puzzled by his unexpected behaviour; but she had decided to invite her son and his new bride to live with her. He was the only one of her children still living at home and she expected that he and Charlotte would be grateful for the offer. William was indeed relieved. There was no possibility of accommodation on the estate. Charlotte would also have to leave her employ. And so it was settled with the least amount of inconvenience to William.

Charles was talking to Ellen about the impending wedding one beautiful August day during one of his regular visits to Lymington, which he had been determined to do since her departure from his home.

"Charlotte has made up her mind to have some dancing after the wedding ... I hope that I am not expected to dance. Dancing is not something I've had much practice at!"

"I can see that you might shy away from such a frivolous pursuit ... have you *ever* danced Charles?" As Charles solemnly shook his head slowly from side to side, Ellen laughed spontaneously. "Do you mean to say that you have never danced?

It might be the most enjoyable thing you have ever done ... really Charles, you must try it. Jack is coming over later and I know he is a dancer ... he could show you how... I would love to see you two prancing about together." Charles visualised this extraordinary idea, and couldn't help himself from laughing out loud too.

They were sitting by the river Hamble on a clear warm evening. The banks of the flowing river were mossy, dry and soft, and the air was full of the sounds of summer, the swishing of the river as it brushed the banks and formed musical folds in the water, the shrill squeaks of the swifts as they circled above, the hungry trout as they splashed their mouths above the surface of the clear water to catch the tantalising insects, the grasshoppers rustling and singing in the grass. There appeared to be nothing which might disturb them.

For a moment, Ellen leant back and looked up at the clear sky. The wedding was going to be something to remember if the preparations for the food were any indication. Charles had told her of his mother's plans, but Ellen had been unsure as to whether or not to accept the invitation when it had come from Charles. She had realised that she had met Charlotte once only, at a time when she had not really noticed her. She had been concerned about Hannah at the time and could not recollect much about her.

Ellen had gone with Charles and Jack to the small engagement party arranged by Maria Coleman. She had been introduced to Charlotte and William, and her vague memory of Charlotte was confirmed. To her surprise though, the evening had been filled with delight and pleasure, the occasion contributing fully to her recently acquired feelings of happiness.

Both William and Jack had danced with her. The local fiddler had been employed and he had brought along another musician, a pipe player, and the resultant music had been lively and very conducive to dance. The parlour had been cleared, the food had been laid out in the kitchen and all had been prepared for what turned out to be a very happy evening.

William was not the most agile of dancers, and Charles had not taken one step onto the floor, clearly avoiding the possibility of his having to dance. So Ellen had to be content with dancing with Jack and then less successfully with William. She danced every dance, and drank large quantities of lemonade. William held her very tight, and she felt awkward being completely unused to being in such close proximity to a man. She enjoyed her dances with Jack more. He held her away from him, and although it proved more difficult to move as one, she was at ease, and she thought she managed to complete the steps reasonably well.

It was after just such a dance that she came off the dance floor looking to Charles so beautiful that he found it difficult to keep his eyes away from her.

She was wearing a simple gown which had been his sister's, but it was a soft pale green with yellow ribbons around the edges of the little sleeves, waist and hem. It perfectly enhanced Ellen's fair skin and her chestnut hair, and with her eyes sparkling and her cheeks flushed from the exertion of the dance it appeared to Charles that she was the loveliest young woman he had ever seen.

She had just celebrated her sixteenth birthday, and although very slender, he had noticed that she had become more womanly and mature in recent weeks. Her health had fully returned, and she had revealed the gleeful side of her nature. Suddenly she had stood beside him, grasping her lemonade glass, and had cheerfully questioned him, "Chassie, who do you think I shall dance with next?"

"Why Ellen I have no idea, but I am sure that whoever it is, he would be sure to enjoy the experience. Who is the lucky man?"

"Why you, of course."

Charles looked at her trying to remain composed and not to show how much he longed to be close to her. He took her hand and began to lead her out onto the floor but it was at this precise moment that the musicians were invited to the table for their well-earned rest and refreshment, and the moment passed. Charles tried to appear disappointed as Ellen bemoaned her missed opportunity to dance with Charles. The dancing had concluded, and with it Charles felt relieved.

As Charles looked at Ellen leaning back on her elbows beside the river, and contemplated the evening of the party, he knew that it was likely that he would be expected to dance at the wedding, and silently vowed to enlist Jack's help in overcoming the ineptitude of his dancing so that he would prepared to stand up with Ellen after the wedding. He realised it was something he was looking forward to, wanting to overcome his fear of being found incompetent; he was longing for an opportunity to hold her in his arms.

Ellen's thoughts had then turned right back to the surprise visit of a family member she least expected, but should, she realised, have been seen as the most likely. Tom had come to his grandparents' home ignorant of all that had transpired since Ellen's departure from his lodgings. He had wondered why she had not contacted him, but imagined either she was feeling a little distanced from him due to his inability to help her when she had come to him or that she was so immersed in her new life that she had unconsciously divorced herself from her past life, particularly as it had been so painful, and had severed her connections with the rest of her family.

This last impression of his had been confirmed as the most likely reason for Ellen removing herself from her immediate family's attention, because during his visit home last Christmas, no one mentioned Ellen, and it was as if she had never lived in their midst.

This belief however was not confirmed by Ellen's actions when he arrived in Lymington with the express wish to see her, and had gone directly to the busy grocer's shop. Ellen was not there but was sent for, and it was only minutes before Ellen burst into the kitchen, and cried out in delight.

"Oh Tom, Tom … it is so good to see you …I did not think for a minute … but you are here … there isn't anything wrong is there?" Ellen was so taken aback at seeing Tom that she imagined that some unfortunate circumstance had brought him there.

"Why no, not at all, there is nothing amiss. In fact quite the opposite. I just felt I needed to see you, especially as it will be your birthday next week … sixteen … well you certainly look a sight better than you did at our last meeting."

"Yes, Tom, I have been taken good care of by good people, as you can see." Ellen smiled at her grandmother and grandfather as they looked at their grandchildren and they felt the warmth of Ellen's love for her brother.

"I have a small gift for you … from the store. You know there isn't much that you can't buy there now. There are so many new departments. You can buy every kind of clothes and accessories too. *You* should see it Ellen."

Tom's thought that Ellen had in some way abandoned her family had been quickly refuted and dispelled. His gift to her was warmly received and Ellen could not restrain herself from giving her older brother a warm and affectionate hug. As she laid her head on his shoulder she remembered the last time this closeness with him had occurred. She had grown since then, she realised, as then, she could only lay her head against his chest. The circumstances of this closeness were very different, and yet she sought for the same reassurance from her brother that he would lend his strength to her and that the months of their separation could be effortlessly overridden; that they would once more be as close as they ever had been.

"I've come to give you news of home ... I don't know if you have been aware but Mary has been stricken with some kind of illness which has confined her to her bedroom for several weeks. Father doesn't talk about it, but he seems well enough. Hannah and Agnes are both doing well ... they carry on as best they can. Agnes has been given the responsibility of caring for Mary. She does her best, but has the care of the younger ones as well. She has finished school, but tries to carry on with her singing ... did you know that she is thinking of performing ... she has a wonderful voice ... she has lessons now in Winchester every week ... Sir Russell takes her to some singing tutor, and brings her home later. I think that father has been reconciled to Sir Russell ... I don't know how but Agnes is the fortunate beneficiary of their improved relationship ... what else has happened? Oh I'm sorry I've not asked you how things have progressed with you ... I must say you look remarkably well and quite grown!"

"Oh Tom it is so good to see you ... that you should have come all this way to see me ... I have often wondered how everyone is ... especially father of course, and have hoped that his heart would be softened towards me ... what do you think Tom? Is there any sign that he has relented?"

233

"Well no Ellen, father never mentions you as far as I have seen, although I am there only rarely, and so I might be mistaken."

"What's father like with the others? Is he the same as he was with me?"

"Well again Ellen, I am not sure of the answer to your question ... I think Henry has had a difficult time, but then that has always been true. I noticed that he has become quieter, and that he shies away from contact with pa. I know that Agnes tries to keep him out of his way if she is around. George and Emily are both well ... Freddie has grown into a very lively boy. He is very robust with an immense amount of energy. Hannah takes him out for exercise every day ... as for father's anger, it seems to have abated."

"You mean that he leaves the little ones alone?"

"As to that I could not say."

"Oh Tom it is not easy to be so far away and not be able to do anything to protect the children."

"Oh there isn't much you could do about that Ellen. You know pa, he won't be stopped when his mind is set ... but I don't think there is anything to concern you ... Agnes, I think, would have said if there was anything going on." Ellen knew that this was true, and she also knew that if their father had been violent towards the little ones she could have done very little about it. She viewed her powerlessness as a burden which kept returning, dragging her down and refusing to leave her.

She wondered if other families' experiences matched her own. She determined to talk to her grandmother alone about what had happened to her, and ascertain as to whether or not this was common practice, or if her experience had been in any way out of the ordinary.

"I know she would, so perhaps pa is gentler with the young ones; but, you, you are happy? Judging from your enthusiasm about the store, things are going well there for you?" Ellen was interested in her brother's life and could see that his smart appearance testified that there was little doubt that he had prospered.

"I have been fortunate in gaining the trust of Mr Plummer ... the son of the owner, you know ... he has promoted me twice ... I am now manager of the gentleman's clothing department. It seems that he is satisfied with my work and with me I suppose, and I have been rewarded. What do you say to that Ellen?"

"Why of course that *is* wonderful Tom, I knew that you were doing the right thing going to Southampton. You had to do it for your own good. I have discovered that I too needed to go away to do the things I had wanted to do ... you know that I have set myself up as a herbalist, I think that is probably the best word for it ... I have always been interested in plants and their medicinal properties ... and I have learnt first-hand what can happen if you are treated by someone who is either ignorant or seeking their own ends ... but that is enough said ... there is so much to learn, and I am fortunate in being able to help the apothecary Mr James for a few hours each week ... so you see we are both furthering our interests!"

Tom was gratified as to Ellen's positive attitude towards him. His conscience had been uneasy for some time, and he had been greatly troubled by the manner of Ellen's departure from his lodgings. He had come to see that Ellen had arrived safely, to see that she had come to no harm through any neglect of her family; he had come to reassure himself that his conduct had not been wrong. Although generally satisfied, he remained uneasy as he had felt there was something that was being partly concealed from him. He decided not to enquire as Ellen looked well enough and he would rather not know of any misfortune.

Tom stayed with his grandparents for lunch, but then quickly took his leave of the family. He felt convinced of his innocence; he had been justified in his way of handling his sister's situation. Ellen watched his departure wearing the silk scarf he had given her covering her shoulders. He began his journey home without a backward thought or glance.

* * *

Thomas and Mary Lambourn had not been seen out together for several weeks. Mary's friends had missed her visits, and the exchanges that had accompanied them. Once or twice they had sought to visit her but had been turned away by the family. Thomas had left strict instructions to Hannah that no one was to disturb Mary, and this had been strictly adhered to. Mary remained alone and unvisited with only her husband and Agnes for company. He had seen to it that he remained with her for the amount of time which guaranteed Mary's dependency on him. He provided her with the tonic she had requested, a recipe known to his mother, who believed it to have a calming effect on persons of a nervous disposition, which Thomas had combined with a drug obtained from Dr Stocks. Using wormwood as the main constituent, Grandma Lambourn had made a liqueur which Dr Stocks diluted with morphine; he had given that Mary could take a spoonful whenever she felt she needed it.

"Is it time for my tonic Thomas? I think it must be just about time." Mary lay in bed beginning to feel anxious about waiting.

"Yes, I suppose it must be about now, I'll fetch it for you." Thomas glanced at his wife whose eyes were listless and darkly shadowed. Her skin had gradually faded over the past few days, and she often complained of giddiness. She occasionally had tried to rise from her bed, but had found that her head had begun to spin, and that she needed to remain where she was. Agnes had seen to her general care, her washing and the emptying of her commode. Thomas had taken his wife her meals, and had sometimes eaten with her if his work allowed him. The days passed with little or no change. Thomas gradually decreased his times of visiting. Mary continued to watch the clock for her 'tonic'. She remained in her bed barely aware of her husband's increased absence.

Agnes grew more concerned as the days passed. Mary spent a considerable amount of her time dozing or sleeping. She awakened and drowsily requested that Thomas should come to her. After a period of time which he had decided upon to keep his wife waiting, for she would, he reasoned, more keenly anticipate his arrival if this was the case, Thomas would enter her room and immediately go to her side, hold her hand and sit on the bed. On a particular evening he had decided to further bring about Mary's dependence on him.

"Why my dear Mary, you are looking so much brighter this evening. Can I be wrong in saying that you are feeling better?"

"I do feel a trifle better though whenever I sit up my head aches horribly and the room begins to spin around me … what do you think is happening to me? I just can't believe that I should be so low for so long … Thomas, could you call Dr Stocks? And I want to see my parents … I've not seen them for weeks."

"Why my dear, do you not remember your dear parents came to see you only last week, but of course I will see to it that they come again very soon."

"Did they really come last week? I have no memory of it ... my mind seems to be so confused these days ... I'm wondering if I am in need of fresh air and exercise and that will put me right ... Thomas I want to get up out of this bed ... please call Agnes to help me."

"If that is your wish, but at least I can help you get into your chair, here hold my neck and I will lift you." Thomas leant over Mary and as she took hold of his neck, he pulled her swiftly to a sitting position.

"Oh ... oh ... Thoma ..." Mary's eyes had begun to swim around from side to side as if she was about to faint and her neck lost its strength. Her head dropped to one side, and her body began to follow but the moment she cried out Thomas caught her and gently returned her to her pillows.

"There Mary, Mary my dear ... my dearest." Mary was sobbing, tears rolling down her face. She hid her face in her hands, and Thomas grasped her to him, holding her close against his chest, feeling her body shake, racked with her sobs.

"P...lease Tho...mas, ge' the doctor, I 'ave to see 'im."

"Yes I will, calm yourself ... rest now my dear ... I will go at once."

Thomas called on Dr Stocks that evening. He spoke privately with him, and came away content that the doctor would call the following day. His conversation with the doctor was one that Thomas would not have wanted to be overheard by anyone. He left satisfied that the doctor would conform to his wishes. He felt only a small amount of disquiet. The overwhelming anxiety he felt in the early days had now left him. But, unknown to him, Agnes was growing more fearful, and did not know who to speak to about her worries. It seemed unbelievable to her that her father seemed to be indifferent and not notice Mary's deterioration;

Hannah had been ordered to keep away; Mary's parents had no knowledge of her condition or Agnes felt sure they would have come; Grandma Lambourn never came to the house these days and Ellen was somewhere probably miles away. Ellen would have known what to do. What would she have done?

Agnes considered the various actions she could take. She knew that whatever she did her father's reaction would be hostile. She knew that he would not approve of her going to someone outside the family for help. But she could not leave things as they were. Ellen would have sought help; she would not have stood idly by. But look where her attitude had led *her* – she had been banished by their father and was never spoken of. What would become of her if she incurred her father's wrath?

Her dilemma was, however, inadvertently solved without any planning on Agnes's part. It occurred on her customary journey with Sir Russell to Winchester for her singing lesson. Sir Russell had taken a particular interest in Agnes, and as he needed to travel there on business each week, he chose to combine his business with making certain that Agnes received her lesson which he paid for.

Apparently Sir Russell's interest in her was born of his love of musical theatre. He was investing a considerable amount of capital in a venture to establish a new theatre in Winchester. He had two partners who shared his love of musical entertainment and drama, and plans to adapt a hotel in the town had been drawn up. The town councillors had approved of the plans as they believed that the theatre would bring prosperity to the town.

Sir Russell was excited at the prospect of music, variety and dramatic productions coming to Winchester which lacked these things. Portsmouth was well provided for and Southampton, as well as Bournemouth which had flourishing entertainment venues.

Now it was Winchester's turn. All of his attention was turned to this enterprise; indeed he had already spent a considerable amount of money on the venture, because he strongly believed that it would prove to be a solid investment.

As they travelled along in Sir Russell's comfortable carriage, Agnes was preoccupied with her thoughts and worries. She looked forward to her lessons so much, but could not summon up as much enthusiasm as usual, and was noticeably quiet. She never spoke a great deal anyway as she did not have much of an idea of what to say to her benefactor. She generally only spoke when she was spoken to first, but, on this occasion was taken by surprise by Sir Russell's question.

"I have heard that Mary is rather unwell. How is she?"

Without thinking Agnes responded, "She is far from well. Indeed I 'ave to say tha' I 'ave been worried abou' 'er this past week."

"It sounds like you are taking responsibility for Mary's care … is that so?"

"Yes, I do 'elp 'er with 'er washin' and such … bu' Sir Russell, she's been like i' for days … oh excuse me, I should no' really talk like this … pa would be angry with me I think, talking abou' Mary outside the family … but …"

"You did right my child, but you need not fear … I will keep what you have said away from your father … he will never know that you have taken me into your confidence … but it sounds like something needs to be done … ay? Am I right?"

"Why, Sir I 'ave been thinkin' all the time tha' somethin' should be done, but I wasn't sure how tha' migh' 'appen."

"Do not worry anymore Agnes, I am sure that now you have confided in me, Mary will soon be feeling a lot better … tell me about the piece you are studying at the moment … I hear you are progressing well … I spoke with Mrs Graham last week and she assures me that you are showing great promise … has she spoken to you?"

The journey continued and Agnes was happy to share her teacher's assessment of her. Agnes for a time at least was not so much concerned about Mary's condition.

Sir Russell's appraisal of future events in relation to Mary's health proved to be correct. Agnes could not believe the change in Mary within a few days. Dr Stocks had called the day after her conversation with Sir Russell and had advocated a change of treatment. Agnes felt such joy when, two days later, she arrived in Mary's room carrying her breakfast and could see that Mary was brighter and that her countenance had changed. Mary was sat up in bed and was looking out of the window at the lilac tree and watching the birds settling in its branches.

"I've missed the lilac blooms this year haven't I? It is such a lovely tree; it's a shame that I have missed so much. What day is it? I don't remember … it's silly I know but I seemed to have lost touch with the days and weeks."

"Oh Mary it's so good to see you lookin' ou' and enjoying the garden … we've been so worried about you … Dr Stocks seems to 'ave found the cure … you look and sound so much be"er."

"Well yes Agnes I must say that it is the first time for a very long time that my head feels clear … the headache and dizziness seem to have vanished … what do you say that you help me get up after breakfast?"

"Wai' until I tell father … 'e will be so 'appy to see the change in you!"

"Yes, I haven't seen him since yesterday evening … is he at home still? I would dearly like to see him."

Agnes deposited the breakfast on the bed, and almost ran out to find her father. She was so excited and relieved at what was happening. Recently she had dreaded each time she had gone in to see Mary as by degrees she had grown worse; but now after days of worry, she now felt enormous relief that Mary showed signs of recovery.

She remembered Sir Russell's words to her and considered that, in some way, it was to him that Mary owed her restoration to health, but it was beyond Agnes's reasoning to understand how this could have happened. Agnes knew that miracles occurred, and she had heard them spoken of during her short life, and she began to suppose, quietly to herself, that a miracle had come about in answer to her fervent prayer.

Divine intervention had become a reality in her life, and Agnes decided that she wanted to change and be a more devout Christian. Now that she had seen God's hand so visibly, she reasoned that she could not ignore it. She thought about giving her life to the Lord, as others had done, but did not know how to do it. She decided she needed to talk to someone who could advise her, but she could not imagine talking to the only person who knew anything about such matters, the Reverend Russell, and so she spoke to no one, and the idea began to slowly fade as ideas do when they are not acted upon.

* * *

Life in Lymington was Ellen's delight. The town had a thriving High Street, despite being on the kind of hill which required a good deal of effort to scale it. The bottom of the hill was even steeper, and the middle part sloped from west to east as well which meant that the shops on the west had to be lifted up with a raised pavement and a wall which was several feet high in places. Ellen loved to look across to the other side of the street, and look down on the bustling heads of shoppers as they slowly climbed the incline. The really old part of the village lay at the foot of the street, curling away to the west towards the harbour and to the east taking the traveller to the quay.

Ellen particularly thrived on going east being so close to the sea, and would walk across the raised sea defences within the reclaimed estuary which crisscrossed between the shore and the beginnings of the land.

The air here was wonderful to her, and she would escape to her favourite haunt, and would sometimes allow her friends Jack and Charles to accompany her. They sometimes came together, and she felt more comfortable and rather pleased as they walked either side of her, occasionally brushing up against her as they talked of their lives and things around them which caught their eye.

Charles seemed to notice so much. She envied him his eye for detail and his inquisitive nature. She knew that she had something of an enquiring mind, but was a little in awe of his knowledge. Sometimes she forgot he was so much older than her, and had had so much more in the way of experience and opportunity. He had literally had more time to learn than she had. When she had heard him explaining about some aspect of nature that she had never considered and felt ashamed, she would catch him off guard by playing a trick on him because she needed to divert everyone's attention away from her ignorance. When he was serious and talking about something she knew nothing about, she liked nothing better than making fun of him by thinking up a game which aimed to make him laugh and distract him.

"Chassie, you have a fly in your hair, hold still … I'll just give it a swipe … Oh sorry I missed." Charles hair was swished back past his ear, and Ellen made a less than gentle contact with Charles's cheek. His hair for a moment stood on end, much to Ellen's delight.

"Why, there never was a fly, I will have to see to it that you pay for that young lady." Charles paused for just a moment and then with a complete element of surprise picked her up and threw her over his shoulder. Jack cheered loudly as Ellen's arms flailed on Charles's back, but he had her and he set off at a trot for the sea.

"No you wouldn't, Chassie. CHASSIE! Jack! Jack, help me!"

"It's time for a lesson."

Just before he reached the sea, Charles suddenly stopped, removed her from his shoulder, and with a sigh gently pinched her chin.

"One day I will do something which will teach you to cheek me … Ellen, oh Ellen." Charles sighed and looked at her rosy face. He knew that he loved her. She could do anything she liked with him. He waited to tell her, or maybe he never would. He had never told anyone that he loved them. Yet he knew from the books and poetry that he had read that the deepest feelings needed to be expressed, and could be with infinite depth and clarity.

He thought that he perhaps should try to write about his feelings as he found it impossible to talk about them.

Ellen had bewitched him, and if he had thrown her into the sea he would have jumped in with her, and he would have held her to him in the water, and not let her be swept away in the waves or pushed down below the surface into the darkness. Then he would have carried her out and wrapped her in his arms and lain with her on the beach until his warmth had been absorbed by her body. He imagined that she would want to remain where he held her, and never be parted from him, that they would kiss gently, and talk softly to one another in complete peace. As he looked at her now he thought that he might kiss her, and looked at her lips.

Her gaze was directed fully on his eyes, and she knew what he was thinking. It would be her first kiss. She was afraid. She loved Charles's eyes. They were such a pale blue, and as he looked at her as close as they stood, she saw a change in them, in that they seemed to be overlaid with tears and become translucent and a deeper blue, diffused with a misty light. His head moved a fraction towards hers.

"So Ellen managed to avoid a drenching then!" Jack had caught up with them.

"It was a close thing I can tell you ... Ellen is an absolute imp ... one of these days she will have to be chastised!"

"Not at all Chassie, it would be totally inappropriate for you to chastise me, wouldn't it Jack? I have done nothing wrong! Isn't that right Jack? Jack, surely, *you* must see that what I am saying is right!" Ellen looked pleadingly at Jack, who had no wish to argue with her and grinned.

"Sorry Charles, Ellen has won me over once again." They all laughed, but Charles knew that Ellen had in fact won them both.

* * *

Charlotte and William's wedding day seemed to come upon the families more quickly than they were prepared. The summer months had hurried by with members of their families and friends fully engaged in those outdoor pursuits which require warmth and sunshine. As much time as possible was spent in the open air, with picnics, walks, rides out, helping with the harvest and preserving the bounty of fruit and vegetables all of which occupied the whole community. Their appreciation and enjoyment of the warmer and lighter times was evident, and the higher temperatures endured until the second week of September. The hedgerows gleamed with rose hips and blackberries. The trees were laden with their fruit, and the harvest and storage of grain had been almost completed.

The busyness continued as preparations were made for the marriage; Maria Coleman and Mrs Webb were at the forefront in the provision of the food as they had agreed upon.

Charlotte knew and was relieved that William would have his appetite fully satisfied at the wedding, and he would, she knew, be happy. She looked forward to watching his evident enjoyment of the feast knowing that the food was one thing that she did not need to worry about.

Sir Russell had, as predicted, offered the use of the lawns at the rear of Botleigh Grange for the gathering after the service, but for a while there was indecision, because the wedding banns were called at Lyndhurst where the ceremony would take place and there was concern about how all the guests would make their way to Botley.

The situation was however resolved. As Charlotte had set her heart on the wedding feast being held at the Grange, calculations were made by Benjamin Coleman as to the number of carriages that would be needed. All the domestic servants from the Grange would need transporting as well as other family and friends. Sir Russell stepped in and offered the use of all four of his carriages, which, he said would be needed to take the servants to the wedding service; and then it made sense for these carriages to be used to transport them back. Everyone could see the convenience of this arrangement, and were grateful for Sir Russell's generous assistance. He, they decided, had been extraordinarily helpful, and gratitude was openly expressed by Charlotte and William. Benjamin's task was in this way simplified, and he used the contacts he had in Lyndhurst to acquire four more carriages which would provide all that was needed to carry the wedding party to the scene of celebration.

Of necessity the arrangements for the wedding party were mostly informal; the tables would be laid and spread by Mrs Webb, Sarah Grace and other servants would lend a hand; all would be made ready for the couple and their guests.

As these preparations were being made a young woman from the village quietly found her way to the back of the Grange Park to silently watch, unseen, from a distance as the tables were brought out and as the servants ran back and forth with plates and trays. She gazed silently holding her child's hand, and thought that this could have been her wedding party. When tears began to flow Hannah crept away, unseen and unheard, and returned to the life she had chosen for herself.

She had been so excited to hear from Ellen. She had written just a week before telling her that she would be attending a wedding party at the Grange and that she hoped there might be some way that she might be able to see her and Freddie. There had not been time to reply. She knew Ellen would be disappointed when she did not hear from her but hoped that there would be a way to explain after the event. Since she had been told by Tom that Ellen was with their grandparents she had secretly hoped that she would see her, knowing that probably it would be almost impossible for her to do so. Her father's original hostility and evident disdain which culminated in his total disinterest in his second daughter did not auger well that a meeting could be accomplished.

Hannah had not been able to resist her desire to glimpse Ellen especially, but also the happy couple. So soon, so soon she had thought. William had chosen a bride so soon after his rejection of her. She knew Charlotte of course, and recognised she was a young woman who knew her own mind and would be determined in her pursuit of something or someone she wanted. She could not imagine William marrying without some sort of persuasion and firm encouragement. She consoled herself with the thought that she would not have been happy with a man who required enticement to marry. No, her husband, if indeed he existed, would have her because he wanted to be hers and for no other reason.

She watched from a copse at the foot of the sloping lawn, and sought for a glimpse of Ellen, the sister that she needed most of all.

* * *

The Church had been relatively full. St Mary's is a large, impressive parish church set at the summit of Lyndhurst's main street. Those that knew the Coleman family were regular church goers and were able to attend; for the most part they were proprietors of business, and because most shops closed early on a Saturday afternoon, the trading neighbours of the Colemans were present. It was therefore a ceremony which was witnessed by a large proportion of the middle class members of Lyndhurst society. There was less evidence of poverty than would have been found at a wedding for a couple from the labouring class. These distinctions existed, and town paupers were present in the town, but the more affluent shopkeepers and craftsmen were growing in number and new competition now existed. It was for this reason that not all the middle class members of society had received invitations, and the church had some empty pews.

The families were complete however. William's mother, brothers and sisters, grandparents and several aunts and uncles had accepted invitations to the service. Charlotte's family was small, but Sophie, Charles and her parents were in attendance and their grandmother. Friends of both families from the Grange, from business and other sources well out numbered the families.

Charlotte appeared with her father at three o'clock. William had arrived just ten minutes earlier looking warm in a rather heavy looking woollen dress coat and fitted trousers. His collar was tight around his thick neck, and his eyes bulged slightly. Whether this was caused by pressure or fright it was hard to tell. His hair had been slicked down close to his square head, and because of his size, he appeared rather bull like. His head was lowered as bulls are known to do, and his forehead was thrust forward. His high collar was apparently causing him some discomfort.

Charlotte noticed his warm face as she came to his side, and smiled as she recognised the effort he had made for their wedding. This would probably be the last time she would see him in a raised collar, with his hair smoothed down. He seemed so different, and yet his familiar solid form reassured her that it was indeed William, the man with whom she was about to promise to stay until her death.

William gazed at his bride and all his fears evaporated. He noticed her beautiful fair hair, coiled around her head with the veil forming a frame around it. Her eyes looked lovingly up at him; she seemed very relaxed and he returned her lovely smile. Her eyes remained lifted to his, her mouth was slightly open and continued to smile, her cheeks were blushing. He looked into her eyes and noticed their glow. He was satisfied that he had made a good choice.

Ellen sat in the church wondering at the mysteries of marriage, and realising that months had passed by and she had hardly given God any thought. She knew that she had lost faith while she was ill and prayer did not come easily to her now. On Sundays in church she had felt very little, and the only time she could feel a slight stirring of her heart was when the organ played and she could hear her voice joined with others in the hymns of faith. Otherwise, she thought sadly, her mind and heart had turned completely to the tasks which she had set herself. She wondered how Charlotte and William had come to their decision to marry, and was a little overwhelmed by the sight of two people who appeared so unreal to her. The unworldly nature of their appearance struck her. Their clothing was not the least practical. Their faces did not hold the everyday expressions which were familiar to her, those resulting from hard work and endless striving. Their hands were held still and quiet; their smiles were in their eyes and their faces were somehow lit up; the total picture resembled a scene from a world which was far beyond what she knew.

There seemed to be a world, she now saw, which was very different from her reality. But, she was dreaming. She had penetrated some form of fantasy world, and she believed that what she had glimpsed was transitory and not real. Life played tricks didn't it? She knew that better than anyone. Charlotte and William would soon become the Charlotte and William that everyone recognised, immersed in the trials and routines of life, and this glowing vision of them would be dispelled. Dreams needed to be recognised for what they were, just dreams and nothing more.

Ellen glanced down the pew to Charles who was sitting on the other side of his mother. She had thought that he would have been the best man to William, but William had asked Isaac Grace. Here was a man who surely must exhibit the reality of marriage and family, having had two children already after only three years of marriage. Ellen had compared his appearance with the bridegroom, and had been pleased to see that her theory seemed to be correct. There was nothing unusual or unexpected about Isaac's dress. He looked very typical of a working man, and although he appeared very smart in his uniform when working, his everyday clothes were slightly worn, his cuffs a little frayed and the material of his jacket showed signs of staining around the neck and buttonholes. His black hair was long, curling and wild, and his narrow eyes were darkened probably by sleepless nights. Yes, what William and Charlotte represented would not endure.

Charles was returning her gaze, and she suddenly became aware of it. He could not know what passed through her mind, but he was looking at her quizzically none the less. Ellen gave him a quick smile and, not waiting for any kind of response from him, turned back to her examination of the happy couple. As she restored her attention to the service, she realised that her thoughts had turned to her own wishes, and found that the idea of marriage was singularly unattractive to her. She could not imagine herself standing at an altar with anyone, and wondered why the prospect held no allure.

The service concluded, and William and Charlotte, gripping each other's hands tightly walked back through the congregation. Charlotte tried to acknowledge everyone as they passed, while William looked only at her.

They passed by without a pause, and Ellen, following the families, left the Church wondering, just at that precise moment, what her own family was doing.

She had no idea that later Hannah was secretly observing her at the wedding party. Hannah seeing her then, found it hard to believe that Ellen had grown in to an elegant young woman.

She had two men with her, who came and went, but who were never very far from her side. One of the men was small, stocky and fair, while the other was contrastingly tall, slim and dark haired. Both spent time with Ellen while Hannah watched. Hannah wondered who they were, and how Ellen came to know them. She could not make out very much from such a distance, but saw that Ellen was happy and enjoying the company of the young men. She danced with both; it was country dancing on the grass, and there was a lot of twirling and skipping, and Ellen's hair flowed and swung around her. The sun caught the chestnut of her hair, and she stood out from all the other dancers. It was probably because she was so very energetic, and seemed to cover more ground than everyone else. Hannah, with tears flowing, realised that Freddie was beginning to lose interest in the bushes around him, and was getting restless. It was time to go. She quietly crept away, thinking that Ellen was well and happy, thinking that she need not be concerned for her anymore.

The Colemans and Mrs Webb were agreed that their wedding food was an unqualified success. The cake was all gone. The cold meats had been consumed. The pickles had been enjoyed. The bread baked in the shape of a sheaf of wheat was remarked upon and eaten with much enjoyment. The pork pies and fruit tarts were equally appreciated. All that remained was a pile of empty plates and glasses.

Once William and Charlotte had left Ellen wanted to help with the clearing away, but Jack persuaded her to leave with him early, as he would be taking her home to Lymington, and he did not wish to delay. After all he was going out of his way to see her home. Ellen felt obliged to agree. Charles remained with his family and left long after Ellen. He had watched her go, and then he had walked away; she had turned to see him and wave goodbye, but he had already disappeared from view.

＊ ＊ ＊

As he walked away he reflected on the change in Ellen, and how a little under a year ago she had appeared very different from the vibrant and lively girl she was now. What had brought her to the brink of destruction? He once again turned his mind to the woman who had had the care of Ellen, and realised that he would not be able to rest until he had fully investigated the circumstances of Ellen's treatment. He reasoned that Mrs Robinson was the instigator of the malpractice if that indeed was what had occurred. He knew with a degree of certainty that Maggie would not be capable of injury. She would be the one to be guided by her mother, and would probably be unaware and innocent of her mother's plans. It was, therefore, to the daughter that he would need to go. His calculations therefore would need to include the removal of the mother in order to approach the daughter.

Enough time had elapsed he reasoned for the mother not to be unduly perturbed by his reappearance if he had a good reason to do so. His next task was to think up just such an excuse for visiting.

Folklore and superstition were endemic and closely intertwined in the society which existed deep in the New Forest. Individuals were seen as casting spells and bringing curses upon other people. The curses might take many forms but would culminate in the demise or suffering of the cursed individual or family. Attitudes were based on acceptance and the knowledge that those who had these powers were to be feared and respected. It was commonplace for explanations of misfortune to be described as the result of a curse which had been laid at the door of the unfortunate victim, and that nothing could be done to prevent such things happening. A fatalistic view pervaded all those who lived amidst these attitudes, and it tended to be unwavering and dogmatic. Some would reason that this was due to ignorance and a stifling narrow mindedness which had existed for centuries. There were practitioners of what may be described as witchcraft who held a strong position in their communities and were not challenged. Their curses and potions, their remedies and intrigues continued as they had done for generations.

Mrs Robinson, known to her neighbours as Jane Root, for that was her name before marriage, and her marriage had been brief, was known for her skill in providing cures for impotence, flatulence, loss of hair, indigestion, gout, melancholy and many other misfortunes. She and Maggie lived slightly apart from those around them, in that they did not seek others out, but remained distant and rather enigmatic which added to their power and influence.

People would come to them for answers to their problems and difficulties. They did not hesitate to request help in solving disputes. They asked that people should receive their deserts, and believed that a payment would suffice and their troubles would be over, whilst the troubles for their adversaries would begin. Arguments with others could be resolved by the infliction of accident or misfortune to those who opposed them. The adverse was also true in that if calamity, illness or any other hardship befell anyone it was seen as either the result of some kind of curse or as retribution for misdeeds. In this way affliction and tragedy could be explained.

It was into this society that Charles was venturing as he sought for the truth about Ellen. He felt a certain misgiving about the two women, and was, he realised deeply suspicious of them. He wondered why he felt this way.

"I have to try and be impartial ... if I'm not then I could easily miss something important ... it would be easy to be prejudiced especially as I feel so uncomfortable about Mrs Robinson." Charles was discussing his feelings with the only person he could, Jack. He did not want Ellen to know anything about his actions until a satisfactory result had been achieved. He knew that this was far from certain, and so he held back from speaking to her.

"Mmm, what you say is reasonable, but if you are to catch a fly you need to set a trap don't you? And you can't do that unless you believe that the fly deserves to be trapped."

"Maybe it's not a trap exactly ... maybe what I need to do is to create a situation which will enable the fly to behave in the same way as it did before, and then judge whether it needs to be trapped then. It's going to be difficult I know, perhaps impossible, I don't know ... maybe it will be enough to study the fly and learn its habits."

"This fly business is confusing me ... although I think studying a situation can often lead to solutions."

"Thank you Jack, you have confirmed what I have been thinking ... I know now that I should plan to study Mrs Robinson's habits ... it won't be easy, especially as I have so little time at present, but I must make time ... will you help me? I won't be expecting you to put yourself into difficult situations, but do you think that we might tackle this together? Can I rely on your confidence? We will need to be very circumspect."

"When will you be needing me? It will be difficult for me too. I work the same hours as you, but if we could do our spying over a few days I think John would cover for me."

"I am thinking the same ... I feel that we will have to look out for one another ... I am not sure how Mrs Robinson is going to react ... so when I approach her you will need to be close by."

"You don't think that you will be in any danger do you?"

"Who can say until we are in the situation? We must plan carefully that is sure ... I believe that Mrs Robinson is capable of evil ... but we must allow her to be innocent until proved guilty ... do you understand me Jack? It will be essential that we stay neutral and natural, or she may react ... and who knows how that would end up."

"Are you sure that you want to do this Charles? I am thinking that it sounds too risky, and no good may come of what you are trying to do."

"I think you will agree with me when I say that if Ellen was nearly killed by her then she needs to know that there are consequences. She has to change or the repercussions would be grave. We also need to find out her motives for her attack on Ellen if indeed she did what she did intentionally. We won't know unless we gain her confidence or Maggie's. I believe that I must try. If you are unhappy about it, then I understand and I will go ahead alone."

"It's not that exactly, but I don't see how you can accomplish anything ... I don't see a way of getting at the truth."

"You are right ... I agree, I am not sure at the moment how I will go about getting Mrs Robinson's trust. It won't be easy but I am not deterred."

"Alright, once you know how I can be of use let me know and I will see what I can do to support you … we must be a little crazy you know … it's that Ellen … she is such a terrific girl … she's gone to our heads!"

"I've noticed how much you like her."

"Yes I do! I think most people would … she has something about her which is very attractive, very appealing."

"Yes she is very lovely."

"Oh yes, she is very attractive to look at, but she has a very engaging manner which has affected my feelings … I have grown … very fond of her."

"I suppose that is why I want so much to solve the puzzle of her past … I have noticed how she has become attached to her new life, and it would be better for her if there could be some kind of end, a resolution to her past life. I don't know what happened to her and her family. I only know that it has been incredibly difficult for her. But she has been courageous and has accepted her new life as it is. I know that if I was to ever accept a life devoid of my past life I would need to make some sense of everything that happened to me in that life … otherwise, it would be very difficult to leave the past behind and look to the future."

"Do you believe that Ellen wants to forget her past completely?"

"I'm not sure … on the surface it seems that way. She is so busy with the shop and the apothecary's, and gathering plants and ingredients for her recipes. She doesn't appear to give any thought to those she has left behind. She told me that she did contact her older sister about the wedding, hoping that she would meet up with her, but she didn't answer, as far as I know, and I gather there is a problem with the father … So maybe she is being forced to forget, for forget she must if she is ever to be happy."

"My word Charles you *have* given this some thought haven't you?"

"I suppose I have ... like you, Ellen has touched *my* heart ... and I do think about how I should help her; she feels so very like another younger sister."

The two young men looked at one another not really knowing what the other was thinking. Charles was probably nearer the mark when he concluded that Jack had grown very fond of Ellen, but a lot could happen over the next two years when Ellen would be eighteen years old. At the moment she was still a very young woman, and would need time to further mature.

Jack thought that Charles thought of himself merely as an older brother, and could not imagine that he could have any designs on Ellen's hand. They drifted into a thoughtful silence, not wishing to talk any further about a subject which they both found disconcerting.

Charles was ready to review the night of the rescue, and remembered the doctor's stated opinion of Ellen's condition. He had not wavered in saying that he viewed her illness as having been caused by poisoning. Charles recollected that the doctor had asserted that belladonna berries had been ingested and this had been concluded because of the patient's dilated eyes, her restless hands, her writhing movements and her inability to speak. The doctor had been convinced of this and had acted swiftly providing Ellen with a dose of water and vinegar and ordering that she should be kept very warm. Watching through the night Charles had kept the fire burning and had lain with her embracing her frail body, holding her close and wrapping his legs around hers, keeping the blankets tightly around her. He had held her so close to him that he had been able to feel the beating of her heart.

At about five o clock he had got up to stoke the fire and had seen in the dullness of the early morning that Ellen was very still and quiet. With the dread of someone who had prayed nearly all night for Ellen to be spared and who had been a little doubting that the prayers would be answered, Charles rushed to touch her wrist and found it warm with a clear pulse. As he touched her he instantly felt such an unspeakable relief and could not help but drop to his knees and his head bowed onto the side of the bed.

"Thank God, thank God … Oh I do thank thee Lord, for being here and for giving this girl her life back … I thank thee for hearing me and ask now that she will fully recover … that she will be well and suffer no more … In Jesus' name, Amen." Ellen had heard the quiet man's tearful voice at her bedside. She knew it was the young man who had carried her out of the house. She knew that he had held her on the front of his horse, and rode somewhere, somewhere where she now was. She could not remember anything else. Only now did she feel safe as the sincerity of the man's prayer sounded close beside her, and she knew that, for the moment, she did not need to fear.

As Charles recollected the events of that night he had no way of knowing of the emotional impact he had had on Ellen. He had warmed her physically he knew but he did not know that he had warmly quietened her fearful heart.

* * *

Charles approached the Robinson's cottage with some dread. Jack had been watching the house each morning for a week and had noticed that the mother had a habit of going out after breakfast. Charles had decided that this was an opportunity for him to interview Maggie and so he met with Jack near the cottage, and while he stayed back out of sight and watched in case of trouble, Charles went alone to meet Maggie.

He knew that the conversation he was to have with her might become awkward and possibly unrewarding. However, he clung to the belief that if he was careful and apparently lacking in any form of deceit, he might be able to catch the girl off guard, and get to the truth. His knock on the door was immediately answered by her.

"Hello Maggie, I wonder if you remember me? Charles Coleman. Is your mother at home?"

"She's no'. Mother will no' be long though."

"I will wait here for her then, I just wanted to let her know that the young girl she was caring for a while ago … who, if you remember was brought here by Jack Woodley, a friend of mine, well I thought you would wish to know that she has fully recovered, and is now doing very well. I knew that you would be anxious about her, as she was very sick when she was with you, and you and your mother had done your best … I am sure your mother would be much relieved to hear the news … it must have been hard for her to have watched her taken away when she had done so much for her."

"Well ma knew that the girl *would* ge' be"er, so she did na fear."

"Oh I am relieved to hear that … she was sure that the girl would get better?"

"Yes, she told me tha' she would be be"er in a couple of days."

"How could she have been so sure? She was after all very unwell."

"Ma 'as 'ad a lot of practice in the art, and could see that it was only a ma"er of time.".

"How amazing! Your mother is an extraordinary woman … she has practiced her treatments for many years then?"

Maggie was nodding and smiling eagerly. "Oh yes, ma 'as 'elped many folk around 'ere."

"But she wasn't able to help the baby?"

"'ow did you know about tha'?"

"I heard about the child and what happened … how the baby was taken by your mother to the doctor … he said that the child had only just died … how awful that must have been for you, I imagine … it must have been terrible for you to lose the child that way." Charles wondered if he had managed to lead Maggie far enough down his own train of thought, enough to get her to innocently share with him what had happened to the baby that he guessed must have been hers.

"I did na think that anyone knew about me daugh'er … ma said that i' needed to be kep' quiet like."

"Some folk know about it, but not many."

"'ow did they ge' to know?"

"At the inquest … you know the baby was taken to the authorities … what did you call her?"

"Jane … after me ma." Maggie bowed her head, and her grief became apparent on her face. She looked up at Charles, "She were a lovely baby Mister, she 'ad golden 'air."

"Golden hair ay? How lovely! So what happened?"

For a moment Maggie looked around her anxiously, but whispered, "She breathed and cried bu' she stopped. Ma took 'er, and tha' was tha'."

"Why did no one know that the child was yours?"

"That was ma's idea … the travellin' man was no' to know abou' the baby."

"Why was that?"

"Oh ma did na wan' 'im to come a calling and 'ave 'im know abou' the baby … ma said 'e weren't no good."

261

Charles understood what Maggie was telling him. He understood that his theory was correct, that the child had indeed been Maggie's; but the reason for the secrecy which appeared to be based on the mother's view of Maggie's vulnerability might not be the true one; there might be other circumstances less favourable to the mother which Maggie was unaware of. Nevertheless it was possible that Jane Robinson was a protective caring mother, but other aspects of what happened pointed again to other motives which were not so benevolent. Charles needed to follow his other theory and it might shed light on the mystery of the baby.

"But what about the young woman, Ellen? She kept getting ill. Your mother seemed to be giving her drugs which were not helping."

"Ma told me tha' she wanted to try out a new remedy she 'ad made, and she gave the girl a bad stomach so tha' she could test it. Just think ma could 'ave found something importan' ... an' she could use it on lots of people and make 'em be"er ... wouldna tha' be wonderful? ... An' folk would look up to 'er and treat 'er kinder."

Charles tried to smile gently at the innocent girl. Maggie simply believed that her mother had done right, just because her mother had convinced her that what she was doing was good. She could not disbelieve; it was not in her nature to question her mother. He instinctively knew that this girl could not be held accountable for what had happened to Ellen or to the baby.

Questions rose rapidly in his mind. How was he to speak to Jane Robinson and what should he advocate as a just consequence? He needed time to deliberate.

"Is your mother not treated kindly then?"

"Sometimes she 'asn't been able to 'elp, and then people won't talk to 'er, and won' 'ave anything to do with 'er ... it's 'ard for 'er, you see."

"Of course, of course ... it must be."

"'ere she comes now."

Jane Robinson saw her daughter standing on the doorstep talking to the young man, and drawing nearer recognised him. She had a remarkable memory for people and felt suspicious when she observed that he was talking in a very relaxed way to Maggie.

"'ow do sir? Do you 'ave business with me?"

"As a matter of fact I do ... Charles Coleman ... I came by if you remem ..."

"I remember you sir, but I wonder why you are 'ere today."

"I was just saying to Maggie that I just felt I should let you know that the young woman Ellen you cared for and who was taken away by me is now fully recovered, and I felt sure that you would be anxious to know that ... seeing as you had cared for her so attentively for so long ... yes, she is fully well and thriving."

"Mr Coleman ...it's no surprise to me ... I knew that she was goin' to quickly ge' well ... but just the same I thank you for your trouble ... letting us know of the fact ... you see Maggie, i' was just as I said i' would be ... I told you tha' she would soon be well."

Charles observed the mother and daughter exchange the kind of self-congratulatory looks which threatened to make his anger surface, but he needed to stay calm and reasoned that a hasty departure was essential.

"Yes, you have had far more experience in these matters than I. I have delivered my message so I will be on my way."

Charles fully believed that he had received the true explanation of the events leading up to his involvement with Ellen, and for the moment he was satisfied but so overcome with anger with the woman who stood before him that he really struggled to contain his feelings. He felt now that he had been justified in pursuing his chosen course. He also felt that despite having come to some kind of conclusion, he might well be at just the beginning of his investigations. He pondered his next move. He wanted to act and assure himself that Jane Robinson would never again use and victimise a vulnerable individual in order to experiment with remedies. If she was allowed to continue in this practice in any way, her capacity to mistreat and harm those in her care might lead to terrible consequences.

He wondered about the true nature of this woman, who had deliberately poisoned a young girl. Was she so cold and unfeeling that she was able to have the possible death of a girl on her conscience and remain unperturbed? Or was she so sure of her skills that she knew without reservation that Ellen would not be in any danger? The latter he found difficult to accept; the treatment which Ellen had received could not be tolerated by anyone who possessed an ounce of integrity towards the care of others. No, how could anyone be responsible for the terrible condition that Ellen was in without being totally immoral, callous and cold hearted? And what was the truth about the child? His blood ran cold when he considered what Jane might have done, because Maggie had been unclear as to why the baby had stopped breathing.

He began to be swayed by the idea that Jane was both calculating and heartless, and that she had to be made aware that there were some who would not stop at reporting her to the authorities if she did not make some kind of assurance that it would never happen again. But was Jane a woman that could be trusted to keep to her word? He had serious reservations. If she could not be constrained to make some kind of agreement with him, which he felt she would be true to, what then?

Charles needed more time. Perhaps the answer would come without his direct involvement. He decided with no loss of anger to leave things in the hands of the Almighty for the time being, found Jack in his hiding place, deciding to tell him nothing, and returned to work satisfied that, for the moment, he had done all he could. But he knew that he could not leave things for long. He knew that if Jane Robinson was allowed to continue and the worst happened, that an unfortunate person became a victim of her callous actions, he could never forgive himself for not acting in time.

Charles's anger did not abate; he felt shamed at the wickedness he had found and vengeful towards the perpetrator; he realised that his feelings for Ellen were beyond what he had supposed. He knew she was safe with her grandparents, but still felt that he needed to protect her, to watch over her and stay where he could guard her. He had not felt this way about any other individual, not even his younger sister. He became restless at work, and lived for the hours on Sunday when he could ride to Lymington and be with her.

* * *

Time passed in the way that time does. For months he wrestled with his feelings and with his need to be with Ellen. He tried hard to reconcile what was happening to him with the knowledge that it would be some time if at all that he could tell her how he felt. He wondered if he should stay away from her, as this might be easier for him. As he struggled, he continued as he had always done, his kind nature overcoming his anguish and no one close to him was aware of the agonising conflict within him.

* * *

With Mary's descent into the living rooms of her family there became a similar downward trajectory in the relationships within the family. There had been, it is true, an uneasiness in the atmosphere prior to her returning to their midst, in that there had been a growing level of anxiety in relation to her state of health amongst some members of the family. Agnes, seeing Mary's gradual decline at close hand, had been particularly affected and had been overjoyed at the miracle which had occurred. This was however short lived as she quickly realised that her father's behaviour changed once again, becoming more erratic than it had ever been before. He tried to continue his attentions to Mary as he had done when she had been ill, but they gradually diminished, until he became unpredictably moody and often silent. He then remained at home very little, and Mary inevitably resumed her discontented view of her husband. This took only a few weeks to evolve, so that the relatively pleasant atmosphere between the family members which had existed while Mary was in her bed, very rapidly vanished. Everyone felt misplaced and on edge with Mary in their midst, caused in the main by Thomas's unreasonable moods and unpredictable behaviour.

Agnes wondered about her father's reaction to his wife's return to the family circle and to health. She could not understand it but she was unwilling to spend time in reflection. She was too interested in her growing musical prowess. Sir Russell had continued to show an interest in her developing talent, and had arranged for her to perform at an evening of entertainment at the Grange.

She had practised two pieces with her tutor Mrs Graham, both composed by Handel, whom she was assured was very popular. She then impatiently waited for the evening of the concert,

To be involved in a musical evening organised by the most influential and powerful family in her enclosed and restricted world was for Agnes something she had had no idea of ever happening. She had never dreamt that she would move in such circles, and was in some measure placated from the unpleasant feelings which had engulfed her the night of Sir Russell's birthday party. She had felt like a nobody then; she had gone unnoticed by all those who had some form of standing in their society. She had felt that her attendance at the party was superfluous and it wasn't until Hannah had spoken to her that she was able to return to her natural cheerful disposition. She had brightened, and had resolved to take full advantage of every opportunity.

She reflected on Ellen's demise, and made the assumption that she had given up her ideals and would remain in obscurity for the rest of her life. Not so herself. She would not allow herself to be in the power of anybody, which she realised in her limited way to be most probably a member of the opposite sex. She would engineer her life with a determination and an enthusiasm which could not be blocked by a man entering her life; she naively decided that she could avoid getting embroiled with any men.

Now that she had been offered yet another opportunity to better herself, she was content for the moment. Mrs Graham, married to a Winchester College master and contentedly housed in a fine house in Kingsgate Street, showed her what might be possible, and she wanted that and more.

She was introduced as Miss Lambourn on the night in question and accompanied by Mrs Graham on the piano sang confidently and with a clarity that made her performance extremely memorable. Surrounded by countless candles in a fashionable room filled with many objects of taste, and occupied by fine ladies and gentlemen who inhabited a superior world to her own, she was not at all overcome. She loved the music so much that she was totally absorbed by it, and hardly noticed the rapt expressions of her audience. They burst into applause after each piece, and after the second she wished that she had prepared more. When she was asked to sing another, Mrs Graham suggested the folk song 'The Ash Grove' which Agnes sang unaccompanied, as it lent itself to the simplest of arrangements, and she performed it with such a pure voice that everyone seemed to be completely spellbound by her presentation of it. No sound other than her voice was heard. At its conclusion everyone applauded so enthusiastically that some stood and cheered. Alfred looked on once again bewitched by Agnes, but she had another admirer, his brother James, who stood beside him in the front row, and who gave Agnes such a wonderful smile that her eye was instantly caught by it. She looked at James and remembered how well he danced the night of the party. She curtsied low apparently to him alone and he bowed slightly in acknowledgement. She turned, knowing she had performed well, and returned to her seat at the side of the room.

Listening to the other performers she realised that she had far from disgraced herself. In fact she thought for just a moment that she had outshone everyone that night, and she felt elated and triumphantly satisfied.

James pursued her at the end of the evening, alongside Alfred. She was standing with the other performers when they both approached her, James taking her by the hand and raising it to his lips.

"Agnes, what a pleasure it was to hear and see you this evening." James stood to one side as his brother also showed his appreciation of her performance.

"It's been too long since father's party ... I have wondered if you would visit again ... I hope your family are all well."

"Why yes thank you." Agnes had blushed at the thought of that night when her father had so unceremoniously escorted her away from Alfred. She felt awkward for the first time in the evening, but quickly regained her poise when James spoke again.

"We hope that this will be a regular occurrence ... that you will come back to delight us again. You know that father is looking to establish a theatre in Winchester I expect. He sees this as being a place of entertainment, a place of music and a variety of performers. I suspect that you will become very popular there ... your gift needs to be enjoyed by many more than are here this evening. There are so many people who would love to hear you ... it would give them so much pleasure ... what do you think of that?"

"Why I 'ave not given such a thing any though' ... I did not know 'ow I migh' be able to sing for people. I am very much dependan' on my pa still, but 'ave been fortunate to 'ave received suppor' from Sir Russell. He 'as been most encouraging ... he 'as been very generous and kind." Agnes knew nothing of theatres and was not able to understand the idea that she would become popular because of such places. However, she was very aware of the need to respond positively to Sir Russell's family as she had concluded that she would need to depend on them until she was quite a lot older.

As both of the young men looked at her, she smiled at them and realised that they admired her. For the first time she ascertained that as a young woman she was able to command the attention of young men, especially if they found her pleasing. Her smiles were returned. Alfred held out his arm to her.

"I expect you would like some refreshment ... we have some here, at the end of the room ... perhaps you would like to come with me?"

Agnes hesitated, reminded of her father's words, but he was not here and so she self-consciously took his arm, laying her hand close to his wrist. He moved slowly through the members of the company, James following just behind her. As she reached the table he came alongside her, and stood watching her. He handed her a small glass of wine. Alfred had a plate of dainty biscuits which he held out to her. The sons of the house were fully occupied. Despite their youth they had moved into the adult masculine world of giving attention to talented and beautiful girls.

Sir Russell joined them to add his words of congratulation and praise to those of the young men, but requested that James should go with him as there was someone he particularly wanted him to meet. James sadly bowed to Agnes and went with his father.

* * *

Hannah had resumed her place in the Lambourn household despite Mary's presence in their midst. She did not disclose her feelings openly, but expended them in private. She had needed Agnes for this purpose. Their relationship had developed in that they sought to talk to one another about those things that troubled them, and they knew that it would go no further. Neither of the sisters wanted their father or Mary to know of their thoughts and concerns. They drew closer, and Hannah turned to Agnes when her feelings threatened to get the better of her, seeking for diversion which only Agnes was capable of.

"Tell me abou' the concer' Aggie ... you sounded so 'appy abou' i' ... did i' go well? I was thinkin' abou' you all evenin' prayin' tha' you would be 'appy ... 'ow was i' Aggie?"

"I' was wonderful ... so wonderful." Agnes lifted her arms above her head and twirled around on the spot. Her action described the way she was feeling. Hannah laughed at her.

"Tell me who was there? Were there many people invi'ed?"

"Oh yes, although I did no' recognise many of them ... I think they were gentlemen of Sir Russell's acquaintance and their wives ... some were no' from round 'ere I am sure ... though the Russells came, and Sir Russell's sister from Romsey ... I recognised 'er ... and James Turner was there of course, and 'e particularly liked my singing ... 'e said he though' I would become popular ... what do you think 'e meant?"

"Popular? ...tha' lots of people would like to 'ear you sing I suppose. Did 'e give any idea of 'ow that migh' come abou'?"

"Oh I don't know 'annah ... all I know is tha' I can't wai' until the next time. I want to keep singin' ... I know i' sounds strange bu' I love to hear my voice ... Mrs Gra'am is so pleased with me ... I can sing 'igher now than I ever could before ... I think i' must be the exercises she gives me, though she says I must no' go very 'igh as I am so young ... but I do love to sing the 'igh notes!" Agnes followed this pronouncement with a rising scale which culminated in a very high note indeed.

With admiration, Hannah looked closely at Agnes and perceived that she was the happiest she had ever seen her. Agnes was glowing with the joy which comes when a talent is practised, worked hard upon, shared and appreciated. Recognition was what

Agnes had wanted, and although Hannah had her doubts about their father's willingness to allow Agnes the kind of opportunities which would advance her singing career, she remained silent. She did not know if and how singers made their own living, but secretly hoped that it might be possible for Agnes.

"I do know somethin' and tha' is Freddie loves your singing too ... 'e listens so inten'ly when you sing ... I think 'e wants to try! Sometimes when we are ou' 'e starts to sing as 'e walks along ... it sounds so pre"y! 'e takes everythin' in you know!"

"He does ... Freddie is so clever I know ... 'e needs to star' learning. Do you think that we should star' 'im on his letters or numbers?"

"I suppose i' could do no 'arm ... 'e can 'ave 'is own slate and chalk ... I'll buy 'em for 'im. Wha' do you say?"

They planned how they would help Freddie and completed their morning chores. Mary had not come down as yet, and so they were free to enjoy themselves as they wanted. They were happy together. Hannah was not envious of Agnes's gift. She had returned to a state of uneasy contentment, relieved that she had not been ousted from the household and had assumed a peace born of gratitude which pervaded her feelings. She could see that she was fortunate, and hung on to the possibility that if she did not antagonise her father, she could live a relatively comfortable and happy life with him. She had forced herself to forget the criticisms and animosity she had felt towards her father. In order for her to maintain a place in his house, she needed to try and view him as a benevolent parent who had done everything he could for the betterment of his children and who cared deeply about each of them. Her mind was distorted by this view, because she was persuading herself to see her father as someone quite different from what reality was telling her. However, Hannah knew that she would need to change her attitude towards him if she was to stand any chance of having a future in his home.

*　*　*

Seven

'The rose distils a healing balm,
The beating pulse of pain to calm'.

Spring had come to Hampshire, a county of forest, river water, heath and rolling downs. Lymington placed on the edge of a forest and perched on the expansive mouth of the sea had truly become home for Ellen. She returned to the land reclaimed from the sea as often as she could. She had, through her herbal remedies and cosmetic treatments, come to know many of the local people, and because of her family connections, had been quickly integrated into the fabric of the merchandising community. The Timms family were hardworking and respected. Jacob and Susannah had invited Ellen often to their little home tucked away in the south of the village. It was small but had a comfortable sitting room and a courtyard at the back where Susannah sometimes sat in the sunshine with her young child, a little girl named Elizabeth, born in July the previous year.

Ellen had liked Susannah and had, when time allowed, helped her with the baby. Ellen was reminded of her own younger brothers and sisters, and particularly Hannah's Freddie. She wondered how he was doing. She thought about Henry and his gentle ways; and there was Emily and George. George would probably not remember her now.

It had been nearly two and a half years, and she realised with a shock that she had not kept her promise to Ada to remember her and do what she could for her. It was true that she had not been in a position to offer her anything. Ada was a long way away, and she had no means of getting to see her. And if she did, what then? She regretted that she had not been true to her word, but she would one day. Her prayers for Ada and for those others who haunted her mind were spoken every day. Her faith had returned because she believed that her good fortune and the many blessings which had come into her life were due to a loving God.

She saw Charles and Jack as being very different. Charles she saw as a man of faith. Jack was less serious. She could not help comparing them. They both came to see her regularly, and she continued to spend most of her free time with them both. Samuel had tried to take up the mantle of Ellen's father, and worried about her in much the same way he had worried about his daughter Hannah. He had stated that for Ellen to be seen so much in the company of two young men might lead to people's disapproval. He also felt that not only would it expose her to unpleasant comments but that the two young men involved might also be viewed unfavourably. He had raised this with Ellen who had been very surprised. She had not expected it at all. Jack and Charles were older brothers, much older in Charles's case. How could anyone view her association with them in such an adverse way? It wasn't long however before her perception of her relationship with Jack was put into question.

A beautiful spring afternoon with a lovely girl is a delightful experience for any young man. Jack, walking beside Ellen, was filled with such a strong feeling of unreserved delight that he was overcome by it, and found that he felt an urgent need to express what was in his heart to Ellen. They were used to sit on a grassy irrigation bank looking out to sea, and this day was no exception. As they sat together Jack gazed at Ellen, and began to express the thoughts which had been going round and round in his mind for months.

"Ellen, I've had something on my mind for a long time ... I feel that I should tell you about it ... it seems like the right time." Jack paused and waited for Ellen to speak, to give him permission to continue, but she just looked at him with a vaguely quizzical expression.

"I have hoped that you see me more than the person who came along all those months ago and stopped to assist you ... I have certainly begun to see you in a very different way over the past months. You have become ... the dearest person to me." Jack again waited for a word or a glimmer of encouragement but found none.

"You must know that you have become the most important person in my life ... I ... I love you most dearly ... you see ... and would wish that we might become engaged to be married ... please Ellen ... choose me to be your husband. I will take care of you ... I will make promises to you which I will not break." Jack held Ellen's hand between his and lifted it to his lips. He kissed the inside of her wrist and waited.

"Jack, Jack ... I need time to consider ... you have surprised me ... I did not expect ... I need time to think about this ... will you allow me some time to think about my feelings ... I know I like you and owe you a great deal ... but I do not know if I can marry you ... please don't be upset ... I would not wish to lose your friendship." Ellen's eyes filled with a tearful consternation and confusion derived from the unexpected nature of Jack's declaration and her unwillingness to lose him. But marriage? She would soon be seventeen. Wasn't that too young to be thinking of such things? How much time would she need? How long would the engagement have to be? Did she love him?

"Yes ... I have surprised you I can see ... I thought you knew how I felt but of course you are inexperienced in such things ... I imagine mine is your first proposal of marriage, and I am hoping it will be your last ... I can't say more than that ... I will leave you to think ... I cannot say more now ... I had hoped that you would have been sure and accepted me ... but I can see I must not press you ... take as much time as you need ... but ... please give me your answer in a specified time ... I don't think I can wait without knowing when your answer will come ... choose a time would you dearest Ellen when you will give me your answer?"

Ellen looked at the disappointment and anxiety in Jack's handsome face. He had been shaken by her reply. He had been so sure. Now all that remained for her to do was to in some small measure try to reassure him that her answer would come sometime.

"Would my ... birthday ... be an acceptable time?"

"Of course, of course." Jack mused on the thought of having to wait two months and realised that he had hoped for an earlier answer. However, he loved her. He could wait as long as it takes. He hugged her close to him. He wanted to kiss her so much but her face was turned away. He could wait. Yes, he could wait.

* * *

Charles had returned home from his visit to the Robinsons angry and perplexed. He had not known how to act, but realised with some relief that Maggie was innocent of any crime and that her mother was solely to blame for what had transpired. He knew now that Mrs Robinson seemed entirely lacking in those qualities which prevent individuals from performing despicable deeds. It was on this conclusion that he was musing two days after his visit to the forest, as he was engaged alone in the workshop that he heard the doorbell ring as someone entered the shop. He hastened to welcome the visitor but was stopped abruptly when he found the same woman of his thoughts confronting him.

"I can see yer surprised to see me, Mister Coleman ... and well you migh' be ... after frigh'ening my daugh'er the way you did ... she 'as told me wha' you said to 'er about the baby ... you 'ave no righ' ... you upse' 'er so much tha' she 'as run off ... I don'' know where she's gone ... and as for wha' you implied abou' yer friend ... an' my daugh'er told you tha' I poisoned 'er ... it's no' true ... an' if you think tha' you can prove i', you won'' ... there aint nothin' you can do Mister ... do yer 'ear?"

"That may be so Mrs Robinson, but I know what I know, and I will, if necessary take what I know to the police."

"You won' do tha' cos if you do you will regre' i' ... misfortune will visi' your family ...illness ... bad luck ... disappointments ... even death ... they will all be yours if you say one word agains' me ... do yer understand me?" Mrs Robinson's expression had not changed throughout this discourse. Her gaze was unwavering. Her eyes were threatening. She spat the words out with such force, that Charles flinched at the mention of each dreadful consequence.

He faced a woman who saw him as her deadly enemy, and she had expressed her hatred without reservation. This woman was indeed a person to be feared. He did not feel afraid of her however. He realised that her words were desperate, that she had seen the precarious nature of her situation. She would try and frighten him off, but he remained indefatigable in his determination to bring her to justice.

"You are threatening me but I am not deterred. I will continue on the course I have set for myself which was to examine the circumstances of Ellen's illness and discover the truth. I have the truth now and what I do with it is up to me and nothing you can say or do will change my chosen course. You see Mrs Robinson I would have been happy for you to make an assertion to me that you would never repeat your experiments. I would have been willing to accept an agreement from you ... but I can see that that would be foolhardy. And so I will visit the police today and tell them what I know ... I will do my duty ... I cannot remain silent."

This verbal exchange had been heard in part by Charles's mother, who hearing the tone of part of the conversation was unsettled, and was moved to come to the workshop from the kitchen. She came hesitantly and arrived just as her son was saying to the visitor that he would do his duty.

Maria could not see the face of the woman as she entered the room, but she saw her son's expression suddenly change from determined and implacable to one of fear.

"My mother is here now and so I must ask you to leave ... our conversation is at an end ... there is nothing more to say." Charles stepped towards his unwelcome visitor and as he did so she turned sharply, gave Maria a malignant look, swept past her and left.

"Who was that son? I didn't like the look of her. What did she want from you?" Maria, frightened by the atmosphere in the room, looked for an explanation from Charles which would calm her troubled thoughts.

"Mother, please do not concern yourself ... she is gone and will not return ... I think I need a cup of tea ... have you any of that delicious cherry and almond cake left?" Charles put his arm around his mother's shoulders and gently led her to the door and to the kitchen where he would spend a few moments with her. He needed to make sure that his mother's disquiet was removed. He would talk to her about her favourite subjects, cooking, his father and his sisters and the ugly woman would, hopefully, be soon forgotten.

* * *

Important decision making had become the prevailing consideration amongst the adults and older children of the Lambourn family. Ellen's choice of husband was perhaps the most significant one to be made and it constantly preyed on her mind hauntingly. Thomas was thoughtfully wondering whether or not to confront Dr Stocks about his wife's improved condition. He had thought that they had an understanding, but it clearly had been broken on the doctor's side. He wanted to know why. Agnes was considering leaving her father's protection and beginning a musical career. She felt impelled to make a decision which would lead to her future happiness, and thought intuitively that she must leave. Young Henry had been feeling very unhappy at home, and his only joy was to be had at school, and when he was out in the open air. He wanted to go away, but he did not know where. Mary, restored to full health, and wondering about the circumstances of her illness and her swift recovery, felt confused by her husband's behaviour towards her and felt bewildered and unsafe. She took to visiting her parents more often, and once she had been informed that they had not visited her at the time of her illness because Thomas had put them off, she became even more puzzled. Thomas had told her something quite different hadn't he? She could not make sense of it. She decided to confide in her mother.

* * *

Just a few weeks after Jack's proposal to Ellen she was submerging herself as she had done before in her duties at Mr James's shop and her own interests in the grocers'. She had collected elderflowers and had dried them successfully. She had branched more into beauty treatments, and had successfully manufactured a hair wash from dried rosemary flowers and leaves. It had sold well and she was now contemplating an attempt at making an almond butter for softening the hands, but she would need her grandfather to supply her with sweet almonds and barley. She had already produced a very lovely rosewater which, it was agreed by those who had purchased it, was beautifully light and very refreshing to the skin.

She liked to work at various recipes and had begun to collect and dry sage which she had cultivated in the garden. She had learnt of many applications of sage infusions; she knew of its use in healing a sore throat and mouth ulcers; it could also be beneficial in treating nervous disorders if taken regularly as a tea. She was absorbed in the painstaking task of laying the leaves out on wire frames which were to be put out in a warm dry place.

She knew that Charles was hoping to visit at some time on a Sunday, as he had informed her at their last meeting that he would extend his journey a few miles more when he next visited Jack in Brockenhurst. He did indeed travel on to Lymington this particular Sunday and found Ellen absorbed in the sage drying.

Charles took every opportunity to visit the Timms family. This was not very frequent as his duties at home prevented him from

281

going about the countryside. However, he tried earnestly to visit regularly but on this occasion it had been over three weeks since he had seen the family. He noticed a change in Ellen, who was always welcoming but she appeared to be almost relieved to see him. He felt this and thought that perhaps she had missed him. She stopped working and came to him immediately.

"Charles, you have been away so long ... had you forgotten us? Look, come and see, I have a new venture ... I have been going over the properties of sage, and have realised that I have not used it as much as it deserves ... see, I have grown some plants ... they are doing well ... I have just picked my first harvest ... what do you think?"

"Clearly you have something important going on here ... how do you do? All well with you? And the family?" The Timms's home appeared to be empty of all its members except Ellen. Samuel and Eliza were visiting Jacob, Susanna and Elizabeth. Charles felt that he had a wonderful opportunity to really talk to Ellen, and, in his relaxed way, took off his jacket, laid it across the back of a chair and sat at the table. Ellen offered him tea and as they sat together their conversation turned to all those things which tend to preoccupy families. He asked about Susannah's daughter. He questioned her on her grandparents' health. He wondered how her work at the apothecary's was progressing. He asked her if she had seen Jack. And so the conversation continued.

"It's been on my mind to tell you about what I have done to get to the truth of your illness ... I wanted to find out for your sake mainly, but also for the sake of others, and so I asked some questions."

"Did you ... oh ... what were the replies?"

"I need not conceal from you that I discovered that Mrs Robinson had deliberately made you unwell ... deliberately, yes, there is no doubt."

"But why should she do such a thing? What could she gain by doing such a thing?" She was startled by the sudden disclosure and could not imagine for an instant why she should have been treated in such a way.

"I am not entirely sure of her motives, but only that she hoped to try out some remedy on you for poisoning, and had to poison you first before she could try her experiment." Ellen's expression displayed her shock on Charles's pronouncement; she could not think clearly.

"This means that she might have killed me ... I can't believe it ... what could possess someone to do such a thing? I don't understand. Do you Charles?"

Charles looked at Ellen's anxious face and realised that she had no conception of the kind of poverty, social rejection and malevolence which can lead to the kind of actions which they were now considering.

"The woman was desperate I imagine, desperate for money or recognition ... it is hard to say what brings a person to perpetrate such wickedness ... I have been feeling very angry about it ... when I have thought of how close you may have come to death." Charles felt unable to continue faced with Ellen's anguished face. He could not guess what was going through her mind. He only knew that he had shocked her and he wanted to comfort her.

"So what now Charles? What are you thinking of doing"?

"I have dealt with it ... it would have been wrong to have let her continue without some kind of action being taken ... it is in the hands of the police ... I told them what I knew ... Maggie has run away but she will be found I am sure ... I think she was driven away by her mother turning on her ... she is entirely innocent of any crime ... her mother will, I am sure, experience the full consequences of what she has done ... I am telling you this because the police will no doubt come here and want to talk to you ... you must prepare yourself for their questions". Charles carefully outlined to Ellen what he knew and what he felt she had to do.

"Oh Chassie why did this have to happen? Why couldn't it all be forgotten? I've dreaded this ... I wanted to put all of it behind me ... I know that you are right but it is very hard to accept ... I know you were thinking of the right course ... you always do ... I wish sometimes that you were less ... honest ... no I don't mean that because then you wouldn't be you." Ellen ended flustered and oddly emotional. She could feel herself becoming as vulnerable and frightened as she had been not very long ago. Charles saw this and wished that he had told her differently, that he had been able to use words which in some way eased the impact of what he had done, that she would find it easier to accept; but he was not able to express himself in any way which could be described as less than entirely truthful. He had an honest way of acting which was intrinsic to him, and he knew of no other way.

"Why don't you have a rest from what you are doing? ... Just for a minute or two my dear, perhaps if we go out for a walk to the sea ... it will make you feel better I am sure ... Ellen?" Charles looked at Ellen in such a kindly way, and spoke so quietly to her that she could only look at him and he drew her to him and Ellen lay without a murmur in his arms. She felt a change within her; she comprehended that Charles understood her and loved her.

"Yes, I can leave this ... I feel I need to walk ... to be blown by the wind ... to see the movement of the sea ... to be away from *this*." She pointed at the delicate leaves which she had painstakingly and gently placed side by side on the rack. He looked at her and smiled, and they left the kitchen by the back door, escaping down the lane at the back of the Street, and almost running down the rough road which led to the estuary. It almost became a race; Ellen cried out as Charles took her hand and dragged her along accelerating until they were both running.

They were both laughing as they reached the path which led to the water, passing along the elevated dykes across the wide mouth of the sea.

They both stopped to feel the air and watch the drifting sky and stirring waves. Still holding hands they were content to be silent. Charles knew that Ellen was present with him as much as she ever could be and he was content. Ellen thought only of the beauty of all that surrounded her, and this was made possible by Charles, her best friend, who had been instrumental in eradicating her nightmares. She was awake now to a reality that held no terrors. Her wholeness however was not complete; there was an unspoken horror which she had not shared with Charles; and when, a little later, he laid bare his own unimpaired heart and laid it at her feet she could not reciprocate and gave no answer.

He took her home once their walk was complete. Their walk together was over. They said goodbye at the shop door, and both, their eyes wet and their hearts shaken, went back to their previous occupations, Ellen to her sage leaves and herbalist occupation and Charles to his shoe making, neither wanting to resume their solitary pursuits but having to do so.

The end of their love had followed as quickly as their recognition of its beginning. Charles had reached for her heart but, as soon as he had grasped for it, had discovered that it was not there, that it could not be his; he believed that her heart was absent. Ellen had not replied to his declaration which spoke of his deepest desire to be one with her, because she needed to speak of Jack and his proposal to her, but found she could not to Charles. She had given Jack no answer. How could she reciprocate Charles's love now? She did not know that he would interpret her silence as a rejection.

*   *   *

A week before her seventeenth birthday Ellen refused Jack. She told him that she could not marry him because she had realised that she did not know her own feelings. She told him that she needed a lot more time and did not expect Jack to wait. She wanted to keep their agreement. So she told him the truth as she understood it. He remonstrated that he was willing to wait, but Ellen would not allow it. The conversation was short and Jack went away aching and wondering if he would ever be happy again. Ellen knew that she had hurt him, and that his disappointment was deep and she prayed earnestly that it would be of short duration.

She continued on as she had before, suddenly bereft of the two men who had sustained her and befriended her, one of whom had left her with a destitute heart.

*   *   *

Marriage is sometimes settled upon easily and without delay or apprehension. Men and women have been known to rush in with varying consequences. Thomas Lambourn was considering his plight as once again Mary was at her parents' home as she had been every evening that week. Sometimes she stayed with them, and apparently they did nothing to encourage her to return to her husband. Thomas had not bothered to go and fetch her home on the first occasion, and he had not altered from this course. Mary went and Thomas did nothing. He reluctantly acknowledged that his plan to bring his wife into subjection had fallen short, and that Dr Stocks had at some point abandoned him and brought this situation upon him.

He had believed that he had a hold over the doctor, but he could see now that it had not been enough to counteract another influence, which he believed to be that of Sir Russell. He believed that somehow the latter had become acquainted with the use of Mary's 'tonic' in her treatment, and had ensured that the overdose of absinthe and morphine was ended.

The large quantities had led to a gradual debilitation of her health. Thomas had wanted this; had wanted a sickly, submissive and compliant woman who would be dependent on him. He would have gradually decreased the dose using the doctor as his accomplice, as Mary would probably demand his attendance on her, but he would ensure that he would only bring Mary back to a place where she could function minimally, and would need him, rely on him and be grateful to him.

He felt sure that Mary did not know of what had transpired, but she had now removed herself from his side; she had grown increasingly indifferent to him and within a few weeks began to demonstrate no interest in him or affection towards him.

He had aimed to see Dr Stocks on several occasions, but had been thwarted in obtaining a private interview with him. He was not at home or he was out and no one knew where. Thomas watched and waited for his opportunity. He needed to know what had led the doctor to desert him. He had been reliable in the past, had remained silent and kept secret those things which he had been called upon to swear to, and had demonstrated a willingness to join with the others involved and hold to the oaths made. So something must have occurred for him to lose his loyalty to him.

But first he would need to see Sir Russell, without others knowing, and ascertain his part in the breakdown of his plan. He needed to act circumspectly and draw no attention to himself. He needed to keep up the pretence of remaining at odds with him so that no one would suspect the alliance between them. He tried to think of a way of seeing Sir Russell without anyone becoming aware.

The city of Winchester was still the centre of culture and learning for most of the county of Hampshire. The town was to have a new theatre. The schools were established, and the College was known to be the educator of many great statesmen and leading thinkers and innovators of the time. Those who lived in Winchester were generally affluent although there were areas particularly in the lower parts of the town which were composed of very small dwellings with their doors opening on to the street. These homes had only just been built and attracted families with little wealth and a large number of children. A very short walk away on the other side of the cathedral beyond the Close and through the Kingsgate a very different atmosphere prevailed.

Lying close to the Winchester College, the streets were inhabited by those of good education and comfortable living standards. It was here that Agnes met with her singing teacher, and it was here that Sir Russell had taken her, and was just about to set off for his first appointment, when the door of his carriage was flung open and Thomas Lambourn's imposing figure stood on the carriage step before him. The driver had not been aware of the extra passenger, as Thomas had swiftly entered and quietly pulled the door to. He sat opposite Sir Russell and staring sternly at him at once began to explain the purpose of his being there.

"Sir Russell! It has been quite a time since we have been able to speak freely … and that is why I am here … I have something of importance to ask you, and I know I can rely on your honest reply. So I won't waste any more time. Did you speak to Stocks about the medical treatment of my wife?"

"If I did, there is nothing to discuss".

"Oh but I think there is. We had an agreement. It has held for many years … I was not aware that anything has changed … the trust that has been held has been broken … we agreed … the four of us … that nothing that transpired on the night in question, and nothing that has occurred since amongst us would be challenged or spoken of outside of us." He looked grimly at Sir Russell and added with a smile, "I state the obvious."

"Indeed I concur I have not spoken of anything beyond what you have described."

"How is it that an arrangement between Stocks and myself has been tampered with? You cannot deny that you have involved yourself in my business, when it don't concern you … what can you give as an explanation?"

"It is true that I went to Stocks. Many in the village were talking of Mary's condition … there were rumours about you and a great deal of unpleasantness … if we are to continue as we have and not raise any suspicion, I believed that whatever you were doing to Mary, it had to stop. With accusations against you, I knew that none of us would feel safe. Surely you can see that each of us is dependent on the others to remain above suspicion?"

"I heard of nothing in relation to myself."

"That was probably due to the fact that most of the rumours were starting close to home … your mother was one of the main instigators … you will have to be careful around her you know."

Thomas sat back and realised that he could not take the argument any further. Sir Russell had the measure of him, and he became silent.

"Now I can see I am almost at my destination … as we slow, you will remove yourself from my carriage … and I don't expect to see you again until all this has died down … you understand me Lambourn?"

Thomas stood and waited to open the door and jump.

"If … what you are saying is true I cannot question you further … I will, however look into the rumours you describe."

"You will not! Just such an action will draw further attention to yourself and will add fuel to the uneasiness felt by some around you … you must do nothing to raise people's suspicions. That's my final word."

Sir Russell stood and, held the door, ready to quickly open and then close it after Thomas's departure. As the carriage slowly turned the corner, he chose the moment to open the door wide and Thomas leapt and ran from view.

Sir Russell immediately hauled the door closed. He considered that Thomas was becoming dangerous, and for a moment, he reflected that he had always believed that Thomas was the weakest of the alliance. He hoped that his words had placated Thomas and that he would submit to his reasoning and not take things further.

The realisation that the tailor had become a menace haunted Sir Russell, and he wondered about the necessity of finding a way of ensuring that he remained silent. He considered what had transpired and decided on keeping a close eye on Thomas. He employed Isaac Grace for just such circumstances as this and summoned him immediately on his arrival home. He outlined to Grace what he expected of him. The servant understood that he was to watch Thomas Lambourn for the foreseeable future and report back to Sir Russell on a daily basis. Isaac had been called upon to perform similar duties in the past, and he was well recompensed for the inconvenience of the assignment. Sarah had found his long absences from home difficult but she was reassured when he regularly returned home with a full purse.

Sir Russell was satisfied that he had done what needed to be done and settled back into his business and family life, no longer feeling particularly concerned about the tailor. He knew that Grace would provide him with all the information he required.

* * *

News of Charles's marriage to Amelia Petty did not take long to travel to Lymington. Charles had not contacted the Timms family since the day of his final walk with Ellen, except to send messages via his friend Jack who had continued to visit just occasionally. Samuel and Eliza Simms had noticed the changes taking place in their household. They had both noted the way Ellen had immersed herself in her work, and now walked out alone. They had discussed the absence of Charles and the gradual disappearance of Jack and had drawn their own conclusions. Ellen's sad demeanour, it appeared to them, was due to the loss of Charles, and they imagined what had led to this. They never spoke of it to Ellen, because they were of the opinion that she would share her troubles with them in her own good time if she desired. In the meantime they tried to keep her spirits up.

The evenings which involved musical entertainment, became more numerous. Ellen participated in these as far as her low spirits would allow her. She was mainly happy to listen to her grandmother play her piano and sing, because she had little inclination to join in, but occasionally when pressed she did contribute, and could not help but be reminded of the time when Charles, Jack and all the family made music together at Christmas.

When Ellen heard of Charles's marriage she could not believe it. It was so soon after he had pressed her hand to his heart, so soon after he had kissed her so softly on her lips that she had hardly known that for a moment they had been joined to his. His warm eyes had been so muted and grey; his manner so gentle and loving. And he had left her suddenly; he had turned his eyes away from her so she would not see his distress, the stream of tears that he could not stop. She did not know that he was broken; she did not perceive his wretched state; she could not tell him why she had no answer; she had to give Jack *his* answer; only later did she realise that her feelings for Charles were very different from those she had for Jack, and that was only when he had been gone for several weeks.

She felt forsaken, wretched and full of regret. Charles had become such an integral part of her life and she had never imagined that there would ever come a time when he would not be close at hand. Now the unimaginable had occurred. She was left struggling to live without him, knowing that there was no possibility of his returning. She knew what grief was and felt it again. She spent long hours working and found a degree of peace as she did so. She participated in the life of her family, but always felt that part of her had somehow been separated from her and the part that remained longed for a reunion, when she might again feel whole.

Her life had continued in this way until she suddenly received a letter from Tom. Her reaction to its contents was one of excitement and a momentary loss of sorrow.

12, Bugle Street

5th September 1874

My dear Ellen

I am writing to you because I have recently seen Hannah and Agnes, and they wanted me to write to you. Hannah is not able at this time to contact you herself. Life at home with father has become more difficult. I am sure that she will explain when she sees you, which is what she hopes for.

Agnes has been accepted as a member of some new choral society. It appears that when she auditioned she did very well. We are all very excited about her success, and are planning to attend her first performance at the Winchester Guildhall which will be in a few weeks. She wants you to be there. I will give you all the details and hope that you will be able to come on the 8th of October. We all want to see you so much. Do you think you might be able to attend the concert?

Please give my best wishes and kind regards to grandpa and grandma. Perhaps they would like to come too?

Your loving brother

Tom

Ellen read and reread the letter and knew that she would do all she could to go to the concert. She was so delighted to hear that Hannah wanted to see her. This was an echo of her own wishes. As for her father, she could only guess at his attitude, but made the logical assumption that he would not be going to the performance, as she believed that Tom would not have written if he felt that an invitation to her would lead to their father being faced with the daughter of whom he never spoke. Ellen wondered why her father was not going. He, of all people, should be delighted to see and hear Agnes perform.

She needed to reply to Tom. She could not imagine anything that was more important than putting the words that needed to be said on paper. The writing of this letter took on such significance that she wondered if all the writing that she had done up until that point had been preparing her for this moment.

She would write to her brother and explain who she was now and what she wanted to become, and why she had felt driven to distance herself from her immediate family; and if she could she would go to Agnes's concert.

There had only been one occasion, one time, when she had felt that she had existed within her family after the death of her mother, and that had been when she had stood in her parents' bedroom and Tom had come and had tried to comfort her, for that was what it was she knew. Then she had noticed the bare lilac tree and the darkness of her brother's face and had experienced for the first time the despair and desperation which someone else was feeling. She had clung to him, and she believed he had to her. She clung to him again in her heart as his invitation to her took on a symbolic significance; that it somehow represented the removal of the darkness of her forced separation from those she loved; she longed for paper and pen but she knew she needed to wait until she had shared her news with her grandparents. She had to tell them as soon as she could. She did not spend long reflecting on the circumstances of the invitation, but hurriedly went to tell them about the letter's contents.

*   *   *

The time Ellen had been away from her home had wrought changes in all the individual members of the family, which, to those who observed them, were accounted as both good and bad. Hannah, terrified of losing her home altogether, and believing her future had been dictated by the birth of her baseborn son, dwelt in a spirit of gratitude that her son had saved her. However, her father was rarely present in his workshop and in their home; he had gradually ceased to provide for his children, and Hannah, faced with the possibility of hunger and homelessness, took to finding ways of acquiring money. She had proved herself to be a reasonable seamstress and took it upon herself to inform her neighbours and other village people that she could offer her services in mending and making a range of garments. Her father's melancholia deepened and he was hardly aware of Hannah's efforts and she was too absorbed to notice his decline.

The covert activity instituted by Sir Russell on Thomas had resulted in nothing to alarm him. Isaac, as assigned, had reported to his employer but had little to relate. Thomas was apparently going about as usual. His wife was away a great deal, but he showed no inclination to accompany her. Isaac reported that they appeared to be living separately, and that Hannah, the eldest daughter and her little boy were the only family who seemed to spend time with him. He went out a good deal and appeared to visit various customers, and once or twice went to Lyndhurst apparently on business. Otherwise he stayed at home.

Isaac had made some enquiries at the local ale house, not directly referring to the tailor, but, in his clever way, ascertaining that there had been a time when Thomas had frequented the inn but it had been some time since the landlord had seen him. Sir Russell was satisfied with Isaac's reports, and felt there was no immediate danger of Thomas causing any possible harm to himself or to his reputation.

The surveillance would continue however, until such time that Sir Russell was satisfied that Thomas had no intentions of jeopardising the arrangements which he had taken years to consolidate. His position in the community and the power which he held could not be threatened by a provincial tailor who knew too much and who could not be trusted. Sir Russell's position, influence and prosperity had to remain intact.

Thomas's mother was equally disparaging of him. Grandma Lambourn noticed her elder son's decline and had continued to have uncharitable thoughts about him as had been her habit.

"I knew that he would regret the day he married Mary ... from the first everyone could see that they were ill matched ... what drives a man to make such a stupid choice? ... And there's his ridiculous decision to take Hannah in when everyone knows that it would have been better for him and his family if she had been sent away." The disappointed mother was expressing her frustrations and incredulity to her close friend Mrs. Prewett after she had seen Thomas out in the High Street heading for goodness knows where. "It's around the village that he has given up the business ... Hannah has taken it on ... is he ill do you suppose?"

"Mrs Lambourn, I know not what troubles him ... I saw him in church and you must agree with me that he looks like a broken man ... the Reverend has been speaking to him a good deal I noticed ... what was that about I wonder?"

"Doubtless it was about Agnes ... I know the Reverend likes to keep up with Agnes's progress ... what else would they be talking about?"

"Well if you don't know I'm sure I don't ... it's those little ones I'm worried about ... Hannah is looking after them all ...

she can't manage to keep them all ... unless she is getting help from somewhere."

"Ah yes, that is something that wouldn't surprise me ... you know she's always seemed to have money ... have you noticed?" The two women were enjoying their conversation. They went on for a little while longer wondering who the benefactor might be, and if Hannah had sold herself in an unspeakable way. It wasn't long before rumours were circulating the entire village which stated the belief that Hannah was the recipient of financial favours which were given in payment for intimate favours received.

* * *

"How is it that you are unable to report of anything of concern, and yet I have from reliable sources that Lambourn is going about implicating me as the father of his daughter's child? I cannot believe that you have been thorough in your investigations ... Grace, have you been watching him as I said you should? Don't bother to make excuses to me ... it has angered me beyond measure to have these reports circulating and I am the last to know."

Sir Russell forcefully berated his servant for it appeared to him that his valet was to blame for his present discomposure. He had made it utterly clear to him what was expected and yet he had failed to pick up on Lambourn's mischief. Isaac Grace had always been able to do what was required in the past. What had gone wrong? He wasn't really interested in Grace's explanation. His servant was an errand boy who was of little consequence, but somehow Grace would have to make amends, and ensure that nothing more came of the rumours.

"Sir, I have not heard of any such reports ... are you sure that the person or persons who gave you this message are trustworthy?"

Sir Russell began to show an increased agitation as he walked away from Isaac.

"What! You question me on the validity of what has been reliably reported to me! Grace, I have no option but to insist that you find out more ... you must make amends for this mess ... I will not have my name slandered in this way ... not by anyone ... get to Lambourn and fix him ... you know what to do ... and, I and my family ... we must not be implicated ... in any way." It was clear to Isaac that the interview with his employer was at an end. He would do anything for Sir Russell, and so, with a plan forming in his mind, he quietly left.

Thomas had been content to remain silent about Hannah's seducer, but once he had heard the rumours about the supposed favours that she was receiving, his pride could not be restrained and he did what he could to end the falsehood. He had had a very brief interview with his mother that had ended in violent words and she had been badly shaken by her son's threats. He had then gone on to speak to the Reverend Russell, supposedly seeking counsel, and had told him that Hannah had been seduced by a leading member of the Turner family, and had been abandoned by her seducer. It hadn't taken long before Sir Russell was informed.

* * *

Isaac Grace had formed a plan which he hoped would satisfy Sir Russell. He became Thomas's shadow and it wasn't long before he was able to find him in a place which was lonely and secluded. Thomas was returning home one night after following Mary unnoticed to her parents. He had turned down the unlit passageway at the side of the shop and had been leapt upon and struck down. The attack was uncompromising and vicious carried out by Grace who possessed a determination to put his victim on the ground never to rise again. He desperately wanted to impress his employer irrefutably, and regain his comfortable and elevated position in the household. He knew that he would if the tailor was dealt with in such a way that he would never again trouble his employer.

He left the body of Thomas in the alleyway unnoticed by anyone and was grimly satisfied that his night's work had achieved his chosen aim.

Thomas was not dead but was carried home a disfigured and broken man. His head had been struck and beaten several times against the wall. He was found with his skull caved in and distorted, his face running wet with blood, unconscious, lying in a pool of rain water stained scarlet from his wounds. He was rescued from death in the dark alleyway by a passing stranger who had noticed his dark misshapen form lying in the alley and had knocked on Hannah's door.

* * *

As Ellen gradually allowed Charles's marriage to dim into the recesses of her consciousness she was able to prepare for Agnes's concert with some degree of enthusiasm retained from when she had first received Tom's letter. She was being escorted by her grandparents, and they planned to take the train and stay in Winchester overnight. The journey was long but the company of her grandmother alleviated the tedium and the nagging emptiness that she felt because Charles was not escorting her; that she had lost him for ever; this thought would not go away; she felt it would always torment her.

The Guildhall had been completed only recently, and was much admired by those who viewed it as evidence of Winchester's increasing prosperity. The entrance was imposing with long, wide steps running parallel to the walls and on either side of the entrance, tall gothic windows looked down below the steeply inclined roof which was surmounted by an impressive clock tower. The tall, red bricked building with various pronounced architectural details and decorations gave the impression that no expense had been spared in its construction.

The steps then turned to enter the wide impressive front doors which were thrown open bringing the beautiful, shining, marble floored hallway and the mass of gas lights into view; the whole interior was lined with pillars supporting a high decorated ceiling. The wall paper was a rich red velour, the edges of the columns and pediments glinted with gold leaf. As the family looked around them Ellen was stunned by the strangeness of a space which commanded her attention because of its opulence.

The doors in to the auditorium were tall and commanding, and as she glanced through them, she realised that a great number of people were already seated.

The hallway was still bustling with a number of people lingering in groups before entering the auditorium. As the family's intention was to meet Hannah and Tom before taking their seats, they did not move far down the corridor, but waited where they hoped they would be seen easily.

They heard the beginnings of the orchestra tuning up, and Ellen began to feel anxious that somehow or other the planned meeting was not going to happen. She knew it must almost be time to take their seats as now the people around her had suddenly become sparse in number.

It was just as she was beginning to think that perhaps they should find their seats without Tom and Hannah when she saw Tom suddenly appear in the doorway looking anxiously around him. The moment he saw them however, he smiled with relief, rushed towards them, but spoke to them abruptly and nervously.

"Sorry ... sorry I'm late ... it's so good to see you." Tom held Ellen to him for a moment and smiled at his grandparents and in one movement he led them all through the nearest doors. He clutched the tickets ready and so they all managed to be taken to their seats as the applause broke out when the choir entered followed by the conductor of the orchestra moving towards the rostrum.

Ellen did not have time to ask the question which was on her lips the moment she realised that Hannah was not with Tom. An empty chair beside her grandmother was evidence of Hannah's absence, and clearly testified that her presence had been expected. She looked eagerly for Agnes and found her easily, standing in the front row of a large number of women all dressed in white high necked blouses and black skirts. Agnes had her hair dressed so that it was off her neck and face and pinned up. She looked older than Ellen had remembered.

......*

I don't think I will ever be able to overcome the feelings I had as the agonising truth of my father's injuries at the hands of an unknown assailant were made known to me.

He was unmoving now, unable to speak and do anything for himself.

He was being cared for by my sister who became his compulsory nurse, forcing others to complete those other domestic duties which had been hers; but she could not do them any longer because they had become superfluous and been removed from her responsibilities by the wicked action of a wicked man. She was displaced from her usual struggles and impelled into a life which she had not chosen. She bore it well. She spent her days performing those acts which were required, feeding and washing, feeding and clothing, feeding and turning his inert frame. Others offered the option of respite. She did not take it often.

I wanted to see father immediately, and having been prepared for the change in him, I did go to see him, and could not be wrenched from his bed the whole of that first wretched night.

He could not be nursed at home I thought. Others, those who needed nurturing, suffered because of the demands of caring for a living corpse who could not help but devour the ones who cared for him.

He did try to speak sometimes I think. He tried to tell me something I am sure, but his mouth did not mouth the words. His tongue moved in his mouth but that was all. I wiped his mouth gently and kissed his cheek and smiled, nodding and hoping that somehow he would know that I believed that words would come, that he would be able one day to utter one syllable and then maybe two, until he could hold us spellbound with the completion of every sound.

His eyes looked frightened but not unkind. His expression did change. Sometimes as I read to him at the side of his bed I would catch a look from him which spoke, "I need to tell you something. If I could then I would be happy".

But he was helpless, beached on a slippery and uncompromising surface which entirely immobilised him. He needed someone or something to launch him, to remove him from the paralysing grip of muscles that did not work and a body that was bound with no chance of being loosed. How could he live like this? It would be a slow lingering death for him, unless … unless the life giving water, the tide came and lifted him, washing over and under his inert legs and back and releasing him from the grip of the dry earth. He would feel his head lift from its anchor, the anchor would have no power, and the rest of his being would follow and float. There would be bubbles forming words around his mouth and tongue. He would taste the saltiness of his rescuer, and feel her tears on his cheek.

......*

I awoke and saw my daughter washing my arm, with gentle strokes upward from hand, wrist to armpit. And then the cloth dipped into the cloudy bowl, was wrung out until no drips remained, and the gentle strokes continued with more warmth than before. I knew that her touch was gentle but I felt nothing. I am wrapped in some kind of covering which has no feeling and leaves me without sensation. I have entered a rigid casement, a cocoon which has been created by someone whose motives may have been either malevolent or benevolent. Perhaps the actions of a kindly creator would be designed to protect me from further pain, to enable me to heal and be untroubled by past sins. Perhaps the design of the protective creator would be to ensure that I could do no further harm to anyone, and that as long as I am trapped there is no injury. Perhaps the cruel creator has devised the worst kind of torture instrument for a sinner who cannot receive any mercy. Perhaps, perhaps, perhaps …

I thought that my fate would depend on the reason for the cocoon. If I change, if I repent, become unwilling and unable to continue on my chosen course to hurt and exploit others and especially those who should be able to trust me, then, at some point, I might be judged as being worthy to be released. How could I convince this unknown being that I am changing, never to return to my cruel ways, and would ultimately be safe to be released? I must ponder this question and reflect on the nature of the creator, for there the answer lies.

I am looking at my daughters and my sons, and the girl who had been torn from her mother and brought unknowing to a place which was not hers to inhabit. Only I had known. But no, I remember now there had been others. Others that had made the decision to do what they had done. Was I as guilty as they? Or had there at some point been a trial at which the creator had measured the blackness of the guilt of all of us, and possibly had declared that more of the blackness had penetrated my soul? Was I as guilty as they or could I have been the worst of them all? My son and the other's daughter. Surely the one who instigated the wrong, the other, was most to blame …

My son … and the other's daughter … she's here now … what can I say to her? She's such a bright and intelligent girl … I noticed it from the beginning … bright in knowing what I was thinking, knowing how to react to me when I felt the guilt she induced. Intelligent yes … she could not be restrained … she was always looking for something better … it frightened me … I could not cope with the fear of her knowing … of her ability possibly to penetrate my conscience and know of the immeasurable wrong I had done her. Blackness … yes, I should imagine that I was measured and He, the creator of my impenetrable cocoon had found that it had spread to the depths of my soul.

I have to tell her. She has to know.

* * *

The family home had once again become home for Ellen but had occurred in the worst of circumstances. The uncaring and vindictive parent lay in his cold, marital bed with his children close by, but not knowing. The room had not changed from the time he had brought his first bride home. She had born eight children and had left him behind, sleeping for the last time in this same bed. One who had cared for her until the end had been unable to stem the weakening flesh, and now she was here again, and he began to slowly gain in strength.

The family noticed how he would venture to lift himself by pushing down on his elbows so that his back arched forming a smooth and rounded mound in the bedclothes made by his rising chest. His head remained immobile but the heart of him he tried to raise up, and the children watched as they imagined that he would lift a little more and a little more until he was no longer touching the bed. Henry stayed with his father for many hours, hoping for the sight of his father rising, like bread being proved. What was it that made the dough double in size, and become rounded and full of life? Henry had always been fearful of his father but now he feared him very little. He watched his father lift himself and hoped that he would rise.

The Saviour had risen but He was a God. Henry watched his father again and felt a burden on his shoulders which weighed him down. He knew what it was. He didn't want to be afraid of his

305

father anymore, but knew that if his father did recover that the most likely circumstance would be that he *would* be afraid of him. The burden was his wish that his father remain as he was … that way he knew he was safe.

"Pa I wan' to tell you that I've been wondering wha' it'll be like when you can walk and talk again … would you frigh'en me like you used to?" Henry did not look at his father as he spoke but gazed out of the window at the flowering lilac tree. It had the most blooms it had ever had. Hannah had asked Tom to trim the branches before the winter, and the tree had responded with renewed growth. It stood alone in the garden, but its uppermost branches still reached to the window, and Henry could make out the insects enjoying the nectar of the flowers.

"Pa, would you look at my drawings? Would you talk quiet to me? Would you come to the river with me and watch the fish and coots? Would you 'elp me with my readin' and writin'? Pa … I would like i' if we could so such things." Henry once again paused. He thought for a moment about his father's anger because he was reminded by Ellen, coming into the room. He knew that his father had been angry with her many, many times.

"Henry, are you alright! It looks like you have seen a ghost! Are you staying while I give pa his wash? I heard you talking … were you talking to pa?"

"Yes". Henry looked at his father for the first time and saw that his eyes were open. He thought that his eyes were turned towards him very slightly.

"Do you want to help? You can if you wish."

"I don" know."

"If I tell you what to do, alright?"

"Alright … yes."

Ellen placed the bowl she was carrying at the side of the bed. Henry could smell the vapors streaming and rising from the hot water, a mixture of lavender and something else which was aromatic and smelled like ginger cake. She held a small pot which contained a creamy yellow substance which she carefully placed on the small table. Her sleeves were already rolled up above her elbows. She smiled gently at Henry and gave him the towel which she had carried over her arm.

"I'll wash and you wipe!"

Henry had heard these words before many times, and grinned.

"Be careful mind!"

"I will Ellen … I'm *always* careful."

Ellen began to gently wash her father's face, around his eyes first, and then his mouth, his ears, his cheeks, his forehead, his hair, his chin, his neck. She rinsed the cloth frequently, and then, having completed the washing as she saw satisfactorily, she beckoned to Henry that he could begin. He hesitated at first, so close to the head of his father, but his father's eyes were no longer open, and imagining that he was asleep, and would do nothing, Henry began. Ellen saw how gently and carefully Henry dried his father's face, and was confident in leaving him to fetch more warm water infused with healing and cleansing plants, marigold, comfrey, lavender and ginger.

She returned to find Henry kneeling at the side of his father's bed.

"Is pa going to sit up today? Will he rise from his bed? Will he talk do you think?" Henry voiced what everyone was thinking. He felt safer now than he had the whole of his short life, and he thought he knew why. Ellen had come home. Tom came every day. Hannah looked after them all. He did not lack anything, and here he was happy with his father, not knowing how long it would last, but content that there was tranquility in his home that he recognized, from a long time before; now it had descended on him almost unnoticed like snowflakes on a windless day. He knew it for what it was, and despite the horror of his father's condition, everyone around him seemed to be content, happy even.

Ellen continued to wash her father's arms and hands. Just as Henry was drying them Hannah came in with a tray. She had prepared her father's lunch, and Ellen helped lift him to a sitting position, supporting him with pillows. Ellen sat against his shoulder to prevent him from slipping sideways, and Hannah, also supporting him, placed a napkin around his throat.

"Father, here's your lunch … some vegetable broth … you like it … here."   Hannah saw that her father understood. His mouth opened a little, and he watched as the spoon was brought towards him.

The meal took some time. Freddie had come in as usual to watch his grandfather. Henry remained, watching his sisters. Ellen spoke to her father about Agnes. They had heard that she was enjoying her time away with the Choral Society. Hannah had met with a member of the society, an older woman, Mrs. Marianne Fox, who was to be Agnes's chaperone, and was satisfied that Agnes was in good hands. They had seen her go two weeks before. They wondered if she would return. So the latest news of their 'song bird' was related to Thomas, who never responded in any way, but Ellen was not deterred.

"Pa Agnes is in Manchester today, and tomorrow I think she is going to York. She is so happy pa, and writes all about the concerts. Let me read what she says … 'We performed Handel's Messiah in Chester and the feeling was wonderful the orchestra was so good I don't know who they were but the conductor spent a lot of the practice time on getting the orchestra to balance with us and it really worked. I am learning so much we are going to Manchester and then to York and I think then we are coming back to London. There is a feeling that we will be singing for the Queen nothing definite though but I will let you know as soon as I do. Love to you all specially to pa. Love Agnes'. You see pa, she is doing so well … she is as happy as she was when she sang here … I'll tell Tom the good news when he comes." Ellen looked forward to her brother's visits and always mentioned them to her father when she had the opportunity.

Tom returned nightly to assist his sisters. They had asked him because they knew that their father would need to be lifted completely at some time every day, in order for him to be made comfortable and clean. They felt their brother might help, and so it came about that he returned home every evening after work, having been given travel assistance from Mr Plummer. As before, he had reluctantly shared his concerns with his employer, that his sisters wanted to nurse their father but would need support from him for a while. Mr Plummer, after having ascertained all the facts and feeling the necessity of Tom's involvement in the care of his father but not wanting to lose an excellent employee, chose to assist him and consequently provided a carriage and driver to take him to Botley and return him home again. This assistance was gratefully accepted and appreciated.

Tom came and went to his boyhood home as regularly as the setting of the sun. He was seen, and his movements were remarked upon by the villagers who took an interest in such matters, but as the weeks passed, interest waned and no one made any comment about Tom's movements.

There were however always certain matters to discuss which demanded revisiting such as the attack on Thomas Lambourn. Nothing had been discovered as to the attacker. No one had seen anything. No one had seen anyone near the place. And so, as in situations where a cloud of mystery prevails and banishes the warmth of a clear day, people would return to the circumstances of the brutal assault probably with an eye to somehow discovering a new fact or detail that would shed light on it.

"I've 'eard that Thoma' Lambourn is ge"ing a bi' stronger ... Ma Lambourn 'as it tha' 'e can si' 'imself up now ... tha's a miracle ain't i'? When I think wha' Dr Stocks said the nigh' 'e was taken 'ome ... didn't 'e say that Thomas wouldna last the nigh'?" The topic of conversation on this occasion was raised by William Judd at the kitchen table at the Botleigh Grange. The servants were all assembled, and enjoying their breakfast. William's source had been his mother who had always managed to glean the tiniest particles of local knowledge and here say from a network of like-minded people.

"Is that right? I don't think there is much truth in the rumour. Dr Stocks is generally correct about such things ... but I agree that he got the timing wrong. Lambourn will not last, take my word for it." The opinion given was presented with such an assurance and fierceness that no one was going to challenge him. Isaac Grace's opinion was always sought first. His place in the serving hierarchy was at the head of all the other servants, and so the company nodded their heads and indicated their approval of his view. How he had reached his position of superiority was difficult to comprehend. It had been a gradual ascent which no one had really noticed.

Grace had lived in fear that somehow the man he had sought to dispatch from this world would open his mouth and reveal to the world the identity of his attacker. He could only wish and wait for the end to come. He had no control over present circumstances, and had to bear Sir Russell's probing questions day after day. No, as far as he knew Lambourn was still alive but unable to communicate. No, he could not go anywhere near. He had no reason to visit. No, he could not finish what he had started. He was sorry. There was nothing he could do.

Sir Russell became more and more impatient. Like a falconer who had set his bird on to the prey, he had expected the prey to be captured and brought to him without delay. The bird had returned but its talons were empty.

He had kept Grace close by him since that time. He had kept him tethered, and hooded. Anything further in this matter which needed to be done would be given to another.

The silence of the man continued and seemed as if it could not be broken. He became stronger physically however, and did indeed develop the ability to raise himself to a sitting position. A chair with wheels was purchased by Hannah and Tom, and once the warmer weather returned, it was a regular sight to see him being pushed through the village by Hannah, with young Freddie holding on to the side of the chair. Tom no longer came to the house every night. Thomas was able to assist his daughters in their efforts to wash and care for him. His hands gradually regained some movement, and his strength returned to his neck and back. His family believed and hoped that he understood their efforts in speaking to him although they detected very little sign that he did.

Once Thomas had been made ready for bed the family would all go to say good night. They all remained until everyone had kissed him; and then it had become a habit that one of the children would say a short prayer of thanks. This had occurred for the first time one night when Henry had suddenly bowed his head after kissing his father good night and prayed, "Heavenly Father, we say good night to thee and thank thee for this day. Bless father we pray, in the name of Jesus Christ, Amen." The family had looked at Henry not knowing how to react, but then they had noticed Thomas smiling at him. Hannah had thanked Henry and they had left, more slowly than usual.

Thomas' positive reaction to his son Henry was duplicated several times and as Henry began to feel his father's approval, although a word was never spoken, he began to spend even more time with him, and when he couldn't be found doing the things that he should have been doing, he was discovered sitting with his father.

He played his own games with him, which involved giving his father a choice as to what he would give to him.

"Pa would you like me to give you this cake or this biscuit?"

Henry waited and watched his father closely.

"Oh the biscuit, here you are. What about this? Would you like a drink or something else to eat pa?" Again he waited. Those who observed this game saw nothing which might be construed as an indication that their father was communicating an answer, and yet Henry would respond with confidence as if he had received an answer. At first no one had taken much notice, but a pattern began to emerge which Ellen noticed first.

"Henry, how do you know what it is that pa chooses?"

"'e tells me."

"How Henry?"

"'e tells me … I can 'ear 'im."

"What do you mean? I've never heard him."

"'e speaks to me … it's like the whistling in the wind … it's quiet like …you 'ave to listen very carefully … it 'as to be very quiet or you miss it."

"You can hear father speak … but his mouth doesn't move, I've never seen his lips move to speak."

"'is lips don' really speak ... 'is voice comes from somewhere else I think." Ellen was confused by what Henry was telling her, but decided to stay with Henry and watch the communication he had with their father. It wasn't long before the whole family was aware of what was happening, but none could make out a sound coming from their pa's lips or from anywhere else. They were amazed by what was happening, and could not explain it, but thought it best not to mention it to anyone, as they were afraid of how people might react to such a strange and unexplainable phenomenon, especially as it involved Henry. Many viewed him with a degree of pity and shame. He was a disadvantaged child with nothing to recommend him. With the impediments he displayed, he was seen by many as a hindrance to his family and to the society from which he came. And so it was that no one was made aware of Henry's uncanny ability to communicate with his father outside of the family.

* * *

A life which becomes steady with routines and where emotional stability becomes the norm brings about changes especially where there has been instability and fear in the past. Ellen found that her mind began to turn to people she had known and had made promises to, and they would not leave her alone. She first felt anxious about Ada, whom she had vowed to remember and to whom she said she would return. Then she remembered the kindness of Maria Coleman. She had without reservation said that she would not forget her, and yet over a year had passed since Charles had visited her for the last time. She reflected on her situation and decided that she must visit Ada, and write to the Colemans. Somehow she would travel to Winchester, with the intention of assuring herself that Ada knew that she was true to her word. All that was left for her to do was to make the arrangements for her journey. She had nothing in the way of savings. Her little enterprise in Lymington had not provided much in the way of income, and Mr James had not been generous in his payments to her. She realized yet again that she had remained in a state of dependency. She knew that Hannah had little. She could not depend on her. Perhaps it was time to once again seek Tom's help.

Ellen explained her wishes to Tom just a few days later. He wasn't sure that he could assist her, for he reasoned that there would be little that Ellen could do for Ada if it was found to be necessary.

"If you were to find her in a bad way, what could you do Ellen? I ask you what could you do for the poor creature? From what you have told me she will probably need new employment, a new home and goodness knows what else ... Ellen, I'm sorry to be so discouraging, but surely you can see what I am saying is true."

"It's been in the back of my mind for days Tom." Ellen did not immediately accept defeat. "You must see that I have a duty to Ada. I can't just put her out of my mind. What do you suggest I do?"

"You must leave it until such time as you are in a position to assist her, but you are certainly not now ... I hope you can see that." Tom once again felt the uncomfortable weight upon his heart of not supporting his sister when she had sought his help. He could not alter his reasoning however and tried to soften the leaden feeling within him by gently stroking her cheek. She had not ceased to look at him, wishing that what he was saying could be disproved somehow but she knew it couldn't. Tom was right,

314

and she placed her hand on his as it rested on her cheek, and slowly acknowledged that she agreed with him.

"Tom why do I have to be so useless and helpless? I've never been able to make a difference to people's lives ... I've wanted to ... there's always an obstacle in the way ... somehow I have to change my life ... I'm always dissatisfied with it because I can't do what I really want ... what's the answer Tom? I believe you know." Ellen had observed her brother's single mindedness and realized that it might have contributed to his growing independence and prosperity.

"I don't suppose that anyone does what they really want ... although I am content with my life ... there are things that I hope for ... it's true that I am learning and opportunities have come my way ... Ellen, give yourself a bit more time ... help Hannah as you have done ... take care of pa ... watch over Henry ... Freddie, George and Emily will all do well with you around ... that's all." Tom hoped that what he was suggesting did not sound too mundane. He felt that Ellen was naturally able and willing to care for others, and she should concentrate on those closest to her. If she did this now, at some future time she might be able to look beyond to those in the wider community who were in need of help and support. He felt that this would come.

"Thank you Tom for helping me to see what I *can* do rather than what I can't, but it is hard to accept".

"Yes, it is better to do what is possible ... I love you Ellen." Tom did not know why he felt such a strong love for her just then. She had quietly accepted his words, despite being a young woman of strong principles and ideals. He knew how determined she could be. Now, he realized she had an added measure of vulnerability since her unfortunate experiences in the wider world. She had become more pliable, more willing to accept another's view. She was different from the girl who had tried to defy and outwit their father.

"I wondered for a while if you did love me ... I know you did when I was a child ... but something was different and I could not fathom it out." Ellen needed Tom to know how unsure she felt about him and instinctively felt that this was the moment.

"I used to watch you getting the better of father, and it worried me ... I can't say that I allowed it to change my feelings about you ... I know how much ma thought of you ... I don't think that she thought of you as her favourite but somehow she treated you differently from all the rest of us ... did you notice that?"

"*Did* she treat me differently?"

"Ma was always gentle with all of us, but with you she was as soft as the gentlest of breezes ... she never pressed anything upon you ... you were never forced to do anything ... she gave you the freedom of a wild creature, never having to be tied to duty or to one place. Did you not notice how little was expected of you compared to everyone else? I suppose you did not detect it. You are looking at me as if I am telling you something which is entirely new to you." Tom watched her face, and understood that she had no conception of the differences he was describing.

"Are you really talking about me?" Ellen did not recognise his view of her childhood at all. She had not been aware of her mother's singling her out.

"Yes of course. All of us were a bit afraid of you I suppose, and we never reacted to the treatment she gave you ... but when she died I knew and Hannah knew that everything would change, and of course it did. It seemed like pa hated you ... and I didn't really know why ... I thought it was something to do with your relationship with ma ... but I could not tell ... I just wanted to be away, and so I left, left you I suppose because I could not bear to see your battles with pa."

"Pa was angry because I let ma die."

"Is that what you think? Listen to me. Listen!" It was then that Ellen received the true account of what had happened in the weeks leading up to their mother's death. Dr Stocks had been involved almost daily. Ma Lambourn had assisted the doctor in nursing her. None of this Ellen could remember. She could only recall the constant effort she had made to care for her mother. Did she really remember things so wrongly? How could her recollections of that terrible time be so distorted? Was Tom seeing things as they really were, or was he just trying to take her pain away? She did not know the answers to any of these questions.

"Are you being honest with me? I must know. Please tell me the truth and swear to me that you are not lying." Ellen's eyes began to fill with tears; her cheeks were soon wet; her anguish was caused by a desperate longing to know that he was giving her a true account of what had happened. For so long she had grieved for her mother and the part she had played in her death. She had taken the overwhelming burden upon her shoulders alone. She had felt that she was responsible, that she had, through her incompetence and inadequacy, sent her mother early to her death. Yet, could she believe what was being said to her now? Tom was saying that she was absolved of the crime, that she was acquitted of causing her mother's death, that she never was responsible. Oh, if this could be true, her heart would be relieved of the most terrible weight which had wrenched at her soul and had cruelly crushed her so that she could feel only sorrow … what gratitude, what joy, what purifying innocence she would feel … she waited apprehensively for Tom to speak.

317

"How can I convince you of something which I know to be true ... speak to grandma, speak to Hannah, ask anyone who was close by ... there was nothing that anyone could do ... you did your part, but you were not expected to do a great deal ... you were only thirteen ... do you believe me? *Ellen*, do you believe me?" How could he persuade her to change her thinking and be relieved of her erroneous guilt? He held her shoulders firmly and shook them a little as he stressed the words he wished her to hear above the others.

Ellen could not reply. Deep within her she knew that for years she had held onto a completely false recollection of what had happened. Why had she seen things so differently from reality?

"I don't understand how I could have remembered everything so wrong ... I don't understand ... I don't understand." Ellen's voice weakened and became lost in her distress. She began to sink to her knees. The effect of Tom's revelation was that all her physical strength ebbed away. She could not hold her body upright, and slumped against Tom, who watching her intently, grasped her and held her fast. He could not prevent her from reaching the floor however, and sank with her, kneeling in front of her and whispering to her.

"Ellen, Ellen, Ellen ... you were not to blame ... not to blame ... no ... come now ... you did nothing wrong ... nothing wrong ... it's going to be alright ... Ellen ... sister."

* * *

The letter to the Coleman's was written by Ellen the next day. It stated that she hoped that she would be able to visit, and that if they were ever in Botley she hoped they would call on her. She asked after Charles, Charlotte and Sophie. She mentioned that she knew Charles had married and hoped that he was happy. She hadn't seen Charlotte since her return to Botley, but that was not surprising as she rarely went out. She told them that she spent as much time as she could with her father. Henry, she said, was never far away from him. Hannah worked at the business. Gradually her father was becoming stronger she concluded. Satisfied that she had expressed all that she needed, she sent the letter, and hoped for a speedy reply.

Visitors at the tailor's home were rare, especially since Thomas had returned there so close to death. Neighbours had viewed the dreadful circumstances of the family in various ways. Some had instinctively wanted to shy away from any association as they tended to conclude that misfortune was in some way a result of sin and signified the judgment of God. Others were more charitable in their thinking and believed that tragedy can strike anywhere, and only by the grace of God were they free of it. The Reverend Russell had called a few times, and had said a prayer or two with members of the family. Henry had assured them that when this was done in the presence of his father, his father spoke the 'Amen'.

"Pa likes 'earing the prayer ... 'e is 'appy when prayers are said, and 'e would like to say a prayer too with all of us ... like 'e used to ... 'e should seein' as 'e wants to, don" you think?" Henry, having gained an understanding of his father's wishes was determined to be his advocate, especially as he was the only one who could. He did not wonder why he could 'hear' his father and no one else was able to. He was content to act upon what was communicated to him, and it gave him a degree of happiness he had never known.

The family looked to him to connect with their father, and then convey what he had learned to them. Despite Thomas growing stronger physically there was no increase in his capacity to speak. He could sit up, he could move his legs, and his hands and arms were becoming more mobile and able to perform tasks such as eating with a spoon and assisting his daughters in getting dressed and undressed. It was at this point in his recovery that Dr Stocks called unexpectedly.

......*

I do not believe that I am dreaming, but I do have cause to think that perhaps I am mistaken. I know that I am very ill, and have thought for some time that I am lying on my death bed. It is not my husband who cares for me. It is a woman, and I don't know who she is. Why would a stranger be in charge of me? There's another person close by too who I cannot remember knowing. I am closeted in the house of strangers. Nothing is familiar. I have one distant memory which is of a kind woman carrying a tray. There are fish tails and sea weed on the tray and people calling out to me "Come and buy". I am lost except for the thought that Tom is not far away. I am drenched from diving deeply in to the sea, and there is no one to save me as the weed tangles itself around my legs and drags me down to the sea's depths. Then I suddenly feel the strength of a tree holding my head in its roots, and then I can't remember any more...

......*

The arrival of the village doctor was unexpected and baffling. Dr Stocks had attended Thomas Lambourn only once on the night of the attack. He had not called since, and had not asked after the patient. He had stated on that night that the lacerations and deep indentations to the head would not heal, and that he needed to be kept comfortable. The night would see the termination of Thomas's life. There was nothing more that he could do after he had given morphine and washed the wounds. He had left satisfied that the morning would bring a call for him to go and certify Thomas Lambourn's death.

The call never came, and as rumours spread about the tailor's hanging on to life, Dr Stocks was still unconvinced that he had been wrong, and remained confident that there was some delay to the man's final demise, but that it was only a delay. The inevitable would come in time.

As the weeks passed, certain members of the higher community began to put pressure on him to find out the true condition of Thomas Lambourn. This was the circumstance of his visit, seven weeks after the attack.

He got as far as the kitchen, but was faced by a young woman whom he knew immediately.

"I don't know why you are here doctor ... you have shown no interest in my father's health ... what is it you want?" Ellen became angry the moment she saw the doctor on the doorstep. She had thought for a moment that she would not invite him in, but realized that a conversation needed to take place, and she did not want any chance passersby hearing what she had to say.

"Why Miss Lambourn I am here as you must realize to ask after your father, and to ascertain as to whether you require my assistance ... I have stayed away because you have not called on me ... but I have been your family's physician since before you were born ... your father and I have always had an understanding ... he would want me to be involved in his care ... you must see that."

"I know nothing as to his wishes and as for your interest in my father I find that difficult to believe."

"Come my dear, you are quite mistaken and I don't know why you should think such a thing."

"I know that father is doing very well, without your help. I am satisfied that he is receiving the care he needs from us … do not try to persuade me to allow you to see him … it will not do … your assistance is not needed … you are not welcome … that is all." Ellen did not wait but held the door for the doctor to pass. Dr Stocks had reddened with anger as Ellen had unhesitatingly rebuffed him. Her insults had maddened him to such an extent that as he left he ranted at her, "If you think that you can speak to me … *me* like that then you will soon find that no one in this village will acknowledge you. You will be shunned … you and all your family … your little sister's so called singing career will be over. You do not know the influence I hold here, and you will regret the way you have spoken to me today."

Ellen's heart was pounding as she leaned back against the door. She was surprised to see Henry looking down at her from the stairs. His eyes were shocked and restless.

"Pa's upset … 'e 'eard the doc'or … don'' wan' 'im anywhere near … you'll keep 'im away … come an' speak to pa." Henry's face reflected the deep fear he had felt as he had observed his father struggle to speak and master his feelings when he heard the doctor. Henry could not make out all that his father had said, but enough to know that he wanted Dr Stocks out of his home, and that his father had become extremely agitated and troubled. The calmness of the home had been vanquished in a few moments.

No sooner had Ellen been upset by her confrontation with Dr Stocks, than she faced further distress which came in the form of a letter from Mr and Mrs Coleman:

322

Dear Ellen,

What joy we felt when we received your letter. We had hoped that you would write one day and had always believed that the closeness we felt to you when you were with us would endure.

Mr Coleman and myself are both well, and Charlotte is happy with William and she will soon have her first baby. We did become grandparents for the first time last month when Charles and Amelia became the parents of a beautiful little girl they called Amelia.

But the most terrible heart break followed, entirely obliterating the joy of little Amelia's birth, with the sudden death of her mother. She lived only for an hour with her baby and then was taken. The doctor came and said Amelia had not been very strong and the birth was difficult.

Charles asked Amelia's parents to look after the baby, as he thought it would be best. He is back living with us again now.

Would you be able to come and see us? Perhaps it would help him to see you – he was always very fond of you, you know. It would do him good to talk to you I feel sure. Please think about coming. You know we have missed you, and would love to see you. Please let us know what you decide.

With kind regards, your friends Benjamin and Maria Coleman

The shock of the terrible events described in the letter was hard for Ellen to bear. Her thoughts were stricken with the idea that Charles was alone, that he no longer had his wife and his daughter was living apart from him; she could not begin to imagine his anguish. How could he cope with the loss of his dear wife so soon after their marriage? She tried to picture Charles's face and remembered how he had turned away when she had not responded to his plea for her to stay with him and never leave him. He had not let her see then, and so she was unable to see now.

She heard steps outside in the passageway, and Hannah's voice cried out, "Ellen, Ellen, what is the matter ... what's happened?"

She could not answer and realized that she was trembling uncontrollably and that she must have made some sound which had been heard by Hannah, and had brought her running. When she saw her sister she knew that Hannah had been really frightened by what she had heard.

"Please ... do not ... I have just received some dreadful news from ... Lyndhurst." Ellen had never spoken of her rescuers as they had departed her life by the time she had got to hear of her father being so close to death. The desperate need to be close to her own family had overridden the time she had spent and the affection she had gained with the Coleman family, and so they had slipped into her subconscious. Now they had returned powerfully to the forefront of her thinking and the deepest recesses of her heart. It was as if they had never been gone, and she wondered at the pain that she felt and the cry that had gone out from her as she thought of Charles. She couldn't explain it, and Hannah was before her seeking an answer.

"What has happened to distress you so? I have never heard you make such a sound ... something terrible has happened hasn't it? ... no, Ellen, don't tell me, don't tell me now ... you don't have to tell me now." Hannah moved to sit on the bed and Ellen moved closer and laid her head on her sister's shoulder and cried, as if she was weeping every tear that needed to be shed by all that knew Charles. And there were other tears too which were nothing to do with Charles.

"Tell me one day if you wish." And Hannah remained with her until the pain had diminished. There was another person present as he had been before when they had been consoling one another at a time of deep anguish, but now he was a spirit in the room, felt by one sister and imagined by the other; but he could not have been more real to Ellen.

It did not take Ellen long to decide on her action in response to the letter. She could not go. Not when she was so delicate and suffering such a strong and terrible reaction to Charles's grief. She knew that she could not face him at a time and in circumstances which would be sure to reveal all her longing for him. She would send a card of condolence, and give his parents hope that one day she would come and see them, but couldn't at present; her excuse was her father's condition; she could not leave him nor her sister; she hoped they would understand; she would be affectionate towards them and they would be pacified.

* * *

Life was ebbing away from the countryside as the tide of winter advanced and the trees' branches became exposed and skeletal; the winds grew colder and fresher; the preparations for winter had been in full flow for some time. As the frost decorated the mornings, so an iciness became discernable in the Botleigh Grange kitchen. Despite the warmth of the hearth and the industry in and around the range, here an unwelcome coolness had been turned on Isaac Grace, who was no longer in the forefront of his master's affections. He had felt the chill of the atmosphere as he had watched Sir Russell promote William Judd to second gardener, and seen various favours bestowed to an increasingly grateful and compliant subject, favours which, at an earlier time, would have been his. Isaac watched and became incensed by his master's reduced interest in him; with the increase of William's benefits came a decrease in his own.

His fall from approval was noted by all the servants and it came as no surprise that Isaac was taken from his personal duties to Sir Russell and given the task of serving James and Alfred. Both young men had had little in the way of support from any of the servants excepting only when Isaac had, on occasion, assisted them in deciding appropriate attire and dressing them for important occasions, but other than that they had been self-sufficient and had needed little in the way of advice. Isaac found himself doing little of the kind of work of which he was accustomed, and more of those menial tasks upon which the smooth running of a large household depends. Once he had been responsible for the immaculate appearance of his master; now he had gradually become no more than an under footman, cleaning and maintaining the clothes, furnishings and possessions of the whole family and fetching and carrying bath water, chamber pots, wood and coal.

His anger turned to a festering and overwhelming resentment which threatened to emerge more and more as he became increasingly volatile, teetering on the edge of actual aggression. He had been replaced; he had been thrown over; he had been betrayed; he had been treated as if he was worthless.

A new young man had been brought in to the household by Sir Russell as his personal aide. This man, employed out of a London agency, was given the task of also waiting on the Colonel when he was in residence. Isaac, embittered and shaken by his master's decision, chose to ignore the addition to their ranks, one John Chester, avoiding contact with him and the prying eyes of Mrs Webb and Mr Spreadbury. His dissatisfaction with his employer

326

grew as his wounded pride showed no signs of healing. After all he had risked prison for Sir Russell; he felt he should reawaken Sir Russell's duty to him, and made a decision that this should be done at the earliest possible opportunity.

The opportunity was not long in coming. Sir Russell had need of Isaac's assistance as he prepared to welcome guests to the Grange one evening but it coincided with John's night off. Isaac took full advantage of the moment.

"Sir, is there anything further that you require of me?"

"No thank you Grace, that will be all until after dinner, when you will serve coffee and brandy to my guests in the library, that will be all until then."

"Thank you sir, it has been a pleasure to serve you as I used to do."

"Yes, thank you Grace."

"Some of the tasks set by you in the past have had serious consequences ... I suppose that you will remember my loyalty to you."

"Indeed". Sir Russell eyed Isaac thoughtfully, wondering where he intended to go with this.

"It has always been a privilege to do every kind of task for you even the *dirty* ones." Isaac returned Sir Russell's unblinking stare, bowed and turned towards the door. "You see I have nothing to lose now, but even so, I have decided that my involvement in your affairs and those of your brother have ended ... unless, that is, you give me what is my due."

"What do you mean? Can you be more specific?"

"Only what I am owed ... as I said before I have nothing to lose now ... but I would prefer you to remain within my protection. If not, then I will have to clear my conscience."

"Conscience! You have no conscience ... I'm convinced of that or I would not have employed you. As for keeping me within your protection, that is easily done. You remain in my employment do you not? What more do you want? I suppose it irks you that Chester has displaced you ... well I am the master here, and it suits me to give the *impression* that you are out of my favour." Sir Russell smiled at Isaac and between his teeth he whispered, "Now is not a good time to discuss this ... tomorrow morning at 6 ... come to the boundary path beyond the farm ... at 6." Sir Russell remained where he was and looked out of the window across the wide lawns at the rear of the Grange. It pleased him to see the splendour of the gardens, spread with mature trees, and smiling, in a way which if Isaac had seen it would have caused him to hesitate to agree to the meeting, he gathered his resolve to find a way to solve a very unsatisfactory position.

......*

I remember the thought that kept recurring – it was there whenever I awoke; but the awaking was not as if I had been sleeping; I knew that another form of consciousness had existed, but I had floated in and out of it, and had glimpsed a light which brightened above me and which beckoned to me to follow it. It was such an exquisite burning that filled my breast and it lifted me from the heavy stupor which had been pressing down on me.

There was pain somewhere in my head, and I wondered if it would forever remain; I was wounded but the light, when it came, took away the pain; someone spoke and I knew it was the Lord. He was in the light; He *was* the light; He was inviting me to come to Him, and I knew that if I did my life would become His, and I would change. His was a simple request.

"Thomas, follow me".

My response would need to be simple too.

"I will"!

Then the torment began. The pain in my head subsided but the rest of me, every part, was tormented with a life time of guilt; I saw every bad choice, every selfish act, every unkindness, I saw the brutality inherently part of my hard heart, the greediness, the bitterness, the anger, the cruelty, the pride and the covetousness. I could not look at the light anymore but sank into the horrors of my life and saw only the misery that I had brought on others and on myself; and then I felt someone lift me and the misery descended beneath me and diminished, and he said, "Take my yoke upon you and learn of me; for my yoke is easy and my burden is light".

I had tasted the gall of bitterness, the pit called hell, but now I knew the sweetness of the Lord's love. He carried me and as He did so over years of regrets and sorrow, He spoke again about a time when I had sought Him, but had not persevered. I had not given up all my sins, nor had I really tried to find Him. He told me, "I love them that love me; and those that seek me early shall find me".

* * *

As Christmas approached and the joyous anticipation grew particularly amongst the younger members of the Botley community, Thomas's health began to show signs of deterioration, and his daughters grew anxious. His breathing became more laboured, and every effort was made to keep his room warm and cosy. The family kept his fire burning day and night as the November days grew colder.

Henry remained at his father's side the most. He read to him and talked to him apparently still having exchanges with him that no one else could comprehend. It began to be known more widely that Henry talked with Thomas, and some grew suspicious of the boy and became wary of him. Henry was unaware, but Hannah had been informed by the grocer's wife that "Tha' brother of yours should be seen to, seein' as 'e is 'earing voices." Hannah was entirely ignorant of what was being said and so asked that she might explain her meaning.

"Why it's all round the town that 'enry is talking' to yer father, and no one else 'as any idea what 'e's takin' about ... 'enry is such a strange lad ... we don't like to say it but it seems like 'e's gone a bit mad in the 'ead ... who knows what 'e 'll do next ... wha' 'e ll get up to ... I for one don' like the sound of i' ... I think..."

"Henry is perfectly in his righ' mind and there is no need to be concerned ... I canno' believe anyone would think such a thing when you all know Henry so well ... he is gifted I know, he's differen' ... but he means no harm, and I would be grateful if no more was said – father is happy when Henry is with him – they have a special bond – please do not be concerned." Hannah was trying so hard to convince the woman of the falseness of her thinking, and had grown agitated in her manner.

"Well, dear girl, you can't see it, but those who are on the outside can ... 'enry has to be put ..."

"I cannot listen to this ... you have not listened to a word I have said. Henry is as harmless as ... my little Freddie," and Hannah took her son's hand and, gathering her groceries into her basket left hurriedly, looking flushed and feeling very disconcerted.

The talk in the town did not ease, but grew in vigor. Unkind and accusing remarks were made regularly, and the family led by

Hannah decided to keep Henry close to them, not allowing him to go out unescorted. This strategy seemed to be working, and nothing untoward had occurred. However, with just a week to Christmas, the family heard a knock at the door, and Hannah, thinking that she might possibly have a surprise customer, hurried to open it, but was shocked to see Dr Stocks, standing close to the door, about to knock again.

"Ah Hannah, how do you do? I hope that the family are all well. I will come straight to the point – my last visit was not a happy one, as your sister did not appreciate my concerns – I hasten to add that those concerns still remain." Hannah did not speak. She had known about Ellen's reaction to the doctor's calling and had been amused by Ellen's description of the altercation.

"My concerns have in fact multiplied, for I know your father is growing weaker and your brother Henry is behaving in a disturbed and unhealthy way; it's probably been brought on by the shocking circumstances of your father's injuries. The child's mind has clearly been broken … he has become sick and must be treated."

"We do not have any money for your bills … but in any case, father is much the same, and Henry is just as he always has been … there is nothing more I need to say I think. I have made myself clear, have I not?" Hannah had reflected on the manner of Ellen's response to the doctor, and was swayed by the knowledge that their father had reacted violently when he had heard Dr Stocks' voice. Their father would not wish for this man to be involved with the family she was sure. But why had he come again? Surely Ellen's reproof had been sufficiently forceful. And yet he had returned. She instinctively believed that his motives were vindictive and malevolent. But his influence in the town was strong. She became afraid.

"I am grateful for your concern, but I must assure you that there is no need. Thank you Doctor, but there is nothing in this house to cause you any bother. I am well as you can see. My father is much the same. My brother does not cause me to fret. So you see we are getting along. We need nothing from you I assure you, but", at this point Hannah recollected that she might get rid of the unwelcome visitor by inventing some future malady, "you will be the first to know if our situation changes." Hannah tried valiantly to conceal her apprehension, smiled bravely at Dr Stocks' implacable face, and closed the door.

Closing the door on mischief does not necessarily make it go away, and this was the circumstance on this occasion. Dr Stocks was not so easily got rid of, and he returned to Sir Russell to consult with him and seek further instructions.

The nervousness which Hannah had felt when in close proximity to the doctor did not leave her. She shared her feelings with Ellen at the earliest opportunity and was relieved to hear that Ellen had also been aware of some underhand and improper undercurrents when faced with the same individual. They knew that what each had felt was confirmed by the other, and so they determined to be watchful and seek help from those they could count on as their friends.

It was at this juncture that Ellen told Hannah about Charles. He had been her best friend. He had wanted to marry her. She had not refused him, but had been non-committal and he had interpreted this as a clear rejection she supposed, because he had gone and she had not seen him since. She had never thought to pursue after him, and then he had, before her tears had even dried, married another girl and had had a child. Then, with her heart throbbing and bursting and her fitful breath choking her words she tried to speak of Charles's tragedy, for how, in a just world, could such a good and gentle man be visited by such a terrible misfortune? Everything which had struck Charles down Ellen could only interpret as tragic because it was so undeserving. He had been an undeviating support to her throughout her miseries and had remained a constant friend long after her situation had improved. She related to her sister all that had long hung over her mind and her conscience. Hannah responded as only a caring sister would, and recognized that Ellen was exposing her innermost feelings. She identified her sister's love for Charles, and wondered if the time was right to reconnect with him.

"You must see Ellen that he would if he could come to our help if you were to ask him … perhaps you might consider it … the time is perhaps not the best … I do not know when your friendship was ended, but would you think that he might be informed of our situation? He sounds like he would be willing to help us. What do you think?"

"I don't know what to think … I have to be sure of my own feelings before I can expose him to the possible renewal of his."

"What say you to giving yourself some time to reflect on the hurt that might possibly be caused if you renewed your acquaintance with him and it ended in failure … I do believe that risks should be taken in matters of the heart … but I have suffered badly because of that philosophy, so it would be wrong of me to press you to take what you see as a risk … what do you say to that?"

"I can't say anymore. My thoughts are far from clear at present, but I do know that we are in need of a good friend … and I know that he was the best I've ever had."

"Let's speak no more about him for the present … but you know that whatever you decide, it will be well with me. I will make some tea, and look at Freddie – he's cuddling up to you! He understands! Come and help when you are ready."

Ellen was grateful to once again feel the closeness of her family. It was something she had always wanted, and at this moment, she was content in recognizing her sister's understanding and relieved that she had at last unburdened herself to another who had proved herself to be the most sensitive recipient.

The fears which had brought about this significant conversation did not abate however. The young women felt they were striving to survive in a hostile world. Even their grandmother gave little in the way of support, although she had assisted them with the care of George and Emily when Thomas had been attacked. This was all they could hope for. But the doctor's motives were unclear, and he had an influence much greater than they. Christmas was almost upon them, but the family's festive spirit was seriously impaired by the doctor's intrusion into their lives.

Ma Lambourn had been prevailed upon to keep the youngest children with her throughout Christmas. It was hoped that Agnes would return, but nothing had been heard from her for nearly a month, and although she had promised to see them all and return to Botley for Christmas, Hannah was not entirely convinced that this would occur.

Christmas lost its preeminence however in the minds of the tailor's family because of unforeseen and terrible circumstances. The local paper, the Hampshire Chronicle, described how in the early hours of the twenty fourth of December an intruder had been ascertained in the home of Thomas Lambourn, the tailor of the small market town of Botley and had been caught in the act of attacking the said Lambourn in his bed. His son, one Henry Lambourn had been sleeping in the corner of the room unseen by the attacker, and had promptly been woken by a strange sound and had "severely struck the assailant with a large chamber pot, which had rendered him incapable of further mischief. The said intruder had turned on the boy but had collapsed unconscious due to the violence of the blow. The police have taken a local man to the constabulary, and after receiving medical treatment, have charged the said Isaac Grace with attempted robbery and trespass".

"What do the police mean by the charges? It's not as it should be." Ellen was voicing what the family believed after listening to Henry giving his account of what happened. "Henry was clear that Isaac was trying to smother father in his bed … he could see pa struggling … his arms were trying to get Isaac off him but he did not have the strength."

"I know", Hannah thought the same as Ellen, "But the police seem to doubt Henry's statement … we know he was telling the truth … he could not have been mistaken and he would not lie … the police have said it was too dark to be sure, but they must have asked the question 'What was Grace doing in pa's bedroom?' If you ask me it was Grace who attacked pa the first time, and he'd returned to finish the job … but why would he want to harm father? It doesn't make any sense."

"That's probably why the police think as they do … and you know about the rumours about Henry, not being in his right mind …so it's a simple case of attempted robbery, although what the objects of his efforts were to be is hard to say … we have nothing of value." It was at this point that they could go no further, and both agreed that they had to believe Henry, and that they would make sure that he knew it.

It was fortunate that Thomas was not harmed in the attack because of Henry's timely intervention. It was his daughters' intention to have Christmas dinner and games in their father's bedroom. They could not enjoy anything at all without him, and realized that if the chairs were taken from the workroom and kitchen and placed around the bed, there would be just about room enough for everyone.

They did not go to the Christmas Eve service, because they did not dare go out. It was difficult enough just to complete essential daily tasks without facing what had become the uncertain reaction of judgmental neighbours. Hannah prepared the children's Christmas stockings, Ellen made some Christmas biscuits, Henry did not move from his father's bedside, and later, on saying good night to their father, they sang a Christmas carol together, one which Agnes had taught them.

The night was very cold, and just as Hannah was making up the fire in her father's room she heard a shout from downstairs. It sounded like Agnes, but could it be? She looked round at her father, and could see that he recognized the voice calling out to them.

"I think its Agnes. Do you think so too?"

"Mmmm."

"Oh pa, I'll go see … wait."

At that moment Hannah heard the shrieks of delight as her sisters excitedly flung themselves into each other's arms and laughed joyously. She ran to join them, and then, on a day when complete misery and grief had only just been averted, the sisters were joined in the happiest moment. Their Agnes was with them, and she, filled with relief that the train from London to Winchester had arrived in good time and that her hired carriage from there to Botley had not been delayed, clung to Ellen, thanking God that her prayer had at last been answered, and that she could be with her beloved sister once again. Hannah lifted

Freddie to kiss his aunt, and she once again cried out with the sheer joy of having a dear wish granted.

As soon as they had composed themselves just a little, they all hastened to be with Thomas and Henry, and sitting close to the fire, and gazing at their pa, they let Agnes talk of her concerts and her plans, and listened with smiles and glistening eyes to the wonderful stories she told. Her gaze was on her father and no one else. He made no sound, but he listened, and as he looked on his children one by one, his eyes became full and tears fell. His children did not know what he felt, but guessed his tears were expressions of joy; they had not seen their father cry before; Agnes could no longer speak; Henry came and took his father's hand; he felt the gentle response of his father; from that moment he never again felt any fear towards him.

* * *

The peace which is spoken of in relation to the first Christmas was felt in some measure in the Lambourn home the following day. As the carol says, 'Glory to God in the highest. Peace and goodwill to all men.'

The shock and the relief of the previous day had given way to a remarkably settled calm which contentment and love bring. The family exhibited no selfish tendencies throughout the day. Although their company was increased by the expected coming of Tom in the morning, the adjustments which had to be made when a visitor arrives occurred without any awkwardness, and when Ma Lambourn, Emily and George arrived for a late Christmas tea, the atmosphere remained tranquil; it seemed that nothing could now displace the feelings of solace and unity that prevailed within this household.

337

The members of the family would later remark on this most special of days of how they had been blessed. The cataclysmic storm had been followed by sunshine and a rainbow, the darkest hour by an all-encompassing brilliant light born of love and trust. Each of those present felt in their own individual way an inner peace which diffused from one to another. The family felt complete.

Tom had wondered if his father would want to come down stairs for his Christmas meal, and Thomas smiled and nodded at his son, making his wishes clearly known. Tom had lifted him from his bed and brought him to the rocking chair beside the kitchen range, and propped him up with pillows; Thomas had watched his family gather and had gazed at their faces; Hannah had been at his side, ensuring his comfort and assisting him with his meal. Tom had later lifted him to see if he could move his legs and stretch himself. He tired soon however after having eaten and indicated to Henry that he needed to rest. Tom returned him to his bed and all the children came and kissed him. Throughout the day there wasn't a single moment when he had been left alone.

The family's endeavour to watch their father unceasingly continued as life returned to the normal routines of everyday life. Tom had returned to work and Agnes, wishing to remain for a week, could only stay two days as she received word from Mrs Graham that she needed to attend an audition for a new music and drama agency in London. Her goodbyes were prolonged because she longed to stay, but Hannah took charge of the situation, and escorted her to the door and then to the Inn. Ellen remained behind, feeling miserable and wondering when she would see her dear sister again. She knew that if Agnes was successful in being taken on by the agency she probably would not be able to return home very often.

With Agnes gone, the house became quieter and a scene of renewed industry as the sisters took it in turns to maintain their home and care for Thomas. The deterioration in his health that they had observed before Christmas and had seemingly arrested over Christmas returned. As the first week in January came to its conclusion, Hannah became alarmed as his breathing became as laboured as before. He slept for long periods, and when awake seemed unable to recognize anyone. Her anguish at what was happening was quickly shared by Henry, Ellen, his mother and Tom who came back in response to a letter from Hannah. She feared that their father was dying, and told Tom that he had to return as soon as he could manage.

The apothecary had been summoned at the first sign of Thomas's decline, and he confirmed the treatments which Ellen had already proposed, that steams and infusions of eucalyptus and peppermint should be administered, together with the regular, careful application of poultices of ground mustard seeds on the patient's chest. He also recommended the use of a tincture of balsam, which he supplied, which might alleviate any congestion in the throat and nose.

Ma Lambourn also gave her opinion, which was that Dr Stocks should be called, but her grandchildren could not agree to it. They explained that their father had not wanted the doctor to attend him before, but then, realizing the sense of what their grandmother was suggesting, wondered if it might be possible to summon another. They had to try everything in their power to stem this illness, and so agreed to try and find another doctor whom they knew they could trust.

Ellen remembered the kindly and efficient doctor who had attended her in Lyndhurst. Could he be persuaded to travel the distance to Botley? Was there any way that he could be involved?

In desperation she asked Tom to ride to Lyndhurst and visit the Coleman family. She begged him to speak to them and find out the whereabouts of the doctor, and see what he could do to bring him back to see their father. Knowing of no other, the decision was made to try and contact the doctor and Tom left, traveling as fast as his horse would take him.

It was during Tom's absence that the police called again and once again spoke with Henry, trying to establish the true events of the fateful night. Henry found these interviews frightening and despite the presence of Hannah, was unable to pronounce more than he had hitherto given.

"The man was on top of pa … pa was struggling … I could see that … I had to stop the man … I hit him."

"Yes, but when you saw your father struggling, what was it that you saw that showed you that the man was intent on harming your father?" This question was posed by a young police constable who had little experience of investigation. The local policeman was Bert Blackburn who had visited the family in the first instance. He knew a little about them including some rumours which he had come across as he had gone about his normal duties. He was a good listener, but could not put together a complete picture of what had happened, despite having talked to all those directly involved. Isaac Grace had not been forthcoming. After his medical treatment from Dr Stocks, he had been questioned by an officer from Winchester, a newly trained and recently appointed individual who had achieved the title of detective. Bert Blackburn knew of the addition of these specialist officers, and recognized the possibility that the fact that this officer had been brought in indicated that the case was seen by his sergeant as being more than a common break in. But the real problem lay in the testimony of the boy. He was clearly handicapped in some way. He had heard of what some called the 'sleeping sickness' and wondered if Henry suffered from this.

The detective, Lionel Reed had begun with an interview with Isaac Grace which proved to shed very little light on the true circumstances of the crime; he maintained as he had all along that he had gone to the house to look for money. He knew that the tailor had some stashed away somewhere, for everyone knew that he had bought the business many years before, and had lived comfortably ever since. His eldest daughter was also never short of money. That is why he had gone there but the boy had caught him in the bedroom, and had floored him.

"No I did not find any money. There was none where I looked, but that don't mean that there weren't any ... I need the money you see ... another baby on the way."

Detective Reed paused and thought for a moment before continuing. He was not fully persuaded that Grace was telling him the whole truth. He had to consider the fact that Thomas Lambourn had been attacked previously, and had lain in bed since that time unable to communicate the identity of his attacker. Why should anyone want to dispatch Lambourn? What motive could there have been?

"So your knowledge of Thomas Lambourn is what?"

"Only that he's the tailor in Botley."

"You must have realised that it was one of his daughters who also worked at the Grange?"

"Yes, I knew Hannah, but not well you understand ... she weren't there long ... just a year or so. When she left I had nothing more to do with her."

"Was it through her that you found out about the money?"

"Not exactly … just talk really … everyone knew that Lambourn was successful … and his daughter was always buying stuff for her little un."

"You have a comfortable living at the Grange … you have managed up until now … you have been quite well set up I understand … it does not really add up that you were willing to jeopardize all that you had to steal from someone who you knew to be well off only by hear say … no, no … I believe that you entered Lambourn's house because you had another motive. You had something against Lambourn which you are concealing … you entered the house with the sole purpose of putting an end to him. That is how it really was, and this talk of money is a lie!"

"Now hold on a minute … you have no evidence … only the statement of a stupid retarded boy who don't know which way is up. I'll have you for making such an accusation!"

"Oh really, is that what you do when someone says something that you don't like … you 'have them' do you"?

"Nothin' more to say." Grace folded his arms and sat back in his chair, staring grimly at the detective.

"I am holding you here until I am satisfied that you are telling me the truth. I shall be speaking to your employer later, and to everyone else who knows you and I'll find out why you were in that house that night." Reed noticed a change in Grace's expression when he made mention of his employer. It was only a slight flicker, a momentary horror in his eyes, but enough to tell him that the employer might hold the key to knowing what really happened.

* * *

The attempt to bring a trustworthy doctor to Thomas's bedside was well on its way. Tom had arrived in Lyndhurst at a fast trot and had quickly established the whereabouts of the shoe makers' shop. He found father and son at home in their workshop and quickly explained the reason for his visit. The two men had warmly shaken him by the hand once his identity was made known to them. The younger of the two, Tom noticed, was particularly pleased to make his acquaintance or so it seemed to him. After an initial start of surprise the young man did not let go of his hand for at least a minute, shaking it and asking in a very kind fashion after his family. He particularly asked after the health of his father, and once he had been informed that the reason for the visit was to get much needed help, both men quickly responded and offered to make contact with the good doctor and see what could be done. Charles took his coat and muffler and left them immediately.

Benjamin led Tom to the parlour where a fire was blazing and where Maria Coleman sat doing her sewing. After introductions, Tom was again struck by the warmth of the welcome he was receiving. He felt something very disarming about the woman, and this was confirmed by her generous offer of refreshments while they waited for Charles's return. They had no sooner begun to sip their tea and enjoy the fruit cake when the front door was heard to open, and Charles rushed in.

"The doctor is not available at present, but it seems that it might be possible for him to travel with us to Botley later. It seems that he has struck up quite an affection for your family. Ever since Ellen was his patient he has had some very interesting experiences and interviews with the police, in connection with the case. His evidence in relation to Ellen's treatment by the Robinson woman was crucial, and it appears that since then he has been called upon by the police to assist in other cases where medical advice was required, and has been very happy to do so. He did not see it as a particular burden to travel outside his district, especially as Ellen has been the cause of an increase in his work and standing in the community ... and in his prosperity. He said he would be ready to leave at about three. I would very much be obliged to you if you would agree to my accompanying him. I have been wanting to see your sister for a while, and although the circumstances are far from happy, I hope you will not object."

Tom looked at the speaker closely. He saw a pale young man, stocky and strong with large hands which he moved nervously to stress and elaborate his words. His face was thin and his cheekbones' upper edges were clearly visible and hollow beneath. His expression was direct and uncompromising and Tom decided that this man was probably not used to opposition.

"If that is your wish then I have no objection ... how will the doctor travel to Botley?"

"He will go in his own carriage and I will travel with him."

"It is difficult to believe that he was so willing to go such a distance ... have you offered him some added inducement I wonder ... excuse me sir, I cannot help wondering."

Charles had offered the doctor an increase in his fee, which was accepted, but which Charles had reason to believe was not absolutely necessary but which he out of courtesy, had offered.

"I did indicate that I would add to his normal fee to compensate for the time taken out of his daily schedule ... but do not concern yourself in this matter, I ... I owe your family a great deal, and believe that this is a small way of showing my appreciation ... please do not oppose me in this ... I am determined to assist your family at this difficult time." Benjamin listened to his son with a concern which he found hard to conceal.

"Charles, I feel this should be discussed further, privately …
later … but time is moving on, and you must go and meet up with
the doctor. Mr Lambourn, will you be traveling in the carriage or
will you make your own way back?"

"I will leave with Charles I think, but I will need to return my
horse to the livery in Botley as agreed, so I will have to ride and
forgo the comfort of the carriage."

"I can only hope that the doctor can avert a tragedy; that your
dear father will soon be responding to the treatment given."
Maria Coleman voiced what everyone was thinking and it only
remained for those traveling to Botley to say their goodbyes.

* * *

Hannah had been listening for the arrival of the doctor for most
of the afternoon. She had desperately prayed that Tom would be
successful, and that the doctor for whom Ellen had such a high
regard would not disappoint them. And so it was that her faith
was rewarded, she believed, when the doctor was welcomed into
their home and hurriedly taken to his patient.

The good doctor was young and had received his training in a
London hospital where in recent times there had been a new
emphasis in medicine on listening carefully to the patient as well
as carrying out a very thorough examination before any form of
diagnosis was attempted. This way of doing things was in some
part impeded in this case by the patient's inability to
communicate directly, but Henry wanted to help, and he
approached the doctor warily but was bold in immediately making
it clear that he was his father's 'spokes'an'.

"I can tell yer sir what's up with pa … I've been watchin' 'im
yer see."

"You are …?"

"'enry sir, I am pa's second son."

"Good of you to offer yourself … to help me, you understand … I am Dr Fairweather. Now what can you tell me about your pa?"

For a young man such as Henry to be treated in such a respectful way by an impressive stranger was, in his experience, an unusual occurrence. Henry responded to this treatment by being relaxed and confident, and not in any way perturbed by the presence of a very smart and educated gentleman who would otherwise have filled him with fearful dread.

"Pa 'as not been 'isself for two days … I noticed that 'is breathing began to be quick like … and then he started a bit of a cough … 'e's not coughed any blood though … 'e feels warm and last nigh' 'e began to swea' a lot. We though' we should keep 'is room warm … and tha' is wha' we've done bu' now we don' know wha' to do."

"Has your pa asked for anything to drink or eat since his breathing changed?"

"'e 'asn't 'ad anything today and 'asn't asked for anything … you can see 'e's asleep, and 'asn't woken since this mornin'."

"So he's been like this all day?"

"Yes, more or less."

"What do you mean?"

"'e did ge' a bi' brighter after Ellen put the poltiss on 'im."

"What poultice?"

"It's something that she knows about which is supposed to clear pa's chest."

"I would like to speak to her if you wouldn't mind. Would you fetch her please?"

"Tha' I will."

"While you do that I shall give your pa a good examination … we won't know what's happening until I've done that … thank you Henry." While the boy rushed away to get Ellen, Dr Fairweather brought the candles closer to the bed and began by observing Thomas, his breathing, his physical movements, his skin colour and amount of perspiration. He was concerned that he had a patient with pneumonia and if this was so, there was little chance of saving him. However, because of Thomas's bedridden state and lack of fresh air over a protracted period of time, there might be another explanation which he hoped would become clear. Thomas's heart beat was strong and regular, but something was causing the fever and the shortness of breath. Could Thomas be suffering from consumption? Then he looked at the patient's eyes and opened his mouth to look back into his throat. The examination was not easy and he was not able to come to any firm conclusion.

"You wanted to speak to me doctor?"

A lovely young woman stood before him, so lovely that he found it difficult to think of what he was going to ask her.

"You are Ellen? Yes, well, your brother has told me that your father showed signs of improvement when you applied a poultice to his chest … can you tell me exactly what you did?"

* * *

Dr Fairweather was not able to make any sense of what was happening to Thomas. Ellen had answered all his questions, and it appeared that something she was doing improved his health, but he could not be sure of what it was. He was not convinced that Thomas had either pneumonia or consumption, and wondered if a remedy of a more psychological kind might be applied. He ventured to tell the family that he felt there was no serious cause for concern, but that it would be imperative to ensure that Thomas received regular meals of a good quality, fresh air and a change of scene as often as it could be managed, and that he was given any combination of treatments which were found to produce a positive response in him. The poultice was clearly one which had proved beneficial, and he also recommended bathing in sea water. It would be important to keep a careful record of everything that happened over the next few days, and he gave Ellen the task of doing this.

"So you want me to write down what I notice … what works and what doesn't … how pa is … is that it?"

"Absolutely … medicine is all about nursing and observing … watch your pa and whatever you see you record … I will return in three days and see how things are progressing … I do think it will be important to get your pa out as soon as possible … he'll need to be kept warm mind … but he needs fresh air and a change of scene, of that I am certain."

"You don't think that pa is going to die … he's got so low … I was so afraid … he's going to get be"er doctor?"

"As I've said, you will have to watch him very carefully, and try your hardest to see what makes a difference … I think your father has been through such devastating events, his mind has been affected. He is low in spirit I am sure, but may respond to the extra care you and your family will give him … that is all I can say at present."

Ellen looked at the doctor with wide eyed appreciation, feeling completely overwhelmed by the events of the day. When the doctor had arrived, so had Charles; their meeting again was filled with a mixture of confusion, anxiety, awkwardness and delight; he had long wished for a renewal of his association with Ellen.

In the months after the death of Amelia he had wished to see her, not to renew his professions of love for her, but to share with her his anger and his grief, for he knew he could speak to her about such things for she had been his best friend; she had been shocked and bewildered by the change she saw in Charles, whose suffering she could clearly see, and to whom she wished to give relief and comfort. The awkwardness between them existed only until Charles was able to speak, and then Ellen, released and unrestrained by his kindly greeting, stepped closer to him; just as the doctor was escorted upstairs by Hannah, he also stepped towards her and she, reaching for his face, placed her hands on either side of his neck and gently stroked him. She whispered, "You're here. I knew you would. Oh Chassie. I'm sorry. Sorry. How could you bear it?"

He shook his head gently as he tried to communicate to her the depth of his feelings at the time of Amelia's death and since then. He had wanted to die as well. Life lost all its beauty and purpose. He had reflected on the words of Jane Robinson, pronouncing a curse on him and had thought that this was the fruit of that curse. For a time he had believed it but then he grew to realise that the woman had no power over him; he had not wished to bear the grief, but somehow he had, but he didn't know how, just that he had kept breathing and getting up each day, and forcing his mother's meals down while she watched him anxiously. Perhaps it was that which had preserved him, the love of his mother; he could not tell, but knew he could not deliberately hurt her. He told Ellen this and waited for her reaction. She said nothing except "I know, I know," and then he felt for the first time with Ellen that her heart was obtainable, and that one day it would be within his reach.

The comfort he felt was extraordinary, and as he gazed at her, at her beautiful hazel eyes flecked with the brightest gold, at the sweep of her hair and at the small, determined chin pointed directly at him, she seemed to become the flower that he had seen the first time he had met her, a glorious bloom created and sent by a loving God.

Moments later she was called by Henry to see the doctor. The vision of a young woman who had just been removed from a world of hardship and purposelessness by the man of her dreams was presented to the doctor. He recognized the beauty of something which had been lying dormant, which had been ruthlessly damned; now this intangible thing had been awoken and set loose, and was now running without restraint through the blood of this young woman and giving her a radiant loveliness which he marveled at.

* * *

The interrogations which Detective Lionel Reed carried out were far beyond anything that anyone would have expected. True to his word he had first seen Sir Russell Turner of Botleigh Grange, requesting information concerning his employment of Grace, and his opinion of the man. The interview went well, and Reed came away convinced that Sir Russell's relationship with Grace was different from what would have been expected. Why else had Sir Russell been so hesitant in his responses? There would have been no reason to suppose that Sir Russell had anything to hide and yet his replies were ambiguous, and he seemed to have some issues with Grace which had not been mentioned by Grace himself.

Next the rest of the staff at the Grange came before the detective one by one and each in turn gave their opinion of the man Grace, and why they believed he had attempted to burgle Lambourn. Their opinions varied, but there seemed to be an underlying contempt for Grace. He had certainly lost the favour of Sir Russell, but no one knew why. It was time to return to Sir Russell, but first, Reed made the decision to return to Lambourn's house for another look. He may have missed something vital. Perhaps the answer to everything lay in that house.

His arrival at the house coincided with the imminent departure of Dr Fairweather. The doctor was known to Detective Reed, and they spent a moment or two acknowledging each other. Reed decided that he needed to speak to the doctor about his involvement with Lambourn and how it came about. Doctors were normally restricted to a specific area, and he knew that Fairweather's practice was around Lyndhurst. Explanations were given, and Reed became aware of Ellen's history. But again there remained many unanswered questions, which were mainly centred around Lambourn's total rejection of his daughter. How did this come about? Charles was present during these conversations, and realized that Ellen did not know the answer to this question, and neither did any other member of the family.

A paradox existed however as it was apparent to everyone that Thomas now adored his daughter. Henry had particularly noticed his father's devotion to Ellen, and it was her treatments that had caused the greatest improvement in his health if only for a short period of time. The doctor was of the opinion that this was not caused by an imbalance of the mind in the patient but some other reason existed with which they were unaware at the present time.

As the hour was getting late, the doctor took his leave of Reed, Tom and the family. He needed to return in case of a sudden request for his services. Charles was not inclined to return immediately, and so asked to stay a little longer. His curiosity and personal inclination had drawn him into the detective's investigation. He was loathe to leave without having established a few more of the facts, but more importantly, having once again felt the extraordinary sensation brought about by being in the presence of Ellen, he could not and would not leave her so soon.

He looked at her, and she returned his gaze. They smiled and both looked away feeling embarrassed because of the presence of some who knew nothing of their attachment. It would not be long before their secret became known, but until then, they seemed to feel it was fitting to disguise what they felt until such time when it would be possible for everyone who was dear to them to appreciate their revelation without the distraction of so many family difficulties and concerns.

The question as to Ellen's previous banishment remained unanswered, despite a thorough unraveling of what had transpired immediately before and after Ellen's leaving home. Reed was none the wiser, and both he and Charles recognized that more than those gathered in the Lambourn home that night would need to be questioned. As the night drew in, Reed left having struck a rapport with Charles, who had a very similar way of thinking as himself, but who he noticed, *was* different to him, in that he tended to rely more on his instincts. This was not necessarily a bad thing, but *he* could not allow himself to stray down that path. He was known for his analytical methods and calculations, his thorough and deliberate problem solving. Reed enjoyed putting a puzzle together. Sometimes the pieces were very small indeed, but they were often, he found, the ones which held significant positions in the final completed solution. No matter how small the fact, or the inconsistency or the coincidence it always held a special interest for him. Charles very quickly admired Reed's cool methodical brain, and recognized that with such an ally on the case he would do all he could to work with him. He knew that his involvement in the future of the Lambourn family was assured, and he was ready to embark on the trail with the detective to find the answers with him.

Reed was not aware of Charles's intentions, as he had not supposed that anyone in their right mind would want to be entangled in police business and, in this case, a very mystifying case, particularly as it was the police and they alone who were expected to do the work. After all he *was* employed to do it. He had not reckoned on Charles's overriding interest in the family, and although he had observed Ellen exchanging affectionate looks with him, was not yet fully aware of the force of the feelings they had for one another.

The detective left at a late hour and the last part of the evening was spent by those who remained making Thomas comfortable. Charles was not present during this undertaking, but remained in the kitchen with Henry.

"I don't know if you knew but I am a good friend of your sister Ellen … I've known her for a few years. Did you know that?"

"No, but if your Ellen's friend you are mine too."

"That's kind … I want us to be friends … are you alright with what is happening? … Do you want to know anything? Are you worried about anything?"

"Only pa … the doctor was kind, but 'e didn' say that pa was goin' to get be"er."

"I only know what you know … but I did hear that the doctor was thinking that you could carry on and do a lot for your pa … getting him ready to go out and keeping him company when you can for example."

"I always want to be with pa … always."

"There'll be a need for someone to fetch sea water for your pa's baths … do you think you could help with that?"

"'ow can it be done?"

"We'll think of something … in the meantime, I'm going to try and stay for a few days and perhaps we can sort something out together … we can work on it, what do you think Henry?"

"Yes … if you think that I can 'elp … I'd like that." Henry sat facing Charles and looked very solemn. Charles was grateful that he had managed to start off with Henry in the right way. It was important to him to establish a way of communicating with the boy, to maintain a way of conversing with him which would put him at his ease. Ellen's brother had revealed a level of understanding and perception which had reinforced Charles's belief that he would continue to play a significant part in all the events that followed.

The local inn provided Charles with a bed for the night. He had said goodnight to Ellen in the company of Tom and Hannah and had hoped that they had not observed any obvious familiarity between them. He tried very hard to be cool and aloof, and wondered if he'd overdone it, but he had only to look into Ellen's eyes to see that she understood why he was trying to be distant. He left her, and as she smiled goodnight he felt an overpowering and all enveloping warmth in his heart which had been absent for many months.

As he strolled up the road to the inn, he looked about him. A few of the shops had oil lamps still glowing from their dark interiors. The sparse gas lamps in the street were dim in the half light. The evening was foggy and there was no one about; he could see how someone could be attacked in this street at night and no one be aware of it; but, as far as he could ascertain this particular night, the village of Botley was apparently sleepily innocuous with absolutely no visible sign of corruption or villainy.

* * *

The process of caring for Thomas had taken on a new focus with Dr Fairweather's suggestions being taken very seriously, and planning was required to ensure that the sea water bathing and the frequent excursions out of doors were included in his daily routines. Charles was very much involved in all these provisions; he had ridden back home the following morning, and had spoken at length to his father, explaining the situation. His father was asked if he would take complete charge of the shop for a week or two or until there was an improvement in Thomas's health. He explained about Tom's obligations, which demanded that he return to Southampton, and so the family would be without a man to assist them in such heavy tasks as lifting Thomas and fetching sea water.

Benjamin Coleman, despite being concerned about his son's expenditure in relation to Dr Fairweather, was a sympathetic father who did not need a lot of persuading, and so Charles returned to the Lambourn home the same day, and arranged his further accommodation at the inn.

The planning of how to fetch and carry quantities of sea water to the house was undertaken by Charles and Henry. They would need transport, buckets and a large water container; Charles had considered that perhaps it would be easier to take Thomas nearer to the seaside, and arrange for his care there. It was this that had prompted him to think of Samuel and Eliza Timms. Would it be possible for them to be persuaded to take Thomas in for a period? Or possibly they might know of someone who could accommodate him in Lymington. He was too unwell to be moved at present, but this was a possible option for the future. He had shared this thought with Ellen who had stared at him as if the idea was entirely nonsensical.

"Yes I can see what you must be thinking ... but it is only an idea for the future ... the doctor seemed to be of the opinion that the sea air as well as the water would prove to be beneficial to your father ... if that's true, a time in Lymington would provide him with both. Just a thought for the future you understand."

"To be honest, I'm only thinking about today at present ... do you have any ideas on how to fetch the sea water? Have you thought how it might be accomplished?"

"The nearest sea is at Tichbourne Haven I gather ... Henry and I have acquired two barrels from the inn, and once we have obtained a couple of buckets we will hire a carriage and be on our way."

"When is this going to happen? ... Charles, I'm sorry to seem impatient but I hope that you can see that it might make a big difference to pa ... as long as there is a chance ... could you go tomorrow do you think?"

"Ellen, I can't stay talking to you, I must be off in search of buckets!" He patted her cheek, and winked, and was gone.

* * *

True to her word Ellen kept a detailed record of her father's condition. She noted when he appeared to rouse himself and she wrote about those times when he seemed to sink into a melancholic state and just wanted to sleep. After two days she had noted that his moods were seemingly dependent on the amount of activity to which he was exposed. He rallied briefly after his meals and his treatments; his walks using a chair on wheels had had a particularly positive effect, but no one could have predicted that the sea water bath would have affected him as much as it did. The water had been heated in the copper and poured over him as he sat in the hip bath. More slightly hotter water was added to the bath, and then his daughters, either Hannah or Ellen sponged his back and his legs over and over again. Their father responded so positively; it was clear that he loved the warmth, the smell and the texture of the sea water, and the struggles associated with its acquisition no longer seemed relevant.

By the time the doctor returned as promised on the third day he could see a discernible improvement in Thomas. The doctor instructed that there should be more of the same, and so the family continued on, hoping that the means of doing so would be available to them. Hannah had not been able to work, being fully occupied in assisting Ellen. Charles was not working either, and so the home had no income coming in. Hannah's savings had gradually diminished, and she wondered how they were to manage. She decided to speak of this at the earliest opportunity.

A week had passed, and they were gathered at the breakfast table. She raised her worries, and waited for everyone's ideas on how to overcome the poverty which was threatening to overcome them.

"I think I will have to learn to manage without you Hannah as if you went back to your employment, we would at least have some income … we need to find a way of freeing you so that you can go back to your tailoring." Everyone looked at Hannah to see her reaction to this suggestion. Charles was needed still and could not provide much in the way of financial support. Ellen was the chief amongst those who saw to Thomas's care needs. Henry provided all the help he could. There was no other possible answer, or so they all felt.

* * *

With all the attention being focused on Thomas, there was little time for anything else. Hannah did try to establish the tailoring business once again and managed to bring back some of her past customers for mending and altering garments. She went about with Freddie in the town, calling on neighbors and others further afield to show them samples of her work, and tried hard to persuade them to give her employment. She received a few valuable assignments and set to work, using many of the materials which Thomas had accumulated, but which would, at some time, need to be replaced.

It was an anxious time for her as she realized that much depended on her, but she was determined and unrelenting in her industry. Of all the Lambourn children, she it was who most depended on work; it had been her whole life; for the responsibility of supporting a family therefore, she was ideally suited, but she struggled with a lack of confidence in her tailoring ability. Her satisfied clients built her confidence over time but some caused her endless trouble, and she was affected more by this small minority. However, she persevered, and money began to come in, and while Ellen, Charles and Henry maintained the care of Thomas as best they could a change took place in the family which was felt and seen by everyone.

* * *

Having been thrown more and more together, Charles and Ellen could not conceal their feelings for one another from those who visited and from those who were close beside them. Their visitors were numerous. Members of family came and went; friends traveled to Botley. Detective Reed was a regular visitor. He came to see if there was any change in Thomas's condition. A charge had been brought against Isaac Grace of attempted larceny as Reed had been unsuccessful in finding evidence to support a more serious charge. Reed had decided to go ahead with the lesser charge and play for time.

He could not ignore the evidence which pointed directly to Grace attempting to kill Lambourn and with this on his mind, he visited Ellen and Charles once again, and noticed immediately their unashamed devotion to one another. They stood together, Charles's arm around Ellen's waist, and she had placed her shoulder so that it was snugly positioned under his arm. They looked as if they were joined, fitting perfectly with one another. Ellen's head was slightly turned and leaning towards Charles, and he was looking at her, despite their visitor.

"So I can see you love birds are getting along just famously! But, I wanted to talk … I need to talk to you Ellen … I'm sorry to go over this again … it can't be easy but I've been wondering … if you have had any further thoughts about why your father disowned you … you must have had some ideas." They all took their places around the kitchen table.

"At first I thought it was because he blamed me for ma's death, but I've since realized that that was nonsense; you see he did change towards me after ma died, but now I put it down to something else; ma was always very close to me you see, and I've kind of imagined that he resented that … but there was definitely something else. My grandparents noticed it, they said ma treated me differently from the others; why that was I don't know; they thought it was something to do with my birth; ma had a very difficult time with me you see and I was delivered by Dr Stocks cutting ma open …that's all I know … I'm sorry … if it's not much help."

"I think I shall ask a few questions about what happened; I have an instinct that your father's actions towards you are part of the puzzle; I can't leave any leaf unturned until I have found the motive for Grace's attack on your father, for I know that he did attack him and had attacked him before … there is no doubt in my mind that Henry's account of what he saw is correct."

It was with a renewed determination to uncover the truth that Reed made his way to Dr Stocks house, and with Charles wishing to accompany him, he allowed it but not to attend the interview with the doctor. Charles waited in Reed's carriage while the dogged Detective went about his business.

After the servant had announced him as 'Police sir, Detective Reed sir', his interview began with the doctor but was brief, and curtailed by the doctor's excuse that he had to be elsewhere. Reed did not hesitate to immediately ask what he had deduced was a crucial question.

"What is your standing with Sir Russell Turner?"

"He is a patient, and that is all I am at liberty to say."

"Surely you can speak freely about your involvement with the family when a case of attempted murder is the reason for the question."

"I don't understand you … attempted murder you said?"

"That is right, and I have reason to believe that you and Sir Russell have had a hand in it."

"You are suggesting that I … that I am involved in some conspiracy to murder? … You have no evidence, no evidence for such an accusation, and I will see to it that you will regret having slandered me in such a way!" The doctor had paled as the full implication of Reed's words penetrated his mind; he had stood facing Reed seething with anger and then begun to advance towards him.

The detective, who was not easily intimidated and unperturbed, continued.

"Whatever you may say, you are covering up another crime which has led to a man nearly being killed, and I think I know what it is. Sir Russell has something over you, doesn't he? I will make my enquiries and will, without a shadow of a doubt find out what it is you are concealing … make no mistake."

"You will find nothing … nothing." Dr Stocks walked past Reed and held the door open for him to pass. He did not look at him, but followed him through the spacious hall to the front door, and again opened the door expecting him to leave. Reed withdrew, remaining professionally polite, leaving with a slight bow of his head, and a brief 'goodbye'.

* * *

The plan was decided upon just around the corner from the doctor's residence, to follow him and discover the doctor's intentions. Charles and Reed were not surprised to see the doctor leaving very soon after Reed's summary dismissal. He might well be attending the appointment which he had mentioned, but neither sleuth reckoned this was the case, and it appeared that they were proved right as the doctor rode to Botleigh Grange and was seen entering there.

"Ah I believe the mystery is about to be revealed."

Charles was surprised at Reed's confident statement, but knew that the detective had been collecting statements from many people. Reed, unknown to him, had been waiting for the opportunity to get Sir Russell and Dr Stocks on their own together so that he could confront them.

So it was that Charles accompanied Detective Reed as an impartial witness. Using his police authority Reed dismissed the housekeeper's assertion that Sir Russell could not be disturbed, and asked brusquely where he and his visitor might be found. Within moments they had been escorted to the drawing room and announced.

The sight of two gentlemen looking at them with unashamed aggression did not perturb either of them. They marched forward and Reed boldly and without any sign of nerves introduced Charles.

"Charles Coleman, an associate of mine you understand … acting as impartial witness … thought you might appreciate someone here seeing as you have so much explaining to do."

There was an ominous stillness in the room following Reed's words which chilled Charles but he need not have feared. He did expect some form of violence but was relieved when it proved only to be verbal.

"*DETECTIVE REED, YOU MAKE A HABIT OF BURSTING IN ON RESPECTABLE PEOPLE DO YOU? WHAT BRINGS YOU HERE? STILL CAN'T SOLVE ANY CRIMES AY? GOT NOTHING BETTER TO DO THAN COME HERE AND BE A COMPLETE IDIOT AY? WELL YOU CAN GET OUT! I'VE NOTHING TO SAY TO YOU AND NEITHER HAS THE DOCTOR.*"

"Well that's a shame because I have come here to arrest you both for the conspiracy to murder Thomas Lambourn and for the

362

crime of kidnapping. There may be more but that will do as a start. DON'T TRY TO LEAVE ... I warn you, there are two police constables outside ready to act."

* * *

"Charles, detective work is piecing things together, to the point when there are no visible holes ... that in simple terms is what I have done."

"It is hard for me to understand, but please tell me how you came to know the actions of those two men ... it is hard for me to comprehend, and I am sure that everyone here would be glad of an explanation."

The kitchen at the Lambourn home was full of people. Reed had requested that all the family be present excepting Thomas and Henry. And so they had congregated - Grandma and Grandpa Timms, Tom, Ma Lambourn, Hannah, Ellen, Agnes and Charles, all waiting to hear what they imagined to be an extraordinary story which would, unknown to them change their lives forever; they realized that Reed would reveal circumstances which would explain and throw light on all those things of the past which had bemused and frightened them, but they had no idea of their full magnitude.

"I have to reveal many things to you today of which you will have had no knowledge, but they concern all of you. I will endeavour to be clear with my account for that is what it is. I will retrace with you my movements over the past few weeks, and share with you what I learnt; but please remember that the two men who have joined Grace and who are all in custody at this present time are the true villains and that others who, in my opinion, have been drawn into their cruel web of deceit and crime, are as innocent as those who are preyed upon ... either because of their weakness or their lack of material means. I will not say more on this subject but as my story unfolds, I hope you will remember what I have said at the outset."

"My time at the Grange was rewarded. My attention was drawn to the time of Sir Russell's wife's death and birth of the child and I realized that for a newborn to lose its mother at the time of its birth a wet nurse would be required. I ascertained from the cook Mrs Webb, that this was indeed the case, and that the woman was one Annie Walters, a local woman, who was a nursing mother from Bishops Waltham. She was known to the family because before her marriage her name was Spreadbury, and she had resided in the grounds of the Grange with her parents, her father being the Head Gardener. It was not difficult for me to find Annie, and we talked at length about the night when she returned to the Grange. I asked her if there had been anything in particular that she had noticed which struck her as being odd perhaps or out of the ordinary. She said there had been a couple of things which she had noticed, but she was not sure if they were the kind of thing I was wanting to know and she had not thought much about them since. After all it was over eighteen years ago, and it was hard to recollect. I called upon her to think hard about what happened and she told me that on her arrival at the Grange she had been kept waiting in a small back room for over an hour. She suddenly heard the cries of a baby, and footsteps, and Dr Stocks came in carrying the child. It was crying loudly, and when he was handed to her she noticed immediately how cool his face was, as if he'd been out of doors. She also noticed that although he was dressed in neat and tidy clothes, the shawl wrapped around him was rather old and thin, and showed signs of wear. She could not account for it, for the child was Sir Russell's first, but she paid no heed to it, and thought no more about it, as the baby was hungry. That was all. She was paid well, and the baby James flourished. She could say no more. I thanked Annie for her assistance, and decided then to pay another visit to Sarah Grace, wife of the suspect. I felt sure that she would have something more to say to me now that her husband had been charged."

"I was intrigued to learn that she wanted nothing more to do with him. He had been a poor provider and companion, and she divulged to me that she had married him only as a favour to Sir Russell. When I asked her what she meant she hesitated for some time looking embarrassed and unsure, but with a little bit of encouragement and prompting she divulged to me probably the most important and critical fact of my investigation." Reed paused and looked about him. Everyone was silently watching him. He inspected Hannah a little more carefully; she had not gazed long at him, but had averted her eyes almost immediately when she saw he was looking in her direction.

Reed hesitated and wondered how he could possibly reveal something which would undoubtedly impact on Hannah, but decided that he would not make a direct allusion to her, and try to ensure her some protection from the full implications of what he was about to divulge.

"Sarah told me that when she had been a maid at the Grange she had been raped and become pregnant by a gentleman of the house, and had tried to get rid of the child. She could not bear the thought of having the man's child, and so she had eventually sought Sir Russell's help, threatening to tell the world the identity of the father if he did not help her. Sarah's father was highly respected in the village, and so her threat did have some weight. It seems that this did the trick, probably because of her employer's determination to keep any taint of misdemeanour away from his family; so Sir Russell arranged the solution ... in the form of an illegal abortion performed by ... you may have guessed, Dr Stocks. Now you may well ask what has this got to do with the case against Grace? Well, from this moment Sir Russell and Stocks became partners of a sort. Russell had knowledge of Stocks which could have ruined his career and his life; Stocks knew something about Sir Russell's family that needed to be kept secret. They formed an alliance making pledges to one another that they would not divulge what they knew. It wasn't long before this pledge was tested to the utmost." Reed could not continue for a moment; he had looked about him and could see that everyone in the room was waiting for what came next.

"Dr Stocks delivered Lady Turner's baby ... the baby was a girl ... the mother ... died. Sir Russell desperately required a male heir, because he could not allow the estate to go ... to a brother whom he knew to be totally unstable, dissolute, lascivious and utterly untrustworthy."

"The father of Sarah's child, and of Alfred Russell and of others I am sure, was Sir Russell's brother Matthew Turner, a man totally without morals who took great delight in seducing and abusing young girls, disgracing them and bringing ruin upon them without any concern for them. Sarah told me all this. She had been but fifteen years of age at the time of her seduction, but was spirited and knew instinctively what she should do. She was allowed to remain at the Grange, and was persuaded many years later that she should marry an up and coming valet in the household who was proving to be very useful to Sir Russell. She owed Sir Russell a great deal and so she agreed to marry Grace. Her father Samuel Prewett received many favours through carpentry commissions on the estate because of her compliance

366

she felt sure. She kept silent about the Colonel, and her family benefited."

Reed strode across the room to stand alongside Charles.

"I feel that this is a time to reflect on what we now know — Charles here has been wonderfully efficient in the labours I have asked him to perform." The detective smiled momentarily, trying in some way to relieve the tension which had arisen in the room. Ellen was shocked to learn of Charles's involvement, for he had never mentioned it to her, and reached for his hand. He looked at her and whispered, "I didn't do a great deal."

"Charles made some enquiries at the inn you see, and it didn't take him very long to find out that Grace had shown some interest in your father, and had visited on a couple of occasions, asking about your father's movements. The landlord was apparently struck with the fact that Grace had visited the inn at all, as he had no reason to do so and hadn't frequented the establishment for as long as he could remember. And so we have a picture beginning to form, of a disreputable alliance between two powerful men, of the concealment of immoral and despicable behaviour of the most depraved kind and of a man in the pocket of one of these powerful men going about showing an unexpected and perplexing interest in your father. As well as this we have reason to believe the events of the night of the birth of the Russell's child were suspicious and again we see the other powerful man very much in the forefront of events."

Again Reed looked about him, and became more solemn in his demeanor as he ventured to continue.

"Your father shortly after this time came into a large sum of money for it was at this time that he bought the business and the accommodation which you now enjoy. It took a great deal of persuasion to uncover this fact. Banks are unwilling to divulge their practices, but suffice it to say, that the bank acted for your father in the purchase of the shop, and there remains a considerable amount of money in an account which has steadily accrued interest. Your father very rarely touched the account. The mystery remains of where the money came from. We can answer that too, as the bank also handled the transaction – the money was transferred from the account of Sir Russell Turner."

"Pa was paid a large sum of money by Sir Russell which bought the shop leaving much more besides … it seems *impossible*! How could that have happened and not anyone know?" Ellen's face revealed her complete shock and disbelief. She could not understand it. She could not fathom out how and why such a thing was done.

"Your father was being paid for a transaction. He was being paid for the transfer of his son to Sir Russell and for relieving him of his unwanted daughter, both born on the same day nearly eighteen years ago."

* * *

The lilac tree was in full bloom. I remember that because I'd looked out from the room where my wife and baby son lay sleeping and the delight which I should have felt at the sight of the flourishing, softly falling purple blue blooms was entirely absent from me. The doctor had come and had offered me an answer to all my prayers; to eradicate my struggles, my debts, my worries, but it was not the answer I would ever have expected.

A very large sum of money – more than I could earn in my whole lifetime; this was the answer, and I would accept it because my wife would never know. She was sleeping, and had not held her baby as yet and could not know – never know that I had given away our son. Another family would have him, provide for him.

The family needed a son; they had an unwanted daughter, born just three hours before our son; her mother had died leaving a heart broken father and husband, a man deprived of what he most needed. He needed a son, and he had wanted mine, and he would have mine. He was more powerful than I; more able to do as he pleased; his chances of having his own son had vanished; and so he had wanted mine and taken him.

He had paid handsomely for my son and then he, the newborn infant, my son, quietly and without ceremony, late on a June evening, was taken and exchanged; he was removed from this room looking out over the blooming lilac tree. The doctor had taken him and then he was given a new name and a new home, no longer mine.

A delicate daughter was given in exchange, a fair daughter, pale and fair, small, fragile, needing to belong; she became Hannah's love child, but never really mine, never mine.

Ellen came into our home, and she never let me forget who she was. I said nothing but gradually, as I watched her grow in spirit and intelligence, I could not carry the burden of knowing she was not mine, and that she was never meant to be mine.

My dear wife Hannah noticed my torment, my constant unease around the child and she perceived that I was different towards her, different from the way I was with our other children, and she did not understand it; how could she ever have seen how despicable her husband had become and understood why; instead, she looked for ways to release me from whatever it was that restrained my love for Ellen; she gave Ellen more and more, not I think to compensate for my lack of giving, but to draw me in to see what a wonderful daughter Ellen was. Ellen who seemed to make everyone happy; Ellen who was like a breath of fresh, perfumed and invigorating air swirling through our home; Ellen, who was entirely unaware of her influence, of the beauty she brought to every place where she stood. I couldn't bear it – nor could I allow anyone to know.

The pact had been made. I had been paid in sterling, but I would have to pay back so much more in consequence of my sin; and the payment would be ruthlessly demanded and I would have to pay; there was no possibility that I would be able to evade what I owed. Darkness invaded my senses and my soul and I could not see or hear or feel except to judge or complain or boast.

Once Hannah was gone I felt no restraint; I would do anything to avoid paying my debt. I would rid myself of Ellen. I would take a new wife to prove to everyone that I was my own master, and that I owed nothing to anyone. I would rid myself of the payment which had hung over me like a gallows, and avoid the deadly end pronounced by my conscience. I attempted to wipe Ellen from my memory, but could not forget the part Sir Russell had played, and despite our pact, I wanted to make him suffer, to see him suffer as I had.

Then, as if I had become a man who had lost all sense of what was right, I sought to destroy Mary. Why? Because she would not allow me to be the master; I had to be if I was to avoid the penalty of what I had done, the penalty of an unremitting shroud of guilt which wrapped itself around my heart and arrested the pulse of my existence.

My testimony of these events is now written as confirmation of what has been discovered. I am filled with gratitude that I have been granted some time to pay, to make restitution for the past. I was happy to be helpless and dependent for a time, but then, I suddenly felt the weight of the burden I had placed on those whom I had wronged, and once again chose to slip deeply into a place where I could sleep and wanted never to wake up.

I could not stay there and sleep. I was flooded with kindness, with care, with tears, with sorrow, with every good thing, with sunshine and air, with cleansing water, with nature, with all those things which I had been given before but had never received, accepted and appreciated. I was immersed in the love of my children.

I awoke and loved my children back.

* * *

'Her face it blossomed like a sweet flower
 And stole my heart away complete ...'

There was no discussion at the conclusion of Lionel Reed's revelations. All was quiet, and no one was willing to break the silence. Ellen was the first to move, and as she quietly excused herself, she said that she wished to see her pa, and was heard going up the stairs. No one knew what passed between them at that time, but Charles was later to be made aware of her intentions.

Once the spell was broken by Ellen, each member of the family went to Hannah one by one and embraced her and kissed her, beginning with her grandmother Eliza, who held her for a long time and said nothing. Hannah responded with tears but stayed where she was, and once Ellen returned, she also hugged Hannah and stroked her hair, laying her cheek against Hannah's. Nothing was said, but much that was unspoken was deeply felt.

* * *

The greatest change that was observed in any of the family members after this day was that of Ma Lambourn. She lovingly visited her son every day until his death a year later. Dr Fairweather pronounced that Thomas's life though cut short had been prolonged by the diligent and loving care afforded to him by his family. No one ever spoke openly of his role in the crimes of the past. Nothing needed to be said; so everyone was agreed and all possible incriminations were eliminated from their hearts. .

* * *

The family connections between the village of Botley and the town of Lyndhurst continued, with no sign of any change. Charles had had to return home soon after Lionel Reed's solution was concluded, but was determined to be at the tailor's shop as often as business allowed. He was not prepared for a further shock delivered by his father. Now that Benjamin was assured that all was well between Charles and Ellen, he informed his son that he had been acquainted with Thomas Lambourn for some time.

"What on earth do you mean? How could you possibly know Ellen's father? I don't understand you."

"Charles it's alright ... Mr Lambourn came to me just after Ellen had left with her grandparents."

"Are you telling me that you have known him all this time and never said a word of it to me ... I am amazed ... but what was the purpose of your meeting with him?"

"He wanted to know how Ellen did. He knew that she had formed an attachment to one of her rescuers, because Eliza Timms had written to him and told him that they had collected

Ellen from Lyndhurst and that she was still seeing her rescuer …
you! Apparently he wanted to know how she got on, and so he
asked his pastor to make some enquiries of the Lyndhurst
minister, and it did not take long for him to be informed that
Ellen had resided with us."

"But why did you never say anything? I can't believe that you
would remain silent about such a thing."

"I could not speak of it … Ellen's father swore me to secrecy
… he was worried that if Ellen was to find out about his following
her she would be frightened … their final parting was, apparently,
far from pleasant. Thomas Lambourn was a man you could not
argue with … he had an aura of desperation about him … he
would come when you were not here, and stay only briefly. I told
him what he needed to know and it seemed to ease his mind."

"But *what* did you tell him?"

"Only what you had told me, what Ellen was doing and if she
was happy… that is all."

"Do you know what I think? I believe that he was thinking
about telling Ellen what he had done. He had fallen out with Sir
Russell … why else would he suddenly show such an interest in
her wellbeing?"

Benjamin reflected on Charles's theory and hoped that it was
true.

"How's Ellen? How does she feel about all that has
happened?"

"She told me that once she had spoken to her father, and had
told him that she knew the truth, she saw in his eyes a wonderful
expression of joy and love. He had reached for her, and she had
told him that he would always be her father, and that would never
change."

"But what of James Turner? His situation is extremely precarious surely?"

"No, Ellen has seen him, and the estate is to be shared between the three young people, Ellen, James and Alfred. The legal papers have been drawn up. The Colonel has left and will not return. James cannot be blamed for the actions of Sir Russell. He had wondered why Sir Russell had been so against his associating with Agnes. He tried to keep them apart by seeing to it that Agnes went away ... he couldn't take a chance on James falling in love with his sister! As Ellen said to me, James was an innocent baby, and his life should go on as it has ... as always Ellen seems to be able to calm troubled waters!"

"And what of Hannah? Her child Freddie must have some right to the Turner property surely!"

"Yes, yes and Ellen once again has thought of a way and will bequeath a percentage of her allowance to her nephew ... she loves Freddie so much, *and* Hannah, she would not see them not benefit from her good fortune."

"She loves someone else too, does she not? She's in love isn't she?"

Father and son grinned at one another. There was no denying that Charles's love for Ellen was now returned and that he was loved unreservedly, and so father and son parted, each knowing that they had been undeniably fortunate in receiving the greatest blessing that can be poured out on any one man; that each had gratefully been given and received the faithful and precious love of the sweetest woman.

* * *

'Gentle love deeds, as blossoms on a bough,
From love's awakened root do bud out now.'

June 1877 Births, Marriages and Deaths
The Hampshire Chronicle

Announcement

It is with pleasure that it is announced that the wedding took place on the 28th June 1877, Coronation Day, at All Saints Church, Botley, of Miss Ellen Turner Lambourn, daughter of the late Thomas and Hannah Lambourn of Botley and Mr Charles Edward Coleman, only son of Benjamin and Maria Coleman of Lyndhurst. The bride was accompanied by her maid of honour Miss Ada Strong, and was given in marriage by her brother Tom Lambourn. Agnes Lambourn, Emily Lambourn and Sophie Coleman acted as bridesmaids. The bridegroom was supported by his best man Mr Lionel Reed. The service was conducted by the parson of the parish the Reverend Russell. The bride's dress made of white silk and organza with pearl fastenings and lace sleeves was made by her sister Hannah Lambourn. The bridesmaids were dressed in pale turquoise crepe de chine dresses with white sashes. Plummers Gentlemen's Outfitters of Southampton provided the gentlemen's hats, morning suits, and cravats. Musical anthems were provided by Miss Agnes Lambourn a member of the Comedy Opera Company, London. She was accompanied by Mr Herbert Smith on the organ. The flowers in the church which were mainly scented roses and lilac were arranged by the bride groom's mother and grandmother.

After the ceremony, the guests returned to the home of the bridegroom's grandmother Mrs Victoria Whitcher, widow of Mr Richard Whitcher, past mayor of Lyndhurst, for a wedding breakfast in the grounds of her home. The bride and groom traveled to Lymington by the sea for their honeymoon.

* * *